SUSAN FANETTI

SLAM
THE BRAZEN BULLS MC

3

THE FREAK CIRCLE PRESS

Slam © 2017 Susan Fanetti
All rights reserved

Susan Fanetti has asserted her right to be identified as the author of this book under the Copyright, Design and Patents Act 1988.

This is a work of fiction. Names, characters, places, and incidents are a product of the author's imagination. Any resemblance to actual persons, living or dead, events, or locales are entirely coincidental.

ALSO BY SUSAN FANETTI

The Brazen Bulls MC:
Crash, Book 1
Twist, Book 2

THE NIGHT HORDE MC SAGA:

The Signal Bend Series: **The Night Horde SoCal:**
(The First Series)   **(The Second Series)**

Move the Sun, Book 1   *Strength & Courage*, Book 1
Behold the Stars, Book 2   *Shadow & Soul*, Book 2
Into the Storm, Book 3   *Today & Tomorrow*, Book 2.5
Alone on Earth, Book 4   *Fire & Dark*, Book 3
In Dark Woods, Book 4.5   *Dream & Dare*, Book 3.5
All the Sky, Book 5   *Knife & Flesh*, Book 4
Show the Fire, Book 6   *Rest & Trust*, Book 5
Leave a Trail, Book 7   *Calm & Storm*, Book 6

Nolan: Return to Signal Bend
Love & Friendship

The Pagano Family Series:
Footsteps, Book 1
Touch, Book 2
Rooted, Book 3
Deep, Book 4
Prayer, Book 5
Miracle, Book 6

The Pagano Family: The Complete Series

The Northwomen Sagas:
God's Eye
Heart's Ease
Soul's Fire
Father's Sun

For the lost: may you be found.
For the alone: may you be loved.
For the broken: may you be made whole.

With special thanks to TeriLyn,
for her keen insight, her support, and her friendship.

Freedom is what you do with what is done to you.

~Jean-Paul Sartre

THE BRAZEN BULLS MOTORCYCLE CLUB
Tulsa, Oklahoma

1997 Roster

Brian Delaney — President
Oskar "Dane" Nielsen — Vice President
Conrad "Radical" Jessup — Sergeant at Arms
Simon Spellman — Secretary-Treasurer
Fernando "Ox" Sanchez — Enforcer
Edgar "Eight Ball" Johnston — Enforcer
Gary Becker — Enforcer
Richard "Maverick" Helm — Soldier
Maxwell "Gunner" Wesson — Soldier
Griffin Hayes — Medic
Neil "Apollo" Armstrong — Soldier

Andrew "Slick" Zabek — Prospect
Walter "Wally" Hansen — Prospect

1997

CHAPTER ONE

Without a single tree to filter it, the sun shone mercilessly down. Maverick stared up at a sky almost white with glare and looked straight into that punishing star, until a ghost of it had been burned into his eyes.

Summer heat baked up from the cracked asphalt and turned the yard into an oven. He could almost feel the rubber soles of his slip-on sneakers melting as he stood there. Less than a minute since the metal door had clanged heavily shut behind him, he felt rills of sweat creeping through his short-shorn hair and down his neck.

The routine noise of perfunctory recreation rumbled around him, occasionally punctuated by the clang of weights dropping onto their stack. As the sun faded from his eyes, Maverick scanned the yard.

If someone set up a camera on a tripod and took a photograph every single day, it would be nearly impossible to distinguish one image from the next. Every single day, the same people took the same positions and did the same things. At the picnic table near the wall: the Indians. Against the far fence: the Mexicans, which meant anybody with Latin blood. The Dyson crew controlled the Blacks, who'd claimed the single patch of hard-pack dirt and the three round picnic tables on it. At the weights was White Pride. Few men straggled apart from any group. It was mortally dangerous to be unaligned.

The asphalt might have been hot enough to cook an egg, but the recreation yard at the Oklahoma State Penitentiary was no melting pot.

Maverick hated every single one of these fuckers.

For four years, he'd been living behind these fences, walls, and bars. Four years since he'd been outside without a gun aimed on him from a watchtower. In all that time, he'd never made a friend. Enemies, yes. But no friends. At first, that hadn't been an active choice. He hadn't been a loner on the outside, and he hadn't intended to be one inside. He'd wanted to keep his head down and get through his time—with any luck, get time off for good behavior. But the guards had had other ideas for him.

So he had lots of enemies. Few who'd do more than glare at him, however. And no friends.

But he wasn't unaligned.

He walked toward the weights. White Pride was not his thing, and the skinheads were just as bad as all the other assholes out here, if not worse, but he'd made room for himself by being a bad motherfucker, so he spent his rec time on the weights and his cell time doing push-ups and sit-ups. The Whites had control of the gym equipment.

Besides, the color of his skin put him here. They tolerated him without forcing their shitty Nazi ink on him because he'd agreed to fight for them. He tolerated them because their chief enemy was the Dyson crew.

And he hated Dyson more than anybody else. For the past year, he'd hated those sons of bitches with a heat so hot his stomach boiled. He owed them a mountain of payback, and someday, he would get it.

As he came up on the weights, Groddo, the skinhead leader, sat up on the bench, where he'd been pressing 200. The rest of his baldheaded minions stood with their arms crossed.

"Helm." He gave Maverick a steely nod.

Maverick didn't go by his road name in this place. He hadn't gotten rung up in the line of duty, and it wasn't a name that belonged in here. Inmates and guards alike used his surname. Or, in the case of the guards, his inmate number. And no one alive called him Richard or any derivation thereof.

"Groddo. I work in?"

Groddo stood up and waved a *be my guest* hand at the vacated bench. Maverick shifted the weight peg to 280 and stretched out on the bench. That was almost a hundred pounds over his own weight. He could do more, quite a bit more for a single press, but it wouldn't do to show up Groddo more than he already was.

Maverick did his reps under the ample shadow of Groddo's bulk. As he set the stack down between sets, Groddo rested his hand on the grip Maverick had released.

"Evans'll serve up Carver. For a price."

The backlight of the sun made the Nazi leader little more than a shadowy hulk hovering above him. Maverick squinted and said nothing, but he thought hard. Evans was one of the head guards. He was also the organizer of the side business the guards had set up—a business that had held Maverick enslaved since the first week of his sentence. A fighting ring, pitting inmates against each other to fight until they couldn't fight anymore. No rounds, no time, no limits. They were forced to fight until one of them was unconscious or worse.

It was supposedly allowable to tap out, but anyone who did was made to regret it later.

Maverick had come to McAlester as a former professional boxer. Evans had practically been drooling when he'd gotten his hooks into him.

Over his four years locked away, Maverick had lost most of his hearing in one ear and most of his vision in one eye. He had a cheap bridge filling in the teeth that had been knocked out of his bottom jaw, and his hands looked like they'd been made out of random spare parts. He woke up every morning well before first count, so he could loosen himself up enough to walk.

But he'd won the lion's share of his fights. He was big but not huge—a middleweight: six-three, one-eighty-five. The guards had put him in with bigger and bigger opponents, meaner and meaner bastards, not understanding that size and strength didn't necessarily mean skill or stamina, and bile didn't always mean power, and he'd taken most of them down. Since he'd stopped giving a shit whether he lived or died, the guards had stopped betting on the winner and started calling the damage Maverick would do.

His success in the ring was how he'd found a home with the Nazis. They'd wanted his strong arm and his reputation. He'd needed someone at his back.

Still thinking about Groddo's news, Maverick began his second set. Last summer, shortly before his initial sentence was up, his club, the Brazen Bulls MC, had assigned him a job: a hit on one of Dyson's lieutenants, who'd started a sentence at the prison. The job came from their Russian partner, Irina Volkov. She'd wanted the guy dead.

Maverick had been inside too long to be in the loop for most club business; he'd given Dane, their VP, his proxy before he'd gone in, and it was rare for anyone to ride down to McAlester to ask his opinion. With the exception of Gunner, it was rare for the Bulls to visit, period.

They'd gotten deep with the Russians since he'd been inside, so he didn't understand the whys and wherefores of the hit. But he was a Bull, and he'd been given a job. He'd done it, knowing full well what he'd risked. He hadn't seen another choice. The club was all he had left, and loyal was the only way he knew to be.

Madame Volkov was a powerful old broad, though, with a lot of influence. She'd set the whole thing up, and it had, briefly, looked like he'd get away clear. Then the Dysons had flexed their own muscle, and he'd gone down for the hit. Volkov had intervened at the last minute to pull him back from a harsh new sentence. He'd ended up with another year added on, and four months in solitary while they'd hashed all that shit out.

And he'd been served up on a platter for some personal retaliation.

Evans had served him up, locking the Dyson crew's inside leader, Clement Carver, and four associates, into his cell in the hole with him. The worst hour of his entire life. Whatever happened in the rest of his life, no matter how long he lived, that would always be the worst hour of his entire life.

He hadn't yet retaliated for two reasons: First, he trusted no one, and he couldn't do it on his own. Second, he'd come out of the hole utterly broken, body and spirit. He still fought for the guards, and for the skinheads, but he didn't know if he had it in him to fight for himself.

And now, months later, Evans was offering him payback on Carver. For a price.

"What's his angle?" he finally asked Groddo.

"Gotta be a show. In the yard."

Maverick laughed. Here he was, close to the end of his sentence again, and, again, somebody wanted him to wad that up and toss it in the toilet. Going for Carver in the yard meant no escape from new charges unless the guards decided to let him slide. And why would they willingly give up their favorite gladiator—especially when another charge would get him doing hard time and dancing for them for the rest of his fucking life?

Violence in the yard also made the way for the guards to have themselves a party on the prisoners. He'd probably face retaliation for that as well.

Win-win for the guards, lose-lose for him.

Evans loved his social experiments. He was probably figuring that he'd create an existential dilemma for Maverick—get his revenge on for all that Carver had done to him in the hole and fuck up his release, or pussy out, let Carver slide, hope to be free soon, and spend the rest of his life knowing that he'd let Carver get away with it.

But Maverick didn't give a fuck anymore if he was released, or if he lived or died. Hope was for pussies and fools. And he wanted Carver.

"Yeah, set it up."

~oOo~

It went down two days later, with virtually no warning for anyone. The guards released the inmates into the yard so that Carver and his people were last out. That was unusual, and Maverick took note. Carver was the first man of his crew out, and that was unusual as well. His habit was to follow his personal bodyguard. The hairs on Maverick's neck stood up, and he walked to the middle of the yard.

As soon as Carver cleared the door, it slammed shut, and a guard moved before it. Carver spun around, and there was a short scuffle between him and the guard. He was stranded in the yard without backup, and there was no question at all that the curtain had gone up.

Clement Carver was in his mid-forties or so, a bit more than ten years older than Maverick. He was comparatively short and slight, but he was no joke. Maverick had learned that the hard way. Five on one had been hopeless odds in any case, but it had been Carver who'd laid the worst kinds of hurt on Maverick in that hour.

Not knowing how Evans had arranged this event, Maverick hadn't put together much of a plan. But he'd been fantasizing about payback for months, so he didn't need a plan. He charged at Carver as soon as the man turned around, and he tackled him to the ground.

He got in a flurry of blows before a white-hot pain sank into his arm, and Maverick wrenched himself back and away. Carver was holding a fucking shank—the guard must have slipped it to him.

Goddamn Evans, playing his games, must have set that up.

Carver jumped to his feet, brandishing the sharpened toothbrush. He grinned. "Oh, biker boy. I'm gonna make you pay for this. I'm gonna make you pay all night long. Longer than that. Not like last time. This time, I'm gonna put a collar on you and make you my bitch."

A thick ring of silent inmates had formed, creating an arena of sorts in which he and Carver faced each other. Maverick grinned back and shook his head. "Not when I'm done, shithead. When I'm done, you won't be making anybody do shit."

Blood washed down his arm, but he didn't give a fuck. He would be dead when this was over, or Carver would be. Didn't matter which. He charged again, feinting at the last second and grabbing the hand that held the makeshift knife. He spun and twisted Carver's arm behind his back, wrenching it until it broke. The ensuing crack filled the air like a firecracker. Maverick's hands, holding Carver's arm, felt the break happen. The shank fell to the asphalt, and Maverick let him go, twisting his arm again for good measure, feeling the bones shift loosely in their meat casing. Carver reeled back.

He hadn't yelled, though, or even grunted, as his arm had snapped.

It was a common downfall with powerful men: They began to believe that the power which had accrued to them because of their associations and their attitude meant true, essential strength. Maverick could imagine the feeling that had likely suffused Carver as he'd realized that a fight was going down, and as the guard had slipped him the shank: a first surge of surprise and worry, and then a rush of adrenaline, fueling a giddy sense of power. And then he'd held a weapon and thought that piece of plastic was all the odds in his own hand.

Maverick kicked the shank away; that was not how he wanted to finish this fight. Carver jumped at him, swinging with his weaker but intact arm, and Maverick deflected it easily, returning a hard jab and connecting with Carver's throat. He followed it with a high kick—he'd picked up a mix of fighting skills in prison, and in the underground fights before that—and connected with his chest. Carver went down, choking and gasping, and Maverick dropped on him, getting him almost at once into a chokehold. Out in the world, he'd have been looking for a submission. In an organized prison fight, he'd have been trying to put him out. Here on the yard, in full view of the guards, he meant to fucking kill the bastard.

But just as the body in his arms began to soften, Maverick was pulled off of him, and Groddo's voice was in his ear. "Don't kill him."

Maverick fought off the hold. "What? Fuck off!" He didn't care what the consequences would be; he was intent on killing Clement Carver.

"There's a plan here, Helm. See the guards still standing down? We paid a fare for that. We got our beef with Black, too."

"This is not a fucking race thing, asshole!"

Groddo's eyes darkened under a dangerous brow. "It's always a race thing, brother. You want payback. We want a message. We got you your fight. Now you work our plan." He nodded, and the two skinheads who'd kept Carver down now grabbed him by the arms—this time, Carver did yell out hoarsely as his broken arm was manhandled—and dragged him toward the workout equipment.

Still holding him by the arm, Groddo pulled Maverick in the same direction.

Carver was maneuvered until he faced the back of the bench press machine—the yard had no free weights, which were too easily made into weapons, but instead a few weight machines and a pull-up bar.

Maverick watched as the two skinheads held Carver in a kneeling position, directly against the machine. Another skinhead pulled his pants and underwear down to the ground. Carver fought hard, and one of the skinheads slammed his head into the machine until he went limp.

It made no sense.

"You're the strongman," Groddo said to Maverick. "Why don't you do a rep?"

Just like that, he understood. "Jesus."

Groddo's face twisted into a demonic grin. "You think he don't deserve it?"

Oh, he absolutely deserved it. With a quick scan of the yard—everyone watched in inert silence, including the guards—Maverick went to the bench press.

Rather than lie on the bench—he'd never again be in a lower position than Clement Carver—he straddled it, facing the weight stack and, behind it, Carver, who was just conscious enough for fear to have widened his eyes into caricature.

He moved the pin to 220—the weight that was just about hip-level with Carver's body. Then he bent his knees, gripped the handles, and curled the weight. His biceps bulged, and blood gushed down his arm.

Harry, one of Groddo's minions holding Carver, grabbed the bastard's flaccid dick and loose balls, and set the whole package on the stack of weights Maverick wasn't lifting. Carver fought like a dazed madman, but two other skinheads came up and added their strength to hold the man in place.

His junk sat there, on top of the weight marked 230. Above it hovered two hundred and twenty pounds of iron.

Maverick kept his arms curled, ignoring the shaking of his injured one, until Carver's eyes met his. Maverick sent him all the hatred he could, and he let go of the stack. The sudden release of tension nearly dislocated his elbows, but he barely noticed. The weights slammed down, a fat, wet noise mingled with the crash of iron, and Maverick took a burst of hot blood in the face and chest.

Carver screamed a scream so piercing and loud it was almost beyond human hearing.

And then the guards leapt to action.

~oOo~

Two nights later, Maverick lay again in his own bunk. They'd thrown him into the hole again immediately after the melee in the yard, and Maverick had spent those forty-some hours sitting on the metal bunk and waiting for trouble.

But no trouble had come. He'd gotten sewn up, and they'd left him alone until they'd brought him back here. Everybody was giving him space. Even the guards were keeping a respectful distance.

It hadn't been his idea, what he'd done to Carver, but he was getting the credit. All he'd wanted was to kill the fucker.

He hadn't done that. Carver still breathed, as far as he knew. But he was going to piss sitting down for the rest of his life. Never again would he use a dick like a weapon. Not his own, at any rate.

Maverick was afraid to consider the chance that he might get away with it. At a minimum, he expected Dyson to come for him again. But maybe the guards wouldn't let it happen this time. Maybe something somewhere had turned. He was due for release in August. Seven weeks. Fifty-one days. Was it possible that he might actually get on the other side of the fence?

Jesus. Was it possible?

As the warning sounded to announce five minutes until last count, Maverick turned to the wall beside his bunk. Two small photos were taped there. Only two; he had no other photos and few mementos of any kind. The oldest, bent and fading, was a Polaroid, taken almost four years ago. Inside a clear plastic bassinet was a tiny baby, wrapped like a burrito in a striped blanket and with a pink knit cap on her head. Only a hint of fair skin and chubby cheeks was visible between the blanket and the hat. On the wall of the bassinet, a pink card named her as Kelsey Marie Wagner and her mother as Jennifer Wagner.

The line for father was blank.

In blue ink, across the white space of the Polaroid frame, was written, *Kelsey, 8/21/93*. That date was three weeks after he'd gone inside. Maverick drew his fingertip over the handwriting he'd once known so well.

Taped beside that photo was a newer one, from a year ago. Gunner had brought it to him: a wallet-size school photo of a pretty little girl with hair the color of butterscotch, twisted into two pigtails, and wide blue eyes, sparkling with clever mischief.

His eyes. His daughter. He belonged in the blank space on that pink card. And in her life.

He'd never met her. He hadn't spoken to her mother since before he'd gone inside, and he hadn't heard from her in any way except for that one Polaroid, sent without a letter, in December 1993, four months after Kelsey's birth.

He was set for release nine days before her fourth birthday.

But hope was for pussies and fools.

December 1992

"It's okay, babe." Maverick pulled the stick from Jenny's clenched fist. Studying the blue cross that indicated "pregnant," he repeated the reassurance for them both. "It's okay. We'll make it work."

He reached deep and tried to figure out how he felt about this unplanned and unexpected development. Ten minutes ago, he'd been sitting on the sofa, watching *Seinfeld* with his girl, playing lightly with her tits and thinking about tying her to the bed and eating her out.

Then Jenny had muted the set during a commercial break and announced, "I'm a week late."

While he'd still been in brain freeze, she'd gotten up and picked up her purse from the floor. Rooting through it, she'd pulled out a purple box—a test kit.

Now they were sitting together on the side of the bathtub. He was staring at the test result, Jenny was crying, and the world was different. He was going to be a father.

She wiped her cheeks and snatched the test stick back. Tossing it into the wastebasket, she got up from the side of the tub. She ripped a few squares of toilet paper off the roll and blew her nose, then tossed the soggy wad into the trash.

"No. There's nothing to work out. I'll handle it."

Still sitting on the tub, he caught her hand before she could turn away. "What d'you mean?"

"You know what I mean."

He did, but there was no way that was the end of the conversation. "No, Jen."

"I'm not ready to be a mom—I can barely take care of myself. And we've never even talked about kids. This is not your call, Mav."

She tried to free her hand, but Maverick held tight and pulled her close, bringing her between his legs. "Fuck that. You're right—we've never talked about it. But we made a kid anyway. Together. So let's talk this out together."

With a sigh, she relented, her body visibly relaxing, and he smiled up at her.

"So, do you want to be a family with me, Jenny?"

He'd caught her off guard, and she laughed. The lingering film of tears dampened its tone. "That's where you want to start?"

"How about here: I want to be a family with you."

"Why?"

"Why? I love you, babe. You know that."

"Do I? You never say it."

"I do say it. I just said it."

"Counting now, any idea how many times you've ever said those words to me?"

He heard the click of the landmine he'd just stepped on, and he didn't answer.

"Four. Four times. The other three times, you were inside me when you said them—once, you were actually coming when you said them. We've been together thirteen months.

That means we had an anniversary last month. Did you realize that?"

No, he hadn't. "Never said I was romantic, Jen."

Another laugh, this one sharp with cynicism. "No, you didn't. But I'm just supposed to believe that you love me."

He did love her. He loved her completely. Not a minute of any day passed that she wasn't in his thoughts in some way. He was happiest in her company, and he missed her when he wasn't. He wanted to share his life with her—he *was* sharing his life with her. He didn't think about anniversaries or flowers or candy or throwing out random phrases because he...just didn't think about that shit.

He wasn't romantic, but he was in love.

"It's not my style, babe. But I know you know how I feel. I know I show you."

He did show her. He had her back, always. He helped her deal with her bastard of a father. He got in that man's way every way he could—and he'd happily do more than that if Jenny would just fucking let him. He took care of her when her migraines laid her out. He'd moved her into his place, away from her old man. He kept her safe, and they were making a life. A good life. A happy one. She was his family, and he'd never wanted anything more in his life than he wanted a family of his own.

He showed her. Every day.

"You do," she agreed and put her hand on his head, stroking through his hair. "I know you love me. And I love you. But you can't expect a little kid to just know. You have to say the words, too. All the time. You have to remember their birthdays. Every one. You have to tell them every day how important they are to you. You can't ever let them forget. Not ever."

Her voice had taken on a tremor as she'd spoken, and her hand had clenched in his hair. Maverick understood everything all at once, and he pulled her down to sit on his lap.

"Babe. I love you—there, that's five." Her laugh was full of tears again. "You're the most important thing in my life. I'll say it more. I'll tell you every day, if you want. I'll tell our kid every fucking night when I tuck her in. I'm not your dad, and neither are you. Our kid will have a good family. I promise you—our kid will have a great life. And so will we."

Jenny studied him for a long time, the focus of her eyes— her fantastic eyes, pale green rimmed with deep blue— moving from left to right, back and forth, like his thoughts could be read.

"You want this? For your whole life, you want this?"

Maverick thought about that. Jenny was waitressing and taking classes to be a legal assistant. He did body work at Delaney's Sinclair. And he had the Bulls. They had the beginnings of a modest but good life. A happy life. Just the two of them. When they were together, they laughed, they played, they relaxed, and they fucked like animals. They almost never fought, or even bickered. They had a good thing going.

A kid changed it all. Forever. Did he want that? God yes, he wanted that. A family of his own? Fuck yes.

He gazed into those lively, remarkable eyes. She was beautiful. Their kid would be beautiful. And she, or he, would be loved. Everything would change, but that didn't mean it wouldn't be for the better.

He glanced down into the wastebasket. He'd taken the trash out after dinner, so it was empty except for the stick

Jenny had just tossed away and the tissue she'd lobbed in after it. The stick had landed with the window up. He reached in and reclaimed it.

That blue cross, changing everything. Forever.

"Yeah, babe. I want it."

CHAPTER TWO

"I want Cocoa Puffs." Kelsey scowled into her cereal bowl.

Jenny poured milk over the Cheerios. "Sorry, pixie. We're out of Cocoa Puffs. I'll sprinkle some sugar over these, and they'll be good."

"I don't like Cheerios!" Kelsey pushed the bowl away, and milk sloshed over the table. A lock of her hair was curled on the placemat, and milk washed over it.

"Dammit, Kelsey!" Jenny shoved the chair she'd about to sit on back under the table. "We don't have time for this!"

Kelsey flinched and whined, and Jenny felt guilty. She'd hit her daughter exactly three times in the almost-four years of her life, and all three had been swats on the hand, getting between her and danger—touching a pot of the stove, reaching for the iron on the ironing board, and trying to stick a key into an electrical outlet. She'd never struck her in the guise of discipline or punishment, and she never would. Long before she'd ever been a mother, she'd made herself a promise that she'd never lay a violent hand on her child.

She didn't hit, but, sadly, she did yell. Being a single mother was hard, every day. Some days, those days when she felt at the limit of her tether, she seemed to do little but yell. Kelsey was a good girl, a sweet girl, but she was smart and curious, and she always wanted to know why and how. She got into mischief, and she already had a sassy tongue.

Jenny loved her curiosity and her sass, but sometimes it would be nice to have a child who just did what she was told because she was told to do it.

On this day, when she'd been up most of the night with a migraine and was still feeling the bruised-brain aftereffects of it, life in general seemed too enormous an opponent to contend with.

With a deep, slow breath, Jenny crouched at the side of her daughter's chair. Sitting in her green plastic booster, Kelsey looked down on her mother, her bright blue eyes wide and judgmental. "You said mean talk."

"Sorry, pixie. Mommy's head is hurting today. I didn't mean to yell. If you'll eat Cheerios now, I'll go to the store for Cocoa Puffs this afternoon. If we work hard and aren't late for school this morning, I'll get some ice cream for bedtime, too."

"Mint chocolate chip?"

"Absolutely. Okay?" Jenny knew she should be more careful about the foods Kelsey ate, but her little girl was a crazily picky eater, and she took her wins where she could find them. At least cereal and ice cream had dairy going for them.

Kelsey nodded and pulled her bowl close again. She sloshed more milk when she did so, and her hair was going to be a sticky mess, but Jenny closed her eyes and ignored that.

"Thank you, sweetie." She stood and kissed her little girl's head. "I love you."

"I love you, too, Mommy. That's one."

They counted how many times they said 'I love you' each day and never let a day go by without saying the words to each other at least once.

"One," she agreed and pulled the sugar bowl over to add some sweet to her little girl's cereal.

The back door opened, and Carlena, her father's day nurse, came in. "Hey girls! How are we on this fine day?"

Jenny glanced out the window at the grey gloom. The sky was pregnant with rain, and the forecast called for thunderstorms all afternoon. She cocked an eyebrow at the always-sunny nurse.

Carlena grinned and opened the fridge to put her lunch away. "Big storm means this heat'll break, honey. That's a fine day, you ask me. Besides, what's a better way to spend a day than sittin' on a screen porch while it rains?"

That sounded like a lovely way to spend the day. It wasn't how Jenny and Kelsey were going to spend it, however. Jenny was almost jealous. If not for the company Carlena would be keeping, she'd be completely jealous.

"How was his night?" Carlena asked.

Jenny's father had two shifts of nursing care five days a week, but from one to nine a.m. on those days, Jenny was in charge. It wasn't usually difficult duty—he was in bed by then and hooked up to his breathing machine, so all she had to do was listen for alerts and deal with it if there was trouble—but she resented it anyway.

On Saturday afternoon and all day Sunday, she was in charge. She hated weekends.

"He was quiet. He's been awake about half an hour, I think." She hadn't gone in to check on him, but she knew the sounds of his machines and had heard that his heart rate was wakeful.

"Good. Best get him movin' then. Usual day for you girls?"

"Yep. School for Kelse and work for me." It was July, but Kelsey was in a pre-school/daycare program that ran year-round.

Being a single mom meant giving up half the raising of her kid to other people.

Kelsey had eaten all the Cheerios she was going to and was chasing floating 'Os' around with her spoon. Jenny took hold of her hand. "C'mon, pixie. Let's clean up your mess and get ready for school."

~oOo~

"Ready for another, Russ?"

Russ, sitting in his usual seat at the head of the bar, nodded. "Sure am." Jenny pulled the tap and refilled his beer. As she pushed it across the bar, he put his hand around hers on the glass. "Someday, you're gonna say yes."

Jenny laughed and gently but firmly freed her hand. Russ was well into his sixties, a sweet old retired guy who spent his weekday afternoons sitting right where he was, on the first stool at the bar in The Wayside Inn. He flirted with her every day. While the come-ons were gentle, and she was slightly more than half sure they weren't intended seriously, she worked to maintain a balance between being playfully friendly with him and leading him on.

"I guess we'll have to see if you live long enough to see that day," she retorted now.

He flattened his hand against his chest as if she'd wounded him there. "We used to call beauties like you femme fatales. You know that?"

Before she could counter that remark, the door opened and let in a blast of sultry air and dusty white light. The storms of the day before hadn't broken the heat at all, and, once the clouds had cleared, the humidity had been even worse. The Wayside's loud, rickety air conditioning unit was working as well as it could, but it wasn't up to the challenge of this summer.

Russ had been the only customer in the bar on this early afternoon, so Jenny focused on the newcomers. The sunlight streaming through the open door cast them in silhouette, and all she saw at first was three sizable blobs. The jukebox wasn't playing, and the volume on the television above the bar was low, so she could hear the clomp of boots as they came in.

Then the door closed, and she blinked and saw that they were all wearing kuttes. They were Brazen Bulls. Gunner and Rad and one she didn't know.

The last time any of these sons of bitches had blighted her bar had been the year before, when Gunner had shown up out of the blue and coerced her into giving him a recent photo of Kelsey. For Maverick, Kelsey's father.

Who had ruined her fucking life and was therefore out of it. Forever.

Now there were three of them walking toward her. She crossed her arms and turned her attention on Gunner. Of all the Bulls besides Maverick, she knew Gunner best. She'd liked him, in a different life. "What the fuck do you want?"

Gunner opened his mouth to speak, but it was Rad who answered. With a chuckle in his voice, he said, "Dial it down, darlin'. We don't mean trouble." He nodded at Gunner, who reached into his kutte and pulled out a fat, business-size envelope. He held it out to her, and Jenny stared at it, leaving her arms crossed.

The Bulls gave her money every month, something she supposed Maverick had worked out from prison. It was for Kelsey, and Jenny took it, notwithstanding her intention for Kelsey and her father never to meet. She saved almost all of it, only hitting it in emergencies—like last year, when Kelsey had had meningitis and been in the hospital for eight days. She never wanted to come to rely on that money for her daily living, and she meant it all to be a way for Kelsey to go to college and get her life started.

She got money from the Bulls on a regular basis, but not like this. Normally one of their hangarounds brought it by. And the envelope was never this thick. From the look of it, it was several times the normal amount.

Russ had turned on his stool and was considering the Bulls. He was a senior citizen whose body had been devastated a couple of years back in a cancer fight. There was quite obviously nothing he could have done against three big, burly bikers, but he still asked, "Jenny? You need anything here?"

For that, she spared her regular customer a grateful smile. "Thanks, Russ, but I'm okay."

Since she'd made it clear that she wasn't taking that envelope from him, Gunner set it on the bar.

"That's more than usual. This whole thing is more than usual. Why?"

This time, Gunner did speak. "He's getting out at the end of the week."

"What? Why?"

She'd kept track of Maverick's sentence. She knew that he'd been scheduled for release the year before and had had time added, and she knew he was scheduled for release again right before Kelsey's birthday. If he was getting out this week, it was early—almost a month early. She wasn't ready. Sharped-edged wings of panic fluttered in Jenny's belly—and something else, too, something fragile and long unnourished. Even after everything, after the wreck her life had become, her love for Maverick Helm made her quiver.

All three Bulls, even the big blond she didn't know, took on the same angry expression, like a shared mask of offense. Rad answered with a snarl. "He did his time. All you need to know." He turned his glare on Russ, who shrank a little but held his seat.

Beginning to understand what that envelope and this visit were about, Jenny didn't want Russ to be privy to the conversation. "Can you give us a few minutes, Russ?"

He glanced sidelong at the Bulls and then studied her. "You sure?"

"Yeah. I'm safe." She believed that, at any rate. They wouldn't hurt her.

"Okay. I could go squeeze one out, anyway. I won't be far." He slid off his stool headed toward the bathrooms in back.

Jenny watched him go. When she turned back to the Bulls, she said, "You think you can pay me to let him in. That's what that is." She tipped her head toward the stuffed envelope.

"He's her dad, Jen," Gunner said. "He wants to be her dad."

"Then he should have been out here, being her dad."

"Jesus fuck," Rad muttered. He slammed his palms on the bar and leaned close.

Radical Jessup was the club Sergeant at Arms. He was big, a scowl rested more easily on his face than a smile, and he was almost as quick to violence as Maverick. Jenny fought the need to step back, out of his reach. She made herself stand firm and meet his dark, angry eyes.

"I don't know what story you worked out in your head to make him a bad guy in this, but he did what he did to protect you—"

She scoffed, unable to hold it back, and Rad slammed his hands on the bar again, even more forcefully. She was also unable to hold back her flinch.

"If your life is shit now, that's on you. You could shove that bastard in a state home and be done with it, but you like playin' Little Miss Martyr, don't ya?"

He was making a lot of assumptions about things he had no knowledge of. "Fuck you, Rad. Get the fuck out of here, all of you."

Nobody moved. Then Rad reached out and grabbed her arm. He didn't hurt her, but he used force to drag her close, until the bar cut across her ribcage, and he put his face right in hers. Jenny wondered whether she'd been right—*would* he hurt her?

"It goes like this, Jenny. Maverick is that girl's father. He wants to be in her life. He's a Bull. The Bulls got his back. So he *will* be in his little girl's life. Whatever we have to do to make that happen. That envelope right there is one way. But there are other ways. You think about that."

He glared into her eyes for another few seconds. His eyes were dark, dark brown, so dark his pupils were barely discernible. It was like looking into him and seeing nothing but abyss.

The words he'd said had been full of threat, but his eyes scared her most of all.

He let her go with a little shove, and she took a quick couple of steps to keep her feet.

Rad spun on his heel without another word and stalked to the door. The blond one followed.

Gunner held back. When Jenny made eye contact with him, he pushed the envelope closer to her. "Jenny, come on. Last year, I told you how bad he needed you and Kelsey. This year has been a fuck ton worse, but he's finally getting out. You know he'll be a good dad."

She knew no such thing. He was a violent hothead who always had to have his way and never thought about the consequences before letting his fists fly. She'd been raised by exactly such a man, and he had not been a good dad at all. Now, because of Maverick and his flying fists, she was saddled with her father for the rest of his life.

Jenny didn't answer Gunner, and she didn't touch the envelope. Finally, he sighed.

"Friday. He gets out Friday." He turned and headed for the door.

When she was alone in the bar, she picked up the envelope and pulled the flap free. It was stuffed with loose bills. Hundred-dollar bills, all of them. Riffling through it, she estimated that there was twenty thousand dollars in that basic white envelope. Several times more than usual.

Twenty thousand dollars.

That was what the Brazen Bulls thought her daughter was worth.

~oOo~

"'Then he lay down close by and whispered with a smile, 'I love you right up to the moon—'"

"'AND BACK!'" Kelsey yelled the rest of the sentence and grinned up at her.

Jenny closed the book. "Okay, it's time for all good little pixies and sprites and fairies and elves to go to sleep. Who do you want a slumber party with tonight?"

Kelsey sat up and considered the giant herd of stuffed animals corralled on the floor. "Mrs. Misty," she said.

Jenny got up from the narrow twin bed and picked up a stuffed Labrador. She handed it to her daughter, who settled it in the crook of her arm, and tucked them both in. She switched off the bedside lamp, switched on the nightlight that cast pink light over the room, and kissed Kelsey's head. "Good night, pixie. Sweet dreams. I love you."

"I love you, too, Mommy. That's...five."

"Yep, that's five."

Pulling the door to, Jenny went down the hall to the living room. Darnell, her father's second shift nurse, was cleaning up the dinner he'd just fed him. The television was on, showing some cable news program. She stood in the entry to the living room and watched Darnell wipe her father's mouth.

Nonstop since the Bulls had stormed the Wayside that afternoon, more than she had since Kelsey was an infant, she'd been thinking about Maverick, her father, and her life.

The man in that wheelchair was not tall, but he had once been barrel-chested and heavyset. He'd had a thick wave of brown hair and a fleshy face creased with suspicion. He'd been a voluble speaker with a biting humor and an arsenal of offensive jokes and observations, which he'd regularly deployed to cause harm.

He'd also been capable of sweeping gestures of love. Jenny had grown up pinging between his warm hugs, his cold words, and his stiff belt.

For the past four years, he'd been the man in that wheelchair: frail, balding, grey, sagging, unable to control his body enough to walk, or feed himself, or handle any of his own needs. For the past four years, he'd had the mind of a six-year-old, and a vocabulary of four words: need, no, now, and Jen.

Before the wheelchair, he'd been held in a wary esteem by the residents of their East Tulsa neighborhood. In public, he was a neighborhood leader, a businessman, active in civic events and politics and admired for his good works. Jenny felt sure that they'd all known the kind of man he was in private, with his family, but no one had interfered in his private business.

The Wayside Inn, the tavern her father had opened as a young man, had been a neighborhood touchstone for Jenny's whole life. For the past four years, she'd run it. And lived again in the house she'd grown up in, with the man in that wheelchair, who'd ruled over her childhood, doling out love and anger in equal portion but wildly erratic manner.

Earlier in the day, Rad had called her a martyr. From the outside, maybe it looked like she was. Her life would have been easier, certainly, to have left him to become a ward of the State of Oklahoma. He deserved it, certainly.

She thought about it sometimes. Even with the nursing help she managed to pay for, living this way was hard on Jenny and on Kelsey, too. If she could have afforded a decent place, a private facility instead of a state-run warehouse, she'd probably have done it. But the two shifts of home nursing were hardship enough.

Still, on the really hard days, she opened her address book to the page for his caseworker and considered arranging any bed she could find for him, anywhere. But one thing stopped her and would always stop her: she needed to be a better person than he'd been. She needed him to know, to the extent that he could, that he hadn't warped her into an image of himself. That she was a good person. A better person, who took care of her family.

Did that make her a martyr? Jenny didn't know. She stared up at the patched ceiling and wondered.

If he hadn't become the man in that wheelchair, she would have turned her back on him. She'd been trying to do exactly that when hell had broken loose in her life. Four years ago, almost to the day.

July 1993

Jenny was in the kitchen fixing supper when Maverick got home. As always, he came straight to the kitchen and stood behind her, smoothing his hands over her huge belly. She was careful to tip her head so he kissed her right cheek.

"My girls have a good day?"

She still hadn't figured out how to talk to him about her day, so she shrugged and said, "Sure. You?"

"Normal and dull, so yeah. Smells good. What you got there?"

"Pork cutlets." She turned one in the skillet, and the sizzle kicked up beads of hot oil. "And you're gonna get us both burned if you're not careful."

Another kiss, and he stepped back. Jenny heard the fridge door open and the snap and hiss as he uncapped a beer bottle. He was on her left side now, so she gave her head a subtle shake and made sure her hair was a curtain between him and her face.

It was stupid. He was going to see; there was no preventing that. She'd had a couple of hours to figure out what to say, how to manage the situation, but her brain had refused to deal with the problem. And it was a big problem. She was thirty-four weeks pregnant. Maverick would lose his shit. He was always on the verge of losing it over her father, anyway.

She poked at the cutlets and tried to force her pregnant brain to organize last-minute words, but then Maverick came up to her left side and brushed her hair back.

For a few seconds, the scene froze. He stood there with her hair lying over his hand, holding his beer in the other. She stood staring at the cutlets, the fork in her hand hovering over the skillet.

"I'm going to fucking kill him."

The words slithered slowly out of Maverick's mouth—he didn't yell; when he got really angry, he got quieter, not louder. He'd never struck her, but she'd seen the damage he could do with his fists. She'd seen that damage several times.

He slammed his bottle on the counter and stormed from the room.

"Mav, wait!" Jenny turned off the burner and hurried after him, as fast as her belly would allow. "Wait! Stop!"

He ignored her, but he'd pulled his boots off when he'd come in, as usual, and she caught up with him as he was yanking them back on. "Maverick, listen to me. Talk to me. Let this go."

"He fucking hit you, Jen." He scanned her face. "Twice—he hit you *twice*, didn't he?"

She touched her swollen lip, and then her cheekbone. Yes, her father had hit her twice. He'd knocked her down, but she wasn't going to tell Maverick that. "I provoked him. I made him so mad. I said things I shouldn't have said when I was alone with him. I knew he'd probably strike out, and I said them anyway."

Though she hadn't planned what had happened, part of her was glad her father had hit her. Sitting on the floor with her mouth bleeding and her eye blackening, Jenny had known that she'd be able to leave him behind. She wouldn't feel the pull of guilt that had always drawn her back in the past. He'd hit her while she was pregnant. For her daughter, she'd stay away. Cut him out for good.

"Jesus, listen to yourself! How many fucking different ways can you blame yourself for getting hit?" Maverick yanked his second boot on and grabbed his keys. "This fucking ends *now*." He slammed out of the house.

"Maverick, wait! Please!"

Jenny didn't care if Maverick beat her father. She didn't think he'd actually kill him, but she wouldn't care if he did. But she would care if he went to prison and left her alone with a new baby, and her father would absolutely press charges. Their hatred was mutual and molten hot. So hot that Maverick wouldn't stop once he got started.

Jenny worked her swollen feet into her sneakers and waddle-ran out to her car.

~oOo~

Maverick must have gone like hell on wheels, because by the time she pulled up in front of the house, she could hear the crash of violence coming from inside.

The front door was standing open, and the ruckus was loud enough that it had drawn the attention of her father's next-door neighbor. Mr. Turner was crossing between their yards with a shotgun in his hands.

"Stay back, Jenny!" he yelled. "There's some kinda trouble inside! I called the police."

"Wait!" she called, but Mr. Turner ignored her and ran into the house.

She got through the door just as the neighbor fired a blast into the ceiling. Plaster showered over him, and Jenny was distracted by the snowy scene. Then she turned and found Maverick and her father on the floor.

The blast hadn't distracted Maverick at all. He was straddled over her father, perfectly silent, dealing blow after blow, all with his dominant arm. The blows had torn her father's face to shreds, and a pool of blood oozed out around his head.

Her father's only movement was the rocking and twitching reactions of his body to the blows. His eyes were open, but he wasn't fighting at all or even resisting.

As Mr. Turner cocked the shotgun again, sirens sounded outside.

A sharp spasm clenched across her belly, and Jenny cried out. That stopped Maverick. He jumped up and came to her, laying his hands on her belly—hands dripping with her father's blood.

"Babe, you okay?"

As a cop outside used a bullhorn to announce their presence, Jenny knew that no, she wasn't okay and never would be.

Maverick had killed her father, and law was right there with them. He was going away for murder and leaving her alone to raise their child.

CHAPTER THREE

At wake-up on the day of his release, Maverick's eyes were already wide open. He wasn't sure he'd closed them, even to blink, all night. He'd lain on his bunk with his two photos of his daughter on his chest, his hands folded over them, and he'd let his imagination run. On that night, for the first time in years, he let himself really think about what he would do on the outside, how he would live in freedom.

He'd gotten word at the beginning of the week that he was being released almost a month early. Just a summons to the warden's office for a three-minute meeting in which he was told he would be released on Friday. No reason was offered, and Maverick hadn't bothered to ask for one because he hadn't believed it was true. He'd simply nodded and gone back to his prison life.

But in the days that followed, he'd been given information about release procedures and told how to handle his scant belongings and insignificant affairs. The guards had left him alone and pulled him off a scheduled fight. Evans had sneered in irritation and said it wouldn't do to mess up his pretty face.

In the early dark hours on Friday, Maverick had dipped his toe into the waters of hope.

Just before wake-up, he rose from his bunk and pissed, then stretched his stiff limbs until he could move. When he was loose enough to function, he gathered his bathroom gear and waited. He completed his morning routine exactly the same way he'd done it for the past one thousand, four hundred, and thirty-five days: wake, piss, stretch out, wait for first count, shower, dress, back to his cell to put his gear away and wait to be called for mess.

He hadn't had a cellmate for a couple of months, since the last one had hung himself in the cell while Maverick had spent a night in the infirmary after a fight. He didn't even remember his name, but he'd been a pimply kid, still in his teens, rung up for vehicular manslaughter. He'd been drunk and had slammed headlong into an oncoming car and killed a mom and three little kids, including a three-month-old baby.

Those eight days in gen pop had not been kind to him.

When Evans called his block for mess, Maverick left his cell to head to breakfast, as he had every morning for almost four years, but the guard blocked his way.

"Back to your cell, inmate. You wait until you're called."

He felt a strange tickle in his belly and didn't understand what it was until he was back in his cell. He was nervous. That was what hope brought you: if you let yourself think you could have something worth having, then you had to contend with the fear that you might lose it, or never get it at all.

He sat and waited in his cell for hours, while the drab routines of prison life went on around him and without him. Never had he felt lonelier than in those hours of limbo. He was like that cat he'd learned about in physics class back in high school—the one who was both alive and dead, who existed and didn't exist simultaneously.

The rest of the inmates were at lunch when Kohn, one of the guards, came by and tossed a cardboard box at him. Maverick caught it out of reflex. It was empty.

"Pack up, inmate. Five minutes." He stood in the open cell door, and Maverick understood he was to pack right then, while Kohn watched.

Another inmate, one more comfortable with the concepts of faith and hope, might have used the hours of idleness to prepare his belongings for packing, but Maverick had only sat and let the clock tick away. He'd been afraid to dip his toe back into that pool of hope.

He didn't have much to pack, anyway, so three minutes was sufficient time to shove his few things, mostly toiletries and a few books from Mo's annual Christmas package, into the box.

When he was done, Kohn led him out of the cell. The thought that he was leaving that forlorn home for good pushed against the door of Maverick's brain, but he leaned on it and didn't let it in. Not yet. Until he was on the other side of the fence, it was better to be prepared for this to be an elaborate ruse.

He was brought to the warden's office, relieved of his box, and searched. Inside the office, he sat in the vinyl chair in front of the desk and listened while the warden explained that he had seventy-two hours to register with his probation officer. He was given the contact information he needed to do that, and then the warden pushed a piece of paper at him and told him to sign. He didn't bother to read more than the heading: *STATE OF OKLAHOMA DEPARTMENT OF CORRECTIONS. PRISONER RELEASE.*

Release. Prisoner release. He signed his name with a hand that shook.

And then the warden of the Oklahoma State Penitentiary, who'd overseen Maverick's four years of despair, stood and stretched his arm across his desk, offering his hand.

"Don't want to see you in here again, son," he said, with a serious smile on his face.

Not knowing what else to do, Maverick nodded and shook the man's hand.

~oOo~

An hour later, dressed in clothes he hadn't worn in four years—the jeans were too big and the t-shirt too tight—he walked outside, still surrounded by high fence and razor wire and accompanied by Kohn. But at the end of the chute, in a gravel space across the road, he saw the sun-glinted chrome dazzle of motorcycles.

Kohn opened the final lock. He held the gate open, and Maverick, without a nod or a word or a look back, stepped through.

He was on the other side of the fence, and damn if it didn't smell different. Look different. Feel different.

The Bulls—the whole club, by the looks of it, including men he didn't know—crossed the road and met him. As Brian Delaney, the club president, held out his arms, Maverick dropped his box and accepted the embrace of his president.

"Damn, it's good to have you back, brother," Delaney said at his ear.

His feelings about Delaney had grown complicated over these past four years. He didn't like some of the choices he'd made—those he knew about—and the direction he'd taken the club, and he didn't like that the president had seemed to forget about him unless there was work that needed to be done inside.

He didn't like that most of the Bulls had seemed to forget him inside. But he hadn't been touched with affection in four years, and in that moment, he realized how desperately he'd needed it. Delaney's warm, sincere embrace was a balm. It gave him new strength. The rush of freedom filled his blood, and he thought he could forgive grudges and grievances he'd been nurturing for four years. He loved his brothers. He was a Bull, first and last. And it wasn't the club's fault he'd been inside.

"It's good to be back, D. So damn good." Maverick swallowed back the emotion that filled his throat and stunted his words.

When Delaney released him, he expected Dane, their VP, to be next in line, but it was Gunner, holding out Maverick's kutte, draped over his arms like a ceremonial offering.

In some ways, Gunner felt like Maverick's own kid. That was ridiculous; Gunner was only five years younger than he. But the kid was a mess, and Maverick had felt protective of him from the first night they'd met. He'd brought him into the Bulls because he thought his skills were useful, and also because he thought the club would give him some structure and an outlet, a way to make his self-destructive tendencies constructive. He'd gone inside less than a year after Gunner had earned his patch, but from a distance, he'd seen enough to know he'd been right.

He also knew, because he saw Gunner fairly regularly, that things were settling down and looking up for the kid. He had himself an old lady, and he seemed centered and happy. And not so much a kid anymore.

"My man," Maverick said, feeling a grin spread his stiff cheeks for the first time.

Gunner grinned back and held up the kutte on his arms. "Brother. This is for you."

Maverick took the kutte from his friend. Someone—had to be Gunner—had polished the pebbled leather to a soft, fine sheen, and the sun had warmed it so that it felt like comfort in his hands. Before he put it on, he held it to his face and breathed deep.

God.

He brushed his fingers over his name. He held it up so that he could see the Brazen Bull across the back. Feeling emotion rush up and fill his throat again, he coughed and swung the leather over his shoulders, shrugging his arms into it. Heavy familiarity settled onto his back, and he could almost feel his muscles swell.

"Goddamn," he muttered, and he grabbed Gunner and held the fuck on.

He was out. He was out. He was really out.

His life was almost within his reach again.

He and Gunner embraced until Delaney hooked a hand on Maverick's shoulder. "Let's get you the fuck away from his hellhole, Mav. Let's get you home."

He stepped away from Gunner, and the rest of his brothers, those he knew and those he didn't, took their turns welcoming him back to the world. He learned that the men he didn't know were Apollo and the prospects, Slick and Wally. Griffin, who'd been a prospect when he'd gone in, was a full-fledged patch now.

After he had back-slapping hugs from them all, they cleared a path so that he could see his Harley—his beautiful, sleek, black FXS Low Rider—parked across the road, shining in the sun.

He was out. He was free.

~oOo~

The Brazen Bulls' neighborhood looked almost exactly the same as the last time he'd seen it. A few of the storefronts had changed, and the church on the corner at the opposite end of the block, the Glory to the Savior Fellowship, had gotten a fresh coat of paint and a new (though still lettered by hand and not very well) sign, but otherwise, it was perfectly familiar.

Sorry for the glorious ride up from McAlester to end, Maverick pulled into the Bulls' lot, followed by his brothers. As they parked their bikes, a line of women came from the back. Mo, Delaney's wife and the queen of the clubhouse, had the lead.

"Hello, love." She smiled and held up her arms, and Maverick gave her a tight squeeze. Shit, it felt good to hold a woman again, even a woman who was more mother to him than anything. When his body stirred at the touch of her breasts on his chest, he stepped back.

"Missed you." He kissed Mo's cheek.

"And we all missed you," Joanna, Dane's wife, said, and came in for a hug of her own. This time, Maverick kept some distance between their bodies.

He hugged Maddie, Ox's old lady, and he met Willa and Leah, old ladies to Rad and Gunner. Willa stepped up for a friendly hug. Leah held back a little, looking up at him with a shy smile. She was a young one. He'd known that; Gunner had told him she was younger—like twenty, maybe?—but it was still a bit of a shock to see such a fresh, innocent face in a place like this.

He held out his hand. "Hey, Leah. Good to meet you. I hear you take good care of my brother."

She set a slim hand in his. When he closed his fingers around hers, she squeezed back, showing strength. "I try to. He takes better care of me, I think."

Maverick turned to Gunner and hooked his arm around his neck, pulling him close. "That's good to hear. Knew he'd turn out good eventually."

"Fuck you, Mav," Gunner laughed and put an elbow in his chest.

"We've a house full of people waiting to welcome you home, love," Mo said and hooked her arm through his. "And a line of girls waiting to ease your aches and show you some love."

Maverick let Mo lead him into the clubhouse. He tried to be excited about the party that awaited him. He tried to be glad to be home. And he was. Fuck, he was glad to be here. But this wasn't the home he needed right now, and the girls inside weren't the love he needed.

He needed what he'd had four years ago. He needed Jenny and his daughter. He needed his family.

~oOo~

A few hours later, as a hot dusk settled over the neighborhood, Maverick sat on a battered old sofa on the patio. He was nursing a beer and had sent off the girl who'd attached herself to him—Kymber or Timber, he wasn't quite sure—to have a minute of peace and quiet.

After the rigid routines of prison life, the clamor of the clubhouse had already worn on him. The loud music, the laughter, the drugs and booze, the practically naked women—his brain and body couldn't take much more.

For all the familiarity of the neighborhood, the clubhouse itself had been a bit of a shock. Mo had been tearing through the place, redecorating and remodeling, and the only rooms that still looked entirely like he remembered were the kitchen—which she was apparently agitated to work on next—and the chapel, which Delaney had forbidden her to touch.

Going through the clubhouse, Maverick had had the feeling of coming home to a place he hadn't remembered correctly. Everything was almost right, and nothing was exactly right.

Jenny wasn't here. He'd known she wouldn't be. She'd cut him out the day he'd been sentenced, and there was no reason to believe she knew or cared that he'd been released.

But in those dark hours of his last night in his cell, when he'd let himself think about freedom, a tiny image, fed by the frailest capillary of hope, had floated in his mind: walking into the clubhouse, seeing Jenny sitting at the bar, watching her turn and see him, watching the anger he'd last seen on her beautiful, heart-shaped face fade out, seeing the love he'd known come back. In his fantasy, she'd produced a pretty little girl from behind her back, a little girl with butterscotch hair, who'd run to him and said, "Daddy!"

And then Jenny, flowing into his arms.

That hadn't happened, of course. Instead, he'd had a mortifyingly quick and unsatisfactory fuck with Timber-Kymber-Whoever, he'd gotten drunk on two shots of Jack and two beers, he'd puked his guts out, passed out for an hour, and now he was sitting alone, mostly sober, nursing a beer he wasn't enjoying, and trying to figure out what the fuck his life would be now.

He was out. He was free. He should have been happy.

Kymber—he decided to go with that; it sounded more name-like—sashayed over on her high heels. She was carrying a beer, its chill made obvious by the condensation beading the brown glass. She leaned down, putting cleavage in his face, and reached for the beer in his hand, hanging forgotten off the end of the sofa.

"Looks like you need a refresh," she simpered and took hold of his bottle.

Maverick reacted without thinking or understanding his own impulse. He yanked his hand back as if that warm, flat beer was the Holy Fucking Grail.

"Did I fucking *say* I wanted a refresh?"

It wasn't until Kymber's face registered real fear and she jumped back that Maverick realized how sharply he'd spoken. In his mental replay, he heard the menace and, shit, hate that had blazed out at this harmless chick.

The cold one dropped from her hand and shattered, and she dropped to the patio floor, crouching on those stupid shoes. "Sorry, I'm sorry, M-Mav. Oh shit, I'm sorry."

Her frightened obeisance made Maverick truly angry, and he had to hold himself back from lashing out again. His most potent impulse was too knock her away. But he didn't hurt women.

Jesus, prison had turned him into a fucking monster.

He got up and left the girl to her mess before he did something truly shitty.

~oOo~

"Hold up, Mav. I got your back." Gunner trotted up as Maverick kicked his bike to life.

Maverick shook his head and raised his voice over the engine. "Don't need a sitter, bro. Just need to ride."

"You shouldn't be on your own tonight."

He'd been surrounded for the past four years—by people, by bars, by walls, by fences, by cameras, by guns. Even in solitary, he'd been surrounded. Crowded in. What he absolutely needed on this night was to be on his own, out in the world, with the wind in his face and the scent of freedom in his head.

"Go back to your lady, Gun. I'm good."

~oOo~

He got on the highway, out of Tulsa, into the country, and rode for hours on narrow lanes twisting through woods and fields, rarely sharing the road with anyone. At first, and for a long time, his brain was nothing but noise, a cacophony of thoughts and feelings and memories that amounted to nonsense. Eventually, the road cleared all that out and let him think in a straight line, and he remembered that feeling. Four years had changed a lot, had made even familiar things different, but the feeling of finding his pitch on the road, that was exactly the same.

This was freedom. The ability to jump on his bike and ride until things made sense. Four years, he'd gone without a good mental cleansing. Four years of shit, really bad shit, pain and hate and anger and fear, loneliness and hopelessness and loss, piling up, gunking up his works, making his brain run choppy. He'd have to ride nonstop for the rest of his life to get everything back in working order.

He'd heard, from inmates landing back inside, usually on parole violations days or weeks after release, that it was impossible to go back to who you'd been before. Prison changed a man, broke him, made him somebody who couldn't function in freedom anymore.

But if that were true, every ex-con would end up dead or back in. So the trick was to find a new way to be.

The Bulls had been a few years into outlaw work when he'd gone in, mostly freelance, just beginning to do some small jobs for the Russians and build that relationship. Now, they were managing all of the Volkov traffic into the southwest and the north, across half the country and beyond. Small club that they were, they were big league outlaws. Eighty percent of their work was dark work. The risk of landing inside on club business was exponentially more than it had been when Maverick had gone in on personal business.

Could he deal with that? He'd done near his full time, so he wasn't on parole, but he was on supervised release for the next year. There would be a spotlight shining down on his head everywhere he went. Could he handle the possibility that he could land inside again? And be a repeat offender, with a sentence reflecting that?

He didn't know. But he didn't have a choice, either. He was a Bull. He loved his brothers, even the ones who'd forgotten him. And without the club, he had nothing.

A stoplight switched from yellow to red before him, and he braked and put his feet down. He was at the bottom of an exit ramp. The intersection was bright with light from the Mobil station on the corner, and Maverick realized where he was. Without consciously choosing to do so, he'd made his way back to Tulsa and was all the way to the east part of town.

He was four blocks from The Wayside Inn. Knowing that he absolutely should turn right and make his way back to the clubhouse, he turned left instead.

The neon light above the door was still on, but the street before the bar was empty. Maverick backed in at the curb and checked his watch. Fifteen minutes past last call. She'd probably locked the front door by now.

Then the door swung open, and two men came out. One paused, his shoulder still holding the door open, to light a fresh smoke. Maverick looked inside and saw a dim slice of an empty bar. And no Jenny standing there ready to lock up.

Maybe she wasn't working tonight. She couldn't possibly have managed the bar for its full schedule, so maybe somebody else was in charge tonight.

The customers sauntered down the sidewalk, and Maverick dismounted. He went to the door and yanked it open.

The juke was still playing: Loretta Lynn admonishing her man not to come home a'drinkin' with lovin' on his mind. That had to be Jenny's touch—she loved her good ol' fashioned country music.

But Jesus, she hated this bar.

Nothing about the place had changed in four years—or, for that matter, in twenty. It was still the same old beer-soaked dive he'd remembered, with the mismatched barstools, the rickety tables and chairs, the bubble-tube Wurlitzer 45 and the row of pin-up pinball machines along the back. Behind the bar were three shelves full of booze and two taps: Budweiser and Busch. No swishy imports or light beers on tap here.

Sitting at the end of the bar, a different bar, but still almost exactly as in his fantasy of the night before, was Jenny Wagner. Love of his life and mother of his child. She was doing some kind of paperwork. As in his fantasy, she turned.

"Sorry, we're cl—" the sentence died abruptly as she faced him and realized who he was.

Maverick stopped, ten feet away yet. In his fantasy, anger had given way to love on her face. In reality, irritation at somebody coming in after hours gave way to shock. They faced each other while Loretta finished her song and the juke went quiet.

God, look at her. So fucking beautiful. Her dark hair had gotten really long; it lay over her shoulders and covered her breasts. She was slim, maybe more than he remembered. She wore jeans and a snug top that bared her shoulders and the top half of her back, and showed deep cleavage in front. Maverick's cock swelled and ached.

"Jenny?" He'd wanted to sound strong and firm, but her name came from his mouth as a plea.

"You're not supposed to be here," she breathed, barely loud enough to travel the distance between them.

"Where else would I be? I love you."

God, he loved her so fucking much. Even now, even after she'd turned her back in anger he hadn't deserved, and left him to rot in prison without any hope, even after she'd refused him his daughter, he loved her.

She'd thought he hadn't said those words often enough, and when he promised he'd say them more, at least once every day, she'd started a habit of keeping count. What he wanted most right now, more than anything else in the world, was to hear her say the words, *That's one*.

March 1993

"That's one."

Maverick looked up from Jenny's neck, where he'd been nibbling at the sensitive, fragrant skin below her ear. "One? Come on, I said it this morning."

"It doesn't count if you say it when you're coming." She grinned and lightly flicked his nose. "Especially not if I'm swallowing at the time."

"But I mean it then, too. Sincerely."

"You would sincerely love a glory hole while you were getting your rocks off. Doesn't count."

He rolled his eyes but didn't protest that statement. He loved the fuck out of her, and she damn well knew it.

"Things're more precious when they're rare, you know. Ever think about that?" He sucked on her lobe, pushing his tongue through the little hoop of her earring.

She sighed and arched her naked body against his, and her voice took on a sultry tone, even as her gentle hectoring continued. "You're just lazy. I'm cooking your whole kid in here. The least you could do is throw me a few words every now and then."

He loved her, and the baby she was making for them. She needed the words, she said them to him all the time, so he would give them to her as often as she needed them. It was indeed the least he could do.

He skimmed his hand over her gently rounding belly. Four months along, she was just starting to look a little pregnant. His kid was in there. Next doctor visit, they'd get an ultrasound and maybe know what flavor she was cooking. Maverick just wanted a healthy kid, but he was pretty sure they were having a girl. He figured most guys wanted a son, and sure, he did, too, but the thought of a baby girl, looking at him the way Dane's girls looked at their dad? Damn. Yeah, he wanted that.

Moving down from her neck, he sucked on her collarbone, then licked over the flaming heart tattoo at the notch between her collarbone and her shoulder. He'd marked her as soon as they'd found out about the baby—and then she'd read in one of her trove of baby books that she shouldn't have gotten ink while she was pregnant, and she'd stressed out for weeks, until they'd heard a heartbeat and the doctor had told her to relax.

As he shifted farther downward, he murmured, "That all you want from me, babe? Just a few words?"

She moaned, arching her back to present her breasts as she spread her legs wide. "I love you. I'll take anything you give me."

"That's..." he'd kind of lost count.

"Four. Mav, make me feel good."

He took the invitation, pushing his hand down her belly and between her legs, over her trim, dark bush, and sucked her tit into his mouth as he slid two fingers inside her. At her writhing gasp, Maverick delved deep and sucked hard, and her nails raked up his back with such force that he broke from her breast with a hiss.

"Should've tied you up."

With her brilliant eyes locked on his, Jenny reached both hands back and grabbed onto their slatted headboard. "Do what you want with me," she purred, her face shining with trust and love.

"Oh, babe. There is so much I want. I love you so goddamn hard."

"That's two," she whispered and closed her eyes.

CHAPTER FOUR

"Where else would I be? I love you."

Jenny's heart raced and leapt, like it was trying to claw its way to freedom. Maverick stood right there, not ten feet away. She wasn't ready.

She'd known he would be released today, and she'd spent most of the day in a jittery state of watchfulness, expecting him to do exactly what he was doing now: pop up right in front of her. But then the hours had waned, and the night had gone quiet. The bar had emptied, and she'd begun to believe that he was going to do what she'd asked. What she'd demanded — leave her and Kelsey alone.

It was what she'd demanded, but now, with him standing there, telling her he loved her, she admitted to herself the thing she'd refused to acknowledge all these years: it wasn't what she wanted. She still loved him; she'd still harbored a tiny, frail, fluttering hope.

Things were so much more complicated than that. Kelsey didn't know about him, not in any concrete sense. She knew her father was 'not here,' and she hadn't yet asked any more incisive questions. As precocious as she was, as curious and insistent about answers, she'd so far been content to be told that not every family had a mommy and a daddy.

Now her daddy was here. Her father, at any rate. No — her daddy. Jenny couldn't, wouldn't pretend that Maverick didn't want to be his daughter's daddy. He'd wanted that since they'd been sitting on the side of the tub, staring at the test stick. He'd barely blinked before he'd asked her to keep the baby, before he'd committed to their family wholeheartedly — this big, bad biker, who'd spent great chunks of his free time punching people in the face, who rode and drank and fought and loved and fucked hard, had turned into a squishy marshmallow at the thought of having a child.

Things were so much more complicated than that now. It was more than Kelsey. It was her father, too. What Maverick had made of him. What he'd made of her life. He'd ruined it and left her in the rubble, alone but for their daughter and what was left of her father. He'd left her to raise their little girl on her own and to care for a man she'd been trying to escape.

She'd told him no. Again and again, throughout their relationship, she'd told him to stay out of the mess that was her relationship with her father. But he'd always believed he'd known better, that it had been on him to handle it his way, since she wouldn't do what he'd thought she should. He'd thought her way was weak, that *she* was weak, and he'd done what he wanted and then left her on her own.

But he'd been wrong—she was strong. She was still standing, and she'd gotten through these years on her own.

And now here he was. Saying the words she'd once had to cajole out of him.

He was changed. He'd always been fit and cut; he'd been a professional boxer and had continued to fight recreationally afterward, and he'd spent a lot of time working out. But now he was noticeably bigger, even more muscular. His plain black t-shirt strained under the swell of his body. But he seemed leaner, too. His jeans hung low and loose, almost as low as a lot of younger men wore their jeans now. His thick black leather belt—she'd bought him that belt, with its sterling silver buckle—cut across his hips.

More than anything else, his face had changed. There was a kiss of grey in his stubble, and his nose bulged oddly at its center, like it had been broken repeatedly and inexpertly reset each time. Scars bisected both eyebrows, and a thick scar hooked around his left eye, which didn't open quite as much as his right. His left ear was misshapen—more than it had been before. Its top was thick and tipped out from his skull noticeably.

His dark hair was shorter—almost shorn, with just a skim of stubble wrapped over his skull. There was grey in that, too. He was only thirty-four; that seemed young to be going grey.

Prison had aged Maverick severely.

During the past four years, Jenny had thought about him often, but she'd been careful to wrap her anger around her like a suit of armor first, to protect herself from despair. She hadn't allowed herself to think long about what his life was like. She'd done what he'd always said was the way to get through: 'head down, shoulder to the day.' She'd kept her mind on getting through each day of her own life, of her daughter's. Of her father's.

Now, seeing the ravages of prison life carved into his face, Jenny knew deep guilt. She had abandoned him, too.

An odd, choked noise came up her throat and out of her mouth, and she put her hand over her lips to prevent any more of them from following. When he moved, she realized that that sound had been the first she'd made since he'd said the words *I love you*.

He strode toward her, his hands—oh, his poor hands—came up and cupped her face, displacing her own from her mouth, and before she could take even one breath, his lips were on hers, fierce and desperate, and his tongue plunged deep.

She was overwhelmed, beyond resistance. He'd always overwhelmed her, pushed her toward new places, new sensations, bigger feelings than she could process, but this was different. This was four years of anger that had crystallized into hatred suddenly blowing apart, sending shards all through her. This was pain and despair and loss and fear slicing through every part of her. And love. God, so much love. Oh God.

Her hands hooked over his forearms — so warm and strong and familiar — and she kissed him back, rolling her tongue over his. He grunted and shoved his hands to the back of her head, grabbing fistfuls of her hair. His breathing was loud and frantic.

In four years, no one had touched her like this. Her life had been consumed by Kelsey and by her father and by this fucking hole of a bar, and she'd never spent a moment of these years in any other way. Her father's nurses and the regulars at the bar were the closest things she had to friends.

Maverick had been the last man to touch her, and the only one who'd ever mattered.

The scruff of his almost-beard dragged at her skin, made it burn and tingle, and she pushed closer, wanting more. Letting go of his arms, she circled his body and caught her hands in his t-shirt, grasping for hold against the snug pull of the cotton across his back.

He grunted again and dropped his hands from her hair to grab her hips. He lifted her from the stool she still sat on, and, following his lead, she hooked her legs around his hips as he slammed their bodies together. The thick, granite-hard ridge of his cock pressed between her legs, digging the seam of her jeans into her clit, and she cried out into his mouth.

All at once, he turned to stone, still clutching her, keeping them pressed as tightly together as their clothes would allow. Even his tongue went still and receded from her mouth. He groaned, his hands clenched, driving his fingers into the meat of her hips, and Jenny felt a throbbing between her legs that was more than her own body's need.

He'd come. She realized that even before his body sagged and he set her back on the stool.

"Fuck," he muttered shakily and let her go. "Son of a bitch. Goddammit." In a burst of temper, he shoved at the papers she'd been working on, and they scattered over the bar and fluttered to the floor behind it.

She was on the verge of saying it was okay, which was nonsense considering she had no clue if any part of anything that was happening was okay, when he stalked away without another word, toward the bathroom.

Quivering and breathless, Jenny slid woozily off the stool and collected the strewn papers—vendor receipts, inventory tallies, and the beginnings of a restocking list. She shoved them in the drawer under the register and went to lock up and turn out the sign. She still had to close out the register and do her usual closing work, but that was obviously going to have to wait a few minutes.

Maverick was back.

Jenny tried to think, but her mind and body were full of noise. And need. And…

Maverick was back.

She poured herself a finger of Jack, and poured a couple for him as well. She had just finished hers when he came back from the bathroom. When she nudged the glass toward him, he picked it up and swallowed it down at once.

He set the empty glass on the bar, and they stared at each other.

Jenny couldn't stand it. Though she didn't know how to make sense, she needed something to fill the silence. "Mav—"

"I need back in, Jen. I'm so pissed at you, and you've made it fucking clear you don't want me. Believe me, I got the fucking memo. I feel like a goddamn pussy for saying it, but I don't know what this is out here, or who I am. I can't do this on my own. The club's not enough. I need you. I need..." His voice caught, and Jenny's heart broke. "I need Kelsey."

She wanted to say yes. For all her efforts to keep her anger stoked to the heat of hatred, she wanted him back. But it wasn't that easy. "It's not that easy."

"You've got somebody." He said the words as if he were handing out a death sentence, but she didn't know whose.

"No. There's nobody. There hasn't been anybody."

Something in his face changed, softened. "Then why?"

"She..." Jenny stopped, afraid to say it. Swallowing hard, she made the words happen. "She doesn't know about you."

His head dropped. There was a jagged scar across his crown. He'd worn his hair longer when they were together, so she'd never seen his scalp, but she could tell that this scar was one he'd gotten in the past four years. She wondered how it had happened.

When he looked up again, the blue of his eyes seemed deeper. "Nothing?"

"No. She hasn't asked much yet, and I haven't told her."

"What did I do to make you hate me so goddamn much?"

She didn't hate him; that had been a lie she'd told herself because it had given her energy to get through her life. She understood that now. "You know what."

"I protected you. Jesus Christ, Jen. You think he ever would have stopped? Why would he—you let him go at you and apologize, over and over in a cycle for your whole life."

That day came roaring back to the foreground of her consciousness, and with it the anger she'd gotten so comfortable with reclaimed its central place in her heart. "He did it because I was breaking away from him. I was done with him. And now I never will be. You didn't listen to what I wanted, what I needed, you didn't even let me get the words out, and then you left me, and I was alone with that man and a new baby. You told me we'd make a great family, and then you tore it all apart before she was even here. That's what you did."

She was shaking again. When she poured more Jack into her glass, the neck of the bottle rattled on the rim. She poured some for Maverick, too.

"I was protecting you," he said again before he drank his whiskey.

"You were doing what you wanted, without listening to me. What you always do."

"I remember that day, too, Jen. It's burned into my fucking brain. I remember you saying that you provoked him. That's bullshit victim talk. Why should I have listened to that?"

"Because you said you loved me, and I was telling you what I wanted to do with my own father. What I *needed*. If you loved me, that should have mattered."

His hands clenched the edge of the bar, and he spoke in careful, measured syllables. "I let him threaten you. I let him grab you and leave a damn bruise on your arm. I didn't do shit about that because you said you had to handle it yourself. I fucking hated it, but I didn't go for him. I brought you to me instead. But then he hit you while you had our kid inside you. *My* kid, while you were huge with her. It wasn't just you he hurt. I'll never sit back when somebody goes at my kid. And I'll never sit back when somebody goes at my woman. Not ever again."

"If you'd listened to me, if you'd waited even one minute to hear what I had to say, I would have told you that I was done with him. It was over. If you'd heard that and let it be, we could have been together all this time. Raising our little girl together. The family you promised me."

Maverick shook his head. "I hate that I missed all this time. Not a day has gone by that I haven't been torn up inside with missing you and her. I'm so fucking sorry I wasn't here with you. But I don't for a *second* regret what I did to that piece of shit old man of yours. Only thing I regret is he's still breathing at all."

Jenny regretted that, too. It made her feel guilty to wish her father dead, especially in his helpless state now, but she did. The pendulum of ambivalence she'd felt for him for most of her life—love and fear, guilt and hate, swinging ceaselessly back and forth—had settled into resignation. She felt nothing for him but the weight of his burden—and that vestige of guilt, the knowledge that a truly good person would have more compassion and forgiveness for such a compromised soul.

"He *is* breathing, though, and I'm stuck with him, and with this stupid fucking bar. I'm stuck in a life I hate, and that's your fault, Maverick. I had it handled, and you destroyed it. Your need to have your way and work your fists was more important than what I needed. That's what you did to make me keep Kelsey from you."

"That's not fair, babe."

The word *babe* struck her like a slap, full of the memory of the life she'd had, they'd had, when he'd used that word routinely, as often as he said her name, maybe more.

"No. It wasn't fair, what you did to us. You're right."

Again, they stared at each other. Jenny kept her arms wrapped across her belly so that Maverick wouldn't see how hard she was shaking. She wanted him to hold her again, to kiss her the way he had, to make her feel safe and loved again, but now that they'd said all this, she remembered why she'd cut him out. It hadn't been petty. He really had torn everything down.

Finally, he sighed. "Don't keep her away from me, Jenny. I need to be her dad. I'll be a good one. You know I will."

"Do I? If some kid at the park is mean to her and makes her cry, are you going to beat him up?"

"A little kid? Jesus! What do you think I am?"

"Or that mean kid's dad? Are you going to beat him up? Right in front of her?"

That made him blink—they both knew that yes, if such a dad gave him lip, Maverick would lay him out. Right in front of Kelsey.

"Jen, come on. There's a lot of shit I need to work on, I know. But I'm fucking lost here. I don't know how much of me is left. I want to be a good dad. I want to be good for you and our girl. I want it all back. I need it."

They'd come full circle, and Jenny could only say the thing she'd started with. "It's not that easy."

"That's not a no. So tell me what I need to do."

Jenny thought about what they'd had before. She thought about that kiss, the feeling of being overwhelmed by him again, and how badly she'd needed it. She thought about the love for him that burned again in her heart, fighting with the anger and quelling it. She thought about the Bulls—that thick envelope, and Rad's threat.

There was no question that she would let Maverick in in some way. She wanted it. He needed it. The club would demand it. And he *would* be a good dad—flawed, but good. She was plenty flawed herself, but she thought she landed in the good range most of the time.

The question was how she would let him in, and how far. She didn't know, but she couldn't put off figuring it out any longer.

"I need some time. I need to figure things out."

That seemed to be a sufficient answer to give him hope; his body visibly relaxed, but not that sag of defeat that had happened earlier. "Can I at least see her?"

Always pushing. She let out a frustrated breath, making sure he could hear its sharpness. "I need some time, Maverick. Give me time."

"You had four years. How much more do you need? I'm laying myself out here, babe. Wide open."

Four years of anger and denial didn't count. This half hour—if that—had changed things, but they were moving into old territory now. They'd rarely fought as a couple, but not because he hadn't pissed her off routinely. He was just so pushy and relentless, never raising his voice, rarely even sounding angry, but always asking for a little bit more, under the guise of 'talking it out,' until she was too exhausted and insecure to continue and simply gave in.

Back in those days, she hadn't been good at standing her ground at all. It had been difficult to feel safety in her own strength, growing up as she had, never knowing whether she was going to get a slap or a hug in response to any word or deed.

These four years had taught her how to stand up. So she replied, "You need to get out, Mav, and stay away for now. I'll call the clubhouse when I have something to tell you."

He held her gaze for a few more seconds, then nodded and walked out of her father's bar.

~oOo~

She was home late that night, and, after another finger of whiskey after she'd locked the door behind Maverick, was a bit more buzzed than she should have been for driving. The trip wasn't long, though, and she got home without trouble.

Darnell was dozing on the sofa, with some old movie playing quietly on the television, its undulating glow the only light in the room. She eased quietly to the sofa and pressed on his shoulder. He woke at once.

"Hey there, girl."

"Sorry I'm so late."

He grinned and sat up. "Not a problem. You don't make a habit of it, so I don't mind. No place I was goin' but bed, anyway. This sofa's more comfortable than my bed."

It was a good sofa—lots of cushy padding, the kind a weary body could sink into. "Thank you. You're awesome."

Jenny was lucky with Darnell, because he loved kids, had been single for the past couple of years, and, for a little extra cash on the top of his home-nurse salary, he happily added Kelsey's care to his duties on the evenings that she had the bar. He really was awesome.

He got up and stretched his long frame until his hands touched the popcorn ceiling. "Everybody's settled down to a good night's sleep around here. Little incident tonight I should tell you 'bout. Earl got agitated over something on the news—who knows what with him, you know—and lashed out. Kelse was standing next to his chair the way she does, patting his arm and watching television with him. His elbow got her in the face."

Her father had little control over his body, but he wasn't paralyzed. Sometimes he lashed out in ways they couldn't predict, and sometimes he simply spasmed. Jenny had been popped repeatedly by her father's flailing limbs, but he'd never hurt Kelsey before.

"What? Oh God! Is she okay?" She turned and looked toward the doorway, as if she could see her daughter from there.

"She's good, it's all good. Cried a little, had a red mark on her forehead for an hour or so, but no lump and no bruising. I talked to her about how his body works, gave her a rainbow Band-Aid just for the kick of it, and she was good. Kissed Grandaddy good night just like usual. No fear. We read *Stellaluna* for bed, and she had a million questions about bats. She's probably gonna be askin' for a pet bat tomorrow."

Calming down, Jenny laughed. "Happens every time we read that one. I'm thinking about getting one of those bat houses, but then she'd probably try to climb the pole so she could see inside." She'd done that when they'd put a wren house in the back yard. It hadn't been enough that the wrens could use it and she could watch them flying around. She'd wanted to see them 'in their house.' Jenny had been working on her little vegetable patch when she'd turned to see her daughter trying to climb up a stack she'd made of random objects—including an upended wash pail, a brick from the flower bed edging, a half-deflated four-square ball—as high as her head.

"Thank you." Suddenly, Jenny was utterly fucking exhausted. What a goddamn day. She yawned obnoxiously, and Darnell laughed.

"Get yourself to bed, girl. I'll see you Monday." He patted her arm, and they walked to the kitchen, where he gathered up his stuff and Jenny saw him out, locking the door behind him.

He'd done the dishes, and they were arranged tidily in the drainer. Too tired to put them away, Jenny turned on the light over the sink, turned off the overhead, and went to check on her family.

She went to her father's room first and peeked in. He was sleeping in his hospital bed, his big wheelchair standing beside it. His CPAP was in place and turned on, making its usual ponderous hum. All the other machines—heart monitor, blood pressure, pulse ox—were doing their thing, and the readout on the screen looked normal.

Someday, they wouldn't. Someday, the trouble alerts would wake her up, or maybe she'd sleep through them and simply wake up one morning to a steady tone. When that day would come, she couldn't say, and neither could his doctors. For a man in his condition, he was fairly healthy. He could live for many years.

She didn't go in. Tomorrow afternoon and evening, and all day Sunday, she'd be on her own to deal with him, and she'd get plenty of father-daughter time then. She crossed the hall to her daughter's room.

Kelsey was sound asleep, curled into the snug little ball that was her most common sleeping position. Tucked under her chin was Mr. Spotsie, a panda she'd gotten for Christmas. He'd made the slumber-party cut tonight. The big pink daisy on the wall that was her nightlight gave its cozy pink glow to the room.

Perfectly centered on her forehead was a little Lisa Frank Band-Aid, rainbow colors with leopard spots. Jenny brushed her daughter's hair back and felt her forehead—no bump.

Kelsey sighed and moved her head, getting closer to her mother's touch. "Run, puppy, hurry," she murmured in her sleep. A sweet giggle followed before she settled back into deep sleep.

Leaning close, Jenny kissed the bandage. "Night, pixie."

As she got to the door, she turned around and considered her little girl, sleeping so serenely, hugging her stuffed panda and dreaming of puppies. There was so much of Maverick in her—her bright blue eyes alight with curiosity, the shape of her smile, her refusal to be dissuaded, even her temper, flashing hot and flaming out in a blink. She saw herself in Kelsey, too, but there was no way to deny that her daughter was more than only her. And there was no way to deny that Kelsey needed more than only her. Teachers and neighbors and nurses were raising her daughter as much as, if not more than, she was.

Temper or not, Maverick would be a good father. At least as good as she was a mother. He'd love their little girl with a fierce and quiet fire. He would take care of her. He would protect her—and that would be the thing Jenny would have to show him how to control.

But there was no question in her mind or her heart, no honest question, that he would be a good father. In fact, it was the first thing she'd ever thought about him.

Okay, the second. First, she'd thought that he was smoking hot. Then, she'd thought that he'd make a good father someday.

November 1991

Jenny maneuvered her cart into the ladies' section, shoving past overloaded rounds of sweaters and blouses. Wal-Mart always packed everything too closely together. In the sections and in the aisles, it was impossible to travel through the store unimpeded, especially late on a Saturday afternoon. It was like it was some kind of nefarious scheme they'd concocted to trap customers in the store like rats.

Usually she enjoyed shopping much more than this, but she was frazzled and tired today. She'd finished a shitty early shift at The Roost, and her feet hurt. It wasn't even Thanksgiving yet, but she was already tired of Christmas carols — especially 'Last Christmas.' Man, she despised that stupid song, and she *really* hated the way it wormed into her head and stayed there for *hours* after she heard it. Seriously, if she ever went postal, she'd blame George Fucking Michael.

But it was Mrs. Turner's birthday tomorrow, and she couldn't let that day pass by. As usual, once she'd put her hands on a cart, she'd gotten sucked into the Wal-Mart vortex and now had probably fifty bucks' worth of shit she didn't need and hadn't wanted an hour ago. And still hadn't gotten over to the housecoats and slippers.

She was headed toward the sleepwear, but something sparkly on a round by the wall of jeans caught her eye, and she left her cart where it was and wended her way over. Oh, it was cute — a creamy mohair sweater with iridescent sequins scattered over it. She liked the wide neckline that would drop off her shoulder and show her new red bra with the wide satin straps. Victoria's Secret — she'd never spent so much on a bra before, but it was pretty, too pretty to hide under her clothes. She felt sexy in it. She could wear this sweater and that bra to The Roost's Christmas party, with her Guess jeans and her tall boots, and see what Brent thought about that.

Flipping through the hangers, she found a sweater marked 'S' and double-checked the price tag against the sewn-in tag to make sure the sizes matched. They did, and the price was okay, so she looked around for a mirror. She was reliably a Small, so she didn't need to try it on, but she wasn't sure about cream with her coloring. A couple of years ago, she'd had her color analyzed and was supposedly a winter—dark hair, skin tone everybody called 'peaches and cream,' light eyes—but she thought she looked like a corpse in white. Maybe cream, though?

There was a mirror by the accessories, so she went back to her cart and pushed her way to the other side of the ladies' section.

She took off her coat and hung it over the side of her cart, then took the sweater off the hanger. Laying it over her t-shirt to approximate its fit on her chest, she pushed her boobs out a little and considered the look. Her hair was still up in the high ponytail she wore for work, like a spout on her head, and she wasn't wearing much makeup.

She looked like crap. Gross.

With a sigh, holding the sweater to her chest, she pulled the elastic out and gave her head a hard shake until her hair fluffed and settled on her shoulders. Then she tried again.

Better. She shimmied her chest a little so that the sequins caught the light and reflected in the mirror. For good measure, she gave her hips a shake, too.

"Looks good," a gruff male voice at her side pronounced.

Jenny jumped and squeaked and nearly wrenched her neck turning toward the owner of that voice while she yanked the sweater off her chest. "Huh?"

Oh God. The most gorgeous man she'd ever seen in the twenty-three years of her whole *life* stood right there. Look at him! Holy *shit*! He wore a black leather biker jacket—the kind with silver zippers, snaps, and buckles—and a plain white t-shirt under it. Dark jeans and engineer boots. No shit, it was like James Dean was standing in front of her—James Dean if he'd been well over six feet tall and had had dark hair. And broad shoulders. What was under that jacket and t-shirt? Something good, no doubt. Something *real* good. He was grinning at her, and his eyes—so blue, dreamy, dive-in-and-die-happy blue—twinkled.

He had four handbags hanging on one arm, and another in his hand. All were dainty, shiny bags for fancy dress.

"The sweater." His voice rolled from his lips like his throat was equipped with a glasspack. "Looks good. I like the sparkles."

"Uh." Fuck, her brain had dived in and died in his blue eyes.

He chuckled—she felt the sound in her belly—and winked, then turned back to the holiday handbag display.

When he turned away, her brain revived and found her tongue. "I think the silver lamé goes best with your jacket." Oh! Good one, Jen. Sassy but not mean. Flirty. Well done.

Those blue eyes swung back to her and brought that grin with it. "Thanks for the tip, but it's not for me."

"Your girlfriend? Or wife?" She blushed—could she have *been* more obvious?

Clearly not. Tall, Dark, and Dean's grin sharpened, and his eyes gleamed. "My...niece, I guess. It's her birthday. Fourteen."

"Oh, cool. Did she ask for a bag like that?" Was that a good question? She definitely didn't want to stop talking, but she didn't want to be rude and put him off, either. He was showing possibly some interest, and she was fairly certain a sign saying COME ON IN WE'RE OPEN flashed over her head.

"Nah. But she likes to dress fancy, and she likes purses. Since she was little, she's always carrying a different one around every time I see her, hooked on her arm like a grand old lady." His tone and expression took on a different aspect, sweet instead of sly. He loved this girl he was talking about. Enough to have noticed her little purses. He did not look like a man with a vast knowledge of, or interest in, women's accessories.

Suddenly, out of the freaking blue, she imagined this guy with a little girl in his arms, resting on his hip, her arms locked around his neck. He'd be a good father, she was sure of it.

Cripes. Two months without sex and her hormones were on red alert.

He held his arm out, with the handbags dangling from it. "Which one d'you think is best?"

Jenny stepped closer, so that his arm crossed before her and his body was at her side. Up close, he was almost imposingly tall—maybe six-two, six-three. Nearly a foot taller than her five-four. She could smell him—something rich and deep. Not cologne, but alluring in a similar way. Maybe just his leather and his soap. She took a deep breath through her nose, trying to be subtle about it.

Keeping her voice and her body steady and assured, she studied the different bags. "She's fourteen?"

"Yep." Now that she was closer, he'd dropped his voice so that it was almost a caress over her ear.

"Favorite color?" One of the bags was bright red. Another was gold sequins. Then the silver lamé, a black beaded clutch on a satin cord, and a black satin drawstring sac with a red crystal heart charm the size of a half-dollar coin.

"Uh...blue, maybe? She's a redhead, if that helps."

She lifted the satin sac. "This one. It's versatile, and she'll like the charm. She could take it off the cord and wear it as a pendant if she wants—if you were into it, you could get her a chain, too, so she could do just that."

He furrowed his brow at the bag. "I don't know. Her old man would gut me like a fish if I gave his fourteen-year-old daughter a heart necklace. No matter what I meant by it."

"Ah. Good point. Well..." she turned to the display and considered the other bags. There was a long hook full of those satin sacs, all with different crystal charms. One had a pink flower. "How about this one? What are her thoughts on pink?"

"I think she's good with pink." He tried to work the other sacs off the hook while his arm was still burdened with the bags they'd rejected. Jenny moved in to help him, and his hands and hers got tangled up. Just for a second, just long enough for his rough fingertips to skim her knuckles. Again, her belly fluttered like he'd touched her there.

They got the bags sorted out so that those he didn't want were back in fairly neat assembly on the display, and he had the one with the pink flower charm.

"Thanks for your help." His smile had turned sly again, but he made no more move.

Just 'thank you.'

Jenny had never made a move on a man in her life. She wouldn't know how to begin. Always, she waited for the man to ask her out, or ask for her number, or start the conversation. It was a small miracle that she'd comported herself with this guy as competently as she had.

"Um. Okay. Well, I hope she likes it. Have a good night."

When he tipped an imaginary hat at her and turned away, Jenny went to her cart and pushed it to the sleepwear, trying to ignore the disappointed bubble in her belly. Mrs. Turner liked matching housecoats and slippers, and she loved that Jenny always bought her a new set for her birthday. That was why she'd come shopping, not to pick up men.

~oOo~

She'd kept her eyes peeled while she'd been in the store and especially as she was checking out, but he must have checked out as soon as he'd had his purse, because she hadn't seen him again.

She scanned the parking lot, too. It had gone dark while she'd been shopping, so she didn't have much hope. But then, parked in a striped space under a light standard, centered in the halo of light, was a big, shiny black Harley. It totally looked like a bike James Dean would ride—the actual James Dean or her new personal favorite version. She supposed there could have been another biker in Wal-Mart. Tulsa wasn't exactly hostile to bikers; they even had their own MC in town, and most people she knew thought they were decent guys. Actually, she didn't even know if he *was* a biker. He'd been wearing that jacket, but that could have been a style choice.

Still, a girl could hope.

Moving as slowly as was reasonable, she made her way to her Escort and opened the hatch. She carefully placed each blue sack inside, and the new tube of giftwrap, and closed the hatch. Then to the cart corral, like a bipedal sloth.

When she turned back, out of ways to delay, there was a tall, dark form leaning on the rear fender of her car.

Oh, praise Jesus and all his disciples.

She walked straight toward him, at a significantly more purposeful pace. When she was close enough, he held out his hand, and she took it without even thinking about whether it was smart to do so.

Big and warm, rough and hard. This was a man who worked with his hands.

"Didn't get your name."

He pulled her close and turned, pushing her back to the side of her car, then leaned in, gripping the roof and framing her between his arms. He was wearing more leather—a vest over his jacket. There were a couple of white strips patched to his chest. It was too dark to read them, but she understood. He was more than a biker—he was an actual Brazen Bull.

He'd asked for her name. "Jenny." She whispered it, afraid to break the spell.

"Hi, Jenny. I'm Maverick."

"Maverick?" She couldn't trust her hearing or any other bodily function just then, but that hadn't sounded like a name. Except for Tom Cruise in *Top Gun*.

"Yep. You got a fella?"

She shook her head, and he smiled.

"Been thinkin' about kissing you since I saw you dancing around in that sweater. What d'you think about that?"

Jenny thought it was one of the better ideas in the history of man. Right up there with flight. And Reese's Peanut Butter Cups.

She nodded, and he bent his head to hers.

Oh yeah. Absolutely brilliant idea.

He didn't have a beard, but his face was rough with the day's growth. That fine sandpaper contrasted starkly with the warm velvet of his lips and made Jenny's nerves stretch out. He kept his tongue to himself, let his lips caress hers until she felt greedy for more. She was surrounded by him, drowning in the scent and heat of him, and she opened her mouth as much to breathe as to ask for his tongue.

When she touched her tongue to his lip, his chuckling breath stuttered across her cheek. He shifted, no longer leaning his weight on his hands, and wrapped his arms around her, sliding under her open coat. The move brought her body firmly to his chest—broad and hard as a brick wall—and she was dwarfed and overwhelmed. As his tongue pushed into her mouth, he leaned forward, forcing her to bend backward, so far that she had to trust him to hold onto her so she wouldn't fall.

He held on, and she didn't fall, not even when her heart raced so hard she thought she'd pass out.

After a glorious, breathtaking, impossibly brief eternity, he pulled back and brought her up. As if he knew that her knees were weak, he held her tightly for another few seconds, until she could support her own weight.

When she opened her eyes, he was smiling slyly down at her. "I gotta go, but I think I'm gonna need your number, Jenny."

She nodded. He let her go and rooted inside his vest. He pulled out a felt-tip pen, handed it to her, and held his hand out flat, palm up. Her hand shook as she took the cap off the pen and wrote the number of The Roost across his callused skin.

"This is where I work. You can reach me there, or leave a message." She couldn't risk him calling home when she wasn't there.

He cocked a curious look at her but didn't ask any questions. While she watched, he pursed his lips and blew over the ink. Then he caught her chin in his other hand and bent his head—oh yay! He was going to kiss her again.

"I hope you work a lot. 'Cuz I'm gonna be in touch real soon." He laid his lips on hers for the space of a heartbeat, and then he stepped away.

"You have a good night, Jenny."

"Thanks. You, too." Ugh, how lame.

With another sly grin, he turned and walked—no saunter, no strut, just a steady, confident stride—to that shiny black Harley. Jenny stood and watched him pull a pair of gloves on, mount his bike, and fire the engine up. He pulled off, sending her a jaunty salute as he rolled by.

She watched until he turned out of the lot. Then the spell broke, and she was standing on a Wal-Mart parking lot, alone in the cold.

But a sexy man called Maverick had just kissed her practically unconscious and asked for her number. She touched her fingers to her swollen lips and smiled.

CHAPTER FIVE

Maverick hadn't slept, not to speak of, in days. Since that last, entirely wakeful night in his cell, he'd been lucky to catch a couple of forty-five-minute naps in a night. The bed in this crash room was too big and too comfortable, the pillows too fluffy, the linens and blankets too soft. The clubhouse sounds and smells were all wrong.

And his brain would not shut the fuck up.

Even so, every morning, even after three nights spent staring at the ceiling, he was on his feet before six-thirty, working the kinks from his long-abused body. He showered and dressed and made his bunk...his bed. Then he went downstairs for breakfast.

The first morning, after that shitty, surreal encounter with Jenny, where he'd creamed his goddamn jeans like a thirteen-year-old, he'd stood in the middle of the room and waited for first count. Even after he'd realized how stupid that was, it had taken him a couple of attempts to make his body go to the door, try the knob, open it, and step through.

He had forgotten how to live a life without permission.

By Monday morning, he'd stopped waiting for first count, but he was far out of sync with the world nonetheless. Even a window without bars or chicken wire was strange and unsettling, and he'd caught himself several times staring out the club's front windows, transfixed by the vehicles and people moving freely about.

Activity already bustled in the party room this Monday morning, when Maverick came down at about quarter to seven. Delaney had called church for seven, and Mo had come with him. Several boxes of doughnuts and pastries were lined up on the bar, and the rich aroma of strong coffee brewing wafted through the room.

Good coffee—absolutely one of the highlights of life outside. No more instant.

Mo smiled when he went up to the bar. "Morning, love. How're we doing today?" She poured him a cup without asking and passed the cream over.

"I'm okay. You?" He ignored the cream. He'd taken cream before, but the crap they'd had inside had been the powdered creamer filth, and he'd never even tried to develop a taste for it. He'd taken the prison swill black, and his first cup of coffee with real cream on the outside had tasted like custard. He was a black coffee man now.

"Two more weeks before I go back to school, and I'm gonna enjoy every second. I was thinkin' you and I could do some apartment hunting, if you're of a mind."

The thought of renting a place gave him a weird, vaguely sick feeling. A whole apartment to himself? Alone? He was too used to four close walls. More space than that made him feel loose and unsteady. He didn't want to be alone. He wanted the apartment he'd had with Jenny. That had been his alone for years, but it had become a home when she'd moved in. He wanted that home back.

But he didn't have it, not yet, and Delaney had already told him that he couldn't live in the clubhouse. He could stay only until he got himself settled, and the implication had been that he should be quick about getting settled.

He had money, at least. That wouldn't be a problem. Delaney and Simon had handed him a fucking sack of bound stacks of bills, and Simon had given him a sheaf of papers accounting his earnings for the past four years, less what they'd paid to Jenny over those years—and an accounting of that, as well. It was all in code, but Simon had explained it. The partnership with the Volkovs had been lucrative work. His cut was smaller because he hadn't worked the jobs, but even so, he had a decent nest egg.

He had money. Enough to put a good down on a little house, if he wanted. It'd be okay if Mo helped him out. Less lonely.

"Sounds good. I got...I gotta get with my probation officer today, and D wants me to put in some hours next door, but after work tomorrow, I could spend some time."

"That's good. I'll spend some time today putting together a list of places to see. Any thoughts on what you'd like?"

Jenny and Kelsey. That was what he'd like. But she hadn't called yet, and he wasn't sure he believed she ever would.

Maverick shook his head. "I trust you, Mo."

~oOo~

The club roster was not much changed since he'd last sat at this table—Griffin had been patched in while he was away, and Apollo had signed on to prospect, done his time, and been patched in during his sentence. The new prospects were strangers to him. But otherwise, he knew his fellow Bulls.

And yet, he felt like the stranger at this table. Becker had taken Maverick's customary seat, and there was a minute or two of awkwardness as they figured out how to reconfigure the table. Ultimately, Becker made way for Maverick, and he sat where he'd always sat, and felt like it was somebody else's place.

Delaney started the meeting by welcoming him back to the fold, and there was more cheering and back-slapping. But then that was over, and a normal club meeting began. As Maverick listened to the financial report and the status of various jobs he hadn't been part of, including the Russian gun routes, he understood that he was out of sync even with his club. As stable as the club roster had been, much had changed in four years. They'd been dominant in local and regional outlaw circles before, but now they were playing on a national stage. They were moving guns for some very bad folks, to some even badder folks.

He was no law-and-order tightass. Hardly. He'd been a rebel from the time he'd first said no. He was far happier handling his grievances himself, with his fists, than looking to any system to do it for him. He fucking *despised* institutional power—even more after spending four years as its bitch. Nothing that the club had done before had given him pause. They'd kept the outlaw work in bounds, only laying down hurt where it was earned. They'd kept innocents clear, and they'd put good out into their neighborhood and town, good they wouldn't have been able to do without the bad. He was proud to be a Bull. They'd earned the respect that patch got them—and it was respect, not fear.

But he wasn't so sure that this work with the Russians was in bounds—not the same bounds, anyway. He'd killed two people in his life: one in a boxing ring, his last fight, and the other in prison, on the club's orders—on Irina Volkov's orders. Maverick had never even met the woman, but he'd killed for her, and he'd paid dearly for it.

Before the Volkovs, the Bulls had never done a contract hit. Even Rad, the patch with the most blood on his hands, who'd put a lot of hurt down on people over the years, and had killed a few enemies of the club, had never, to Maverick's knowledge, killed for anyone but the club, in retaliation for harm done to one or all of them. Taking the life of someone with whom they had no personal beef? That was next-level shit.

It was going to take some work to get his head lined up with where his club had gone in his absence.

After they discussed the gun routes and the schedules for upcoming runs, none of which Maverick would be in on, since he couldn't leave the state, Delaney said, "Now. I wanted to get all that out of the way before we talked about what happened last night."

Everybody's attention drew to a fine point. Maverick looked around the table and decided that Delaney, Dane, Rad, and Eight Ball were already informed, but whatever was coming would be news to the rest of the members.

"The prospects got jumped last night, comin' out of Callwood Auto Supply. They'd picked up an order. Got the shit kicked out of 'em, and lost the van."

"Fuck!" Gunner barked. "They okay?"

Delaney nodded, and Dane picked up the talk. "Willa patched 'em up. We sent 'em home with a couple of girls to take care. They'll be okay. The van was full of off-book parts, but D already talked to Tulsa PD, and there'll be no blowback if they're still in the van when—if—law finds it."

The club van had delivered Maverick's bike to him at McAlester. It was no great prize for a car thief. Same one they'd been rolling before he'd gone away. "That van's a piece of shit. Were they after the cargo?"

"I don't think they were, no," Delaney answered. "Callwood is near Northside, just on the edge of Dyson turf. They've been setting little fires with us all around Tulsa for the past year or so, ever since…ever since you took Jennings out, Mav. Just trivial nuisance shit, slinging back and forth. But you're released, and two nights later this happens across the street from their border? Still not big, but real harm this time. Prospects say the guys that jumped 'em were black. I think Dyson's looking to beef."

91

Maverick was *very* interested in this. The hit on the prospects he didn't know wasn't the focus of his interest. The notion that the club might beef with the Dyson crew, though—he had a mountain of payback due on those bastards. He thought wiping out that whole fucking crew would go a long way toward getting his outlaw head screwed back on straight.

His hands curled into fists. He was all for this beef.

"Jesus fuck," Rad growled. "We don't do this shit in town. Not where we live."

"We do if that's where it's dropped on us," said Gunner.

Maverick turned and studied his friend. He really had changed a hell of a lot during these years. He'd always been the club's loose cannon, loyal as fuck and great in a fight, but crazier than most, and he'd always carried himself like somebody who thought he was already halfway in trouble before he'd gotten out of bed in the morning. Maverick had spent a lot of time with him, helping him find ways to keep his head tied to his shoulders without bringing trouble on himself or the club. There'd been times when that had been nearly a full-time job.

Now, though, he seemed calm. Even just sitting in his seat, he was different. He didn't fidget, for one thing. No infuriating shaking of his leg, his knee thumping against the table nonstop. Was that all about that pretty young blonde he'd marked?

"Right now, we need to know more. Apollo, get with your cousin at TPD and see if there's word on the van. Rad, Eight, Ox—go to Callwood, see if anybody saw anything. I'm gonna go talk to the kids, see if they remember more after some sleep, some food, and some head. Everybody else, get on with your regular day."

"D." Maverick jumped in before Delaney could gavel the meeting closed. With the president stopped and nodded, he said, "I want in on anything Dyson. I want to sit up front on any move we make."

"Could get dirty fast, brother," Dane said. "You sure you want that risk already?"

"Positive. I got my own shit to work out on that crew."

"Your head straight enough for it?" Delaney asked. "You're not steady yet, from what I see."

"I'm steady enough. If I'm not, that'll get me there. I paid hard for doing that hit. I'm owed now."

The table was quiet. Delaney narrowed his eyes and examined Maverick. Maverick stared right back. "Alright. You say you're ready, you're ready. But you hold tight until we decide what to do."

Maverick nodded. As long as he was on point when the Dyson crew got hit, he'd wait for the plan that would make it happen.

~oOo~

After church, Maverick did a few hours at the Sinclair station. Simon had been doing all of their auto body work on his own these years, getting some help with the heavy stuff from a couple of the guys. He'd spread his shit all over the body-work bay, like he owned the damn place. So most of Maverick's first shift was spent muscling himself back into place where he'd once had seniority. After that, he'd hung out in front with the codgers from the neighborhood. A couple that he'd known had died, and a couple who'd been working men back then had taken their seats. Sitting with the old men in the hot sunshine, being pulled into their aimless conversation, was the first time since his ride on Friday night, before he'd stopped at The Wayside, that Maverick felt some peace.

How long was Jenny going to make him wait? He was Kelsey's father. No matter what she thought, he'd done nothing to warrant being kept away from his child. If Jenny didn't want him, that would tear him up, but he'd abide by that. But not being kept from Kelsey. No fucking way.

He reached into his pocket for his wallet and pulled out the little school picture Gunner had brought him.

"What you got there, Mav?" Horace, one of the old men, asked.

"Picture of my little girl." He held it out so Horace could see. It was the first time he'd ever shared that photo, the first time he'd ever introduced her as his own. "Kelsey. Kelsey Marie. She's gonna be four soon."

"Well, lookit that little miss. What a beauty. She looks smart, Mav. You must be proud."

"I am."

Horace handed the photo to Fred, who cooed over it as well. All the old men took their turn and made some comment or another that made Maverick's chest swell with pride and ache with loss. When it came back to him, he stared down at that sweet face, his own eyes shining impishly from it. He brushed his thumb over the matte surface, a gesture he made often, like he thought he could touch her that way. He'd done it so much that the gilt had rubbed off the small printing, showing the name of her school and the year the photo had been taken. He could barely make out the words: *Alphabet Acres Children's Center, 1996.*

The name of her school. It was the end of July, though—she probably wasn't in school now. But she was only in preschool, and Jenny ran The Wayside. She'd need child care. Did preschool run year-round? Did *this* preschool run year round? Was Kelsey still in this school?

Maverick had no answers, but he knew where to start to get some. He went into the station, around the desk, and pulled out the Yellow Pages. Still holding the photo between his fingers, he opened the book on the counter, flipping it to the As and sweeping pages by until he was on the right one. Using the photo as a guide, he found the listing, with a number and an address. There was a note pad stuck to the side of the register; he ripped a sheet off and wrote the information down.

"What're you doin', Mav?" Gunner asked. He'd come in from the pumps.

Maverick didn't answer. He shoved the paper in his pocket, put Kelsey back in his wallet, and slammed the Yellow Pages closed.

"I think that's a bad fuckin' idea, brother. This is the wrong time to piss her off."

That was rich—Gunner Wesson giving him advice. It'd be a cold day in hell. "I gotta go. Meeting with the probation officer."

"I'll ride with you. It's a light day on the pumps. Apollo can handle it on his own."

"I don't need an escort, Gun. I'm good."

Gunner stared at the Yellow Pages on the counter. Maverick picked up the tome and put it away.

"I said I'm good." He headed to the clubhouse to change out of his uniform.

~oOo~

The meeting with his probation officer was no big deal. He laid out the terms of Maverick's supervision and gave him a bunch of papers to fill out. It was a lot of bureaucratic bullshit, but in his case, Maverick would be clear of all this shit after a year, and out here in the wide, free outside, a year didn't seem bad at all. The officer—his name was Franklin—was impressed that he already had a home and work address. Slightly less impressed when he realized that it was the Brazen Bulls clubhouse and Delaney's Sinclair, but the guy was civil enough.

Back at his bike after that was done, he fished the notepaper from his pocket. He'd grown up in Tulsa and knew every street and alley of the place, so he knew exactly where Alphabet Acres Children's Center was.

Gunner was right; if Jenny found out he'd been lurking around Kelsey's school, she'd lose her shit. He could destroy any chance of getting his family back the way he wanted.

It didn't matter. He had—*he had*—to see his girl. Right now. He couldn't wait for Jenny to decide he was worthy. Kelsey was almost four years old, and he'd waited long enough. He needed to see more than her image in fading, tattered photographs. He needed to see her running and laughing and playing. He needed to see her *living*.

~oOo~

Alphabet Acres was a single-story brick building on a corner at the entrance to a subdivision. It looked nice enough, and well kept. Big elm and sycamore trees shaded a playground enclosed by a chain-link fence. The chain-link was higher-end, with green vinyl coating the wire.

There were kids playing all over the yard. Maverick pulled up at the curb across the street and killed his engine, and the sound of their laughter filled the air.

Was Kelsey one of those happy kids?

For a minute or two, he stayed astride his bike and tried to make her out from there, but he was too far, and the trees obscured part of his sightline, and there were too many playground apparatuses for a good view. He dismounted and walked around to the long side of the fence, trying to be inconspicuous. He didn't want to be perceived as some perv, and he knew that somebody might see his lurking around a preschool playground as decidedly wrong.

Beside one of the sycamores, he crouched down and scanned the yard through the fence. Still he didn't see her, and he began to think that she wasn't out there. Maybe her little class wasn't having playtime or recess or whatever they called it now. Or maybe she was home with her mom.

Then a path cleared, and there she was, sitting on the soft playground surface, drawing on the rubber with chalk. He'd expected her to have pigtails, like in her picture, but her hair was loose over her shoulders, caught back from her face with a pink clip. That butterscotch silk lay on her back and over her shoulder, fluffing gently in the light breeze.

She sat alone. Not laughing or running. Just drawing, concentrating, sitting with her little legs tucked under her bottom.

Maverick felt a tickle on his cheek and swiped the wet away.

As he watched, his daughter looked up and right at him, as if she'd known he was there, and their eyes locked. His chest hurt, like things inside him were breaking apart, but he didn't look away.

Kelsey stood and came toward him. Maverick stopped breathing.

When she got to the fence, she hooked chubby little fingers over the chain-link and smiled. "Hi. Do you want to play?"

Her little voice, sweet and high, was music. But he didn't like how she'd come right up to somebody she didn't know. "You shouldn't talk to strangers, honey. Didn't your mama tell you that?"

"Uh huh. It's Stra-nger Da-nger. Mommy says don't talk to strangers and hold her hand when we cross the street and say please and thank you and lots of stuff. Miss Betsy and Miss Connie say it, too. Are you a stranger?"

No. No, he most certainly was not. But to her, he was, and he didn't like that she'd just come up to him like this. Yet he couldn't make the word *yes* come out.

As he tried, she said, "Your eyes look sad. Are you sad?" and Maverick thought he'd die.

Then a woman's voice called out "Hey! No!" and a heavy young woman wearing a smock over her jeans ran up and took his daughter's hand, drawing her back from the fence.

"It's time to line up to go in, Kelsey. Will you please start the line for me?"

Kelsey nodded and turned back to him. "I have to go now. I'm sorry you're sad." She spun, her hair flying around her, and he watched her run away from him.

"I don't know what the hell you want, and I don't want to know," the woman snarled at him. "But we called the police." She stalked back toward the building.

Maverick knew he needed to get his ass in gear before law got there, but he couldn't move. He could still see her, standing near the door, while other kids lined up behind her.

God, she was even more perfect than he'd imagined.

When the line was long enough that he couldn't see her anymore, he was able to get up and get back to his bike.

Gunner was parked behind him, sitting sideways on his saddle, his arms crossed.

Had the tables turned so far that *Gunner* was watching out for *him* now?

"What're you doin' here, man?"

Gunner laughed and cocked up his mouth in its crazy grin. "That, my brother, is the question I should be asking you. This is straight-up insane behavior right here. Skulking around a preschool? Kelsey's preschool? Jenny will have your dick for supper and save your nuts for leftovers."

"I know. They called the cops. We gotta roll." He mounted his bike.

"Fucking fuck, Mav." Gunner mounted up, too. "Follow me."

He wanted to tell him to fuck off, but Gunner would just dog him all over town until he gave in anyway, so he nodded, and they pulled away.

They passed a Tulsa PD cruiser two blocks from the school.

~oOo~

He followed Gunner to a drive-up taco joint. He hadn't eaten since downing one of Mo's pastries with his coffee that morning, so he wasn't entirely opposed to getting some greasy food. All food on the outside tasted like fucking Thanksgiving now.

They sat at a round plastic picnic table, under a round umbrella. Gunner was alone among his brothers in that he'd already fully assimilated the fact that Maverick was now mostly deaf in his left ear, and he always stayed to his right.

For a few minutes, they just ate. Maverick felt raw and desolate. It had been a mistake to go to Kelsey's school, and not just because he'd probably fucked everything up even more.

Now his daughter was more than a concept, a dream. Now she was a living, breathing little girl. He knew the sound of her voice and the rhythm of her walk. He knew the light in her eyes. He knew that she was kind and friendly, and that she liked to draw. Now he really would die if he couldn't have his family back.

And there was absolutely no chance in hell that Jenny wasn't going to hear about his visit. The softness he'd felt in her on Friday night, the need he'd known that she still had for him, that would be gone.

He'd made his need more acute and his chances more bleak.

Gunner watched him, chewing his taco contemplatively.

"What?"

"I want to give you some advice. I know it's weird coming from me, but gimme a sec here. If there's anything I know, it's what a noisy head sounds like. Remember what I call it?"

Maverick remembered. "Like a gear that can't catch."

"Yeah. That's what you're feeling, right? I see it in you."

"I've been out four days. What the fuck d'you want?"

"I just want to throw some of your words back at you. Maybe help you remember who you are."

"I'm not him anymore. He got lost at McAlester."

"I think if you want Jenny and Kelsey, maybe you need to find him again."

"Don't try to be profound, Gun. It doesn't suit you."

He'd hurt his friend's feelings, but he was offended himself. He didn't like this table-turn. Gunner was the fuckup, not him.

Gunner shook off his offense and wadded up the paper from his first taco. "I love you, Mav. You are my best fucking friend, and I'd probably be dead a dozen times over if it wasn't for you. I'd've run out of lives before I had Leah if it wasn't for you. I'm gonna start paying you back by propping you up while you figure this shit out. And I'm gonna remind you that you gotta look close for now. Don't think about what you want and don't have. Don't think about what'll make everything perfect. Think about what'll make this day okay. And the next day. When all your days are mostly okay, think about what'll make 'em good. Every step toward having what you want. Remember what you told me."

"Fuck off."

"C'mon, brother. What do you say?" Gunner reached out and hooked his hand over Maverick's arm. He wore a new ring now; a big grinning skull that probably did serious damage in a fight. Maverick had never worn the big rings his brothers did. He wanted to feel the full impact of a punch directly on his hands.

He sighed. "Head down, shoulder to the day."

"That's how you get through. Thinking about the first time you told me that got me through some hard shit, Mav. It's good advice."

Maverick managed a laugh that was mostly sincere. Damn, he loved this kid. He'd turned out to be a fine man.

Proud as he was, it hurt in some way as well—sharply enough that he rubbed at his chest. Gunner had needed him once. Now he was the one who needed.

He still vividly remembered meeting the tornado in a meat suit that Gunner had been back then. He hadn't been Gunner yet. Just Max, spinning out of control.

September 1991

Jesus *Christ*, Sherman was going to kill that kid. "Stay down, kid, stay down," Maverick muttered under his breath, moving around the edge of the circle, trying to get close enough so the kid would hear him. He needed somebody in his corner.

But the kid got up. He was a bloody, broken, swollen mess, but he kicked out and knocked Sherman back, and he got to his feet. He was making some weird kind of noise, like a wobbly howl—or maybe he was crying.

Then Maverick got close enough, and he understood that the kid was *laughing*. Blood ran from his mouth in streams, and from his forehead in a rush, his face looked like the Elephant Man already, but through all that, the kid was back on his feet, laughing and swinging wildly. It was like he wasn't trying to hit Sherman so much as keep him pissed off—like he *wanted* that tank to roll over him.

Sherman was happy to oblige. He unloaded both barrels and landed a monstrous right jab straight on the kid's chin, and that was it. He went down flopping like dying fish. He was out.

No, he wasn't—shit, he was trying to get up *again*, and, seeing that, Sherman dropped down and sent a flurry of fists, rocketing back and forth into the kid's head and shoulders. The kid was trying to get up, not protecting himself at all.

Maverick had been fighting in this underground league for a couple of years, and there were some crazy-ass motherfuckers who liked to fight bare-knuckle with few rules, but he'd never seen anybody like this kid—he'd still be trying to get up ten minutes after his heart stopped.

This was nuts. He jumped into the center of the circle. "ENOUGH!" While the crowd around them, wild with blood thirst, booed, he hooked an arm around Sherman's neck and got under his chin until he had him in a rear naked choke. "Back off, man. Back *off*. You're gonna kill the kid." The kid who was still trying to keep going. Jesus.

Sherman grunted and fought the hold, trying to pull Maverick's arms loose. But he'd fought Sherman and won three times—he was likely due to fight him again tonight—and he knew his tells.

Finally, Sherman backed off, and Maverick eased up just enough to let him talk. "If he wants to die, what d'I care?" he gasped.

"Cops, man. It's a mess. You won. Kid's too crazy to know he's knocked out."

That got through, and Sherman relaxed and nodded. Maverick let him go to take his victory, and he went to the kid, who was still trying to get his feet under him. When Maverick crouched before him, he took a blind swing and dealt him a glancing blow in the temple.

"Easy, idiot. I'm trying to help you."

"No help!"

The words were almost too slurred to be understood, but he was still trying to fucking fight. Maverick grabbed the kid's head and tried to make him see him. Inside their swollen lids, his eyes were wild and unfocused. Shit, he really was crazy.

All around them, the crowd was yelling, and Montgomery, the guy who organized these fights, stood over Maverick, shouting for him to get this loco, half-dead boy up and out of the way.

"Kid! Look at me! C'mon. It's over. You're not dying tonight. What's your name?"

"Fuck you!"

"Yeah? That's your name? Your mama sure hated you, didn't she?"

"She's dead, asshole!"

Maverick winced, sorry he'd made that verbal jab—but the kid had made sense reacting to it, so he was coming back. His body was settling down, too. Maverick shoved his shoulder under the kid's arm, hooked his arm around his back, and heaved him to his feet.

"C'mon, kid. Let's find a place to clean you up and get your head on again."

"Where the fuck're you goin' Mav?" Montgomery got in his way. "You're taking on the top contender tonight—two more fights before that."

"Not tonight, Monty. Tonight I'm cleaning up your mess. You should've stopped this one ten minutes before I did. Kid's near dead."

Maverick had once killed a man with a punch, but that had been in a professional ring, with rules and procedures, and he'd unfortunately hit just the right—just the wrong—spot full-force and broken the man's jaw and neck at the same time. He'd been dead, wide-eyed, when he hit the mat.

Beautiful Ben Brodsky. Twenty years old. And never older.

Maverick had been Rumblin' Ricky Helm back then, boxing in a regional division, trying to make his name—and starting to get noticed. He himself had been twenty-five—still young, but not for much longer, by boxing standards.

He'd picked up boxing at an after-school program in middle school, trying to put off going back to the group home for as long as he could every day. The home hadn't been some horror house, it had been decent as far as places like that went, but it had been relentlessly chaotic, and he'd liked having something that was his.

He'd known a lot of men fighting a lot of ways for a lot of reasons—and some women, too. For all the years he'd been swinging his fists, he'd never seen anybody chase death the way this kid had tonight.

Montgomery made to block him again, and Maverick stood at his full height, still propping the kid up. "Do not fuck with me, Monty. I'll be back another night. You can keep my buy-in for tonight. I'm getting the kid out of here."

When Monty cleared out, Maverick dragged the kid to the edge of the circle and waited for the group—about fifty men looking to scrap on an abandoned parking lot at the farthest northern reaches of Tulsa—to part and give him passage.

~oOo~

"You ready to tell me your name?" He handed the ice bag to the kid, who took it and pressed it to his left eye, which was all kinds of fucked up.

Shawna, one of the Bulls' sweetbutts, who didn't live far from the fight location, tightened her silky robe and lit up a smoke. She leaned against her kitchen counter and watched Maverick trying to get through to the kid.

He'd had his bike at the fights, and he'd known he wouldn't go far with the kid hanging off his arm. So he'd dragged him to a phone booth and called for some help.

"Max."

"Hey—we're getting somewhere. I'm Maverick. Shawna here's being nice enough to let you use up all her first aid supplies and sleep on her sofa tonight so you can get your feet under you a little bit. You have a car out at the fights? Or a bike?"

"Car."

"Good. She'll get you back to it tomorrow. If you're not ready to drive, I'll come back up and get you home."

"Why?" He bent his head over the Tupperware bowl Shawna had put on the table and spat out a wad of thickening blood, into a deepening pool of the same. Behind them, Shawna made a grunt of disgust.

"Seems like you need a friend."

"Fuck off."

Maverick had grown up in foster care from the time he was four, all of that time in the boys' home. He had intimate knowledge of all the different suits of armor boys in pain wore. So he only chuckled.

"Okay, Max. We got you as cleaned up as we're going to, I think. And Shawna's got her sofa made up all comfy for you. You need help getting over there?"

He shook his head.

Maverick stood. "It feels like hell, I know. I've been there, too. But it's never as bad as it feels. If you can keep your head down and get through, just lean in and put your shoulder to each day, you'll come up on a day that's not so bad. Then one that's pretty good. If you keep going, keep fighting, maybe you'll get to have a great day. But you gotta fight to *win*, Max."

"Fuck off," the kid said again.

He wasn't a kid—he'd been fighting bare-chested, as most of them did, and he had a fair amount of ink, far more than Maverick. Sitting here tending to his many wounds, Maverick had had opportunity to study some of the work. Most of it was shitty quality, but a few were well done. One of the better pieces was military—some kind of Army insignia, with a battalion number and the words *Operation Desert Shield/Operation Desert Storm* under it. Desert Storm had gone down earlier that year—Max wasn't long out of the service, and he'd seen action, so he was no kid.

It had been a short war, with few American casualties, but they'd done some significant damage to their enemies. Maybe that was this poor guy's pain. Maybe he had blood on his hands. That was no easy burden, even when there wasn't much blame.

"I'll see you, Max. Get some sleep."

Shawna followed him to the door, and he caught her hand and pulled her close for a kiss. "Thanks, sweetheart. I know this is a lot to ask."

She smiled and pushed firmly up against him. "I don't mind, Mav. It's sweet you thought of me for help."

He kissed her again, lingering this time, to show her he appreciated the help. Then he set her back. "Call the clubhouse if you need anything. I'll crash there tonight and check in in the morning, if I haven't heard from you."

"That's fine. Mav—can I ask you somethin'?"

"Sure. Shoot."

"It don't seem like you know this guy."

"I don't—but I think you're safe. He's in no shape to do you any wrong."

"I know—I ain't worried about that. Poor guy's a mess. But…why're you doin' all this for him? You don't know him, and it don't seem like he's grateful."

Why was he doing all this? He hadn't taken the time yet to think about it. Maybe it was guilt for Ben Brodsky, ending that young life and all its potential. Maybe it was seeing the kid's crazy death wish and remembering the boys like that he'd grown up with. Maybe it was like when he was a kid and he'd find a stray dog in the neighborhood—he'd go door to door all over the place, sometimes miles from the home, looking for where it belonged.

Yeah, it was that, all of it. He was a sucker for lost things. He'd been one himself.

He looked back at the broken man slumped at Shawna's table. "Just trying to do some good where I can, sweetheart."

CHAPTER SIX

Hours after she'd picked Kelsey up from school, Jenny was still shaking. Every time she thought of Maverick at the fence, talking to Kelsey, her heart squeezed.

She'd caused a scene in the classroom, when Betsy had explained what had happened. They hadn't called her. They'd been worried enough to call the *cops*, but no one had bothered to call Kelsey's *mother*. Just *hey, good to see you, and by the way, there was a strange man talking to your daughter at the fence today.*

Not a stranger. Maverick. Doing things his way, as usual. She'd been reasonable and far more flexible than he deserved, and goddammit! She'd told him to wait, that she needed time. Three days later, he was stalking Kelsey at school. *Talking* to her.

She sat on the closed lid of the toilet and watched her little girl playing in the tub, singing nonsense to herself and piling pink bubbles on her head.

"Hey, pixie?"

"Yeah, Mommy?"

"I want to talk to you about what happened at school today."

Kelsey frowned. "You did mean talk at Miss Betsy."

"I know. I told her I was sorry."

"Your sorry was mean talk, too."

That was true; she'd barely managed to get the words out of her infuriated head. All she'd been thinking through the whole scene was YOU STUPID BITCH YOU STUPID BITCH. In fact, she liked Betsy and Connie and everybody who worked there, and overall, they did a good job of teaching and caring for the kids. But today, they'd dropped the ball, and that ball had been her daughter.

So yeah, she hadn't been kind, even in apologizing.

"That's not what I want to talk about, Kelse. I want to talk about what Miss Betsy told me."

"I talked to a sad man and that was bad."

"It wasn't bad, pix. It was unsafe. Do you know why?"

"Stra-nger Da-nger." She nodded seriously, dipping her head low, and the bubbles slid off her head and over her face. Sputtering, she pushed them away.

This was dicey territory. Maverick was her father. If Jenny did decide to let him into their lives—a much less likely scenario now—then she didn't want Kelsey to be afraid of him when she was properly introduced. If she'd never seen him, that wouldn't have been a problem, but now she had, and if Jenny made her think of the 'sad man' she'd met—Jenny's heart had cramped a little at that—as dangerous, things could get complicated when she found out that man was her father.

Fuck you, Mav. Just *fuck* you for having to get your way every goddamn time.

"Right. You have to be careful when you meet somebody new, and you should always be with somebody you trust when you do. Right?"

"Uh-huh. A good grownup. But he was a good grownup, Mommy. He was nice, and he said to not talk to strangers, just like you say."

"Why did you talk to him, then, Kelse?"

She shrugged and pushed a boat through the disintegrating bubbles. The water was probably getting cold by now. "I don't think he's a stranger, Mommy."

Jenny's breath stilled. There was something lurking in her daughter's statement. Something profound. "Why not?"

Kelsey's only answer was another shrug. Her attention had returned to her bath toys, and Jenny knew that the conversation was over, whether there had been a resolution or not—and there definitely had not.

~oOo~

Once the house was quiet and she was in bed, her room dark and still, Jenny's mind went haywire. She didn't know what to do, and all her brain could offer was a constant barrage of questions and images and fears.

If only he had just *waited*. Just given her the time she'd told him she needed. Just for once, done what she'd said she needed and not what he thought was right.

Sleep was impossible, but she didn't want to ramble around the creaky old house in the middle of the night, either, so she lay on her back in the center of her bed, perfectly still, staring up at the shadows. The back yard backed onto a rain culvert that was lined with trees, so they had a lot of privacy in that direction. She never closed her bedroom curtains; she didn't like the closed-in feeling of four solid walls.

The moon was bright, and the trees and leaves, the utility poles and wires, and the skeleton of the old swing set made an elaborate pattern on the ceiling. Some of the shadows moved; others simply shifted with the moon.

She wasn't sure how long she'd stared without noticing, but one shadow was wrong. It was too thick and heavy to be leaves or wires, and moving too much to be a tree or a pole. As she focused on it, she decided that it was a human being. Somebody was in her back yard.

Rather than go to the window to see—if there was somebody out here, she didn't want to give up the element of surprise—she eased from her bed and into her closet, leaving all the lights off. By feel, she found the gun box and turned the combination. With her .38 in both her hands and her finger safely across the trigger guard, she left the room, worked her way around all the creaks in the floor, and moved to the back door.

Please let it be Mav. Please let it be Mav. Maverick, she could deal with. She might shoot him anyway, just on principle, but at least she'd know what he was about. A stranger with some other purpose would scare the fuck out of her, and she didn't know if she'd be able to do what she needed to do.

Taking a big breath and blowing it out, she opened the door and stepped out onto the back porch. It was screened, but the moonlight was almost as bright as sunlight, and she could see the yard clearly. She could see that the dark figure sitting on top of Kelsey's Little Tikes picnic table with his head in his hands was Maverick.

She went through the screen door and stepped into the yard, keeping her gun aimed. He looked up as the door shut behind her, and then he stood.

Kelsey's father. The sad man she'd met that afternoon.

The gun shook in her hands, but she steadied her grip and walked toward him, still aiming.

"Are you stupid? What the *fuck* are you doing out here, Maverick? And after the shit you pulled at school!"

"I taught you how to shoot that thing."

"And you did a good job, so answer my fucking question before I show you how much I remember." She cocked the hammer.

"Don't cock a gun you don't mean to use, babe."

Jenny cocked her head, too, challenging him.

He laughed. "Maybe you should. Maybe that's what needs to happen. Just aim true and get it done. 'Cuz I can't fucking deal out here. Not without my family. I got nothing under my feet, Jen. This is freefall."

"Don't put this on me, Maverick. Don't you dare tell me that I'm standing between you and a bullet."

His mouth quirked up and dropped, a spasm of humor. "Actually, you're behind the bullet right now."

She decocked the gun and dropped her aim. "You know what I mean."

His eyes rested on the lowered gun. "Talk to me, Jen. We can work this out if we can just talk."

Because he could talk circles around her, and he knew it. She'd get emotional, he'd stay 'reasonable,' and she'd start thinking she was being silly. The only thing she'd ever been able to hold him back on—until that final, fateful day—had been her father. And that was because she'd been terrified of what he'd do if she gave in.

And rightly so.

"I told you I needed time."

"I don't have time. I've been on ice for four years, and now that I'm out, I'm rotting away."

"Why did you go to her school today?"

If the change in direction threw him, he didn't show it. "I had to see her. I didn't mean to talk to her—I just wanted to see her. I needed her to be more than a picture. When she came up to me, I didn't know what to do."

"You made everything more complicated. Now you're a stranger that she's supposed to be afraid of. I don't know how to undo that."

Maverick smiled suddenly and stepped closer. Surprised, Jenny realized that she'd just told him, with other words, that she was willing to try.

Also, she was fucking talking to him. Dammit.

"You need to go, Mav. Go home. I'll call."

She turned, meaning to get her ass back inside, but he grabbed her hand, and the touch, its familiarity, set off a chain reaction inside her, like switches going off, up her arm and into her chest.

"Jenny, please. I'm begging. I will kneel if you want me to."

It was much harder to think while he touched her. He took another step closer, and Friday night at the bar was going to happen all over again. From the day they'd met, her body had craved his. Her heart had craved his. How could she stand up for herself when everything inside her clamored to be consumed by this man?

She took a step back. "Porch. You can't come inside. We can talk on the porch."

When she tried to pull her hand free, he tightened his hold and drew her closer. "Thank you."

He was going to kiss her, and she wasn't strong enough to resist. "Mav, n—"

His mouth came down on hers, and her whole body wanted to form itself to his and let him have his way.

But her brain held back. She was strong enough, after all. Instead of cleaving to him, her hands went to his chest and shoved, hard, so that he took a step back.

"Dammit, Maverick! If you want a chance to know your daughter, you have got to *listen* to me. I know you think if we talk you can spin your webs and get me trapped into thinking your way. But here's how it's gonna go. *I* am going to talk. You're going to shut the hell up and listen — really listen — for once. You start talking over me, and I'm done. Do you understand?"

She didn't like his grin — well, truthfully, she'd always loved that smirk, but now she understood the patronizing bullshit behind it.

"Do. You. Understand."

"Oh — you mean I can answer? You told me not to talk."

"Fuck you and your fucking games." She turned. He could stay a stranger to Kelsey for all she cared.

"Jenny, Jenny. Sorry. I'm sorry. I understand. I'll listen."

She kept walking, but when she got to the porch, she held the screen door open for him.

They sat on the ancient metal glider. She'd freshened the paint and changed the cushions a couple of years ago, but the glider itself had been on this porch longer than Jenny had been on this earth.

Right behind them was her father's bedroom window. She liked that. He usually slept a heavy sleep aided by medication, but his machines showed that sometimes he was awake in the night. She liked the thought that he might hear them talk. It was unlikely he remembered Maverick's voice, or who Maverick was, but if he did, he'd hate it.

That was the kind of woman she'd become—petty enough to wish her brain-damaged father a little extra dose of unhappiness. It was probably a good thing that Kelsey had other role models in her life.

Would the man sitting beside her become one of them?

"You still thinking about using that thing?"

"Hmm?"

Maverick nodded at her lap, where her pistol was still in her hand. "Oh." She set it on the weather-beaten table at her side.

"What do you need me to hear, Jen?"

How to say it all? She hadn't figured anything out yet; she'd never been able to think clearly about everything, not in four years, and certainly not in these past few days. What did she need to say? What did she want?

Suddenly, she realized that she did know what to say. She had been living it for all of these years, and what she needed and wanted *had* become clear. Her anger had a source and a purpose.

"Do you know why I cut you out?"

A frown winced across his face. "Yeah. You told me. But I was protecting you."

She threw her hand up. "Shut up with that. And no, that's not it—or yeah, it is, but it's not all of it. It's bigger than just that day."

When she paused, he kept his mouth shut. A good sign—normally, he'd leap on the slightest opportunity to take over the talk.

"It's because what you did that day is who you are. In everything. You always have to have your way. You have to win every fight. The way you see things is the only way that matters, and everybody else is wrong. Your truth is the only one you know. That's how he was, too." She tipped her head toward her father's window.

Maverick's eyes went wide, and his mouth opened, but he didn't speak. Good boy.

"I'm not saying you're just like him. But in that way, you are. I was trained to it, I didn't know any better, and I let you have your way in almost everything. The one thing I held fast on was how to handle him, and it drove you completely batshit."

"He *abused* you, Jen. The way you wanted to handle him was to be his victim."

Her hands clenched together in her lap. "Shut. Your. Mouth. Last warning." When he slammed his mouth closed, his lips now sealed in an angry line, she continued, "That doesn't matter. I think you're right. I was afraid of him, love and fear and hate and all kinds of crap was all tangled up in me, and I was slow to break away. But I had to do it on *my* terms. It took me a while to figure that out, and now I need you to see it, too. It had to come from me, when *I* was ready. If I'd let you do what you wanted, I'd just have been hiding behind you. Moving from the shadow of one man to the next. I needed to get out into the light. I cut you out because you wanted to keep me in your shadow, and you would have done the same thing to Kelsey. I couldn't have that for my little girl."

"*Our* little girl." The words came out through his still-clenched mouth, barely moving his lips.

She let it slide. "Our little girl."

With every word she said, Jenny dug more deeply into her own understanding of not only Maverick but herself. She was putting thoughts she'd barely allowed herself to think, ever in her whole life, into words for the first time. Expressing herself in the most real and crucial way. She had to do it right, but what was right? What words, dug from the deepest part of her psyche, would make him understand, when he never had before?

He stared at her, his mouth a grim slash, his eyes blazing at her in the sparse light. He was too angry to hear her; it was obvious. She imagined his head so full of all the words she'd refused to let him speak, all the arguments he thought would make her see things his way, that there was no room for her.

But she had to try. Something fluttering inside her demanded that she try.

"You know, I always thought you'd be a good dad. From the day I saw you at Wal-Mart, standing there with sparkly purses hanging all over you, I thought that. But on the day you beat him, seeing for the first time the violence you were really capable of, and having you completely ignore me when I asked you not to go for him — that day, I saw that maybe you could turn out like him. If enough bad things happened. If I pushed you hard enough, or if our child did. I saw that there was a switch inside you, and if it flipped, you'd be gone and I'd be trapped with another angry stranger. You were gone that day, Mav. Just like my father. He was my daddy until my mom died the way she did. It was after that he turned into what he was." Her voice broke as a burst of emotion flooded through her, and she cleared her throat and breathed deeply. "You were an angry stranger that day. You were gone. That's how you left me alone."

She thought she'd said everything, but she wasn't sure. She'd said all she knew to say, so she sat back into quiet. Maverick didn't speak, either, but in the shaded moonlight, Jenny could see a million words warring behind his eyes.

They were quiet for what seemed like hours before he asked, "Can I talk?" His voice was a low growl, like a warning.

She nodded.

He blew out a breath. "I'm trying as hard as I can not to tell you you're wrong. But I don't know what else to say. I'm not him, Jenny. I'm just fucking not, and I want to punch him because you think I am."

Did he see the irony in that? Rather than follow that rabbit hole, she said, "I don't think you are, Mav."

"Then what did you just say? I don't understand."

"I think you could be. If you don't learn to listen."

He stared at her, his eyes jumping with emotion. After a beat, he shook his head. "I don't know what you want. I listen."

"You listen to gather ammunition to advance your case. You listen so you can throw my words back at me. You listen so you can catch your chance to take over. You don't listen to understand."

"God, that's so fucking unfair. You think I'm an abusive son of a bitch like your old man. I beat him up because he was abusing *you*. He fucking punched you while you were eight months pregnant! I was supposed to let that just *go*?"

"You were supposed to let me handle it!"

"But you weren't handling it!"

"I *was*. I *had*!"

"By letting him get away with it! He needed to pay!"

Jenny opened her mouth to yell back at him that it had been over with her father that day, that she'd been *free* of him, until Maverick had stormed in and turned her father into one of her children and trapped her with him forever. He'd made *her* pay, too. And Kelsey.

But she'd said it before. It didn't matter to him. He couldn't see it. He couldn't *hear* it.

This was hopeless—and comprehension flashed: she'd had real hope. That flutter in her chest—she'd hoped they could work this out and be together again. The family she'd wanted. The one Maverick had promised her. Tears welled up, and Jenny let them fall. "You're not listening right now. You haven't listened this whole time."

He let out another long breath and calmed again. "What do you want, Jenny? Tell me what you want me to do. I will do it. Just please say it straight out."

"I've been saying it straight out. I just laid my heart out, and all you hear is that I was a victim who needed to be saved. You always have to be the hero of the story. You're not a hero, Mav. You're a bully."

Before she could lose her nerve or get pulled into his web again, she stood up and went to the back door, as quickly as she could without running. Behind her, as he realized what she was doing, Maverick jumped up—the glider slammed into the wall behind it.

"Jenny, no! Wait! Talk to me!"

She pushed into the kitchen and slammed the door shut, turning both locks and hooking the chain.

"Jenny! Don't do this!" He slammed his fists into the door. "Don't cut me out! Talk to me! Don't fucking do this!" A heavy thump, and the door rattled hard, then another thump, and another. He was kicking now. "JENNY! NO! LET ME IN!! SHE'S MINE! MINE!"

She'd never heard him yell before. She'd pushed him to an entirely new level of anger and violence. Just like her father. Folding over, Jenny wrapped her hands around herself and sobbed.

"Mommy?" a tiny, frightened voice cut through the din of rage on the other side of the door. Jenny looked up. Kelsey stood there in her yellow shortie pajamas, her hair a nest of wild sleep, clutching Mrs. Fifi, her stuffed kitty. "Mommy, is it Stra-nger Da-nger?"

Was it Stranger Danger? Yes, it was. An angry stranger, shouting and pounding, huffing and puffing, shaking everything down. Everything she'd feared. Since the day he'd beaten her father, Maverick had made her every fear come true.

Jenny ran across the kitchen and picked her daughter up. Hugging her close, she said, "We'll be okay, pixie. Let's go to your room. We'll close up snug in there, and I'll call somebody to make the angry man go away. Okay?"

Kelsey nodded, staring wide-eyed over Jenny's shoulder. Jenny grabbed the cordless off its base and dialed 9-1-1 as she hurried to Kelsey's room and closed the door.

She hadn't been much older than Kelsey when she'd seen her parents fight for the first, and the last, time. She hadn't understood anything that had gone on that night.

She'd hidden in her room then, too. This very room.

The night her mother died.

June 1974

"WHAT THE HELL DO YOU THINK YOU'RE DOING?"

Jenny shrank back against the wall, letting the leaves of her mommy's jungle plant cover her. Her daddy stormed into the dining room and grabbed her mommy by the hair. Her mommy screamed, and Jenny slammed her hands over her ears. But she could still hear everything.

"Earl, no! It's mine! It was Nana's!"

Her daddy snatched out of her mommy's hands the fancy glass ball with the pretty trees and swirling snow in it. Sometimes, when Jenny was good, and if she promised to be still and quiet, Mommy would shake it carefully and let her hold it while it snowed inside.

Daddy crashed it to the floor. It broke into a million pieces, and her mommy screamed.

"You WHORE! If you want him, then get the fuck out and HAVE HIM. But you take NOTHING! IT'S MINE — MY SWEAT PAID FOR EVERYTHING YOU HAVE!" Daddy pushed Mommy hard, and she fell over a chair. He slammed the door where Mommy kept her fancy dishes, and the window in it broke. Glass rained down into the mess from the snowy glass ball.

Jenny didn't know what was happening, but she was scared. So scared she made wee. It ran down her leg and made a puddle at her feet. Oh, Daddy would spank her for the mess.

"Baby!" Mommy was crawling toward her, through crackling glass, trying to stand up. "Baby, come here."

Afraid of everything, afraid of Daddy yelling like a monster and Mommy crying, afraid of having to touch her toes and take her punishment, Jenny bolted down the hall. Her bare feet, wet with wee, slipped on the wooden floor. As she slid into her bedroom, she saw Daddy shoving Mommy out the front door.

"Jenny! Baby, Mommy loves you!"

The door slammed shut, and Jenny slammed her own door and ran to hide under her bed.

~oOo~

"Jenny. Twinkle, come out from under there. It's okay."

She'd fallen asleep. Now Daddy was on his knees, peeking under the pink ruffle around her bed, holding his big hand out to her. He wasn't yelling anymore.

She took his hand, and he pulled her out. "Is Mommy home?"

At first, he made his mad eyes, but then he was sad instead. "No, Jenny. Mommy don't love us anymore."

"But she said she did. When you pushed her, she said she loved me."

"I just told you—she don't. She's a bad lady and she don't love you. Do I always tell you the truth?"

"Uh-huh."

"Your mommy wants a different family. She don't love us anymore. That's the truth."

Her mommy didn't love her? That made Jenny sad, and she cried.

"Oh, Twinkle. Daddy loves you enough for ten mommies. We'll be okay, you and me. We don't ever need nobody else."

He hugged her tightly, and she felt a little better. But then —

"What the fuck? You pissed yourself? Goddammit, Jennifer!"

"I'm sorry, Daddy! I'm sorry! I didn't mean to." She was crying hard now, so hard her tummy felt funny and she couldn't breathe. She was going to have to take her punishment now, and Daddy used the belt when he gave it. He used it hard when he was mad enough to say the baddest word.

But then, his mad eyes went away, and he was sad again. "Shh, Jenny. Shhh. It's okay. I'm not mad." He picked her up and hugged her hard, and she felt all swallowed up and warm. Maybe it was okay that Mommy didn't love her like she'd said she did.

"Let's get you in the bath and cleaned up, Twinkle. It's past your bedtime."

~oOo~

When Jenny woke up the next morning, she went out to the kitchen like usual, but Mommy wasn't there making breakfast, and Jenny remembered that Mommy didn't love her.

That made her sad, but her tummy made her hungry, and Daddy loved her, so she went to find him. Sometimes he made her peanut butter and honey sandwiches, so maybe he knew about breakfast, too.

She went through the dining room. It looked like always, but there wasn't a window in the dish door anymore. On the sofa in the living room, she found Daddy. All the curtains were closed, and it was almost dark like nighttime. There was a big bottle of the grownup soda between his legs. She'd sneaked a drink of that soda one time, but it wasn't like Pepsi, and it burned bad.

His head hung back on the sofa, like he'd fallen asleep. But he was awake. Jenny knew he was awake because he was crying.

Jenny was afraid, but Daddy had made her feel better when she'd cried last night, so she went to make him feel better. "Daddy?"

He jumped, and his head came up fast. "Jenny! Come here. Come here."

He set the bottle on the table and held out his hands, and she went to him. He sat her on his legs and hugged her to his chest. She liked to sit with him like this, because he smelled like his cigarettes and the green stuff he slapped on his face every morning after his shower, and because his voice was all rumbly when her ear was on his chest.

This morning, he smelled like the yucky soda, too.

"Twinkle, I have to tell you something. You need to be brave for Daddy. Okay?"

She was afraid, but she nodded. She could be brave when his arms were around her.

"Mommy died last night."

Jenny tried to understand. She thought about Petey, Mommy's yellow bird who'd sung in the sunshine every day. They'd found him on the bottom of his cage one day, all quiet and stiff, and Mommy had cried and put him in the box from Jenny's shiny black shoes for her Christmas dress. Then she'd dug a hole under the roses and put him in the ground.

She'd said that Petey had died and gone to Birdie Heaven.

"Did Mommy go to Mommy Heaven?"

Daddy's arms got tight and made her hurt, and he cried some more. When he was done, he said, "I'll always tell you the truth, Jenny. I promise you. Your mommy ain't going to Heaven. She's not good enough for Heaven. She did a bad thing, and a lady got mad and killed her."

"The bad thing that made you mad, too?"

His eyes were sad and mad all at once, and Jenny didn't know how to feel. "Yeah. The same bad thing. She hurt a lot of people. But you and me, we love each other, and we're gonna stick together. You and me. Okay?"

"Okay, Daddy." She snuggled deeper into his arms.

CHAPTER SEVEN

Maverick leaned against the concrete block wall and closed his eyes. He took slow, deep breaths and tried to calm the stormy seas that filled him up and crashed against the backs of his eyes.

Everything was completely fucked to shit.

Jenny had called fucking *law* on him, and now here he sat, in Tulsa Police lockup. She'd left her gun on the porch. He hadn't even known that, but the cops sure had.

It wasn't her fault. People talked about 'snapping,' when somebody went off the rails and did something stupid and violent. Now he understood how apt a description that was. It was like he'd been stretched farther and farther, from the day he'd gotten stuffed into a squad car outside Jenny's old man's house four years ago, until tonight, watching her run away and lock him out of the same fucking house. He'd been stretched and stretched, everything inside him going taut and thin with the tension of it. And then he'd literally felt something let go in his head. Something had snapped.

And he'd punched and kicked and yelled his throat sore. Jesus Christ. And gotten stuffed into a squad car yet again.

She'd called him a bully, but that was bullshit. He'd never been violent with her; he'd barely ever even *raised his voice* to her before. He rarely yelled at anybody, ever, except to be heard over noise. No matter how angry he got, he wasn't a yeller. Yelling was a weak man's response to anger. Reason or action were the only strong responses to conflict.

He still believed that. The man he'd been had lived that. What had happened at Jenny's...he didn't know who that man was.

He opened his eyes and stared down at his hands. They were scarred and discolored, and his knuckles were oversized and gnarled from years of relentless abuse. He'd hardly felt the impacts of his punches on her door, but the knuckles of both hands were bloody and ragged. He could flex with only bearable pain, so he hadn't broken anything. All surface damage. It was like they'd built up extra bone to protect themselves.

His daughter had been in that house. Had he woken her? Probably—how could he not have? He'd woken the goddamn neighbor, who'd come out with his shotgun and held him there until the cops arrived.

All Kelsey knew of him: stalking her school and trying to break into her house.

He was going back inside. He didn't even know what to expect—he'd served his full time, but for a few weeks, so there wasn't any time he could finish. But he'd sure as shit violated the terms of his release. What did that mean for what came next?

Could he do more time? Could he survive it?

Didn't matter. Life inside was death. Life outside without his family was death. What the fuck did it matter where his body dropped?

~oOo~

At some point, the stress and despair overwhelmed his body's processes, and he slept. A short series of sharp, metallic clangs brought him back. At first, waking on a jailhouse cot, so much like a prison bunk, he thought that his release had been a dream, and the world around him spun violently. He grabbed hold of the edge of his bunk until the vertiginous dread let him go.

"Maverick. Get up, bud."

He knew that voice; it wasn't from McAlester, and it used a name he hadn't been called there. He opened his eyes and remembered—Tulsa lockup. Jenny had thrown him to the pigs. He sat up and faced Jim Novak, Chief of Tulsa PD. Longtime friend of Dane Nielsen, the Bulls' VP, and thus of the Brazen Bulls MC.

Seeing that friendly face and remembering how far up the Bulls' allies went in Tulsa, Maverick felt a feeble tremor of hope. "Chief."

"Shit, Mav. Yours is not a face I want to see behind these bars."

"How fucked am I?"

He shook his head. "Made some calls this morning, when I saw your goddamn name on my blotter. Jenny's decided it was a misunderstanding. Your PO is willing to let this go, after he promised to throw me under the bus if you cause more trouble. Dane's on his way to pick you up. And the next time I see you, I want to be tossing back shots with you at the clubhouse. Right?"

Maverick's heart was beating so erratically that he could hardly form words—and in his reaction to the news that he'd be free, he saw that real hope still had a root inside him. He wanted to be free. "Yeah...yeah. Yeah, Chief. Thanks."

"It's hard getting your land legs back under you, Mav. I know. I see it just about every damn day. Guys violating back to the house because they can't make it work outside.

Some of them are trying, but they can't get decent work, or a decent place to rest their heads, or because their folks don't want them, or they don't have folks at all. Those end up violating to get by. Others just don't know how to be free anymore, and they go looking to get sent up again. Mav, you got work. You got rest. You got folks. Don't be one of those sad sacks who can't remember how to be free."

Novak was right. The Bulls gave him work, rest, and family. As conflicted as he currently felt about that family, he loved his brothers, and he knew he was luckier than most ex-cons. Novak knew as well as he did that the club's work carried a real risk that he'd go back inside for another reason entirely than not being able to make it work outside, but Maverick took the point the chief was making.

The Bulls weren't the family he needed most, but they were a family, and he was part of it. If he could get his head back in their game, maybe he could be okay, no matter what Jenny did.

If nothing else, the club would help him make damn certain that he got to be his daughter's father, no matter what Jenny wanted.

"I hear ya, Chief."

"Good." Novak unlocked the cell. "Get on out here and collect your shit. Dane should be here any minute."

~oOo~

It wasn't Dane waiting for him; it was Delaney. The club president stood at the desk, his arms crossed over his chest, his face impassive, as Maverick took the envelope with his wallet, watch, and keys and signed the clipboard.

When he went through the door to the lobby side, Delaney said nothing, showed no expression. He simply watched Maverick approach.

Maverick said nothing, either. He harbored some ill will toward his president, and he hadn't had time yet to work out how to get over it. Or if he could.

"Let's get out of here," Delaney finally said. "I'll buy you breakfast."

"I just want to get to my bike."

"After breakfast. Let's go." He put his back to Maverick and walked to the front door.

His other choice was to walk all the way back to Jenny's street, so Maverick followed Delaney. He guessed he was having breakfast.

~oOo~

In Oklahoma, you couldn't get by with just a bike. There was too much weather, and the winters could get harsh. Delaney drove a big, flashy red F-350 dually with the full feature package—it was new; Delaney swapped out his cage for a new one every couple of years. Maverick had had a '69 Impala before he'd gone inside, but he'd had Gunner sell it rather than let it sit while he was away. He supposed that was another thing he'd have to attend to.

Sitting high in Delaney's luxury pickup, Maverick looked out the passenger window and kept his mouth shut. Delaney didn't press him, and they rode in silence until he turned into The Roost, a mom-and-pop, greasy-spoon diner that was a local favorite.

Jenny had been a waitress here when Maverick had been with her. He wondered if Delaney remembered that—or if he'd ever known it. If so, he was an asshole.

"Come on. We'll talk over biscuits and gravy." Delaney got out and slammed his door.

Maverick sat where he was for a few seconds and breathed. He had to get his head straight, and the first step was getting right with the club. The first step to that was getting right with its president.

He got out and followed Delaney into the restaurant.

~oOo~

The Roost had been remodeled while he was away, and it barely looked like the restaurant he remembered. The staff was all different as well, so Maverick was just another customer. He figured Toots Bingham, the owner, still manned the grill, but as long as he stayed in the kitchen, everything could be cool.

The food was the same, though—good, rib-sticking country fare. Delaney ordered his biscuits and gravy, and Maverick ordered eggs over easy, crispy bacon, and a short stack.

While they waited, Delaney pushed his coffee aside and leaned in. "I'm putting you on the bench, Mav. Just until you've got your wits about you."

He was half on the bench already. He wasn't on the guns, and that was most of their work. The only club business he was active for was legit security work and any move on Dyson. What Maverick heard now was that Delaney wouldn't include him on Dyson.

"No fucking way, D. I'm owed."

Delaney stared down at his coffee cup, like he was reading the swirls of cream. When he looked up again, Maverick couldn't get a bead on his expression.

"I know what happened to you inside, Mav."

Maverick's fists clenched, but he stayed outwardly calm and didn't respond. Delaney waited, letting the silence draw out, like he was making sure Maverick had nothing to say. He hadn't—there was no way he was speaking out loud about it. Ever.

When Delaney got that, he gave a quick nod and sat back. "I understand that you feel owed—"

"I *am* owed," Maverick cut in. "You offered me up to your Russian queen and then left me to rot when I did what she wanted."

Delaney frowned, but he also nodded his head. "I'm sorry, Mav. I don't know what I can do besides say that."

"You can not bench me. That'd be a start."

"It's more than what you're owed. It's the whole club's security on the line. Even with the little jobs, I can't have a wild card in the deck. That's absolutely true with any move on Dyson. I want you to get what you need out of them, but we're on the brink of a Tulsa civil war here. That's not good for anybody. The beef is the beef, and we need to answer their challenge, but we have to be careful. We can't be blowing up our own house."

"Tell me how Gunner's active, then. Talk about a wild card."

"Because his brand of crazy is known and useful. I bench him when I have to. And he's not so crazy anymore. I don't know what's going on with you right now. Goin' after your own woman? You?"

Their breakfast came, but Maverick wasn't hungry. He pushed his plates aside and rested his head in his hands. "I don't know. I feel like the world is a merry-go-round, and I'm trying to jump on while it's spinning."

"That's what I'm talkin' about, son. When you get on the ride, I'll put you to work. That includes Dyson. For now, focus on finding your chance." He used his fork to slice off a piece of gravy-soaked biscuit. "Mo says you two have a date to do some house hunting today. That's a start. Get yourself a place. Put things in it. Move back into your life."

Fuck. He'd forgotten about Mo. "I can't move back into a life I lost."

Delaney sighed and set his fork down. "Then start a new one, brother. You got two choices—live or don't."

~oOo~

"It's fine."

Mo wheeled on him, her manicured hands on her hips "You know I have a gun in my bag, right? If you shrug and say 'It's fine' at one more place, might be I'll use it and put an end to your misery and mine."

He laughed, feeling a twinge of real humor. "Sorry, Mo. But remember where I've been putting my head down the last four years. Every place you've shown me is a fucking palace after that."

She stared on, drumming her fingers on her hips. Then she grabbed him and pulled him over to the window seat in this empty living room. "Sit."

He sat, and so did she.

"Tell me what you thought about while you were inside."

No. He knew what she was doing, but it wouldn't work. With a shake of his head, he said, "That won't help, Mo. I didn't have pretty dreams about life outside. I lost what I wanted when I went in. I thought about that."

"Oh, love." She reached out and grabbed his hand. "It's over now, though. You're back with us now, and you can start afresh."

He laughed again—but no humor powered it this time.

Mo tried again. "Right. Tell me what you want right now. What would make you happy?"

"Jenny and Kelsey." That, he could answer without hesitation.

"What kind of house would you want them to have?"

Again, Maverick saw what she was doing, and he saw the danger in it. If he got a place thinking that his little girl might spend time in it, that was a big sack of hope. If he never got to see her again, he'd burn the place down before he'd live in it alone.

He'd ruined his chance with Jenny. She'd said she'd seen her father in him, and, wrong as that was, he'd gone and given her a real good show to cement her thinking. So he couldn't let himself imagine Jenny living with him. That was a deadly level of hope.

But the Bulls would help him get to be Kelsey's father. At least that, he'd get. Jenny might hate him forever, she might never trust him, but she couldn't withstand the will of the club.

"A good yard. Maybe a swing set." She had a lot of toys in the yard at Jenny's, and they all looked well loved. "A little playhouse, too." He'd build it from scratch. It would be better than the plastic one she had at Jenny's. "Maybe a puppy. Or a kitten."

Mo smiled and opened her handbag. Instead of her gun, she pulled out a little flowered book with a small pen attached. She pulled the pen from its loop, opened the book, and began taking notes.

"So a nice big yard, with good grass and a strong fence. Keep going."

"A safe neighborhood. Not too much traffic, so I can teach her to ride a bike on the sidewalk." As he spoke, the image of his descriptions rolled out in his head like unspooling film. "A sunny bedroom. I'll paint it her favorite color. A good place to sit down to eat together. A fireplace."

"Fireplace?"

Maverick refocused on Mo and saw that her head was cocked. "To hang stockings at Christmas."

He'd only done that one time in his whole life: the single Christmas he'd spent living with Jenny. Right after she'd found out she was pregnant. The fireplace had been one of those electric things you could buy at Wal-Mart, but pretty enough, with a mantel and a ledge like a hearth. Jenny had brought home matching stockings with their names embroidered on the cuffs, and they'd hung them before their fake fireplace.

Mo stared, her gold pen poised above her flowered notebook. Maverick didn't realize he'd made her cry until she lifted the hand holding the pen and swiped a tear from her cheek with her knuckles.

"You break my heart, love."

"Yeah. Mine, too."

~oOo~

Late that afternoon, they found a house with a lease-with-option offer. It had all the things Mo had jotted down, plus some things Maverick liked but hadn't thought of—like big trees in the yard.

He took it on the spot. While the agent filled out the paperwork and Mo fussed at her about details, he stood at the back door and looked out on the wide, green lawn. The slab patio had plenty of room for a grill and a table and chairs.

He thought about the night before, the monster he'd been, throwing himself at Jenny's door that way. Scaring her. Probably scaring Kelsey, too.

She'd called him a bully. She'd thrown that at him and run, without giving him a chance to respond.

That had been her point, he thought—that he always had to respond. That he always had to be right. That he had to be the hero. It wasn't true. Or fair.

Was it?

If he *was* right, shouldn't he press his point? Wasn't that what a discussion was? When you had to make a decision, somebody had to be right. He saw reason. Fuck, he was all about reason. If not, he'd have punched Delaney at breakfast, when he'd told him he was benched. He'd sure as shit wanted to.

It was true that he'd gotten his way in most things with Jenny. But that wasn't all on him. She'd been deferential when they'd gotten together, giving way easily to him, with hardly any resistance at all. When she'd gotten more secure and started to push back, her counters had been all *It makes me feel...* or *I don't know, I just think...* Why would he have given way to that? If his points were better formed, was that him being a bully?

Please.

He'd given way where he shouldn't have. The one thing she'd fought hard on — really fought, not just disagreed — had been her fucking father. She'd fought with fire about something that shouldn't have been a fight at all.

He wouldn't have had to play the hero if she hadn't been so damn insistent on playing that bastard's victim.

February 1992

Maverick stood behind Jenny and unfastened the little pearly buttons that ran down the back of her blouse, kissing the skin he bared as he did so.

He was proud of himself—he'd done something nice for Valentine's Day. No flowers or heart-shaped box of candy or anything like that; all that stuff seemed just silly and fake. But he'd taken her out for a nice meal, and now he was going to make her come as many different ways as he could imagine.

He liked this girl a whole lot. She was sweet and beautiful, and damn, he loved to fuck her. It was getting to the point where he thought about her just about all the time. Sometimes those thoughts had downright embarrassing side effects.

It had been a long time since he'd spent so much time with one girl, but he wasn't feeling restless at all. Quite the contrary. Lately, he'd been happy to just stay at his place with her to watch TV and fuck. She cooked, too, and she was pretty good at it. When she was there, his apartment felt like a home.

She moaned prettily and dropped her head as he pushed the blouse off her shoulders. It fell from her arms to the floor.

He unhooked her bra and pushed that off as well, then slid his hands around her and cupped her tits. Her nipples tightened against his palms, and his cock surged in the confines of his jeans. "Do you trust me, babe?"

A little nod was her only answer.

God, that was so hot. She really did trust him—to keep her safe and to give her pleasure. She put herself in his hands. Someday soon—hell, maybe tonight—he wanted to play with that a little bit, take her places she hadn't been before. He tweaked her nipples just sharply enough to make her gasp and pull her shoulders back, then released them and brushed his hands over her arms. He caught one to turn her to him, and a tiny, almost insignificant wince passed through her.

Maverick moved his hand and looked at her arm. "What happened here?"

She pulled away and laughed—but it was a weird, shaky little syllable. "I ran into the edge of a shelf in the kitchen at work."

Yeah, that was bullshit. If there was one thing Maverick knew, it was bruising. That wasn't the mark of an impact. It was pressure. Suspicious now, already forming an infuriating deduction, he caught her hand to hold her, then reached over and flipped the switch to turn on the light on the ceiling fan over his bed. With enough light to really see now, he lifted her arm and examined the mark.

"Mav, it's fine."

"This is a hand, Jen." He turned her arm. "These are fucking fingers." He bent down and grabbed his t-shirt off the floor. "Put this on. We're talking." She did, and he sat her on the edge of the bed. "Your old man did that."

She didn't deny it.

"Tell me what happened."

"It's not your business, Maverick. I've told you a hundred times—things with my dad are complicated."

A hundred times was an obvious exaggeration, but she wouldn't have had to tell him even twice if her father weren't such a prick. "Jennifer..."

"Don't fucking call me that."

The fire in her tone shocked him. She used his full name when he'd irritated her. He'd never used her full name before, but it had seemed appropriate now, a rebuttal to her use of his. But he had more pressing concerns, so he pushed the curiosity to the side. "You can't sit here and think you can have a bruise like that and I'm not going to need to know about it. That's a deep bruise, Jen."

She turned her arm and studied the mark. "It's not bad. Just red."

"It's 'just red' because it's deep. Tomorrow, the next day, it's going to look like Jaws took a bite—and feel like it, too. Why'd he grab you so hard he about tore your arm off?"

"It's not important. Mav—you and me, we've been together two months. You can't think you can fix a relationship that's almost twenty-four years old. You can't even understand it."

"What do I need to understand? You're his daughter. He's your father. There is no situation where him hurting you is understandable."

She grunted and stood up. "God, will you just listen?"

"Hey. I'm listening. If there's a way to understand, then you need to explain it to me so I can." He took her hand and pulled her back, tucking her between his legs. "I want you safe. I don't like somebody hurting you. Is that a bad thing?"

"No..." She chewed on her bottom lip, and he reached up and pressed on her chin until she stopped.

A thought occurred to him, and he tested it out and decided he liked it. "Then let me protect you. Move in with me."

Her eyes went wide. "What? No!"

"Yes—why not? You're with me most of the time, anyway. I like having you here. You need to get away from him. It's perfect."

She studied him, and he got the sense that there was something she was looking for, but he didn't know what else there was to say—not until she said something more, at least.

"We've only been together two months, Mav." Again, she chewed on her lip. "I don't know—I just think it's a big step to take already."

"I didn't propose, Jen. I'm asking you to move in. If we don't work out, then we'll figure that out then."

Her eyes continued to move all over his face, scanning back and forth between his eyes, down to his mouth, back up. She took a long, deep breath. "I love you, Mav."

She'd never said that before. He grinned. "Is that a yes?" After a beat, she nodded, and he set her on his lap. "That's my girl."

~oOo~

"YOU THINK YOU CAN JUST SNEAK OUT ON ME LIKE A THIEF?"

At the shout and the crash that followed, Maverick put down the box he'd just picked up, the last box of Jenny's old life. He left her room and ran down the hall, his fists already tight and ready.

The front door was open, and Jenny's father had her up against the wall. Father and daughter were staring at each other. Earl wasn't tall, but neither was Jenny, and he had her trapped. Jenny's expression was full of fear and anger—and there was guilt in there, too. He despised the way this fuckhead had her so twisted up.

Maverick had kept her with him the night before, and he'd come with her today, while her father was supposed to be away, to move her shit out of his house. He'd have been lying if he'd said he wasn't a little glad ol' Earl had shown up, though he'd have wanted to be the one to meet him first.

"Back the fuck off, asshole." Maverick didn't yell; he growled the words and grabbed Wagner by the back of his canvas coat, throwing him across the hallway. He gave Jenny a quick once-over. No new hurt; just the bruise on her arm—after a day to ripen, it was just as vicious as he'd predicted it would be.

"You okay?"

She nodded. When he then turned to make sure Earl Wagner understood that his days of hurting his only child were well and truly done, she grabbed his arm.

"Mav, no! Please! Don't hurt him!"

Goddammit. "Jen—"

"No! Shut up! You got what you wanted! So let's go. Let's just go."

What *he* wanted? It wasn't the time to challenge that, so he filed it away. He needed to get her out of this diseased house. Letting her keep hold of him, he turned to her father. "You touch her again, and I will kill you."

Wagner didn't even look at him. He kept his eyes on his daughter. "Jennifer, don't you do it, too. Don't you fucking leave me, too."

His words were quiet now, but they were just as filled with anger, and with fear, as his shout had been. The relationship between these two was all about anger and fear. And guilt. A great big heap of guilt, at least on Jenny's part, which was outrageous. If there was any real love in there, too, it was stunted and dying. Or already dead. Just its corpse lying there to remind them it had once existed.

Maverick didn't remember having parents, he'd been raised with a staff of adults whose responsibility to him had begun and ended with food, bed, and shelter, but even he knew how deranged things were in this house.

"I'm not leaving you, Dad. I'm just moving a few miles away. I'll see you tonight."

Maverick turned back to her. "What? You're still working the poker thing? No. You're not."

She helped out at her father's bar when there was some kind of party or other. He hated that, too, and he'd sure as fuck thought she'd give that up when she moved in with him. How the fuck could he keep her safe if she wouldn't stay away from this man?

"Yes. I am." She looked him dead in the eye. "Let's fucking go. Dad, I'll see you tonight."

She walked out of the house and straight to his Impala, which was loaded with her belongings. Maverick watched until she was sitting in the passenger seat, staring out the windshield.

Then he turned back to Earl Wagner. "I *will* kill you. Any mark on her. Ever. She even gets a new *freckle*, and I'll string your guts across Tulsa."

He left her father standing against the wall, silent and shaking in impotent rage.

CHAPTER EIGHT

Over the past four years, Jenny had had cause to be in the neighborhood of the Bulls' clubhouse a few times, and she'd driven by the corner with Delaney's Sinclair once or twice. She'd always felt a shiver of...not fear, exactly, and not guilt, either, but a tweaking sense that she was behind enemy lines.

The clubhouse had never been her favorite place, even while she'd been with Maverick. Everybody had been nice enough, for the most part. She'd been his old lady, and she'd been treated with respect. There were a couple of Bulls she wasn't wild about, but she'd gotten along okay with them all and really liked a few. But there weren't a lot of women around that she could relate to. Mo, Joanna, and Maddie all had their own deals, real careers, and they were a lot older, anyway, so they'd treated her like a kid.

And then there were the sweetbutts. A whole bunch of women hanging around to serve, and to service, the Bulls, and dressed the part. Jenny knew she was okay-looking, maybe even cute, but she always felt schlubby around women dressed to maximize their physical attributes. Just handing Maverick a drink, they performed the act like they were offering him themselves as a bonus, even when Jenny stood right beside him. She hated it.

It was just a scummy, dark, stinky place full of discomfort and stress, and she'd been happier to be at home alone with Maverick—and he'd seemed happy with that as well.

When she parked on the Sinclair lot, she was facing the clubhouse, and for a minute or so, she stared out the windshield, focused on the Brazen Bulls MC sign, and felt all that old discomfort and stress bubble up and blend with all the new discomfort and stress. She really hoped she didn't hurl all over the floor when she went into the station. It was a possibility, though. Maybe a probability.

She couldn't believe she was doing this. Almost two weeks had passed since Maverick's explosion at her back door, and she hadn't heard a peep from him. That was a good thing. He was leaving her alone, like she wanted. She should let that stand and get on with life.

But she couldn't. She jumped like a frog on a hotplate every time the phone rang, or the doorbell rang, or the door at the bar opened. Every time, it might be Maverick—or worse, another Bull, maybe Rad or Eight Ball or Ox—coming to demand Kelsey. There was no way he would just fade away. She knew that for a certainty. And when he came, he would do all he could to force her to his will. After that scene at her back door, she no longer believed that there was a line he wouldn't cross to get what he wanted.

She no longer trusted him not to hurt her.

Which was why this was such a horrible idea, coming alone to the lion's den. And also why she absolutely had to. There was no one in her life she could have asked to join her, and she had to face him and know what was in store.

So she pulled her shit together and got out of her car.

As she walked toward the station, a car pulled from the full-service pumps, and she heard her name. Without breaking her stride, she turned and saw Gunner trotting up to her.

"Hey, Jen. What's going on?"

"Looking for Maverick." She didn't stop, and he grabbed her arm. He didn't grab hard, but she jerked away with a gasp nonetheless, and finally stopped. "Don't."

"Sorry, just—this is a bad place to get him fired up, Jen."

"Is that a threat?"

"Fuck! No. It's just...it's not cool to come up on him unannounced like this."

She laughed, because that was fucking funny. All Maverick had done was pop up unannounced—at her bar, her home, Kelsey's school.

"Fuck you, Gun." She started for the station again, and pulled up short after one step. She didn't have to go in. Bulls were coming toward her—through the main door and from the bays, like an advancing front.

That urge to puke clamored in her belly and began to swell.

Maverick came from the far bay, where they did auto body work. Even with one, two, three, four, five other Bulls, in addition to Gunner, arrayed before her, scowling, even sick with dread, Jenny had a fluttery moment as Maverick came toward her. He looked so good in that uniform; she'd forgotten how good. Just a service station uniform, a couple of shades of bland green, dark pants and lighter shirt, but he made it as sexy as a GQ cover.

He always tucked his shirt into his pants for work, showing slim hips and firm belly. He left three buttons undone so his snug white beater showed, with a hint of the curve of his pecs. The contours of his biceps swelled from the short sleeves of the shirt, which he'd cuffed so they cut across the midpoint of his upper arm. Still the most gorgeous man she'd ever known.

When she'd seen him at the bar, she'd noticed that his hair was nearly shorn, barely longer than the stubble on his face. The past two weeks had put actual hair on his head.

Still shorter than he'd worn it before, but enough that the arc of his skull was softer. His stubble was the same, however. During their time as a couple, he'd cycled from clean-shaven to stubble to full beard and back a few times. She liked stubble best—like it was now.

He wiped his hands on a red shop towel and shoved it into his back pocket. "Is Kelsey okay?"

That was the first question a good father would ask in this situation—thinking of his little girl before anything else. God, what would Kelsey's life had been like if she'd been born with a mom and a dad who loved each other and lived together and made a family for her?

It was a stupid thing to wonder, because the reality was nothing like that, and the past was unchangeable.

"She's fine. I wanted...I want to talk." She glanced at the line of Bulls. Gunner had backed off and was watching like the others, but without the same dark distrust in his eyes. "Is there a place we can go to be private?"

"You're not afraid to be alone with me?"

She was, a little. But face to face with him now, remembering her love for him, and surrounded by angry Bulls, he was the safest person around. "Should I be?"

"No. You're always safe with me."

"Then can we talk?"

"Yeah." He cast his eyes around like he was looking for somewhere to go. "The clubhouse is the best place I can think of. It's empty, as far as I know. You okay with that?"

He knew she didn't like it there. But there weren't many options—something she hadn't considered when she'd dropped Kelsey off at school and decided to do this.

"That's fine. That'll work."

"Guys, I'm taking a break."

"Mav…" Gunner began.

"It's cool, brother. It's all good." He held out his hand to Jenny.

She almost took it. She wanted to take it. But she locked her arms at her sides and began to walk to the clubhouse.

Maverick sighed heavily and followed.

~oOo~

The clubhouse was empty, not even a loitering sweetbutt or a prospect doing chores. Jenny looked around, surprised. "They fixed it up."

"Yeah. Mo's been on a tear for a few years, going through room by room, I guess."

It was…nice. Homey and warm. A big improvement over the flophouse it had been. "It looks good. She did a good job."

"From what I hear, the old ladies did the shopping and the guys did the work. But yeah, I guess it's okay."

He reached for her again and stopped. Instead he waved toward the bar and headed behind it himself. "You want a drink?"

"It's not even ten o'clock in the morning, Mav."

Returning the bottle of Jack he'd just picked up from the back of the bar, he turned to the coffee machine. "Coffee?"

"No, thank you. Just talk."

He picked up the Jack again. "Well, then, I need a real drink." He poured his drink, then stayed behind the bar. Jenny got the feeling he kept it between them on purpose. "What do you want to talk about?"

She wished she'd taken him up on the offer of whiskey after all. With only her will to rely on for strength, she took a breath and said, "I'm ready to tell Kelsey about you."

That was the conclusion she'd come to, the night before, when, yet again, she'd nearly leapt from her skin at the ringing phone. She couldn't sit back and wait for the Bulls to force her hand, and she knew they would. At some point, they would come, and they would stomp all over her. If she wanted to control the situation, then she needed to fucking control it.

She hadn't decided to just show up here until this morning, when she'd pissed herself off second-guessing the decision.

Maverick had been taking a drink. Now he stopped and stared at her over the glass. His eyes stayed on her as he slowly set the glass on the bar. "Yeah?"

"Yeah. I'm not...I'm not ready to just hand her over to you for an overnight or anything like that, but I'm ready to tell her and—if she wants it—I'm ready to let you meet her."

"Yeah? Jen, Jesus. Thank you." He reached across the bar and wrapped his hand around hers. The heat of him pulsed through her arm at once. "Thank you."

She drew her hand away. "I'm not ready to just hand her over. She stays with me, but you can see her while I'm there. Not on your own—at least not until I know she's comfortable with that, and I'm comfortable with it, too."

He stared at the top of the bar. Jenny studied his face, learning all his new scars.

"What did you tell her about the other night?"

"She thinks it was an angry man who was mad at somebody else and came to the wrong house. She doesn't know it was her father. She never saw you, and the cops didn't talk to her."

"Thank you. And thank you for dropping it with the cops."

Jenny nodded. She began to feel a new layer of watchfulness. Maverick wasn't saying much. He hadn't argued at all about not spending time with Kelsey on his own. He hadn't even pushed to define the parameters of the situation. All he'd said was 'thank you.'

There was another shoe hovering around somewhere, waiting to drop, and if she wasn't careful, it would smack her in the head.

"I still need to talk to her, but after I do, I was thinking we could meet somewhere—like a park or something, somewhere with a playground—and you could meet her there."

He stared at her—not aggressively, but like he was trying to work out how to behave. Jenny grasped something important: he was trying. He might fail, and the shoe might still whack her, but he was quiet because he was trying to listen to her.

"I'm okay with that. But can I make a different suggestion? I guess it's more of a request."

Waiting for the shoe, she nodded.

"I got a place. Pretty nice one. It's a house, in Ranch Acres. I'm fixing it up." He smiled. "How'd you feel about bringing her there? You could take a look, tell me how I'm doing, if I'm making a place she'd like."

"You bought a house?" They'd been looking for one together when everything had gone to hell.

"It's a rent-to-own deal, but yeah. Got a fireplace."

Remembering that flimsy thing in their apartment and how much he'd liked it, Jenny smiled—and then wanted to cry. She dropped her head so he wouldn't see her struggle for composure.

"If that's too much, okay. The park is fine."

God, he really was trying. Jenny wanted nothing more just then than to hug him. She cleared her throat and made herself look calm. "No, I think that's a good idea. It would help me to know what your house is like, and Kelse would like that, too, I think."

"Yeah?"

"Yeah. We'll do that."

The smile that broke across his face was wide and bright, full of relief—and of happiness—and Jenny saw the man she'd loved.

The man she still loved.

She had to get out of here. "Okay. I'll talk to her tonight, and I'll call you to set something up about coming over. I'll be in touch."

As she stood up and started for the door, Maverick came swiftly around the bar and stepped in front of her. Jenny flinched, and he held out his hands like a plea.

"Wait. Thank you, Jen. I mean it. I've been losing my mind, and you just gave it back to me. So thank you. Can I—I want to hold you."

"Mav..." If he touched her, she'd melt.

"Please, Jen. If I blew it with you, I get it. That's not what I mean here. I just..." Words seemed to fail him. "Please."

She could see him try, and she loved him all the more for it, despite the mess between them. She nodded, and his arms came around her, and she melted. It felt so good, so perfectly right.

After only a second or two, she felt the shift in his body that signaled his intent to pull away, but she couldn't let him go. He relaxed again, resting his head against hers, and they stood together, entwined and silent, while Jenny wished everything between them away.

"Jen." His voice rumbled at her ear, and he turned his head so that she felt his lips on her cheek. If they stayed like this much longer, he was going to kiss her, and she was going to welcome it.

She leaned reluctantly back, and he released his hold. For a heartbeat, as they moved apart, their lips nearly touched.

"I'll call you. Soon," she said and stepped out of the range of their embrace.

"Okay. Thank you."

As she got to the door, he called, "Jen!" and she turned around.

"What's her favorite color?"

She smiled. "Green."

"Green? Not pink?"

"She likes pink, too, and yellow, but green's her favorite. Mint green, not dark. She says it makes her belly happy. Mint chocolate chip is her favorite ice cream."

He grinned and gave her a nod, and Jenny left the clubhouse feeling warm and happy and sad and anxious—deeply confused and more hopeful than she'd have thought. Too hopeful.

He was really trying.

~oOo~

That evening, while Darnell did his checks on her father's equipment, changed his bedding, and prepared his bath, Jenny sat at the kitchen table with Kelsey and her father, and they ate supper together.

Her father couldn't chew well, so he ate only soft foods, like grits and oatmeal, mashed potatoes, and pureed fruits and vegetables. His fine motor skills were almost nonexistent, and his gross motor skills were erratic at best, so he had to be fed. He could swallow what was spooned into his mouth, and he could use a straw. He got most of his actual nutrition from protein drinks. But at supper, on those evenings she was home at suppertime, she always tried to give Kelsey the closest thing to a family meal she could have.

For Kelsey and herself, she'd made beef and noodles—a variation on a stroganoff recipe Mrs. Turner had given her, without the ingredients her picky little girl wouldn't touch.

This was basically just chopped sirloin and egg noodles in a cream sauce, without mushrooms or onions or garlic. Pretty bland. Jenny sprinkled a ton of pepper and garlic salt over her own serving. But Kelsey always gobbled it up and asked for seconds, which was a minor miracle and not to be dismissed.

She set up Kelsey with her Beauty and the Beast dish set, pouring milk into her mug. She fixed her own plate and set it at her place, then hooked the adult-sized bib around her father's neck. He watched her, his eyes wide and mobile. His muscle tone as it was, he had to actively keep his mouth closed, and he rarely did, so it sagged open most of the time. He didn't drool much, because his meds tended to dehydrate him a little, but he always looked — and probably was — profoundly confused.

"Jen," he said.

"I know, Dad. I've got cheese grits for you tonight. That sounds good, right? And Granny Smith applesauce."

"Jen."

She sat down and scooted her chair close to her father's wheelchair. When she held up a spoon of grits, he opened his mouth and closed it over the spoon. Just like she'd done for Kelsey when she was a baby, she used the empty spoon to scrape the residue from his lips.

"Hey, Kelse," she said as she spooned up more grits. "I have something I want to talk to you about."

"Did I do bad?"

Jenny turned to her daughter, leaving the spoon hovering, mid trip. "No, pixie. Not at all. Why would you think that?"

"I don't know. Is it about my birthday? 'Cuz I want to go to the zoom and I want Maisie to come, too. And I want ice cream cake and presents and a balloon."

"It's not about your birthday, but that's the plan. We're going to the *zoo*, and we'll have cake and presents and a balloon after."

Maisie was the Turners' granddaughter and Kelsey's only real friend. Jenny hadn't yet figured out why she had trouble making friends. She wasn't shy, she wasn't bossy, she wasn't mean. She could be a little sassy, but that didn't seem to bother kids. She got along with other kids fine and would talk to any who came up to her. But even when Jenny tried to rig the situation, to start kids at the playground playing a game or something, Kelsey would separate out pretty quickly and play by herself.

Maisie was the exception. She was a few months older, and Mrs. Turner was her full-time babysitter, so she and Kelsey had grown up together.

"Jen!" her father yelled, and Jenny flinched. He sounded like his old self when he yelled her name, although his old self would have yelled her full name if he were angry. She fed him his spoon of grits and got back to thinking about this talk she needed to have.

How to tell her almost-four-year-old about her father? She'd been tearing up her head all day trying to practice and, as usual, her brain refused to do the heavy lifting. Whenever a high-stress problem arose, her mind crossed its arms and turned away with a huff, and she was left flailing. Usually, she ended up squeezing her eyes shut and just jumping in, which she did now.

"It's about your daddy."

"I don't have a daddy. Not all families have daddies. My family has a mommy and a granddaddy."

Her own words coming back to punch her in the face. "That's true. If you could have a daddy, would you want one?"

Kelsey set her fork down and looked up at the ceiling. She pinched her little chin in her hand like she was pulling a beard, and Jenny smiled. She's seen that on television, a character taking that pose to think, and since then, when she had a serious thought to think, she did the same.

"Would he be a daddy like Maisie's?"

The Turners were African American, as was their son-in-law. Jenny didn't know if that was what Kelsey meant. It wasn't easy to know the mind of a preschooler. "What do you mean?"

"He brings the yard eater over to eat our yard after it eats Mr. and Mrs. Turner's yard, and he takes Maisie to the swings and he sits in back with Mr. Turner and makes hamburgers and has beer. He puts the sprinkler out and we can play in it."

Jenny laughed. "Yeah, I think he might be like that."

"Did you meet him?"

"Yeah, pixie. I know him. We loved each other when we made you."

Kelsey frowned. "But then he went away when I came."

She'd never said any such thing. She'd never said anything about Maverick except that not all families had daddies. Kelsey had made this leap on her own, and it hurt Jenny's heart. "He didn't want to go away, Kelsey. He was really, really sad when he had to. But now he's back, and he wants to know if you would like to know him."

"NO!" Jenny's father shouted forcefully and swung his arm, knocking the spoon to the floor. "NO!"

He stared at Jenny, his eyes steady and fierce, and she knew he understood that they were talking about Maverick being back.

She stared right back and put as much meaning as she could into her eyes. "Calm down, Dad."

"Granddaddy, it's okay," Kelsey said. "I don't like grits, either."

After watching her father to be sure the outburst was done, Jenny picked up the spoon and went to wash it in the sink. "What do you think, Kelsey? If you don't want to meet him, that's okay."

Again, she pulled on her chin and looked up at the ceiling. After she'd had her thought, she asked, "Is he nice?"

"I think so, yes. I think he'll be very nice to you."

"Is he nice to you? I don't want a daddy who isn't nice to my mommy."

Jenny went and crouched beside her daughter's chair. "You are a wonderful little person, Kelsey Marie. I love you."

"I love you, too, Mommy. That's three."

"Three, uh-huh. And yes, your daddy is nice to me."

"Will he come live with us? Maisie's daddy lives with her and her mommy, and the baby in her mommy's belly, too." A new thought happened. "Oh! Will you have a baby in your belly, too? If you do, I want a boy baby."

"Slow down, pixie." That was all much more complicated and fraught than Jenny could sort out, and it made her woozy to try. "You haven't even met him yet. Let's start there. Would you like to meet him?"

"Okay, if he's nice. I'm done with my noodles, and I ate three green beans. Can I have a cookie?"

With a relieved laugh, Jenny wrapped her little girl up in a hug. "Yes. Clear your place, and you can have one cookie." She helped her out of her booster seat.

As Kelsey set her dishes at the sink and picked out a gingersnap from the cookie jar, Jenny sat back at the table.

Her father stared at her with that steady, perceptive look. His breath came loudly and quickly, like a violent pant, and his face was flushed.

She hadn't seen him truly angry in four years.

She wasn't afraid of him anymore.

~oOo~

It was a nice house.

A sprawling brick ranch in the middle of a huge yard full of mature trees. His bike was parked on the driveway, next to a new, or new-ish, black Jeep Cherokee. Jenny considered that SUV and wondered if Maverick had other company. That would suck, if he did.

Kelsey tugged on her hand as Jenny led her to the front walk. "Is this his *house*?"

"I think so, yeah. Do you like it?"

"It's like a *castle*."

It wasn't—it was just a nice, middle-class brick ranch house in a neighborhood full of nice, middle-class brick ranch houses, but compared to the rundown bungalow they lived in, maybe it was a bit palatial.

Just then, the front door opened, and Maverick stepped out. He wore jeans and a plain white t-shirt, in his usual snug fit. He grinned at them.

Kelsey tugged on her hand again, and Jenny leaned down. "What is it, pix?"

"Mommy, that's the sad man from school. Miss Betsy said I couldn't talk to him."

Crouching to her daughter's level, Jenny turned her so that they were face to face. "He was a stranger that day. Today, you're going to meet him. What's the rule about meeting new people?"

"Be with a grownup I trust."

"Do you trust me?"

She laughed. "That's silly. You're my mommy!"

Jenny laughed a little, too. "So do you?"

Still giggling, Kelsey nodded. "Yeah, silly. I trust you to the moon and back!"

"Okay. Then it's time to meet your daddy." Standing up, Jenny took her daughter's hand again.

Maverick had stayed on the slab porch when they'd paused for their little talk, but as they began to approach him again, he stepped off.

"Hi." He smiled at Kelsey and crouched to her level. "Hi, Kelsey."

"Hi, Daddy."

Jenny's breath caught—she didn't know why she was surprised; for the past twenty hours or so, she'd been calling Maverick Kelsey's daddy, so why wouldn't she greet him that way? But to hear her say that, with such ease—God.

Maverick took the greeting liked she'd stabbed him with it. All over his face, Jenny could see the raw pain and the struggle for control over his emotions.

Kelsey saw it, too, but she couldn't understand the reason. "You have sad eyes. Like at school. Are you sad to meet me?"

"No, sweetheart," he said, trying to smile. "Not at all. I'm happier to meet you than anything. I just—can I give you a hug?"

Kelsey nodded. "I like hugs." She lifted her arms and went right to him. Maverick pulled her tightly to his chest and tucked her head against his.

Jenny saw tears make wet trails down his cheeks, one from each eye. She hated herself for cutting him out. Whatever her reasons, right now, standing right here, she knew she'd been wrong.

"I'm sorry, Mav," she whispered.

He heard her and shook his head. "Doesn't matter now. It's okay now."

When Kelsey began to squirm, Maverick let her go. "You want to come inside?"

"Yeah! Your house is like a castle!" Kelsey took Maverick's hand—he hadn't held it out to her, she simply folded her hand over the edge of his, under his thumb. His head jerked down at her touch, and then he glanced at Jenny, like he was guilty.

She liked that bit of deference to her, but it hurt her heart, too. "It's okay. I'm glad."

With her blessing, he led Kelsey through the front door, and Jenny followed.

~oOo~

Oh—it *was* a nice house. And fully decorated. He'd been out of prison for less than a month. How had he acquired so much stuff already? Had he bought it furnished?

Her questions must have been clear on her face, because he answered them. "Mo went on a shopping spree. There's still a couple of empty rooms, but she got the important stuff done for me. You know how Mo loves to shop."

The living room was just off the front hall. There was a long, stacked-stone fireplace with a heavy mantelpiece. The furniture was comfortable and masculine, and actually had a bit of Maverick's personality. Mo had done a good job.

The dining room was empty, but the kitchen had a round oak table and four chairs in a bright bay-window breakfast nook that looked out over the back yard—big and green, with handsome trees making cool shade. A slab patio ran from the back door to the outside edge of the bay window.

Kelsey gasped theatrically. "Mommy, look! A princess house!"

At the back of the yard stood a dainty house, creamy white with pink trim, and even a little porch with a pink railing. A playhouse. The day before, he'd asked about her favorite color and sounded a little disappointed that it wasn't pink. Jenny thought she now knew why.

"Daddy, is it for me? Can I play in it? My birthday is in four days, you know. I am going to be four years big." She held up her fingers to show her father.

"I know! The house is for you, but we need to ask your mom if it's okay to play in it."

"Mommy, can I play in my new house?"

Jenny stepped around the table and chairs so she could see more of the yard. A tall cedar fence. Well-tended grass. Good shade trees. No sharp fence posts or rocks. "Sure. That sounds fun."

"Yeah!" Kelsey looked frantically for the door. Maverick chuckled and opened it for her, and she ran out. After a few steps, she spun and ran back, throwing her arms around Maverick's legs. "Thank you, Daddy!"

Just as quickly, she spun away again and ran to her house. Maverick stood there, his face a portrait of shock and awe.

Again Jenny said, "I'm sorry. I'm so sorry."

Still stunned, he shook his head. Then he blinked and focused on her. "I am, too. I'm not holding a grudge, Jen. I'm just so fucking glad she's here now. And you, too."

"You have to watch your language now." She smiled, wanting him to know she was teasing—and also true.

He laughed. "I guess I do. Hey—can we step away from her for a second? The fence is solid, and the gate's locked. I want to show you something before I show her. Is that okay?"

Jenny stepped past him to lean out the open door. "Kelsey!"

Kelsey opened a little casement window and peeked her head out. "Yeah, Mommy?"

"I'm going to be inside with your daddy for a few minutes. We'll leave the door open. You stay in the yard. Understand?"

"Yes, ma'am. I'll stay in the yard. I'm making tea and crumpets!"

Jenny cocked her head at Maverick. "Tea and crumpets?"

She thought he might have blushed. "There's a kitchen set in there, and a table and chairs, and a little easy chair. It was all set up at the store, and I got everything. Didn't seem right to give her an empty house. I don't know about the tea and crumpets."

"That's in a book she likes."

"Shit." He slapped his forehead. "Books. I didn't get her any books. Oh — shit, I said shit."

Jenny laughed. "It's okay. She loves to go to the library and pick out books to borrow. And she'll yell at you for using ugly words and mean talk, so be careful."

"You made a great little girl, Jenny. She's — she's amazing."

"Yeah, she is. I don't know how much of that's my doing, though. I'm not Mom of the Year material."

"I don't believe that."

With a shrug, Jenny changed the subject. "What did you want to show me?"

"Yeah. This way."

When he took her hand, she didn't pull away.

He led her through the living room and down a long hallway. Several doors lined the hall, all but one of them closed. The open one led to a bathroom, and Jenny noticed a fabric shower curtain and towels hanging on a rod, all in brown and white stripes. Even the bathroom had been carefully decorated.

As they continued down the hallway, the sharp, not-unpleasant scent of latex paint hung in the air. Maverick opened a door, and the scent became instantly stronger. He led her inside.

"Oh my God," she muttered. "Mav…what did you do?"

He walked around to stand at her other side. It felt like he did that a lot, put himself on her left side. She wondered if it was some kind of prison thing, like a habit he'd built up to keep people on his stronger side.

"I wanted her to have a room here. Of her own. If it's too soon or too much, I understand. That's why I wanted you to see it first."

She was standing in a confection of a little girl's bedroom. The furniture was simple and white, typical kid furniture, except for the little three-mirror vanity in the corner and the pink puff sitting before it. But the walls were mint green, and the linens had a pink rose pattern with mint green stripes, and the curtains matched. Even the pink mini-blinds in the window matched. A few fluffy pink throw rugs were scattered over the hardwood floor, and there was a toy chest, like a white treasure chest, under the window.

A ring hung from the ceiling, just above the head of the bed. White netting hung down from it and draped over the bed. A canopy. Kelsey's heart would explode.

"You did all this since yesterday?"

He shook his head. "Since then, I painted and put up the window stuff, and Mo picked up the bedding and rugs. The furniture I'd already bought. And the playhouse was the first thing I did—I built that right after I took possession, before I had anything to move in here."

Her heart pounded in her ears, drowning out sound or sense. Emotion surged like a tidal wave through her, and she couldn't hold it back. She put her hands over her mouth as a last resort, but the sobs came anyway.

"It's too much," Maverick muttered. "I'm sorry. Goddammit."

She shook her head, trying to stop. When he put his arms around her, she needed the comfort and didn't fight it— and she was comforted.

"You bought our house," she finally choked out against his chest.

"What?"

"When we were looking. This is what we wanted. You have our house."

His hand smoothed over her hair. "Say the word, babe. One word, and it *is* our house."

In that declaration, for the first time since she'd gone to the station, she heard the old Maverick—the one who'd push and push and push until he got his way. The real Maverick. Was all this a show? Had he *planned* this?

No—that was ridiculous. Not even Maverick would go so far as to buy a house to prove his point. Still, she broke from his hold and sniffed herself calm.

"It's not that easy."

She watched him fight not to argue with her—and, to his credit, he succeeded. Ultimately, he simply nodded. "Okay."

With another wistful look around Kelsey's dream room, she sighed and faced Maverick again. "It's beautiful, Mav. It's perfect. But it's too much. For today, at least—I don't want to overwhelm her. Or confuse her." She thought of Kelsey's questions about where her daddy would live and if she'd have a baby brother. "The playhouse is enough for today."

"Okay. Fair enough. I got mint chocolate chip ice cream. Can she have that?"

Jenny smiled. "Only if I get some, too."

~oOo~

That night, before she went to bed, Jenny pushed open Kelsey's door and leaned against the frame. Kelsey slept in a little ball, with Mr. Spotsie tucked firmly in her arms.

This room had been Jenny's room when she was a little girl. The walls were covered with the same busy, pink and blue floral wallpaper, and the curtains were the same white, ruffled, dotted Swiss tie-backs. The vinyl pull-down shade was the same. The furniture was different—she still slept in the double bed that had been hers growing up, so Kelsey had a new bed and other pieces—and there was a plush area rug on the floor. The toys were different and more plentiful. And the love was more real. Kelsey's room was better than her own had been, though they'd both occupied the space within these four walls. But it was nothing like what Maverick had made for her.

This house, this life, was nothing at all like that fantasy Maverick was creating. A fantasy close enough to touch. But a fantasy nonetheless.

It was the life they were supposed to have. The life Jenny had thought she'd have, when she was huge with Kelsey and planning a future with Maverick.

Instead, he'd gone away and left her alone to raise their daughter and care for her father, whom he hadn't quite killed.

And she'd given birth alone in a hospital room, one floor down from her comatose father's room, with no hand to hold through her pain and her fear but that of a nurse she'd never met.

August 21, 1993

"No! No! Please! It's not supposed to be this way! I can't do this by myself!" Jenny sobbed and wailed. A small voice inside her said she was making everything worse, but the rest of her didn't care. This hurt, and she was alone, and Maverick was supposed to be here. She was supposed to have a good life ready for her little girl, not this...this hopeless, homeless emptiness.

The contraction let her go, and she settled into quiet sobs, trying to roll onto her side so she could hug the pillow and bury her face. She could only make it about halfway.

The nurse—it was a different one now, another stranger who'd no doubt have her whole hand up inside her any minute—was talking to somebody at the door.

Jenny didn't care. About anything. She closed her eyes and tried to go away.

A cool hand brushed over her head. "Jenny? Can you open your eyes for me?"

More sobs happened, and tears leaked from her sealed lids. The room spun like she was drunk.

"Jenny, Jenny. Shhh. Can you take a deep breath for me?"

Jenny didn't even try.

"Oh, honey. Let's talk. I want to try to help you. Dr. Ingersoll wants to give you a sedative, but things are pretty far along here, and baby's gonna get sleepy, too. That can make everything take longer and go harder. If you can't get calm, we need to do that, but first I thought I'd see if I can help."

The nurse's voice was gentle and soothing, and Jenny calmed down enough to take a deeper breath. She opened her eyes. A young nurse with short blonde hair smiled down at her. "Hi. I'm Willa. Debbie asked me to try to help you. Can you tell me what's got you so scared? What exactly is the scariest part?"

She heaved in a stuttering, painful breath. "It's...it's...not supposed to be...like this."

"Like what, honey? Is it something I can help you fix?"

"No!" A fresh crying jag hit her at the same time that a new contraction took her over, and she screamed, "I can't do it! I can't do it! I can't do it!" until the pain was too much and she could only grunt.

It one was the worst yet, and when it was over, she was too spent to cry.

The nurse—what was her name?—put down the side rail on the bed and got in next to her, sliding her arm under Jenny's back. That was strange and unexpected, and Jenny tried to draw away, but the nurse simply held her.

"The next contraction, I'm going to help you curl up, and you're going to grab me just as hard as you can, okay? Put all your tension from your whole body in your hands, and let everything else stay soft. Don't worry about hurting me. I'm from West Texas. We're tough stock."

Jenny heard the nurse, but it was impossible to focus on anything but the turmoil inside her, in her head and in her body. "I'm not supposed to be alone."

"Is there somebody we should be calling for you, honey? I know your dad's upstairs. A friend, maybe? The father?"

Weeping with renewed vigor, Jenny shook her head and buried it against the nurse's shoulder. "I'm alone. I'm not supposed to be alone. I can't be a mom all by myself. I don't know what to do!"

Another contraction hit, and without thinking, Jenny did what the nurse wanted. She grabbed on, digging her hands into this stranger's body, and the nurse helped her curl up. The pain was exquisite—each one was worse than the one before—but the horrible pressure came off her back a little, and there was focus in her hands that pulled her mind up out of the some of the pain.

When it was over, she sighed. "What's your name?"

"Willa. You did good, honey." Willa reached over and hit the nurse call button.

A male voice came from the speaker. "Can I help you?"

"Otto, it's Willa. I need an assist in here to do a check."

"You got it. I'll send Janet."

"Thank you!"

Jenny knew what 'check' meant. "Already? It hurts!"

"I know, but these are good contractions. I think they're getting you closer. So let's see how close."

"It's not supposed to be this way." This time the words came out as nothing but a whisper.

Willa brushed her wet hair back from her face. "I'm sorry this is so hard for you, honey. I wish I knew more so I could try to help." She hesitated, then added, "If you want, I can have an adoption counselor come visit you after—"

"No! I want her! I need her!" The thought of losing the baby, too, made the tears and breathless fear come back. They hadn't decided on names yet when everything went to hell, but Jenny was going to name her Kelsey. Kelsey Marie. "I need her! But I don't know how!"

"Okay." Willa gave her a reassuring squeeze. "We're going to take things one at a time. You want your baby, and she's about to be here with you. That's a good thing, right?"

Jenny nodded.

"So let's get that to happen the right way, and we won't worry about anything any further ahead until that job is done. Then, you and me, we'll take on the next thing. And the next. You're not alone, Jenny. I know I'm not who you want to be with, but I'm here, and I'm going to stay with you. Right here. Okay?"

The door opened, and another nurse came in. The only person she had right now in the whole world was Willa, whom she'd met only minutes before. But she held onto her for dear life.

~oOo~

"Would you like me to take her to the nursery so you can get some rest?"

Jenny lifted her eyes from her daughter's perfect face. "I want her here, with me. Is that okay?"

Willa smiled. "Sure. I'll bring in some extra supplies. You should sleep now, while she is. You just worked hard, and your body needs a breather." She picked up the pink card Jenny had already filled out. "Kelsey Marie. That's lovely. We have a Polaroid camera at the nurses' desk. I'll bring it in later so you can have a picture of this day."

"Thank you." She felt better now, more like herself. Still scared—she'd spent the past month scared out of her mind every single second—but holding her little girl, finally having her in her arms, was too big, too astounding to be anything but wonderful.

About to slide the pink card into the holder at the back of the nursery bassinette, Willa paused. "Are you finished filling this out?"

Jenny had left one line blank. Maverick wasn't a father. A father wouldn't have done something to risk leaving his family behind. Not even her own father had done that. She nodded, and Willa slid the card into its place without further comment.

"I'm getting evicted on the first of the month. I don't know what I'm going to do."

Willa came up to her side and smiled down at Kelsey. Jenny did, too. She was so pretty, with wispy curls already. Both she and Maverick had dark hair, but Kelsey's was fair, like Jenny's mother's had been.

"Okay, that sounds like the next thing. You get some rest, and I will make some calls and get somebody up here who can help you find a place to go."

She had a place to go, she supposed. The thought horrified her; she'd only been free of it for less than two years. "I have a place. I can go to my dad's house. I just...I don't know how to get my stuff there." Her stuff and Maverick's. The remnants of the life he'd ruined. "I don't have a job or a home or even a friend. I have my dad, who's a vegetable now, and I have her. This isn't how it was supposed to go. He promised me he'd take care of us and she'd have a good family, and now all she has is me, and I'm nothing."

Willa put her hand on her shoulder. "Hey. You are *not* nothing. You're a good role model for your girl. These hours we've been together, I've seen a woman who was terrified and fought anyway. That's strength. You delivered a baby without drugs, Jenny. That's something you can brag about for the rest of your life. If you want, you can be all sanctimonious when mommies are swapping their stories and say, 'Me, I had a natural childbirth.' They'll all think you're a superhero."

"I only fought because you made me. I only had to do it without drugs because I was too scared to come to the hospital until it was too late for drugs."

There was no other way to think about what had happened when the contractions had started: she'd had a breakdown. Alone in the apartment she'd shared with Maverick, she'd been trying to pack up the life he'd destroyed, panicking about the fact that she had nowhere to go but the house she'd grown up in, that she would have to bring her baby into that house, when she'd realized that the contractions were the real thing. She'd totally lost it and spent she didn't know how long lying on the floor, screaming *NO NO NO* through them all, until a neighbor had burst into the apartment and gotten her to the hospital.

"I told you when I came in—you could have had drugs. Doctor was ready to sedate you. But you protected your baby, and you toughed it out. I think this is a lucky little girl."

She wasn't; neither of them was lucky. But Jenny offered Willa a smile anyway. "Thank you."

"You're welcome. Now, get some rest. I'll make some calls and see if I can find you some help to move."

Willa had been with her through the last part of her labor, the long, terrible time of pushing and delivery, and the recovery. "Your shift has to be over soon."

"My shift was over before we met, honey. I've been here with you because I want to be."

CHAPTER NINE

After the station closed, the Bulls who'd been on shift always walked over to the clubhouse for at least a couple of drinks. Sometimes, usually when there was a decent sampling of girls around, those couple of drinks turned into a low-key party. Other nights, it was a couple of drinks and then everybody went their own ways.

On this night, most of the guys had either gone home to their families or upstairs with a girl or two. Maverick and Gunner were alone in the party room, sitting side by side at the bar. Slick, one of the prospects, drew two fresh beers from the tap and set them on the bar. Maverick nodded and took his.

"Thanks, man," Gunner said as he took his. "Now fuck off."

Maverick watched the prospect walk away. He still showed some damage from the beat-down he'd taken more than a week ago, but he was back at full power. Wally, the other grunt, was still in a sling.

"What d'you think about Slick?" Gunner asked.

Maverick shrugged. "No opinion yet. Why?"

"He's been prospecting two years. Si's agitating to put him up for a vote."

"Simon sponsored him?"

When Gunner nodded, Maverick turned again in the direction Slick had gone. He'd left the room, so Maverick turned back and contemplated his beer. "You tell me."

It was shit like this that made him feel most out of sync—he didn't know Slick at all. The kid had been out of commission for almost a week of the short time Maverick had been back, and Maverick's attention had been elsewhere, anyway. He had no idea if Slick was patch material. But he'd be expected to vote on it.

Gunner finished his beer. "He's a good guy. Loyal. He's been hurt a few times in the line. With the gun business getting bigger, we need the bodies. He's quiet, but I think that's as much him being a grunt as anything. I think he's ready, and I think we need him."

"Then I'll vote with you." Again, Maverick considered how much Gunner had grown and settled while he'd been gone. "Maybe you should sponsor a new prospect."

Gunner laughed. "Fuck no. I got enough trouble keeping myself in line." After a quiet second, he added, "I don't know who I'd call up, anyway. We could use the bodies, though."

"Maybe I should put a name in. Last one I sponsored turned out okay."

He was fairly sure Gunner was blushing under his thick beard.

The front door opened, and Delaney came in alone. He'd been off on some club business he hadn't seen fit to share with the club, and he'd refused backup. There's been some controversy about that when he'd left a couple of hours earlier.

"Mav. Glad you're here. Come on back." He walked past Maverick and Gunner, heading toward his office.

They exchanged a glance. Gunner shrugged, and Maverick hopped off his stool.

"I'll hang out," Gunner called after him. "Leah's got school tonight, anyway."

Maverick nodded and headed to the president's office.

"Have a seat." Delaney closed the door as Maverick sat in the chair beside his desk.

"What's up? Problem?"

"Not at all. I need to take your temperature first. Seems like you've settled down since those first few days. How're you doing?"

He had settled down. That fucking breakdown he'd had at Jenny's had shaken him up more than a little. That wasn't who he was—it hadn't been him before prison, and he wasn't going to get what he needed to have, be who he needed to be, if he lost his shit like that.

Getting the house had helped. Spending time in Mo's no-nonsense, unflappable presence had helped. Making up a home for Kelsey had helped. Nothing had helped as much as hearing his daughter call him Daddy, though. That was who he wanted to be, who he needed to be: Kelsey's daddy. And her mother's man. Most of his energy and effort these past two weeks had been on Jenny and Kelsey and trying to get that life back.

The club barely made his notice. It didn't matter; he'd been benched, so it wasn't anything but a job and a place to drink, anyway. And it sounded like he was about to vote to patch in a guy whose last name he didn't even know. Right now, the connection he most wanted, most needed, was not here.

He'd thought for a minute that he'd had Jenny. She loved the house. When she'd cried in Kelsey's room and let him hold her, he'd thought she'd finally seen that they didn't have to be over. But she'd backed off, and he hadn't heard from her in a couple of days now. He was trying to do this her way, but if she didn't call soon, he'd go over there. He'd have to.

"This just a status check?" he asked his president.

Delaney's head swiveled left and right, but his eyes stayed on Maverick's. "I got news. If you're thinking straight."

"I am."

"Good. Just got back from a face-to-face with Melvin Dyson."

"On your own." Rad would bust a vein when he found out. His number-one job was protecting the club president.

An irritated line creased Delaney's forehead. "Melvin and I've been doing this shit a long time. Most of that time, we've been good with each other. We don't need backup to have a conversation."

Maverick said nothing. If Delaney had news, and it had to do with Dyson, then he didn't want to delay hearing what it was.

"Most of what I've got to say belongs at the table. I've got Dane callin' everybody into church tonight. But I want to hear from you first."

Maverick waited.

"Melvin says that the ambush on the prospects wasn't sanctioned. He says none of the bullshit we've been catching from Northside is sanctioned. He's got an insurrection building, and he's looking to quash it hard."

"Was what happened inside sanctioned? What happened to me?"

Delaney's answer was a silent stare.

"Then I want him dead."

"You're saying you want the head of a king, Mav. It's not that easy."

Fucking hell, was he tired of hearing people tell him that what he wanted 'wasn't that easy.' Like anything in his entire goddamn life had been easy. "I don't give a fuck."

"It's bigger than you. You say you're thinking straight, so I'm gonna trust you to understand that. The truth doesn't change reality. We can't blow Tulsa up over a turf war, and that's what'll happen if I give you what you want. The Volkovs'll get involved on our side, and the Street Hounds'll get in with Dyson, and we'll all leave scorched earth in our wake. Melvin doesn't want that any more than I do."

"You're saying you want the man who okayed the hit on me to keep breathing. More than that—you're having private *chats* with the bastard."

"I know you got payback for what happened in your cell. I know what you did. There had to have been some satisfaction in that."

"And I told you I want Dyson off the map."

"Even if that could happen, it makes a vacuum, and the Street Hounds come in from outside and fill it up. Right now, Dyson's holding them off with a partnership. But if Dyson folds, they'll be here before the bodies are cold. The Hounds turn every neighborhood they put a stake down in into a wasteland. We don't want that. The Dyson crew's been working Northside longer than the Bulls have been a charter. We have balance. We need to keep it." Delaney took a deep breath and leaned back in his chair. "You're a thinker, Maverick. Always have been. I need you to think now. There is more at stake than revenge, and you know it. We're strong because we think before we act, and we don't go chasing short-term satisfaction at the cost of the future. But I'm not selling what happened to you short. If you'll hear me out, just hang on and fuckin' listen, I've got something for you."

Maverick was also getting mighty sick of people telling him he wasn't listening enough. He crossed his arms and glared at Delaney.

"Melvin needs to step on trouble inside his crew. We need satisfaction for the hurt his rogues have been putting on us. You need satisfaction for the hurt you took. He's offering it to us. He ID'd three ringleaders, and he's offering them to us as scapegoats."

"He's handing over his outcasts for us to take care of. That us cleaning his house. How's this a win for us?"

"All three've been hitting us. And one of 'em is Ellison Carver. Clement Carver's baby brother. Raised up by his big brother after their mama OD'd. You left Clem alive. You want more hurt on him, you take it out on the boy he raised."

That caught Maverick's interest. He didn't know Ellison Carver, and he hadn't been around for the trouble with Dyson on the outside. He didn't bear him a particular grudge, other than his association. All he knew was that Clement Carver was the man he hated most in the world. If Delaney was right, and the Carver brothers were that close, then killing Ellison would cause Clement more pain than flattening his dick had. Lasting, eternal, unbearable pain.

"I'm in. When?"

"Let's bring it to the whole table. But soon. Tonight. Tomorrow latest. And Mav — we do this, it squares us with

Dyson. That grudge is ended. Anything from today back is settled. You understand?"

"This is all I get—three guys Dyson doesn't want."

"And killing one of them will tear Clem Carver up. That's the terms."

He was thinking straight enough to understand that it was the best chance he had. But he had to control what happened when they did these guys. "I'm on point. Rad stands back unless I say otherwise."

"Agreed. I'll talk to him." Delaney sighed. "But, brother, take some counsel here. I'm the only one here who knows what happened to you. If you don't want anybody else to know, then you think hard about what you do to these guys. What you did to Clem—that says loud and clear what kind of payback you needed. You do that, or anything like it, inside a circle of Bulls, and they'll understand why."

~oOo~

There was a room in the basement of the Bulls clubhouse— just an unfinished room, with two concrete-block exterior walls and two sheetrocked walls still showing tape and mud. Between the studs of those two walls, the Bulls had packed heavy-grade insulation, and the door was solid oak.

The floor was bare concrete. It sloped subtly inward from all directions, to a slotted drainage grate.

In this room, the Bulls exacted vengeance or extracted information. Sometimes both.

It had been used only three times in the six years Maverick had worn the Bull before he'd gone away. They'd had cause to inflict hurt more often than that, but they had a place off site, out of town, on Dane's property, and they used that location when they could, because it was safer. Incapacitating or killing a man in a basement in the middle of Tulsa meant a complicated cleanup, with any number of opportunities to be seen. Killing somebody a mile from any road or neighbor meant more security and more leisure with the job and the cleanup.

But Maverick wanted these guys done in the Bulls' house. He wanted them to know where they were. He wanted to be in the heart of the club when this went down. He thought maybe this would sync him up with the club, doing this thing with his brothers.

There were three men, all of them young, in their twenties. Rad had taken Eight Ball and Ox to collect the cargo, and they'd set them up in the basement before Rad had called Maverick down.

Maverick and everybody else. Even Slick. At the end of the meeting when they'd made this plan, Simon had put up Slick's name, saying he should be in on the payback as well, since he owed Dyson some hurt, too, and these three were the ones who'd done him the damage.

The club had voted to patch him in right there. The ease of the vote gave Maverick some assurance that the kid was worthy.

Now, every member of the Bulls, from Delaney to Slick—his last name was Zabek, Maverick now knew, and his given name was Andrew—stood in the basement, outside the bare room. Rad stood near the door. Ox and Eight Ball had rolled out two big tool chests from the storage room.

They'd sent the women and the hangarounds away and the old ladies home. There was no one in the clubhouse but the Bulls and their prey.

"Room's not big enough for everybody. We got 'em naked and hog-tied right now, like you wanted." Rad glanced at Mav, who nodded. "Slick, Eight, Becker, and Apollo are on cleanup. When it's done, you wrap and pack, then out to Dane's in the van. Bury 'em deep. Stack em in. Got it?"

"Yeah, Sarge," Eight Ball agreed. The others nodded.

"Slick, you want in on the doin', right?"

The kid looked sick, but he nodded. "Right." His voice was steadier than Maverick had expected.

"Mav, I'm told you want to lead this, so what's your plan?"

He didn't have a plan. For all his experience beating people up, he wasn't an enforcer with the club, and putting this kind of hurt on people wasn't normally his job. Rad was their SAA and did most of their wetwork. Ox was his right hand in that work. Maverick had been like Gunner and the rest—just muscle when he was needed.

He'd killed two men before this night. One had been an accident, and one had been an assignment.

"You gotta go in there with a plan, brother. How much hurt you want 'em to feel?"

This was different from Carver. Carver had hurt him, had nearly killed him, body and spirit. Paying that back had filled in part of the hole in his head that son of a bitch had dug. And even at that, Maverick hadn't killed him. But he'd wanted to, intended to.

The three men on the other side of that door had to die; that was Melvin Dyson's price for offering them up. But Maverick didn't feel any ill will toward them. They hadn't come at him inside. They hadn't sanctioned that attack. Fuck, they weren't even Dyson anymore.

He'd hurt the man who'd done him most hurt. He couldn't get to the man who'd okayed it. These were just scared young idiots who'd done other people some damage.

"Slick—these are the guys that beat you and Wally, right?"

The kid nodded.

"You get first crack, then. Leave Carver alive. The others, do what you want, long as they're dead when you're done."

"You sure, brother?" Delaney asked. "This is the payback. There's no going for more."

He understood. But this wasn't what he wanted. He'd get no satisfaction from torturing these kids who'd done nothing to him. He'd kill Carver's brother, because that would give Carver more hurt, but he'd do it quick. He owed the kid no pain.

"Yeah. Slick's the one with the claim against these guys. He should get to do the damage he wants." He went to the stairs. "Call me when it's time to end Carver."

"Mav!" Delaney called, but Maverick ignored him and went back up to the party room.

~oOo~

Alone in the party room, with a bottle of Jack and a glass, Maverick picked up the phone and dialed The Wayside

Inn. He didn't know Jenny's schedule, but she'd had quite a bit of free time earlier this week, so he took a guess that she'd be working tonight.

"Wayside Inn." Her voice rolled over the honkytonk tune playing in the background.

"It's me, Jen."

A beat of silence. "Hi. What's up?"

"You haven't called. Starting to freak out over here."

"It's only been a couple of days. I haven't had time to bring her over, and I'm not ready to—"

"Hand her over. I know. You keep saying that. Like you think I'd snatch her and run."

She didn't respond, and as her silence stretched, Maverick knew what he'd done. He'd cut her off and taken over. He sighed and took a swig straight from the bottle. "Sorry. I'll shut up."

"Her birthday's the day after tomorrow."

That was a date he would never forget. He closed his eyes and saw the blue ink of Jenny's handwriting, drawn across a white border: *Kelsey, 8/21/93.* "I know. Can I see her? You got a party planned or something?"

"I'm taking her and her friend to the zoo, and we're having cake and presents after."

She went quiet, but Maverick could sense that she wasn't done. Afraid to say something and foreclose the chance that she was about to ask him to come along, he kept his mouth shut.

"You can come with us, if you want."

"Yes. When? I'll be there."

"I'm going to try to get her to take a nap first. So about one? We'll meet you there."

Jenny still drove the shitty Escort she'd had when they'd met. He'd just bought the '95 Cherokee, and a car seat that Mo had said Kelsey would need. "I could pick you up. I bought a Jeep. It's safer than your little car. Room for her friend, too."

"Maverick." Icicles hung from his name. "We'll meet you at the zoo at one o'clock."

He opened his mouth to make a case for taking the Jeep, but slammed it shut when he saw that he was doing it again. Shit, was she right? Did he always need his way?

No — the Jeep was better than the Escort. Simple logic. He was right.

But she'd shut him out if he pushed the point, so he took another swig and dropped it. "Okay. I'll see you then."

She hung up.

Gunner came into the room as Maverick put the phone on its base. He was flushed and sweaty. "We're ready for you."

Maverick took another swig before he followed Gunner to the basement to kill a man he'd never met.

~oOo~

Slick stood just outside the room, panting noisily and staring at a wicked hunting knife in his hand. The blade dripped blood. Maverick recognized the hilt of that knife: Rad's.

He stepped into the doorway of a room that stank of sweat and blood and piss. Two of the young men, the scapegoats, were dead, their throats slit. Their bodies were still naked but no longer hogtied. They'd been shoved off to the side, in a jumble of limp limbs, but Maverick could see that Slick had had some shit to work out. These boys must have hurt him and Wally bad. By the look of Rad and Gunner, the new patch had asked for some assistance in getting his revenge.

Blood rolled like a river from that pile of bodies toward the drain in the center of the floor.

One man remained hogtied and alive: Ellison Carver. He lay in a pungent puddle that streamed to the same drain and mingled with the blood; he'd pissed himself. What was he, twenty-one? Twenty-two? Fucking Christ.

His frightened eyes were round as silver dollars. The wadded shop towel in his mouth forced his frantic breath through his nose in ragged gusts. But he was unharmed. It seemed that no one had yet touched him; they'd simply left him to lie there and watch his friends' brutal deaths.

Maverick was meant to be the agent of his end.

"Ellison Carver?" he asked, crouching before the terrified kid.

The kid nodded, his head jerking as if a part in his neck had gone rusty.

"Clem Carver's your brother."

This time, the kid's head didn't move, but those huge, frantic eyes managed to widen still more. Good enough as a yes.

"I owe your brother a lot of pain. You understand that? You know how these things work."

The boy began to weep.

He patted his trembling shoulder. "But I don't owe you any, kid. You got debts, but not to me. So I'm sorry."

He stood, pulled his Glock from his waistband, and shot the boy in the head.

Now he'd killed three men in his life, and not a damn one of them had felt right.

~oOo~

He didn't quite trust Jenny not to walk on across the bridge and into the zoo entrance without so much as a pause to wait for him if she'd gotten there first, so he was at the zoo at twelve-thirty. He bought two adult and two child tickets, and he went back to stand at the head of the bridge and wait. It was crowded for a Thursday, he thought, but he guessed it was probably the last week or so before schools started, so maybe parents were getting in a last outing before the summer was over.

She walked up at ten past, with Kelsey holding her hand and a little black girl about the same age holding Kelsey's other hand.

He waved.

"Hi, Daddy!" Kelsey said as they stepped onto the sidewalk. She shook free of Jenny's hand and dragged her friend to him. "This is Maisie. We're forever friends. She has a daddy too and now I have a daddy and Mommy can get a baby in her belly like Maisie's mommy and I can have a boy baby like Maisie gets."

"Kelsey..." Jenny muttered.

Maverick didn't know how to respond to that barrage of preschool logic, so he merely laughed and crouched to their level. He held out his hand to Kelsey's friend. "Hi, Maisie. I'm Maverick."

Maisie shook her head. "I'm supposed to say Mr. and Mrs. to grownups."

"Okay, then. You can call me Mr. Mav. Will you shake my hand?" She did, smiling sweetly. Maverick turned to Kelsey. "Happy birthday. Can I have a hug today?"

"Uh-huh. I like hugs."

Damn, he did, too. This tiny girl wrapped her soft arms around his neck and snugged her sweet-smelling head to his, and for that short capsule of time, the whole world made sense.

"You have a itchy face." She rubbed her cheek when he let her go.

"Sorry. Should I make my cheeks smooth like yours?"

She put her hands on his face and rubbed back and forth. Maverick closed his eyes so he could focus completely on his daughter's touch. "It's prickles. I like it."

"Then I'll keep it."

"Okay. Can we go to the zoom now? I want to see the giraffes first because I like them best." She took his hand and Maisie's hand.

Maverick stood and turned to Jenny. "I bought tickets already."

"Oh, okay. I've got cash. I'll pay you back when we get inside."

"No, Jen. My treat. Please." He felt like he had to beg for every concession from her, but if it got him close enough to Kelsey to hug her and hear her call him Daddy, then he'd keep begging.

She seemed nervous and unhappy, but she smiled. "Okay. Thank you."

Maverick took a step toward the bridge, but Kelsey held back. "Mommy! You said we need to hold hands and make a chain!"

"You're right." She went toward Maisie.

"No, Mommy. Hold Daddy's hand. Then it's grownup, grownup, girl, girl. That's called *sorting*."

Jenny stared at Kelsey, then at her hands, and finally at Maverick.

For his part, he struggled with his temper. She behaved as if he were a monster she was afraid would eat her alive, but he could feel that she still loved him. It was all around her, all around them when she was close. When he'd had her in his arms, he'd known for a certainty that she wanted what he wanted.

But even the idea of holding his hand made her stand there, paralyzed.

"Mommy, come *on!*" Kelsey's tone was impatient and imperious.

"Watch your tone, pixie."

Maverick heard that word and flinched. When Jenny had been pregnant, they'd called the baby inside her a little pixie. She'd started it, and he'd picked it up. Even after they'd known she was a girl, they hadn't yet settled on a name, and they'd kept calling her their little pixie.

"I'm sorry, Mommy. I didn't mean to do mean talk at you. I love you."

"I love you, too."

"That's two."

Maverick heard that and took a punch to the gut.

Jenny hadn't seemed to notice his reaction to the word 'pixie,' but her eyes met his when Kelsey said 'that's two.'

"Yep, that's two." She took his hand. "You want to see some giraffes?"

He nodded and let her pull their chain toward the entrance.

He was still struggling with his temper, and now he was hurt and aching, too. She'd said the other day that he'd bought their house, and she was right. But she'd lived their life. She'd had Kelsey, kept her all to herself, and she'd passed on to her the things that she'd shared with him. But she'd never told Kelsey that those things had come from them, from Jenny and him and their love for each other and for their baby. Until a few days ago, Kelsey had had no understanding that she'd even had a father, much less one who wanted her, who loved her.

Jenny had left him to rot and claimed all the good for her own.

He'd been in shackles when she'd turned her back, and she had him in shackles now, begging for the smallest scraps.

August 2, 1993

Maverick sat alone in the dingy courthouse meeting room and rubbed his wrists. The shackles they made him wear when he was in the same space as free people weren't excessively tight, but it was like the metal burned him. Just the feeling of the steel lying on his skin made him itch and ache.

In here, they'd released him, so he sat on a hard chair and rubbed his wrists.

He didn't know why he was in here. He had a plea deal—nine months in county jail and a five-hundred dollar fine, in return for his confession and saving the County of Tulsa and the State of Oklahoma the expense of a trial. Today was supposed to be a formality: stand before the judge, confess that he'd beaten Earl Jack Wagner of North Joplin Avenue and done Great Bodily Harm, get his slap, and do his time sitting on his ass watching daytime television. Maybe get time off for good behavior and only be inside four or five months.

But the guards had shoved him in here instead, and he got antsier with each passing minute. Something was wrong.

He was hoping he'd see Jenny in the courtroom. He'd asked if he'd have a chance to see her alone before he was sent back to County, and Percy had said he'd work it out. He'd only caught glimpses of her in the short time since he'd been arrested; he'd been denied bail while they'd all waited to see if Earl would croak. He hadn't, and it no longer looked like he was going to, so the charge was Aggravated Assault.

Jenny was so pissed off, and she was frightened. That was a bad combination for trying to get through to her. He fucking hated that she'd have their little girl while he was cooling his heels, but he'd be out just a few months afterward, and they'd be okay. He just needed like five minutes to get her head straight, and she'd be okay while he was away, and then they'd be okay when he got out. The Bulls would watch out for her. She wouldn't be alone.

The door opened, and Maverick tensed. Percy Clayton, the club lawyer, came in. Delaney was behind him. Neither man looked at ease.

"What happened?"

Percy sat down at the table, across from Maverick, before he answered. Delaney stood behind Maverick and put his hand on his shoulder. Oh, this was going to be bad.

"DA pulled the deal. She's got new terms."

"What? We signed off on this—*she* signed off."

Delaney put steadying pressure on his shoulder, but Maverick wasn't ready to blow. He didn't understand enough yet to be angry. Just confused and anxious.

"I'm sorry, Mav." Percy really did look sorry. "She got a lead on something, and she wants your help. New terms are same deal, but to get it, you talk."

Now he understood why Delaney was in the room. Using the club lawyer hadn't even been a question for Maverick—he was a Bull and had nothing to hide from the club he loved—but it meant that the lawyer was working for the club first and the patch second. Delaney was here because he wanted to make sure Maverick wouldn't talk.

"D, you know I won't talk."

The president sat beside him at the table. "I know. I just want you to know that we got your back like you got ours. Jenny's taken care of. Anything she needs."

"The DA's not getting shit, but what's she after?"

"The Russians. She got a lead that we're connected to the Volkovs, and she got a lady boner."

The Russians were penny-ante shit for the Bulls. They did a couple of runs a year for them. But it was interstate, and that could bring the Feds into the mix. ATF. "Jesus Christ." He turned to Percy. "I'm no rat. What'm I looking at now?"

"She'll recommend the max. Five years, five hundred dollars."

Five years? Their little girl would be ready to start kindergarten. He'd miss her first everything. And Jenny— Jesus, what would she do? She wanted to stay home and be a full-time mom, and he'd promised to take care of his family, so she'd quit her job. They'd only just started looking for a house. He hadn't made a good home for her and their kid yet. He couldn't go away for five fucking years.

But he couldn't rat. Delaney didn't need to be sitting at his side for that to be true.

"What's Jenny know?"

Delaney answered. "She's here, waiting outside the courtroom. Mo got her to come. We told her you had a deal for short time, and you'd be staying close by. She knows something is wrong now, but not what. She's a mess, Mav. I won't sugarcoat that. But we got hold of her, and we won't let her go."

"We could go to trial," Percy offered. "The vic is stable now, so I can probably get you bail, get you outside until the trial is over. That way you can be there when the baby comes, at least."

Delaney stared hard at him but didn't speak. Maverick knew he was letting him work out the problems with that plan for himself: a trial would bring their business up. The Russians would come up, and anything else they did that wasn't in bounds. He couldn't go to trial. Besides, there was a witness, unimpeachable, and Maverick wouldn't let the club nullify the old guy who lived next door to Jenny's old man. That guy had been good to Jenny.

He was going to do time. Real time. In the pen. If he had to do it, he'd better do it so he did the least amount of damage to the people he cared about. Get in, do his time, get out. Head down, shoulder to the day.

"No trial." He met Delaney's eyes and held fast. "You'll take care of her?"

"You know we will."

"Send her my take of everything that comes in. All of it."

Delaney shook his head. "I'll send her half of it, and I'll keep the rest back for emergencies—yours or hers."

"She's having my kid, D. She's gonna need the money."

"And she'll have everything she needs. But I'm not gonna leave you with nothing when you get out."

"I'll have her and the baby." She wouldn't be a baby anymore by then.

Delaney laid his hand over Maverick's arm. "Think about it like a savings account, son. Trust me. We'll take care of your family."

Maverick's heart pounded, and his stomach rolled and twisted, but he nodded at Delaney and turned back to the lawyer. "Let's just get it over with. I need to see Jenny first."

~oOo~

She'd lost weight—a noticeable amount in just a couple of weeks. Dark shadows hung beneath her eyes. It couldn't be good to *lose* weight at eight months pregnant.

She came in just through the threshold and stopped. When the guard closed and locked the door, her back was almost against it.

He walked to her, meaning to hold her and kiss her, but she shrank back, so he only took her hands. "Babe. I missed you so much."

All she did was blink at him. Her eyes blurred with tears, but she didn't cry.

"You're not eating. You need to eat. For you and the little pixie both."

"You don't get to tell me what to do. Never again." She pulled her hands from his.

He'd wanted this meeting, when he'd first asked Percy to set it up, to talk her into patience, to cheer her into believing it wouldn't be long that they'd be apart, and to keep her in the bosom of the club while he was away, so she wouldn't be alone. She didn't like the club much. She'd never been comfortable with his family. Not obviously uncomfortable, either. Just always on alert—for what, he'd never figured out.

But now, he had news that might break her, and he didn't know how to deliver it. With her standing before him, nearly weepy and clearly angry, he was actually afraid to tell her.

He didn't have a choice. Or time to dither.

"I need to tell you something, Jen. It's not easy, and it's not good. But if you love me, we'll get through it. I swear we will. The Bulls will be there when I can't be. The club'll have your back. You won't be alone."

She blinked and didn't speak, but a more focused fear sharpened her eyes. He swallowed and went on.

"I didn't get the deal. The DA is recommending the max. It's five years, Jen."

At first, nothing happened. Then her knees gave, and Maverick caught her as she overbalanced forward. She pushed him away as soon as she had her legs under her again.

"No." The word had hardly any sound.

"What?"

"No. No club. That's not the family you promised me. That's not the way things are supposed to be." Her voice reclaimed its power with every syllable.

"They're my family, Jen. They'll step in for me until I can be with you again."

"No."

"Jenny, I can't have you out there on your own with our little girl. You need the help. You need to listen and do what's right for you and her."

A harsh, furious laugh burst from her lips. "Fuck you, Maverick. Who are *you* to tell *me* to listen? You did this. All of it. To yourself. To me. To our baby. You did this. I don't want your fucking club checking up on me. I don't want anything you have to offer, because all you offer is lies. My little girl and I will figure this out on our own. We don't need the Bulls, and we don't need you."

She turned and pounded on the door. Maverick had reached out for her, but he dropped his hand as the guard's face came into view, and Jenny waddled from the room as fast as she could.

She never looked back.

When he was finally before the judge, he and his to-that-point clean record got three years in the penitentiary. Three, not five. By then, three years seemed a relief, maybe even some hope—with good behavior, Percy assured him, he could be out in half that. He turned and scanned the gallery. He saw Delaney and Mo, Rad, Gunner, Dane, Becker. But no Jenny. He didn't know where she was or who was with her.

~oOo~

Four months after his intake at McAlester, he got a Polaroid of a swaddled baby in a beanie, and he learned his daughter's name and date of birth. No other words than that. And that was the best information he'd gotten that his woman and his child were okay. She'd refused all contact with anyone associated with him.

Jenny had slammed the door between them and locked him in the cold.

CHAPTER TEN

Jenny got the aura while they were still within sight of the zoo entrance behind them—a dead spot in her vision, a hole into which the thing she tried to focus on fell. It meant she had forty-five minutes before the pain set in.

And here she was, at the Tulsa Zoo on a sunny, late-August afternoon, with two four-year-olds and one anxiety-inducing ex-boyfriend.

More than ex-boyfriend. Ex-old man. She brushed her hand over the left side of her chest, where her only tattoo was, near her shoulder.

She'd gotten her first migraine when she was fourteen, a few days before her first period. She'd thought for sure she was dying and had run to her father for help. He'd taken her to the emergency room, and they'd done a bunch of painful tests and decided it was 'just' migraine. They'd given her a morphine shot for the pain, and they'd sent her home when it wore off.

Her father had been angry that he'd 'wasted' most of his day off over nothing but a headache.

Since then, she got them once a month or so. Doctors said it was hormonal, but it didn't seem as connected to her period as that first one had suggested. Then again, while she was pregnant, she'd had them two or three times a month, which would indicate that wacky hormones brought them on.

Still, Jenny herself thought it was stress that triggered them. So she shouldn't have been surprised at this aura— and she wasn't, not really. Scared and angry about it, but not surprised. After fifteen years, she'd gotten about as used to headaches so bad she wanted to kill herself as it was possible to get. With Kelsey to care for and a life to manage, she'd even coped well enough to live around most of them—driving, working, parenting, all while half blind and three-quarters crazy with pain.

The aura would last about five minutes, and then she'd be okay until the pain. After that, it could be a couple of hours, or it could be days. Considering that she was stuck at the zoo and unable even to get away from the sun, this one would likely be a long one.

She could cancel. Turn around right here and now and go back home before the pain came. Carlena was on vacation and her father's fill-in nurse wouldn't watch Kelsey, but Mrs. Turner would keep her for the afternoon. She'd gotten migraines, too, as a young woman, and she understood.

But it was Kelsey's birthday, and she was happy and excited, swinging arms with Maisie, chattering up at Maverick, telling him all about the giraffes as they walked in their chain deeper into the park. She couldn't cancel this day.

Okay, then. Suck it up, buttercup. She and her migraine were just going to have to coexist today.

Jenny glued her smile on. Head down, shoulder to the day.

~oOo~

"You okay?" Maverick brushed his hand down her bare arm.

"Yeah. Fine."

No, she wasn't. The pain had just arrived, like an air drop of anvils behind her right eye. They'd gotten through the giraffes and the bears, they'd stopped at a cart for Bomb Pops, and now Kelsey and Maisie were playing in the little playground. Jenny found a shaded bench and sat down.

Maverick sat next to her. Without asking, he took her sunglasses off and squinted at her. "Migraine. Right?"

She snatched her glasses from his fingers and shoved them back into place. "I'm fine."

"Babe, I know what you look like when one hits. We need to go."

Jenny wished he'd stop calling her babe. Every time he said it, she felt it like a touch, like a caress. Everything about him was so confusing.

Actually, it wasn't. Nothing about Maverick was confusing. Everything he wanted was laid out for her to see: he wanted to pick up the life he'd destroyed. He wanted her to move into the house he'd bought, to bring her daughter there and be the family that they'd meant to be.

As if that were possible.

What was confusing was how she felt about it all. She still loved him — she thought she loved him as much as she ever had. She still craved his touch and felt safe in his arms. Maybe even more now, after four years alone. She hadn't told him to stop calling her babe because it felt so good to hear it. No one had loved her since Maverick. Maybe no one had loved her *but* Maverick. She'd been more than alone these last four years; she'd been lonely. She had Kelsey, and that would always be the most important relationship in her life, but it was different from having a partner.

She wanted what he wanted, as much as he wanted it, but, unlike him, she understood that it was impossible. She wasn't the person she'd been, and he was. He was, so obviously, the same domineering man. Before, she hadn't understood how controlling he'd been and how much she'd deferred to him. Now, after his willful disregard of her had turned everything to rubble, she'd changed. She couldn't live like that, always deferring her will to his. No matter how much she loved him, or how much she wanted the life they'd planned.

And her head hurt far too much to deal with these confusing, frustrating thoughts.

"Go if you want. It's Kelsey's birthday, and I'm not ruining it." She turned from him and smiled at the playing girls.

"You sure? You can gut it out?"

At Maverick's question, Jenny remembered that, before Kelsey, she'd always been incapacitated by her migraines. She'd taken to her bed with every one. That was the Jenny he remembered: weak.

"You think I've had a choice for the last four years? Who was going to take care of her if I didn't 'gut it out'?"

She hadn't shifted her attention from the girls as she'd spoken, but she felt him flinch at her side. Good. He needed to remember that he hadn't been the only one living a fucked-up life since he'd gone away.

As if he heard her thought, he muttered, "I know I fucked us up, Jenny. I know I let you down. That's not news to me. But I wasn't away on vacation. You understand that, right? Prison almost killed me. The shit that happened to me was fucked up, but it was knowing you weren't waiting that made it hell."

The hammer came down on the anvil in her brain, again and again. Her heart pounded with the stress of this day, this talk. She felt ill and knew she'd be puking here at the zoo fairly soon. She hoped she'd at least make it to the restroom to do it.

The little train tooted its horn, and Kelsey stood up to look for it. "Mommy! Can we ride the train?"

Jenny took a slow, deep breath and got her game face back on. "Sure, pixie!"

As she moved to stand, Maverick grabbed her arm. "You call her pixie. And you keep count."

She nodded; she'd seen his shock earlier when Kelsey had said 'That's two.' Until she'd seen his reaction, she hadn't thought about its impact on him—and she'd been surprised to discover that it hurt him. She'd started calling Kelsey pixie because she'd been calling her pixie for months before her birth. She'd started keeping count with her because it was a happy memory at a time when she'd needed one. And because she wanted Kelsey always to know that she heard those words every day.

"I'm part of that, Jen. Those were our things. I've been in your life all this time."

Her head hurt too much for this. "I can't do this now. I can't."

Concern softened his expression, and his hand eased around her arm and became a caress. "Sorry. Okay. Let's get you through the zoo in one piece, then."

When she stood, the change in position made the pain surge to a new high point, and she reeled like it had literally hit her. Maverick's arm came around her waist and steadied her. She leaned on him.

"I'm okay."

"I know. And I'm right here."

~oOo~

Three hours at the zoo. Long, painful hours. Half an hour in a loud, crowded food court. Two trips to ladies' rooms, where she bent over public toilets and hurled, then leaned against the stall wall, crying silently and trying to pull herself together.

Puking made the pain worse. Crying made the pain worse. The greatest torment of migraine wasn't the excruciating pain but all the things it made you do that made the pain worse.

But she got through it and, with Maverick's help, managed to keep the girls from knowing. Kelsey had the birthday trip she'd wanted. They even did the gift shop, where they got big clear balloons with little balloon animals inside, and Maverick bought them each a new toy. Maisie got an articulated wooden snake, and Kelsey got a big stuffed giraffe.

At her car, Maverick helped her get the girls into their car seats. She watched him fasten Kelsey in and was surprised to see that he knew what he was doing.

When she opened the driver's door, he caught it and stepped in her way. "I know you can do it. I've seen how you can deal with the pain. But I see that you're hurting. Let me take you home. Let me drive, Jen."

She'd decided to ask him to join them for cake and presents. Having him here today had helped a lot, and the thought of driving made her want to cry again—driving with a migraine was a special level of hell. But if he drove her car, how would he get back to his? How long would he stay? How would it all play out?

Her screaming head wouldn't entertain these questions. But she did manage to ask, "What about your car?"

"I need to run over right now to get something out of it, but I'll just leave it here and get it when I can."

"They tow after hours."

He smiled. "I know. Delaney's has the contract. So that's not a problem. So I'll drive, then?"

Her brain wouldn't think. She wanted to be home in a dark room with a cool washcloth over her eyes.

"Jen, please."

She wanted somebody to take care of her.

"Okay, yeah. Thank you."

He bent his head and kissed her, right in front of Kelsey, and she'd been thinking and moving too slowly to see it coming. It was just a gentle kiss, barely more than a peck, but Jenny felt it all around and through her. When he stepped back to lead her around to the passenger side, she saw their daughter watching, her eyes wide. Blue eyes, just like her father's.

Her head hurt too much to hold all this confusion.

~oOo~

She made it through the squeaking balloons in the back seat on the drive home. She made it through ice cream cake and even sang 'Happy Birthday,' with her hands clenched behind her back. She made it through Kelsey's squeals of delight at her gifts: a Dentist Barbie from Maisie, some books and a Barbie Dream House from Jenny, some clothes 'from Granddaddy,' and a big art kit from Maverick, with pastels, colored pencils, watercolors on a palette, sketchpads, an apron, and a little easel.

There was a lot of delighted squealing. Kelsey was so happy that, every now and then, Jenny almost forgot that she was enduring the worst migraine she'd had in years.

Maverick took the girls back to Kelsey's room to help her set up the Dream House while Jenny cleaned up the kitchen. She'd bagged up the gift trash and had her hands in soapy dish water before it occurred to her that she'd let him go back without a second thought.

He was loose in her house, and her father was sleeping in his room. His fill-in nurse sat in the living room, watching television. An innocent bystander.

The man who'd gone to prison for beating her father nearly to death was in the same house with him, and the import of that had missed her completely.

She hovered over the sink as a new spike of pain went through her eye, and her stomach revolted. It settled down without rejecting the half a bite of cake she'd had. Shutting off the tap, she turned, slowly, keeping her bearings, and went to make sure no violence was brewing.

Maverick came into the kitchen before she'd crossed the room.

"Everything okay?" she asked.

"Yeah. I have them in charge of taking all the plastic parts off the forms and sorting them out. We'll see how that goes. I want to ask you to do me a favor."

"What?"

"I want you to go to bed. I'll get you a cool washcloth. You look like hell, Jen. You need to close your eyes and rest."

She shook her head. "I'll get through it. It's happened before, and it'll happen again."

He came up to her and closed her arms in his hands, gently. "What are you afraid of? I'm not going to run off with her. I'll build her house and let her play with Maisie, and when you're feeling better, I'll go. I'm not going to hurt her, Jen. Or you. Ever."

"My dad…"

A shadow moved through his eyes. "I'll keep my distance. I'm not going to hurt an invalid, either."

An invalid he'd made. Jenny remembered her father's agitation when she'd spoken to Kelsey about Maverick. He knew more than he could say. He had a child's mind, but clearly, there were things he remembered and understood, even if his understanding had been compromised. He remembered enough to be angry. Or afraid—for her father, those two emotions had always been so similar that they might as well have been the same.

"Mav, I can't." As she said it, nausea overwhelmed her, and she spun toward the sink. Vertigo nearly brought her to her knees as she puked into the empty side.

He was right behind her, holding her ponytail, rubbing her back. "Now you're being stubborn and stupid. Jesus Christ, Jen. Let me help. Please."

He was making the stress worse, which was making the headache worse, but at this point, his leaving wouldn't make anything better. Kelsey would be sad, and she'd be guilty, and it was all more than she could take.

"Okay," she gasped and ran the tap to rinse her mouth and wash her sick down the disposal. "Okay."

~oOo~

She pulled her heavy drapes so that the room was as dark as she could get it, and she turned the box fan on right in front of the air conditioning vent so that the room would be as cool as she could get it. She stripped down to her panties and took a knit camisole from a drawer. Ideally, she'd be naked—even the touch of fabric was too much sensation when she was in pain like this—but she couldn't risk Maverick coming in and seeing her.

Which he did, knocking but opening the door without waiting, as she pulled the camisole down over her chest. He stopped and stood there, holding out a washcloth.

Hurting too much to make a fuss about it, she slid into bed. He came and got down on his knees at her side. "Do you take anything for them now?"

"Nothing works. I took some Excedrin. Sometimes that takes the point off, but I think it's too late to do anything with this one but survive it."

"Okay. Close your eyes."

She did, and he laid the washcloth—cool and damp but not too wet, just as she needed it to be—over her forehead and eyes. She sighed. Though it didn't help the pain, there was comfort in it.

Before his lips touched her, she felt him coming, in the shift of the mattress and the nearing heat of his body, in the caress of his breath. He kissed her lightly at the corner of her mouth and lingered there.

"I'm here if you need me. I'll take good care of our girl."

He got up and left, closing the door so carefully that Jenny had to lift the washcloth and check to know he'd done it. He still knew exactly what she needed during an attack. He still knew how to take care of her. She knew he would take care of Kelsey. She even trusted him to stay away from her father.

For the first time in four years, she could collapse under the weight of a migraine, could give in and rest while Kelsey was home, and know that everything would be okay.

If Maverick had asked her right then to move in with him, to forgive him and pretend that they'd been living the life they'd wanted for the past four years, she very likely would have said yes.

What he did better than anything else was take care. Until that last day, when she'd needed him, he'd been there. He wasn't much for proclamations of feeling; they'd started keeping count because he'd hardly ever said 'I love you,' and she'd told him she needed to hear it at least once every day. But when he was needed, he was always right there.

She'd understood that she loved him—and that he loved her—the first time she'd had a migraine with him. It had been a particularly bad one, the kind that made her lose her mind. Though he never got headaches of any sort, he hadn't minimized her pain; he hadn't called it 'only a headache.' He'd accepted the pain as real. He'd asked her what she needed, and he'd done it.

That was how he showed his love: by taking loving care. By being there, and by wanting to be.

It was also how he'd betrayed it: by leaving her on her own.

But right now, that seemed insignificant. Right now, feeling cared for in her need, she could only be glad he was with her, could only remember how it felt to be loved.

January 1992

The pain was so bad she couldn't be still. But moving made it hurt more. But she couldn't be still and just lie there while her brain was pureed. She had to move. She had to get away from it. God, why wouldn't this just kill her and be done with it? Just let her rest.

Jenny paced around Maverick's apartment, trying to keep enough sense together to keep her hand from rising up to punch her head. That was crazy, that little voice of sense insisted. That would hurt more. But fuck her head! It needed to stop! To stop! Stop!

She tried to lie back down on the sofa and put the washcloth over her eyes, but it had gotten warm, so she threw it across the room and got back up. The floor tilted sharply, and she barely made it to the toilet. All that was left was dry heaves and foamy bile, and each retch was like venomous fangs carving through her brain.

When she was done, she let herself fall to the floor. At least the tile was cool.

The pain pulsed in her right eye, making it swell and recede, swell and recede. Her heartbeat slammed in her ears like a bass drum.

She wanted to be away from this. Anywhere else, even hell, as long as the pain didn't follow.

~oOo~

The light flashed on, and Jenny came back to consciousness screaming. She slammed her hands over her face and rolled away from the pain.

"Shit!" Maverick switched the light back off. "Jen? Babe, what's wrong? Jesus!"

He was on the floor at her side, picking her up. Her head was still trapped in its horror, but sense dawned a little, and she tried to talk. "Hurts."

"I'm taking you to the hospital."

"No. It's...migraine. I get migraines. Hospital won't help me. Need to deal."

"Passed out on the bathroom floor isn't dealing, Jenny."

With sense, the nonsensical conviction she could escape the pain receded, and all that was left was despair. She knew the hurt would end eventually, but right now, if she'd had a cyanide capsule, she'd have bitten the shit out of it. She was trapped, and that always made her cry.

"It just fucking hurts. It hurts!"

"Okay." He gathered her up and stood. "Let's get you to bed, at least."

He carried her to his room, laid her on his bed, and set her head gently on the pillow. "What can I do?"

She hurt too much to answer. When his fingers brushed over her forehead, she flinched from the touch, and he backed off. After a second or two, she heard him leave the room.

He was back after not much time. Jenny wasn't sure how long; the clock moved erratically when she was so focused on the horror show inside her skull. But the first thing she felt was a cool washcloth over her eyes. She whimpered at the fragile fragment of ease it gave her.

"Babe," he whispered at her ear. "I talked to Maddie. She gets these things, too. She said you need dark, cool, quiet, and still. It's dark outside now, but I closed the curtains anyway. I turned the furnace down. I'm not going to bug you. I'll check in and make sure you're okay, and you call out if you need anything. I'm not leaving."

He was supposed to fight tonight. That random fact pushed through the haze. "Fight. You and Gun."

"Not tonight. Gun's gonna have to watch his own ass tonight. I'm here with you."

He kissed her lightly at the corner of her mouth, and Jenny felt each hair of his beard. When he began to stand up, she flailed her hand out and grabbed his. Normally, she needed to be totally alone with her migraine, with as little as possible touching her or stimulating her in any way at all. But suddenly, right now, what she needed was Maverick's arms.

"Jen?"

"Hold me?"

"You got it."

She heard his boots and clothes come off. He slid slowly into the bed, like she'd break at the slightest jostle — and that was how she felt. He maneuvered his body so that he sheltered her without encroaching on her. And he was perfectly still, giving her exactly what she needed.

Jenny knew then that she loved him. She opened her mouth to say the words, but the ease he'd given her had made her sleepy, and she only thought them.

CHAPTER ELEVEN

Kelsey looked up as Maverick came back into her room. "Is Mommy's head ouchie?"

He sat down on the floor between the two girls. "Yeah, it is. Does that still happen a lot?"

His little girl nodded seriously. "Sometimes it makes her make her mad face. Sometimes she has to go to bed and cry. Sometimes she wears her sunny glasses inside. We have to talk real soft like this." She breathed out the last words, hunching her shoulders to make herself small.

"Okay," he whispered back. "Do you think we can build your house quietly?"

"It's not my house, silly. It's Barbie's house. My house is at your house." Kelsey and Maisie giggled in that way women had when they thought a guy had done something particularly dumb—they learned that this young? Maverick grinned and brushed his hand over her soft, soft hair. It really was the color of butterscotch, a golden brown so rich his mouth watered to see it, and fairer, almost white, at her hairline.

At his touch, she smiled at him. His own little girl. Jesus.

"Daddy, can we make the house now?" Impatience nipped lightly in her whisper.

"Yeah, yeah. Let's get Barbie set up in her fancy crib."

"Cribs are for babies," Maisie corrected. "Barbie has a bed." She picked up an elaborate pink and purple plastic thing. "It has a cap-ony. Like for a princess."

Pink and purple and princesses and 'caponies.' He had a lot to learn about little girls.

~oOo~

When he had the dollhouse put together, he left the girls playing in Kelsey's room and went to check on Jenny, who was sleeping quietly in that disconcerting way she had during a migraine—on her back, still as a post, her hands straight at her sides, her face completely slack, her chest rising in short, shallow breaths. But for her breathing, she looked like a damn corpse, and it freaked him out, though he'd seen it plenty of times before.

He checked her washcloth; it had warmed to her body temperature, so he eased it from her forehead and went to wet it again. She didn't stir when he brought it back, except to take a slower, calmer breath when the cool touched her head.

Knowing that she still got those headbangers, and that she'd had to function despite them because she'd been alone, made Maverick even more guilty for being away. It also made him more angry at her—she hadn't needed to be alone; there was a whole club full of people who would have made sure she had everything she needed—and it made him admire her more, too. She was stronger than he'd realized. He thought she was stronger than she'd realized, too.

It was this house that made her weak. This house and the bastard who owned it. He hated that she was back here, and that she'd been raising their daughter in this place, around that man.

He'd told Jenny he'd keep his distance, but Maverick went looking for Earl Wagner anyway. He just wanted to get an eyeful of the man who was the real reason his life and Jenny's had gone to shit.

The closed door across from Kelsey's was, he knew, the old man's room. Maverick opened it, turning the knob slowly, and pushed it inward. Earl lay on a hospital bed, naked from the waist down, showing a desiccated body. A bulky nurse was cleaning him.

She was changing his diaper.

She saw Maverick standing there, and protective anger clenched her face. "Excuse me!"

Maverick didn't apologize. He barely noticed the nurse as she came to push the door closed again. He kept his attention on Jenny's father, whose head had turned to follow his nurse. His eyes met Maverick's and went wide.

As the door closed, Maverick heard a guttural grunt, and he smiled.

~oOo~

Jenny was still asleep when Mrs. Turner from next door came over to pick up Maisie. She recognized Maverick and was surprised, to say the least, to see him standing at Jenny's front door. The old broad asked an arm-long list of questions before she was content to accept Kelsey's assurance that 'My daddy is taking care of me because Mommy's head is ouchie.' She left with her granddaughter's hand firmly clamped in her own, with stern instructions to Kelsey to 'Come over if you need anything, chickie. Anything at all,' and with a threatening glare at Maverick.

Safe to say he was not the most popular person on North Joplin Avenue tonight.

Around the same time, there was a shift change with Earl's nurses, and he got to do the whole suspicion/confusion thing again, this time with a big black guy who had a couple inches on him and thirty or forty pounds. Darnell, Earl's second shift nurse.

And still, Jenny slept. That wasn't unusual. Sleep was about the only relief she got, and when the pain got bad enough, her body simply turned itself off until whatever was wrong got fixed.

How she took care of Kelsey through one of those things, he couldn't fathom. Hell, it sounded like she *worked* through them, too.

The only head pain Maverick had ever experienced had come from injury — getting punched in the face or cracked in the head, some trauma or another that his life had inflicted on him or he'd gone out seeking. He'd never had any kind of headache that had just come out of the blue, just his head trying to kill him on its own.

He'd had several concussions, and that pain was no joke. So he thought he could understand at least a little. Jenny and Maddie, Ox's old lady, had explained it in similar terms, which amounted, in his mind, to an auger boring, incrementally, through their eyes and into their brains.

Yeah, that was no joke.

With Jenny sleeping, and Earl agitated whenever he was in his sightline, Maverick devoted all of his attention to Kelsey. He rooted around in the kitchen and made her a sandwich for supper. He helped her tidy her room and get ready for bed. He learned that she liked to choose from her vast collection of stuffed animals to bring one into her bed each night for a 'slumber party.' On this night, she selected the giraffe he'd bought her at the zoo that afternoon, whom she'd named 'Miss Goldie.'

He didn't give her a bath, because she told him that her mommy helped her do it, and he…well, he worried that Jenny would freak out if Kelsey got naked in front of him. It was ridiculous; Kelsey was his daughter. But he was on eggshells, especially in this house, and he decided that she didn't need a bath from him until everybody was comfortable with him being around.

It was a disruption to her nighttime routine, which caused some consternation, but the whole day had been a disruption of routine, and she rolled with it pretty quickly.

He sat on her bed with her and read her one of the books she'd gotten for her birthday, about a young yellow snake who didn't want to become an 'old green.' She stopped him on almost every page to talk about the snake and what he was doing, asking a lot of questions about his feelings about snakes.

When the book was finished — she made him read the last page, with some scientific information about snakes, and had even more questions he didn't know the answers to — he set it on the top of her little bookcase and stood up.

"Okay, Kelsey. I think it's time to get some shuteye." He pulled the light quilt up over her shoulders.

"What's shuteye?"

"It's a word for sleep."

"Oh! Because you shut your eyes when you sleep, like this!" She closed her eyes tightly, her eyebrows clenching and her lids creasing.

"Just like that," he laughed. "Good night, sweetheart. Thank you for letting me be with you on your birthday."

"You're welcome. You can come to all my birthdays now, because you're my daddy and you came home. You took care of me when Mommy's head was ouchie, and you took care of her, too. That makes you a good daddy."

"I hope so." He bent down and kissed her head. "Sleep tight."

"Wait! You have to turn the flower light on."

Maverick followed her pointed finger to a big pink daisy on her wall. He found the toggle switch on the cord and turned it on, and the daisy glowed. When he flipped off the overhead and saw the true effect, her room aglow with soft, warm pink light, he smiled. "Pretty."

"Too pretty for monsters."

"That's right. Hey, Kelse?"

"Yeah, Daddy?" She'd settled and snuggled into her pillow, and her voice was muffled with coming sleep.

"I love you." Was it too soon to say that to her, true as it was? He didn't care. The words wouldn't be denied. He'd loved her since before she was born. Getting to know her damn sure wasn't making him love her less.

"I love you, too. That's one."

"That's one." The words barely came out; Maverick's throat had clenched like a fist.

~oOo~

Maverick went to the living room; Darnell had Earl in his complicated wheelchair, parked in front of the television, watching *Law & Order*. Ironic.

He grunted when he saw Maverick, but he was calmer than he'd been before. Darnell looked up from the sofa. "I gave him something to keep him calm. Earl does not like you at all, friend. I sure as hell hope I'm right taking Kelsey's word about you."

"I'm her dad." He studied Earl for a few seconds, then added, "I made him like he is."

Darnell nodded. "I know. Jenny told me what happened."

This guy was not just a nurse, but a man who spent forty hours a week with *his* family. Maverick's fists clenched. "What'd she tell you?"

Staring at Maverick's fists, Darnell said, "Why don't you take it down a step, friend? I'm not the threat in this room. Just doin' my job."

"For how long?"

"'Bout four years. I helped her get him set up when he came home. But I got no grudge with you. I know why you did what you did. Can't say I'd do different in your shoes."

Earl grunted again, and his arms flailed for a second. In response, Darnell patted his patient's shoulder and said, "Just saying truth, Earl."

"He understands?" Maverick considered Jenny's father; with his slack face and rolling eyes, his flailing limbs and inarticulate grunts, it didn't look like he understood much.

"Don't think because he doesn't talk much and his body doesn't work much that he doesn't understand. It's hard to know what he knows. The tests say he thinks like a kid not much older than Kelsey. But I think yeah—just like a kid, he knows the important stuff. He knows what happened to make him like he is. He knows his girls. He knows me and his other nurse. And he sure as shit knows you. He hasn't been upset like he is today since he was first home. He doesn't like having you in his house."

"Can't say I care. I'm here for Jenny and Kelsey. They're *my* girls, not his."

"No!" Earl barked. "No!"

Maverick had been standing at the doorway, leaning against the frame. Now he walked in and stood between Earl's chair and the television. He crossed his arms and stared down at the man he blamed for everything. "Yeah, Earl. *My* girls. And when I get things worked out right, you will never see them again."

Earl's arms flailed wildly. "No!" he grunted. "No! Jen! Need!"

Maverick only smiled. Maybe he was a monster, but he enjoyed making this man suffer.

Darnell stood up. "Damn, friend. Making me work for my paycheck tonight." He moved the wheelchair back, away from Maverick, and faced his patient, taking hold of his wasted, flailing arms. "Easy, Earl. Easy. How about a shake. You want a shake? I'll put some ice cream in it. But you have to calm down first."

Just like a kid, Earl calmed at the promise of a sweet.

When the nurse went to the kitchen, Maverick followed him. "How's this work—you taking care of him?"

While he poured a protein drink into the blender and scooped vanilla ice cream on top, Darnell answered, "I don't like to talk out of school, especially not about Jenny. But I'll tell you the service I work for covers two shifts Monday through Friday and one shift on Saturday. That's me and another nurse. We alternate Saturdays. Jenny does the rest on her own."

"Why's he not in a home?"

Darnell stopped and gave him a hard look. "Not my place to say."

He took a couple of dish towels from a drawer and wrapped them around the blender; when he turned it on, the towels muffled the sound. Darnell had some experience with Jenny's migraines, too.

He turned the blender off. "Look, I don't mind being in charge of Kelsey at night. I take care of her pretty often in the evenings, and she's no trouble. So if you want to go, everybody's covered here."

The hired help was not going to tell him to leave. Fuck that. "I'm good. I'll stay out of Earl's way, but I'm not leaving until Jenny says she wants me to."

"It's been rough for her, living this way. She's a good woman, and she doesn't like much in her life but her little girl. It'd be good if you didn't make things harder."

Maverick narrowed his eyes, trying to read this guy. "You got some kind of personal investment here?"

Darnell shrugged and turned back to his work, pouring the shake into a plastic tumbler. "Nothing more than friendly. Like I said, I'm no threat to you. But I like Jenny, and I wouldn't like to see her hurt."

Jesus Christ, even the help had opinions about Maverick's worthiness to be in his own family. He wanted to make her life better, easier, not harder. He wanted to take care of them both. It was Jenny slamming on the brakes at every turn. Jenny, who for some inconceivable reason had chosen to keep her sack of rancid shit of a father home and take care of him. Jenny, who should have had enough money coming from his take to at least be able to live in a decent rental and have a normal job. Jenny, who blamed him for everything, when all he'd done was try to protect her. She was changing the fucking diapers of the guy whose fault it really was.

Maverick wanted to punch this nurse, acting like he was so close with his woman, sharing opinions he had no business having. Instead, he simply left the room.

~oOo~

It wasn't a big house, and he didn't really have anywhere to go, so he went to Jenny's room. She was still asleep, so he sat at her desk and simply watched her.

She'd rolled to her side. That was a good sign; unless it was so bad that she went a little crazy and tried to run away from it, she rarely moved during an attack. So it was probably over.

All those nights in prison, he'd been afraid to think too long or hard about her, afraid to let his mind draw her portrait or remember the feel of her body in his hands. But God, she was beautiful. He'd had plenty of reminders in the past few weeks of her touch, her scent, the sound of her laugh. The glittering light of her eyes. The curve of her ass, the way his palms fit perfectly in the sweep from her waist to her hips.

All he could think of anymore, in the dark and quiet, was her. Her and Kelsey. His girls. *His.*

He'd thought he could deal if she wouldn't have him. He'd thought that he could get by with only Kelsey, but he'd been wrong. He needed his family. His whole family. Dad, Mom, kids—something he couldn't remember ever having except for that short time with Jenny, waiting for their little girl and planning their future. Something he'd always wanted.

He had to find a way to get her back. Whatever it took. He'd give her what she needed. He had to make her see that. He had to, or he was going to go crazy or die. Or both.

~oOo~

Maverick sat, watching and thinking, letting time pass unnoticed. She finally stirred and woke, then sat up abruptly with a squeaking gasp. "Fuck, Mav," she breathed. "Fuck. How long've you been sitting there?"

"Don't know. How d'you feel?"

"It's gone. Just the soreness is left."

He remembered—for several hours after, her head would feel, as she described it, like somebody had been playing soccer with her brain.

"What time is it?"

He checked his watch. The blue glow of the dial showed that the night had gotten quite ripe. "About ten past two."

"In the morning? Shit. Darnell—"

"Been and gone. Your dad's in bed. Kelsey's asleep. Everything's fine."

The room was still deeply dark, but Maverick could feel her eyes on him. "You took care of her. And me. Thank you."

"It's my job, Jen. And it's my life." He stood and went to the bed. She didn't protest when he sat on the mattress near her legs. "You feeling up to talking?"

This close, he could see the wary expression cross her features. "Depends."

"I promise I'll shut up and listen, but I need you to tell me exactly what it is that's holding you back from me. I need to understand. I won't try to talk you into seeing it differently, not right now. Right now, I just need to understand, before I lose my shit."

It took her a long time to say anything. When she did speak, Maverick found his fists curled and pressing down on his thighs. "What if I don't know?"

"I think it would be all kinds of shitty for you to say you don't know why you've got me this scrambled up. Try to know. Try to explain. Please."

Again, she was quiet, and his fists curled more tightly. His short nails dug into his palms.

"Do you love me, Jen? And don't say it's not that easy. I understand that it's more complicated than that for you. Just answer that question."

This time, she didn't hesitate. "Yes. I love you. But I don't want you to say love is enough and we'll figure out the rest."

"Then something else is keeping you back. What?"

Silence. She looked down at her lap.

He'd told her he'd shut up and listen, but she wasn't giving him anything to listen to. "You know why I talk so much when we argue? Because you do this—you shut down. You'll sass me all up and down when we're trying to figure out which movie to watch or if we're going to party at the clubhouse, but when it's really important, forget about talking it out, you won't even *think* it out. You call me a bully, but I'm just trying to figure our shit out, and you're not helping."

He'd pissed her off, and that loosened her tongue. "I'm afraid to tell you what I think or feel, because you'll jump all over the parts you like and not hear the rest. That's what you do. You take the parts you agree with and puff them all up and act like anything else I think isn't worth your time." She laughed sadly. "Mav, that's why I had Kelsey. I love her so much, and she's the best thing I ever did, the only good thing in my shitty life. I don't regret having her at all. But I was young and scared and didn't feel ready to be a mom. You told me you loved me and you'd take care of us. You told me we'd make a family. You pushed the scared part of me away like it didn't matter. You never let me just be worried. I stopped saying anything about my fears that I'd suck as a mom or that something would be wrong with her or even that you'd stop wanting me when I got big — all the stuff I was afraid of, I couldn't say, because you'd laugh and give me a long list of reasons why I was being silly or weak or paranoid."

She took a breath, and Maverick sat there, stunned, trying to sort through that barrage. She'd really been scared? He remembered those days vividly, but he didn't remember that. Jenny had always been inventing some silly thing or another to stress out about — like getting her tattoo — but they'd been based on nothing, and he'd shown her as much. They hadn't been real fears. Had they?

"I'm not saying I wasn't being all of those things," she continued. "But I needed to be able to say what I was afraid of, and I couldn't. And then you made all those things I was afraid of come true. I was alone with a new baby and a broken father, and I'm not good as a single mom, Mav. It's a lot to keep afloat, and something is always sinking. She deserves a better life than she got. So yeah, I'm afraid to fall into a life with you again. I love you like I always have, but love is not enough."

"I didn't know you were really scared about the baby." He was still hung up on that point.

"I know. Because you didn't listen. I told you the things I was afraid of, and you thought they were silly and brushed them aside, so I stopped trying to tell you."

Everything in Maverick wanted to explain to her why he'd set aside her fears. Because they *had* been silly, and he'd wanted to assuage them and give her some peace. He'd been trying to reassure her. He'd thought he had.

But now, here, he'd heard her—she'd needed to work through those fears, and he hadn't let her. He'd made her feel small. Silly or not, wrong or not, she'd needed him simply to listen, maybe hold her, while she'd sorted out her feelings. Instead, he'd shut her down. He'd never thought of it that way before.

So instead of offering a defense, he said only, "I'm sorry."

Another spell of quiet, this one dense with the tension between them.

"I think I actually believe you," she said at last, in a whisper full of wonder.

He reached out and found her hand in the dark room. "I heard you. I understand. And I'm sorry."

Her fingers slid between his. "I'm sorry I didn't share Kelsey with you before now."

He closed his hand around hers and scooted closer. "Jen—babe. Are we…can we be good again?"

Only a few inches separated them now; they were close enough that he could see the turmoil in her eyes. "I can't jump. I can't run. I need to walk. Slowly. I need to be sure you're okay with the way I am now. I won't give in like I used to, and I'll fight when you try to make me feel dumb. I need to be sure that won't make you mad. I need to know nothing like what happened that night at the back door will ever happen again."

He'd never tried to make her feel dumb, but he'd begun to understand that she'd thought he had, and to understand why she'd thought so. The past few weeks had given him a pretty decent picture of the strength of her will now. It was fucking maddening, but not in the way she feared. If they were together—if they were even working toward being together—he'd keep his cool.

"Okay. Whatever you need."

"Thank you. Right now, I need you to go."

He'd been feeling a wash of hope all through him, and he'd begun to feel settled in—for the night, at least. "What?"

"You can't be here when Kelsey wakes up. She's already jabbering about how mommies and daddies live together and mommies have babies in their bellies, and if you're here for breakfast, it's just going to confuse her. She won't understand why we're not together all the time, and I'm not ready for that. So I need you not to be here when she wakes up."

He couldn't have argued that point if he'd wanted to. It made sense. "Fair enough. But it's only two-forty." He picked up her hand and pressed his lips to her fingers.

She chuckled. "Not yet, Mav. That would definitely not be taking things slow. Besides—I'm just coming off a migraine. I don't feel too great."

He wasn't trying to get in her pants—not that he'd have denied her if she'd wanted it. "I just want to hold you, Jenny. I just want to have you in my arms and not feel like you're trying to get away. I want you to want to be there with me. I love you."

"That's one," she whispered and turned back the covers.

Since he'd been released, he'd hoped to hear her say those two words, more potent than the three words she was counting. Those words meant that they would be okay. He knew, right then, that he would have his family. Not tonight, but soon.

His body thrumming with emotion, Maverick toed off his boots and slid, fully clothed, into Jenny's bed. She curled her barely-clothed body to his, resting her head on his chest. They fit together perfectly, as they always had, like she had been designed to nestle at his side. His hand settled on her ass, cupping one soft, warm globe.

He remembered the night that he'd understood that what he felt for Jenny was love—not merely desire, not infatuation, not even obsession, but truly love. It had been a revelation to him, jarring him like a lightning bolt, and the words had spilled from his mouth reflexively, before he'd had a chance to overthink them.

He'd been fucking her at the time, and she'd insisted that the words didn't count when he was inside her. That had hurt, always, but he'd always laughed and teased and set aside her doubt.

Because on that night, he'd said words he'd never said to a woman before, because he'd felt something he'd never felt for a woman before, and where his cock was when he'd said them had made them no less powerful or true.

March 1992

"God, babe," Maverick murmured against Jenny's skin. "You feel so fucking good." He continued to work his way down her spine, kissing the swell of each bone, all the way down to the cleft of her ass. Her skin had risen up in tiny beads, rough against his tongue. "You taste so fucking good."

He laved the dimples centered above each beautiful, pert cheek, then grabbed the globes in his hands and spread them. He licked through her cleft, over her pussy and up. When his tongue touched her anus, she gasped and twisted, escaping from his grasp.

"Mav, no! Not that."

Easing his way up the bed, keeping his body on hers, pressing kisses as he went, he finally hovered over her, face to face. "You don't like that?"

She shook her head.

"Ever done it before?"

A hesitation, then another shake of her head.

"Then how do you know you don't like it?" As he asked, he swept his hand down her side and over her sweet, sweet ass.

She turned again, shifting so that she was fully on her back, pinning his hand in place beneath her. "It seems like it'd be gross."

"Jen, it's not gross. Trust me."

Maverick could see that he hadn't convinced her, but she was too tentative to say no again. He could push that around if he wanted—Jenny was tentative about most things they disagreed on, and she always caved eventually. He considered that option and discarded it—he didn't want to push her tonight.

Well, actually, yes. He did. But not that way. Not so directly. He smiled and gave her a light kiss. "Okay. Can I try something else?"

Relief lit in her eyes, and he was glad he hadn't pushed the way he'd first considered. "What?" She smiled and bit her lip.

Maverick got up and grabbed his jeans from the bedroom floor. He pulled his belt from the loops.

Jenny sat up, folding herself tightly. "Don't hit me. Please don't hit me."

Maverick dropped his jeans and sat on the bed. "Babe, no. That's not what I want. I am never going to hit you. Not even in play. I promise." He'd gotten her out of her father's house just a few weeks before—he knew well why she wouldn't be into spanking or anything like it. He wasn't into that, either. He didn't have any need to cause a woman pain, for any reason.

She stared at the belt. "Why do you need that?"

"Because I don't own any ties, and the rope is out in my trunk."

"You want to tie me up?"

Running a finger down her arm, he leaned in and said, "Just your hands. I want to tie your hands to the bed and cover your eyes."

"Why?"

"So you can relax and not worry about what I'm doing."

"You think I won't worry if I'm tied up and blindfolded?"

"I think I'll make sure you're not worrying." He caught her chin on his finger and lifted her head. "Have I ever hurt you?"

Without answering, she got up, and Maverick thought he'd found her limit. He watched as she crossed the room to the dresser he'd bought her. She opened a drawer and pulled something out—a scarf. Long, silky, and red. Then she pulled another one, also red, but with a pattern. He hadn't hit her limit after all.

"I don't like the belt." She handed him the scarves. "Will these work?"

"Those are perfect." He ran the silky material through his rough hands. "Perfect. Lay down in the middle of the bed and put your hands over your head."

She did what she was told, wrapping her hands around the slats of the headboard. The position shaped her beautiful, soft body into something from a painting. After pressing his lips to each nipple and then to her mouth, he wrapped the patterned scarf around her wrists and around a slat of the headboard, making sure that the binding was tight enough to hold her but not so tight it would cut off her circulation.

Her arms trembled so hard, he worried that she might tighten the bonds herself. "Easy, babe. Trust me."

When he moved to cover her eyes, she shrank back.

"Trust me, Jenny. No hurt. If you tell me to stop, I will. I promise."

She closed her eyes, and he tied the other scarf around her head.

And there she was, naked and bound and fucking perfect. Jenny usually followed his lead and let him go where he wanted—in fact, tonight had been the first time she'd resisted him during sex, and she'd done it twice. He found that especially hot.

Then she'd let him tie her up, as much as it obviously scared her, and he found that profoundly hot.

"Mav?"

"Right here, babe." He hadn't planned any of this, and he wasn't sure what to do. Food? No—he didn't want to leave her, even to go to the kitchen; she was nervous, and he didn't want to shake her faith in him. Feathers or beads or something? He didn't have anything like that. Jenny might, but he wasn't going to root through her stuff.

Scanning the room without hope that the answer would just pop out at him, the answer did just that. A bottle of lotion sat on her dresser. She rubbed it all over herself after her shower in the morning and at night before bed. Unscented. Jenny wasn't a fan of perfumes or scented lotions. She always smelled like her shampoo.

He'd massage her. All over. That would calm her and turn her on, and he'd be completely gentle. He picked up the bottle and went to the bed. She gasped when his weight came down on the mattress, and her body went tense enough that she bowed upward a bit. The headboard rattled lightly with the force of her shaking.

"Easy, easy." First, without the lotion, he simply caressed her, calmed her. Running his hands, slow and steady, from the scarf at her wrists, along her arms to her shoulders, over her collarbones, down, sweeping around her quivering tits, over her belly, out to her hips, down her legs to her ankles, then her feet, pausing there to smooth his thumbs over her arches, then back up the way he'd come. He hadn't touched her tits or her pussy, but by the time he reached her wrists again, she breathed more deeply and had begun to writhe against his touch.

"Feels good, right?"

She nodded, and her tongue slipped out to wet her lips. They looked so plump and inviting that he bent and claimed her mouth, sucking on her lips, sweeping his tongue over hers. She moaned and opened her mouth wider, offering him more.

He had her—already, she was wholly focused on her own pleasure, and she would let him do what he wanted. The heady power of that made his chest feel tight. He didn't understand it—there was a clubhouse full of chicks who'd do what he wanted. This girl right here on his bed had done what he wanted until this night, but the way she was giving over to him now, after he'd already pushed her too far—this wasn't deference or shyness or naïveté. This was trust, and it bowled him over.

He pumped lotion onto his hand and rubbed his palms together to warm it. Then, starting at her wrists again, he began a long, slow, sensual massage of every inch of her skin he could reach.

Again, he took the path that detoured around her most sensitive parts, but this time, when he was back at her chest, he didn't move away.

As he approached her tits, her back arched sharply in time with every sweep and knead of his hands. She was panting now, and little whimpery moans escaped her lips every once in a while.

Lingering over the top of her chest, her sides, her ribs, he waited until she was rocking toward his touch and moaning with every exhale. Then, and only then, he swept his palms over the rock-hard nubs of her nipples. Her gasp at that touch was nearly a scream. He caught her nipples between his fingers and plucked, and she did scream—short and stunted, but a scream nonetheless.

His cock bounced every time she made a sound, and the tip wept with his need, but he wasn't ready. Jenny was a great lay, responsive, vocal, and pliable, but he'd never seen her this worked up before. What a thing of beauty this was. He was going to tie her up regularly—and maybe do some research into bindings, to play around with that a little bit. Because holy shit, this was the best sex he'd ever had, and he wasn't even fucking her yet.

He massaged her tits again and plucked her nipples, and she screamed that chopped scream again. "Please, Mav. Fuck, please. *Please*."

And now she was begging. Maverick resisted the urge to grab his cock and give it the pump it so desperately needed, because he'd blow his wad all over her.

"You need to come, babe?"

Her head bobbed wildly up and down. "Please, please, *please!*"

Wanting to watch her, to be entirely in control of her, he left her tits and filled his palm with lotion again. Massaging his way over her belly, taking his time until he'd kneaded the lotion into her skin, he pushed one hand between her legs—oh hell, she was *dripping* wet—and slid his fingers, first one, then, on the next thrust, two, into her.

She took in a great, noisy gasp of air and planted her feet on the mattress, heaving her hips up. He grabbed her legs and dropped her back down. Then he gave her what she so clearly wanted—he fucked her with his fingers, hard and fast, pressing up, finding the spot behind her clit.

At once, she came, so wildly and wetly that they'd have to change the sheets before they settled in to sleep. She shrieked and flailed, and he kept at her, keeping her going until her body began the twitching that meant her climax was truly over.

But he wasn't done. He reached into the nightstand drawer and snagged a condom. He hated the thought of the cool slime of the lube touching his swollen, frantic cock, but he rolled it on, because he needed to get inside her, and he wasn't in the mood to play the pullout game. He was way too close already.

The idea that he could have her ass now if he wanted it occurred to him, but he discarded it instantly. He could go up her ass—tongue, fingers, cock, she'd let him take what he wanted. But he didn't want it now. Because he knew she didn't. Whatever she'd allow in her languid afterglow, she'd told him that she didn't want it. He couldn't break faith with her. That was more important than moving her limits.

He wanted her trust. He wanted to be worthy of it. So badly that his chest felt tight as he pushed into her. He wanted her to know she was always safe with him. Always.

God, the feel of her around him, holding him, keeping him. The feel of her body beneath his, molding to him, joining with him. The sound of her pleasure, the sweet whispers of *yes oh god yes please*—inconsequential words, but so full of love and trust. Nothing had ever felt like this. Jenny was special. Important. Life or death. Love.

Jesus—he loved her.

That truth slammed through his body like a thunderclap, and he thrust hard. With a trembling hand, he reached up and pulled the scarf from her eyes. He needed to see her, needed those dazzling eyes on his, needed her to see him. He thrust and thrust, and stared deep.

"I love you. I love you." His body's effort turned the words into a growl.

Her brow creased—just a flash and gone—and it wasn't pleasure that had shaped her expression. But it was gone, and she was coming, and so was he, and yeah, it was life or death. This love. This trust he would never break. Ever.

He would love her forever.

CHAPTER TWELVE

Jenny was in a foul mood as she worked the bar the next evening. Fridays were her least favorite days of the week. Weekends were hard at her house, when her father was entirely her responsibility, and closing the bar on Fridays sucked. The Friday night crowd drank harder and got ornerier than any other night of the week.

The Wayside Inn wasn't a big bar, and neither Jenny nor her father had ever gone in for 'Ladies Night' or 'Happy Hour' or any other kind of promotion. In his day, he'd run a big poker game or had a special event for the neighborhood occasionally, but those hadn't been intended to draw strangers in. The only advertising they did was sponsoring a few kids' sports teams.

But The Wayside had been around for a long time, had a complement of regulars and good word of mouth, and was located in a primarily industrial area. They did a decent business every evening and were jammed on Friday nights, mostly with people who started drinking right after work and reeled onto the sidewalk when the lights went up.

She kept the bar running with a staff of two other bartenders, three waitresses, and a couple of teens working as bar-backs. On weekend and holiday nights, she usually put two bartenders on the schedule together.

On this particular Friday, she'd gotten sick calls at home from two people scheduled to work with her: a bartender and a waitress. The other waitress was off at eleven, as would be the seventeen-year-old bar-back on the schedule. Jenny was running the bar on her own all night, with a single waitress, and then, for the last two hours, she would be entirely on her own. On a Friday fucking night.

She suspected that Dave, the 'sick' bartender, and Tawnie, the 'sick' waitress, were fucking. If she got anything remotely like proof that they'd blown off work to play together, she'd kick both their asses right out the door.

Of course, that would leave her short a bartender and a waitress and saddled with the hassle of replacing them.

Jenny fucking hated running this goddamn bar.

Her mood was even worse because Kelsey had pitched a fit that morning when her daddy wasn't there for breakfast. She'd already decided that he'd moved in—the very confusion Jenny had been trying to prevent had already happened, while she was unconscious, trying to survive her murderous head.

She'd taken a puffy-eyed, pouty little girl to preschool that morning, half an hour late, and picked up a sassy, obstreperous little girl in the afternoon.

And Darnell was working a shorter shift today because it was his week to take Saturday morning, so Kelsey would be staying with the Turners tonight. They had Maisie tonight, too, so they'd be in full grandparent mode, stuffing the girls full of sugar. Kelsey would have a great time, but she wouldn't sleep well, and she'd be even crabbier and whinier all day tomorrow.

In the twenty-four hours from last evening to this evening, three different people would have charge of Kelsey at some point—four, if she counted Mr. and Mrs. Turner separately. As a single parent, Jenny was not measuring up.

Just say the word, babe. Maverick's voice in her head. Goddammit. She *wanted* it. After last night, it was the only thing she could think of besides Kelsey. All afternoon and evening, she'd cast sidelong glances at the phone behind the bar, thinking about calling him and simply saying *yes.*

Jolene gave her the kind of smile that meant she'd decided humoring the snarling creature her boss had become was the best course of action.

A customer leaned far across the bar and waved his hand. "Hey, sugar tits, I'm waitin' on a Bud."

She turned on her fakest smile. "And you're gonna keep waiting, until you learn some fucking manners." She moved past him, bringing the change in her hand to a customer down the bar, but the guy grabbed her arm and gave it a hard jerk, pulling her off balance. The money in her hand went flying, and she slammed into the side of the bar, hitting her hip on the underbar and her shoulder on the edge of the bar.

"No stupid bitch is gonna give me lip." He managed to spit those words in her face before he was yanked away by a couple of regulars. By the time she'd stood straight again, Jenny had a brawl on her hands.

If Dave had been there—six-foot-four-inch, former high-school offensive lineman Dave—he probably could have gotten control of the thing. But short of firing the shotgun her father had installed under the bar, which she'd never actually fired, Jenny could only make sure Jolene and Kevin stayed safely in back while she tried to protect the stock behind the bar, wielding a Louisville Slugger, the other weapon that had been behind the bar since long before her time. The shitty bastard who'd grabbed her had about four equally shitty friends, so even her regulars, who'd normally have her back and try to settle the situation down, had no choice but to fight.

It went on forever, and she nearly called the cops—which would have brought a host of problems of its own—but eventually, as these things usually did, it died on its own.

Most of the customers had gotten themselves gone as quickly as possible—this was the kind of bar where fights sometimes broke out, not the kind where the clientele came looking for one—and the rest were breathless and hurt and, now that their energy had been expended, mostly sheepish, looking around at the damage they'd done.

"Okay, everybody out!" she yelled. "We're closed!" It was more than two hours before closing, but Jolene and Kevin were off soon, and she had a fucking mess on her hands. For this night, looking at a substantial net loss anyway, she was done.

Al, Chester, and Tom, three long-time regulars, heaved the instigators out the door. It was they who'd pulled the asshole off of her, thus starting the melee. Jenny didn't know whether to thank them or punch them, but she settled on drawing them all a Busch before they hit the road.

Broken furniture, broken glass, beer and booze. Everywhere. Jolene and Kevin stayed a little while past their shift to help her clean up, but after about twenty minutes, Jenny just needed to be alone, even if it meant she'd spend the whole night picking up the mess.

"I got this, guys. Go on home."

Kevin looked up from the trash bag he was filling. "You sure?"

"Yeah. You're off the clock. Go on home."

Jolene had two kids with a babysitter, so she didn't need to be told twice. They said their goodbyes. They went out the back, and Jenny stood in the middle of the rubble and gave herself a minute to cry.

~oOo~

After she'd pulled herself together, Jenny finished stacking the broken furniture in the back room near the alley door, and she grabbed the big push broom, the smaller straw broom for corners and tight spots, and the dustpan, and she went back to clean up the glass and mess. It was past midnight, and she easily had another hour, maybe two, before the place would be remotely ready to receive customers. And then she had to do the regular closing work.

She supposed she should be grateful they hadn't broken out any windows—though the vintage neon Budweiser sign had been knocked from the paneled wall and was a total loss.

At least Kelsey was at the Turners' tonight. She was grateful not to have to worry about that. Sending out a thought to her wonderful next-door neighbors, Jenny hipped the swinging door open and dragged her armload of brooms into the bar.

The jerk who'd grabbed her and started the fracas stood near the back end of the bar, not ten feet away. His friends were with him. They'd all converged near the back, like they'd been on their way to seek her out in the back room.

She'd fucking forgotten to lock the fucking front door.

Bruised and swollen, with blood still crusted around their mouths and noses, they'd clearly found somewhere else to drink. She faced five furious, violent drunks. The grabber smiled—he'd lost a tooth in the fight. That smile was not cordial or happy. It was victorious.

The bat she'd wielded earlier lay on the bar, inches from his hand. The shotgun was in its cradle, out of her reach. For self-defense, all she had were two brooms, a metal dustpan, and her wits.

In the second or two that it took her to understand and assess the danger she was in, one of his friends slid behind her, blocking her path backward.

Maybe she could get out of this without violence. If he wanted an apology, she'd give it to him. Fuck, she'd pay him, if he'd just leave her and the bar without further damage. "What do you want?"

His sinister smile grew. "You're a mouthy bitch when you got backup. On your own, though, you're just a puny little cunt afraid of her own shadow."

The men with him laughed, and they all came a few steps closer to her. The one behind her was close enough to grab her; she turned and stepped to the side, putting her back to the wall. That was probably a terrible position, but it was the only one that gave her any sense of security at all—at least she could see them all coming.

"What do you want?" She kept her voice as steady as she could and tightened her fist around the push broom. When the time came, she'd just throw the other things in her hands; the big broom was the best weapon available, and she'd need both hands to wield it.

A broom was her best weapon, and it was barely a weapon at all. Her mind began to conjure images of the terrible things that would happen to her when these apes tore the broom from her hands and overpowered her, but she slammed the curtain shut on that horrifying footage.

Grabber came closer still. He stood at the end of the bar now, five feet away at the most. "What I *want*, sugar tits, is payback. Your big mouth caused us trouble tonight. So I'm gonna need to give you some back."

They were too close now, all of them, for throwing anything to be of use to her, so she dropped the straw broom and the dustpan to the floor and grasped the handle of the push broom in both hands.

"Look at my bar. I got plenty of trouble already. Just go. Please, just go."

"Oh, I like that you're beggin'. A woman begging—that's about the sweetest sound in the world." Sniggers from his peanut gallery. "I think I wanna hear you do that some more."

If they got any closer, the push broom would be useless, too. Seeing one chance, she spun the handle in her hands, so that the breadth of the broom turned up vertically, and she swung it upward, between the legs of the man who'd cut her off from the back room and was closest to her now.

Her aim was true; the short edge of the broom landed firmly in his junk, and he howled and doubled over. That reaction, and the step back he took, caught the head of the broom between his legs and yanked it from her hands.

She was empty handed. Nothing between her and, now, four furious men.

They all converged on her at once, even angrier. One man grabbed her, then another, and she was trapped between them, positioned like an offering to the guy who'd started all this.

The only words in her head were *Please no! Please no!* but she kept her teeth clenched, afraid that begging would only get this guy more excited. He came right up to her and grabbed her breasts, clenching his hands around them like he was testing grapefruits for ripeness.

More like oranges, really. She wasn't that stacked. What a strange thought to go through her head right now.

"They are sweet tits, ain't they?" He squeezed harder. Jenny kept her mouth shut, but she was going to cry, and she just knew these guys would get off on that. "I can't decide whether to fuck you before I beat you or after."

One of the ones holding her leaned close to her ear. "Fuck her first, so we all get some before you start the beatdown."

"I want in. I'm gonna shove that fuckin' broom so far up her cooze she'll be coughin' up splinters for a month." That was the guy she'd hit; he gasped out the words. She faced five men again.

"Please," she moaned, but she wasn't talking to them. She was talking to God. She hadn't prayed since she was little. Her mother had been Catholic, but her father had been indifferent, and God was one of the many things of her mother that had been erased from her life. Right now, alone in the middle of the night with five thugs who meant her terrible harm, all she had was a God she'd forgotten, if He would still listen. "Please. Please."

"Yeah," Grabber grunted and released her breasts. She didn't look down, but she heard the jangle as he opened his belt. "I fuckin' *love* it when they beg."

And then God answered her prayer.

Grabber's head rocked forward, spraying blood and bone in a fountain, at the same time that a thick thud resounded in the air. His eyes did a strange thing—they bugged out, nearly straight out of his head—and he fell forward, into her, taking her down to the floor.

What she saw as she fell backward was a miracle. Maverick. Holding the Louisville Slugger, which now dripped with blood and brain matter. His face was warped into a mask of monstrous rage.

The other men turned, all of them shouting incoherently, and leapt at him. Pinned under a dead man, Jenny couldn't see what was going on. She heard grunting and shouting, and none of it sounded like Maverick.

Finally, she worked her way out from under the man who'd been about to rape her, for his opening act, and struggled to her feet.

Another man was already down, and Maverick fought the remaining three. Jenny went for the shotgun, yanked it free, and then stopped, stunned, as he took down another one, using the bat and his feet and his body. He fought all these men at once, and he was winning. He blocked almost every blow. When they grabbed at him, he used their weight against them. When a blow connected, he used their momentum against them.

The men he fought were noisy as hell, roaring, grunting, groaning. Maverick was silent. He'd been like that in the ring, too. She'd seen him fight a few times—she hadn't gone often, because the street fights were much more violent than anything she'd seen on television, and they stressed her out—and he'd always been quiet in the ring, too. He'd been quiet like this when he'd beaten her father near to death.

"Put it down, Jen. I got this." Right in the middle of this raging battle, he addressed her. Calm as you please, like he was telling her they didn't need milk. She looked at the shotgun in her hands. She didn't even know how to cock the damn thing. Or if it was loaded.

She put the shotgun back in its cradle. And then she knew what she needed to do. She picked up the phone and dialed.

~oOo~

Radical waved a wallet at one of the bloody men kneeling at his feet. "Do we understand each other, Elliot Bundy of Porter Street?" The man nodded, and Rad tossed the wallet at him. "Good. I'd hate to have to pay a visit to your family."

"How about you, Charles Peters? I got a good friend lives in Bixby. Know that area real well."

"No trouble from me...sir."

Rad chuckled. "Sir. I like that." He tossed another wallet.

The third guy was nodding before Rad started to speak. The fourth guy, the one who'd taken a broom to the goods, was barely conscious. Rad crouched down and slapped him in the face with his wallet. "How about you?"

He groaned. Rad looked up at Ox and Eight Ball. "This one we keep ahold of until we know he gets the situation. He can sit in the back of the van with his friend over there." He nodded at the body of Grabber.

"You got it, Sarge." Eight Ball yanked the groaning man almost to his feet, then dragged him toward the back. The club van was parked in the alley, waiting for Grabber's body—Ronald Edwin McCook III, they now knew—and also, now, his friend, Clark Godwin.

Jenny sat at the bar and watched it all happen. Maverick's arm was around her. He hadn't stopped touching her since he'd come to her after disabling all of the attackers. Except to ask if she was okay, he hadn't said a word to her yet. He'd spoken to Rad when he, Eight Ball, and Gunner had come in, and he'd said a couple of reassuring words to Gunner, but otherwise, he'd been silent. He'd sat back and let the club SAA handle everything.

Not that there was anything but cleanup to handle. Maverick had finished the fight.

Rad stared down at the three still kneeling before him. "You three, get the fuck out. You darken this door ever again, you ever mention even a word of what went down here tonight to anyone, ever, and I will hunt down you and your family and wipe you all off the face of the earth. If fifty years from now on your deathbed, you feel the need to bare your soul and scrub your conscience clean, my son will find your children and grandchildren and wipe them out. Are we fuckin' clear?"

The men all nodded and struggled to their feet. Gunner cut the bonds from their hands, and they limped and lurched toward the front door.

"Hold up," Maverick called and stood up, bringing Jenny with him. The men stopped and turned wary, blackened eyes back. "You owe my woman an apology. Get over here and do it right."

"Mav, no," Jenny muttered. The last thing she wanted was to be face to face with these assholes, for any reason.

"Yes," he growled back.

She was about to push her point, but movement from Gunner caught her eye. She turned a little and saw him staring at her, shaking his head slightly. Getting the message, she let it drop. This was about Maverick and these men, and some kind of power thing. Not about her. It sucked, but she understood it.

They apologized. She stood still and let them, but she offered them no kind of concession or acceptance. Fuck them.

When they were gone, Rad turned to Jenny. "Stay closed for the day. We'll send some guys over to help get things to rights later on. You take the day off."

"It's Saturday. I don't come in on Saturday anyway. But I have people on the payroll who need to work, and I need to earn so I can pay them."

Rad huffed. She remembered this about him—he didn't like people pushing back on him. Most of the guys were like that, they all wanted their own way, but Rad didn't even like to have a damn conversation. At least Maverick would talk about things. He'd talk her in circles, but he'd talk.

"I'll talk to her," Maverick cut in. "Thanks for this, Sarge."

Rad clapped him on the back. "We got your back, brother. And you're a fuckin' beast." He smiled at Jenny. "You did good, callin' the clubhouse. Right thing to do."

She knew it was. It felt strange, to think of the club as help, as rescue, but when she'd picked up the phone, there'd been no question whom they'd needed.

"Okay. We'll deal with the trash. See you later, Mav?"

"Yeah, Sarge. Yeah, I'll be in."

Rad nodded and headed toward the back. Gunner had already dragged Grabber's body back.

"Rad, wait." Acting on the sudden impulse, Jenny went up to him and hugged him. He stood stiff and surprised, and it was like hugging a tree, until his hands came to her back and patted her awkwardly. He supposedly had a different old lady and a kid now, but Jenny found it hard to imagine Rad as a father.

Still, seeing him tonight, as one of her rescuers, was a far cry from the last time he'd been in her bar, when he'd threatened her.

"Thank you," she said as she stepped back.

His expression softened, and for a second, she could almost see the partner and father he might be. "We were always here, Jenny. All you ever had to do was ask."

With nothing to say to that, she simply took another step back and let him leave.

And then she and Maverick were alone in her ransacked bar.

She turned and saw him standing there, a bruise flowering on his cheek, his hands scraped, his t-shirt bloody and torn almost all the way down the middle, showing half his chest beneath it.

God, what a night.

He'd killed a man for her. He'd saved her from—God, what? A gang rape. A beating. That had been a certainty. Death had been a likelihood. Then she'd sent out a prayer, just a feeble, hopeless little prayer, and Maverick had been delivered to her like her own personal avenging angel.

As she walked toward him, he starting talking, making Rad's case. "You have to close the bar, babe. There's—"

He stopped in midsentence as she reached him and grabbed his t-shirt in both hands, tearing it the rest of the way open.

"Shut up and fuck me."

"Jen?"

Yes, please, take her and Kelsey away from this shitty life. Make the family they were supposed to have made from the start. God — to just be able to be Kelsey's mom and to be good at it? Yes, yes, yes. Right now.

But fuck! He'd been out of prison a month. One month. After four years away. She didn't really know him, and he certainly didn't really know her. Not anymore. They had to take things slowly. They had to make sure.

And what about her father? She didn't love him, but he was her father, and he was helpless. Because of what Maverick had done to him. She couldn't have the two men in her life living under the same roof, she couldn't put her father in a state home — she just *couldn't*, no matter what — and she couldn't afford to put him anywhere with better care.

That was a problem without a solution. But she wanted it. On this bullshit day, with the bar crowded and loud, fending off passes from drunk men and hating everyone around her, she wanted nothing in the world like she wanted Maverick and the life he was holding out to her on his open hands.

"Jenny?"

"What?" She slammed the register drawer shut, spun around, and faced Jolene, the waitress slogging through this night with her. In Jolene's flinch and frown, Jenny saw that she'd barked. "Sorry — what?"

"Ice is low, and Kevin's AWOL. He's probably smoking in the alley. I'm going to run back and scrounge him up."

Jenny nodded. "Grab him by whatever you have to and get his ass back to work."

"Shut up. Shut up. Shut up." She wrapped her hands around his head and pulled, bringing him down so she could reach his mouth. By the time their lips touched, he was all in.

"Oh fuck, yes," he mumbled against her mouth. His arms went around her, clutched her tightly, and he took her down to the floor—a floor still filthy from the violence of the night, smeared and spattered with blood and booze, strewn with chunks of furniture and shards of broken glass. Somehow, like what they were doing was predestined, there was no broken glass where they were.

Frantic and ravenous, they snatched clumsily at each other's clothes and their own, until they were finally naked. Oh God, his body. His beautiful, beautiful body, how she'd missed it. He lay on her, and she felt the warmth of his skin, the gentle exhilarating scratch of the hair on his legs, his torso, his arms, brushing over her. The wet, brilliant heat of his mouth on her breasts, sucking her nipples, his tongue flicking over skin he'd made taut and needy. The fine grit of his palms skimming over her body. Oh God. Oh *God*.

He nuzzled and laved the tattoo—a flaming heart with his name inked across it—that marked her as his old lady. Not a title she deserved any longer, but she wanted it again. Fuck it, she wanted it *right now*. She did *not* want to move slowly. They'd lost so much time already.

"Fuck me, Mav. *Please*."

He shifted over her, and she reached down for his cock—hard and hot, thick and heavy, and ready, so ready. He groaned at her touch and curled his hand around hers. "Wait. I don't have a fucking condom."

That didn't slow her down at all. "I don't care."

His eyes went to hers, and he went still. "Jen. I don't know if I'll be able to pull out in time."

"I don't care. I don't care. Be inside me. Please. I love you, Mav."

He flinched at her words, and a spasm tightened his features. Staring up into his eyes, Jenny might have sworn that they'd filled with tears. "That's one," he murmured, and, with his hand still around hers around his cock, he pushed in. He brought her hand up and kissed it as they both groaned at his entry.

"Jesus *Christ*, you're so fucking *tight*."

She couldn't reply; his entry had taken her breath and her words. Not because it hurt—the stretch was surprising, but the pain dissipated before it had made an impression—but because it was so right. So perfect. As he filled her, it was like he'd never been away from her. They fit together like they'd been custom made for each other. He'd said that often, before, and thinking it now, Jenny was overcome with nostalgia. No more waiting. No more.

When words and breath were possible, she whispered, "There's been no one else. There'll never be anyone else."

He dropped his head to her shoulder and began to thrust. Jenny wrapped her body around him as tightly as she could. At her ear, faint but clear, she heard him whispering, over and over, *I love you, I love you, I love you*. Like he was trying to catch up for all the time he'd missed, all the I love yous they hadn't counted.

He came quickly, fiercely, clutching her so close that she couldn't breathe. As far as she could tell, he hadn't even tried to pull out, and she didn't care. A prayer had brought him to her on this terrible night. If a baby happened because of it, then it was meant to be.

She didn't come, but it didn't matter in the slightest. She was full of him, closed in his arms. She was safe and complete.

In many important ways, Jenny was a different woman from the one who'd first fallen in love with Maverick Helm, that girl who'd been instantly besotted by her own James Dean, standing in the ladies' accessories section of Wal-Mart, festooned with fancy handbags. But in other, equally important ways, she was the same. She loved this man. He was the only one who'd ever taken care of her, who'd ever made her feel safe and secure. He was the reason she'd been able to grow—and, yes, he was also the reason she'd been forced to change. He was the only person who'd ever really understood her—even his infuriating way of 'reasoning' with her was founded on understanding. He knew her, and he loved her. He would love the woman she'd become, too. He was already showing her that he loved her and wanted to give her what she needed. He wanted to understand who she was now.

He lived a violent life. He was a violent man. But until that last day, he'd never brought his violence into their lives. With her, in their life, he was calm and steady. He'd been a strong support while she'd struggled to separate from her father. It was little wonder he'd taken to managing her and shaping her wants. The girl he'd met hadn't known how to know what she wanted for herself. That girl had shaped herself to an erratic, angry father, and the process of discovering what *she* wanted, who *she* wanted to be, had been long and painful.

She'd been wrong to compare him to her father. Maverick was nothing like him. He wasn't a bully. He was strong and willful, but it wasn't his fault that she'd bent so easily.

On that last day, when she'd stood up to her father, that had been the day that the Jenny she was now had begun to be formed. Until she'd been able to do that—for her entire relationship with Maverick—she'd been like soft clay, allowing the men in her life to shape her in their hands.

That was on her, and her father. Not Maverick.

"Can I still say the word?" she whispered. Her heart slammed against her ribs.

He reared up and stared down at her, his eyes sparking with heat. "Jen?"

"I have to figure out my father, and I don't know what that's going to be, and I have to talk to Kelsey so she understands everything, but I want the life we were supposed to have. I want it now. If it's not too late."

"It's not too late. I love you, Jen. So goddamn much."

"That's...I lost count."

He grinned. "Infinity."

July 1993

Jenny's father opened the door.

She could smell the bourbon on him. Since she'd moved in with Maverick, her father, always a heavy drinker, had dived deeper and deeper into alcoholism. Second-guessing her intent, Jenny stood on the porch, two steps down from him. He was already drunk. What she had to say could go very badly. She swept her hands protectively over her huge belly.

"What d'you want?" He sneered down at her hands. His only reaction thus far to her pregnancy and his impending grandfatherhood was resentment.

Which was why this talk couldn't wait any longer. "I want to talk to you."

He shrugged and stepped back, clearing the way for her to enter the house she'd grown up in.

It was dark and musty inside. From the entry, she could smell that he hadn't washed dishes in a while. Newspapers were strewn in careless stacks across the dining room table. Various empty bottles and overfull ashtrays littered the tables in the living room.

"Jesus, Dad. What happened?"

"My daughter abandoned me and let some piece of shit biker put a bastard up her twat."

So they were starting with nasty right off the bat. Okay, then. Good. It would make this easier.

He walked into the living room and picked up a half-full bottle of Wild Turkey from the coffee table. "You want a drink?"

Cradling her belly, she laughed. "No, Dad. I don't want a drink."

"You want to talk. So talk."

She could feel tension tightening the strings through her body, making it want to shake, but she took a deep breath. "The baby is coming next month."

He grunted and drank from the bottle.

"I can't have her around this mess between us, Dad. I can't let her grow up like I grew up. After last week, I know we're not ever going to be okay, you and me."

The week before had been his wedding anniversary. That was a hard day every year. When she was little, it had been an especially terrifying day; several times, she'd been left alone the whole day, until she'd gotten hungry and gone next door to ask the Turners for something to eat, and he'd returned bombed out of his head and dragged her back home.

When she'd gotten old enough to understand what the day was, she'd started trying to make it okay for him—being extra careful to be good, making his favorite foods, seeing to it that there were things he liked happening all day, to keep his mind off the darkness.

Like a fool, she'd come over last week to take care of him on his hard day. He'd shown his appreciation by glowering at her belly all day, and snarling at every word she'd said. When he'd called her unborn daughter 'the little cunt,' she'd stormed out.

She hadn't told Maverick anything about that day. But she'd realized something crucial: her daughter wouldn't be safe with him. Ever. He wouldn't be a better grandfather than he'd been a father. In fact, he'd be worse. The little girl she was carrying was Maverick's child, and her father despised Maverick.

Understanding that, she'd made a decision she probably should have made a long time ago. Today, when her father wasn't working, was the day she meant to act on it.

"What's that supposed to mean?"

Someone had changed out her heart for a rabbit's. It seemed to beat dozens of times a second. "It means…" Her voice quavered, and she stopped and steadied it. "It means that this is the end, Dad. My daughter deserves a good life, surrounded by people who love her. I deserve that, too."

"Are you sayin' I don't love you?"

"No. I'm saying you don't love this baby. And I'm saying I don't want her to know the fear I've known being around you."

He threw the bottle, and she should have left then, before he crossed the living room. The front door was right there. But her feet were glued to the floor—and something else. Something strange. She *wanted* him to come at her. That was crazy. She had to protect her baby. But desire for a real confrontation was there, holding her in place.

Ninety-five percent of her tried to run for the door, but the other five percent knew that if he hit her now, she wouldn't feel bad for him anymore, she wouldn't feel the relentless, irrational pull of guilt and need that made her keep trying to make him love her like he should. She was twenty-five years old. He was never going to love her like he should. He would always see her mother in her, and he would always swing back and forth between outlandish declarations of love and terrifying demonstrations of rage. Hugging and hitting—how her father showed his feelings.

When he stalked up to her, she stood her ground. Then she had the thought—what if he punched her in the stomach? That fear broke the five percent's hold, and she turned for the door, but it was too late now. He cut her off and blocked the door.

"That fuckin' thug is fillin' your head with shit, Jennifer. You never been smart. You don't know what's good for you. Just like your mother. I shoulda locked you up the first time you brought him around here. I know what's good for you. I know what you need. Now you got some biker bitch growin' inside you."

"Dad, let me go." He hadn't touched her yet, and she had a small twinge of hope that he wouldn't. She tried to reach around him for the door, and he pushed her back, with his hand on her shoulder.

"You're mine. *Mine*. I knew when I let you move out he'd turn your head against me."

The impulse to give in, to cajole and concede, grew inside her. All her life, it had been her only hope to avoid the belt or his hands—if she could catch him at just the right time, say just the right thing, she could defuse him. She'd come to think of his beatings as her own failures—she'd pushed too hard, or misread the signs that would have allowed her to change the scene.

Right then—standing in the entry, facing her father before the front door—Jenny understood something that changed her whole life. Past, present, and future, all different, all at once. She'd been blaming herself for her childhood. She'd believed it was her fault that her mother had left when she was six. She'd believed that it was her fault that her father beat her and terrorized her and controlled her. She'd believed that *he* was the victim in this house. Even when she'd been victimized, even when she'd been angry or hurt. Even knowing that he was abusing her, even being able to talk about it with Maverick, to the extent that she had—despite all that, deep down, under it all, she'd believed that he was the victim. She'd seen him as a sad man, lost in his life.

He wasn't sad. He was mean. Her mother hadn't run away from her. She'd run away from him. If she'd needed a man at her side to give her the strength to do that, well, Jenny sure as fuck understood that now.

What was more—Jenny remembered that night when her mother had died. She remembered how her mother had reached out to her, how she'd *crawled*, trying to reach her—*Baby, come here! Jenny, baby, Mommy loves you!*

Her mother hadn't run away from her. She hadn't left her alone with her father. She'd wanted to take her with her. Jenny's father had thrown her out. But she'd have come back. If she hadn't died that night, if her mother's lover's wife hadn't killed them both, her mother would have come back for her. For the first time in all these years, Jenny remembered that night the way it had happened, the way she had *seen* it happen, not the way her father wanted her to see it.

"What're you grinnin' at?" her father sneered. Jenny hadn't realized she was smiling.

"I understand why my mother ran away from you."

Bam. He moved so quickly, she didn't see the backhand slap until his knuckles slammed into her cheekbone. She grunted and sidestepped, but she kept her feet. He rarely lashed out like this and almost never went for her face. He preferred the meaty body parts that didn't show damage in public. He'd still been using a belt on her when she'd graduated from high school—long after, in fact, though she'd stopped making it easy for him.

Cupping her cheek with her hand, she stood straight and faced him. He still blocked the door, but she didn't care. They were done, and it needed to be said. She'd turn and run to the back door if she had to, even eight months pregnant. "This is the end of us. You will never see me again."

"You're just like her, you filthy, disloyal little CUNT!" He slapped her again, catching her mouth with such force that this time he knocked her off her feet. She landed hard on the wood floor, and her back slammed against the wall. The impact jostled the picture hanging there—a photograph of The Wayside Inn, taken on the day he'd opened the bar—and when it hit the floor, he forgot her and dove for the broken frame.

Jenny used the chance to get her waddling ass up and out of the house.

She was two blocks away when she pulled over and opened her car door so she could puke on the street. After, she closed the door and sat there, shaking, her eyes closed, trying to feel inside her belly and know the baby was okay.

When her baby girl kicked and rolled fussily inside her, Jenny laughed. And then she cried. Not with sadness, but with joy. She was free.

She had to figure out how to tell Maverick about this, and already her brain kicked away the mere thought of that conversation. But she'd figure it out, and everything would be okay.

Better than okay. Everything would be wonderful. Life spread out before her, all sunshine and smooth seas. The life her little girl deserved.

She had hours yet before Maverick got home. She'd make a nice supper, and she'd figure out how to talk to him about this. If he could see past whatever her face looked like, he'd be thrilled and relieved that she'd finally cut her father out.

Everything was going to be perfect now.

CHAPTER THIRTEEN

Maverick unfastened the restraint in Kelsey's booster seat, and she raised her arms. He lifted her out of the back of the Cherokee, and she looped her arms around his neck, hugging him.

He'd meant to set her on the ground, but instead, unwilling to let her go, he held on, turning his face into her soft hair. Shifting her a bit to the side, he took her weight on his forearm and came around the back of his car.

She turned in his arms and looked at the station lot. "This is where you do work?"

"Yep. I fix cars. And over there"—he twisted and pointed at the clubhouse next door—"that's where I see all my friends and family."

"You see family at my house, too. You're my daddy, and Mommy's my mommy, that means family."

"That's right. You want to meet some more family? I've got lots of uncles for you."

She screwed up her little brow. "I don't have any uncles."

"Sure you do. You just haven't met them yet."

Gunner was heading their way, so Maverick nodded toward him. "And here's one right here. Kelsey, this is your Uncle Gunner."

"Hello, cutie." Gunner held his hand up to her. "Nice to finally meet you."

Rather than shake his hand or offer a reply, she laid her head on Maverick's shoulder. He kissed her head. "It's okay, sweetheart. You don't have to be shy."

"He has a scary face," she whispered back. "Hairy like a monster."

If facial hair scared her, then she was going to be a nervous wreck before they made it through just the Bulls on shift at the station. Maverick had another twinge of doubt about introducing her to the club. His first had come when he hadn't told Jenny that this was his plan for his first outing alone with his daughter. He'd only told her about the second part—spending the day at his house—because he'd known she'd resist having Kelsey meet the Bulls. Jenny had never gotten fully comfortable around his people, and her distaste had only grown while he'd been away. Last night's excitement at The Wayside might have thawed her some, but he didn't think she'd warmed enough to be comfortable with this part of his plan.

Understanding she'd be mighty pissed that, first, he'd done this without her okay, and, second, he'd essentially lied to her mere hours after that intense, fraught, astonishing connection they'd made on the filthy floor of the ravaged bar, Maverick had indeed had second thoughts about evading this truth. But he wanted it enough to cope with the consequences

This was how he really came home. He had Jenny back. He had his little girl. Bringing her to the club—this was how he found his steady ground and made himself whole and real again.

But he hadn't considered that Kelsey would be afraid of these men.

Hearing what she'd said to Maverick, Gunner chuckled and brushed a self-conscious hand over his thick beard. "Hey, Kelsey?"

She didn't answer him, but Maverick felt her head turn to look at Gunner again.

"It's just hair. You can give it a pull, if you want. I don't bite."

Gunner came close and lifted his chin toward her. Kelsey squinted at him suspiciously, then reached out and patted his beard. Apparently satisfied that it was safe, she clenched a little fist around the part below his chin and tugged, and Gunner pursed his lips and make a smooching sound.

"See? I don't bite, I kiss."

Lifting her head, Kelsey smiled and tugged again, and this time, Gunner turned his head and planted a kiss on her arm. She giggled. And Maverick's doubts were assuaged.

His family would be whole.

~oOo~

"Hey, babe."

Grabbing her hand, Maverick stepped back and pulled Jenny in the front door. He didn't like that she'd rung this doorbell and waited for him to let her in. He wanted this to be her house, too. But not even a day had passed since she'd said she didn't want to go slow, and he knew she still saw complications in every direction, so he would continue to be patient—but persistent.

"Hey. I can't stay long. I have Mr. Turner with my dad."

On weekends, she was her father's caretaker. One of the complications between them.

He shut the door and drew her close. There was no more resistance in her, and that was a beautiful thing. When he bent his head to hers, she licked her sweet lips, ready to form her mouth to his. Need charged through him as he took her kiss, and he pushed her against the door.

Her body was perfectly pliable, yielding to him, shaping to him, following his every lead. *Christ*, he wanted her. He wanted to fuck her properly. Not on the floor of the damn bar—that had been transcendent, but it had been his first time inside her in more than four years, and he'd blown in about a minute and a half. He hadn't given her pleasure, and he wanted that. He wanted to watch her come, to watch her pleasure, to *feel* it, the pleasure he gave her, to feel it grow and grow until she was wild with it.

He'd come inside her, too. And she'd wanted it—or, at least, hadn't *not* wanted it. Holy fuck, if he'd made her pregnant. If he could raise a child with her, be with her from the start.

Growing frantic with need, he thrust against her, rubbing his throbbing cock against her belly, and she tore her mouth from his with a gasp. "Where's—where's—"

"She's taking a nap. It's okay. Fuck, Jen, I need you."

But the willing partner in his arms stiffened; her hands came between them, and she pushed on his chest. "She's napping? It's five o'clock in the afternoon." Though she was still flushed and breathless from the brink of sex they'd been on, Kelsey's mom was quickly replacing Maverick's lover.

He took a step back and a deep breath. "She was tired. Should I have kept her up?"

"A nap this late, she'll be awake until ten or eleven."

"Oh. Sorry." Deciding to get the pain out of the way now, while they were already diverted, he added, "She had a big day. I took her to the clubhouse, and she met almost everybody. Delaney gave her a stuffed Dino, and she hasn't let it go yet."

Yeah—this was going to go badly. The lingering softness of their kiss disappeared from her face, supplanted by the sharp edges and deep creases of anger. "You did what?"

"It's my family, Jen. I wanted her to get to know them."

She pushed him farther back and stepped around him, stalking away, into the living room. "And you knew exactly how I'd feel about it, so you lied to me."

"I didn't lie." He was twisting the truth around semantics, and he knew she'd only get angrier for it, but the words came out anyway. He'd begun to understand what she meant about the way he argued, but it was his nature and not so easy to change.

"Nothing's different. You still think you can manage me, and I'll just give in."

"Jen, stop—"

Before he could finish, and offer an apology, she wheeled around. "Don't fucking tell me to stop! You don't get to shut me down! You know what? I'm an idiot for thinking things could change. I got caught up in my feelings these last couple of days, and I let myself see you as my rescuer, and I forgot the truth. You just do what you want." She huffed a humorless laugh and walked to the front window. "The very first time I trusted you to be alone with Kelsey, you pull this."

He went to stand behind her, but he didn't try to touch her. "She's my daughter. The club is my family. She was going to meet them, Jen."

"It's not that she met them. It's that you went behind my back." She turned to face him, and he saw not anger but sorrow in her eyes. "Don't you get it, Maverick? You knew I'd have concerns, and rather than be straight with me, rather than hear what I was worried about and work it out with me, you went around me and figured you could talk your way out of it later."

She was right. Completely. "I'm sorry. I...don't know why I didn't tell you. I guess it's a habit."

Her huffing laugh was so bitter now, it stung. "That's not better." She turned back to the window. "You know Rad threatened me?"

"What?"

"A couple days before you were released. He and Gunner and another Bull I didn't know, they came to the bar and threw a fat envelope full of cash at me, trying to pay me off to let you back in. When I wouldn't take it, Rad told me I didn't have a choice, that you were going to be in Kelsey's life, and the club would do whatever it had to do to make it happen. They were trying with money, but if that didn't work, they didn't have to be so nice."

His fists curled at his sides. He'd killed his fourth man the night before, the first kill that didn't weigh on his conscience at all. He'd kill anybody who hurt Jenny. Stranger, brother, it didn't matter. "I didn't know."

"I would have told you, if you'd told me your plan for the day."

He took hold of her arm and tugged, only lightly, without force. She turned around and crossed her arms.

"You're right. I fucked up. Jen — don't back away from me. I need to learn how to do this right, and I'm still just figuring out how to be *free* again. But I want to be better. You say I do what I want, well I want that. I want to be right for you and Kelsey. Give me time to figure this out."

She stared at him, and he let her read whatever she could in him. At last, she sighed and uncrossed her arms. "Last night—that was...that was intense, and I was shaken up. I wasn't thinking clearly. We do need to go slow. I need to be sure that shit like this is *over* before we make any changes. If we make any at all."

"What if you're pregnant? I came inside you last night."

Her eyes closed as she took in another deep breath. He could sense her search for calm. "Well, that was a mistake, wasn't it?"

The bleakness of her voice chilled him. "Don't tell me you'd—"

"I won't. But that doesn't mean we'll be together." Her head dropped for a second. When it came up, her expression had smoothed, though the turmoil between them still lurked in her eyes. "I need to get home. Is she in her room?"

The room he'd made for his daughter. Kelsey had squealed and clapped and danced when she'd first seen it. Now she was snuggled up with her Sinclair dinosaur, under the canopy like a princess.

He nodded, and she stepped away, toward the hall. Maverick grabbed her hand before she got too far. "Jenny, wait." She stopped but didn't turn back to him. "I need you. I love you."

They stood like that, joined only by their hands, their arms spanning the distance between them. The silence of the home he'd found for his family seemed to roar.

"That's one," she whispered and pulled her hand free of his.

~oOo~

Later, Maverick stormed into the clubhouse, pushing past neighbors and friends of the Bulls, here partying with the club on a Saturday night. Rad stood near the pool table, leaning on a support beam, holding a bottle of Rolling Rock by the neck. He was talking to Curtis, a longtime club hangaround.

Ignoring everyone he passed, Maverick strode straight to Rad and grabbed him by the neck of his kutte. When the SAA turned awkwardly, pulled off balance, Maverick punched him in the face, catching his cheekbone and feeling the full force of the impact all through his ringless hand. Rad's head rocked back, and his beer went flying. The people around them made way.

"What the fuck?"

"You *threatened* her?" He swung again, but Rad blocked the blow. When he followed the block with a cross, Maverick ducked and charged, slamming his shoulder into Rad's chest. They landed on the floor together.

Maverick was a few inches taller than Rad, but he was leaner, lighter by maybe fifteen pounds. So he took his advantage while he had it, settling his left arm across Rad's throat and slamming right jabs into his head as fast as he could, paying no regard to the protest of his knuckles, which were already sore from taking down Jenny's attackers the night before.

Then Rad got his arms up, and he flipped them. He got three good, solid hits to Maverick's face before Ox loomed over them and pulled Rad off.

Gunner grabbed Maverick's arm, helping him to his feet. Still burning with fury and violence, he shoved his friend off. Gunner had been at the bar, too.

"Easy, brother. What the fuck?"

"He threatened Jenny. I want his goddamn head."

"I wasn't gonna hurt her, fuckwit. I was tryin' to *scare* her." Rad spat blood onto the floor. "For *you*. She was keepin' your kid away from you."

Maverick lunged, but Gunner held him back. "I was there, Mav. It's like he said."

Maverick twisted his arm free and punched his friend in the stomach. Then he went for Rad again, but this time it was Simon diving in his way, slamming him to the floor.

"GODDAMMIT!" Delaney's voice roared over the commotion. "MAVERICK. RAD. CHAPEL. RIGHT THE HELL NOW!"

~oOo~

Delaney, Dane, Maverick, and Rad all sat in their usual seats at the table. With no one else in the room, the configuration made Maverick feel like he was sitting in court: Delaney, Dane, and Rad, the top of the food chain, clustered at the top of the table. Maverick a fair distance away on the side.

"Somebody explain to me what the fuck just went down," the president snarled.

Rad crossed his arms and glared down the table. "You'd have to ask Mav."

Focused with glowering satisfaction on Rad's swelling face, Mav said, "He threatened to hurt Jenny. I will kill anyone who does."

"You're talking about the visit to Jenny before you got out."

Delaney hadn't phrased it like a question, but Maverick nodded his answer anyway.

"That was me, Mav. Rad was on assignment. With Gun and Apollo. I wanted you to have your little girl. We all did. The whole club went in on that payoff. What Jenny did—that wasn't right."

Maverick slammed his throbbing fist on the table. "You think you made it *better* for me? You think the Bulls trying to intimidate her made things *easier* between us?"

"You got your little girl, don't you?" Rad asked. "I heard you had her here today."

"Not because you threatened to hurt her, asshole."

Rad's eyes narrowed, but he didn't respond.

Delaney leaned forward. "Maverick. This isn't on Rad. He did what I sent him to do. Nobody here was ever gonna hurt the mother of your child, and deep down, you know it."

Yes, he knew no Bull would hurt a woman, certainly not a member's woman. "Jenny didn't know it. I can't get my family back together if she's afraid of the club."

"Then it was a mistake, going to talk to her, and I'm sorry."

Maverick stared at the table and didn't answer. As he cooled down, he understood that all this he'd just caused, his anger at the club, it was all misplaced. He'd done far more damage to his relationship than any of his brothers would do, and he'd never laid an angry finger on her.

"Maverick," Delaney pressed. "We good here?"

"Yeah." He looked up and met the president's gaze. "Yeah."

Delaney turned to Rad. "You need to balance anything out?"

Rad had taken quite a bit of damage in Maverick's storm. He stared long and hard down the table. Then he shook his head. "Nah. We're good."

~oOo~

"Jesus Christ, Maverick. No."

Jenny began to push the door closed. Maverick wanted to shove himself against it, prevent her from shutting him out, but he held back, locking his arms at his sides, and only said, "Jenny, please."

She stopped. For three seconds—Maverick counted them off in his head—the door was ajar by a couple of inches. Then the porch light flipped on, the door opened again, and she stepped onto the threshold. It was late, and though the lights glowed through the windows, indicating that she hadn't turned in for the night, she was dressed for bed, in pajama bottoms and a little thin-strapped top. He used to know what she called those things. She'd pulled a zip-up hoodie on as she'd answered the door, and she had it wrapped around herself, crossing her arms over it.

"You've been fighting."

"I kicked Rad's ass. I'll never let anybody hurt you, Jen. Not even threaten to. Whoever it is. Whatever happens with us, that's always gonna be true."

He saw her soften, let her guard down a little. "Why are you here?"

"I don't know. Because ... because I feel ... rootless... anywhere else?" It was a mistake, though. He was pushing again, trying to make her give him something she wasn't ready to give. "It was a mistake. I'll go. I love you."

He turned and slumped down the sidewalk toward his bike.

"Mav, wait." Her voice was closer than he'd expected; he turned, and she was coming toward him. She'd left the door open. He stood still and let her come. When she got there, she looked up at him silently, her arms still crossed over her belly. They were beyond the glow of the porch light, but the streetlights and moon made enough illumination that he could see her face clearly, tinted with the blue gleam of night.

"That's two," she said.

His heart stopped. "Jenny?"

"You have to figure out what you need to figure out to stop pulling bullshit like today. You have to stop stalking and lurking, too. Use the fucking phone."

"Yeah. Okay. Understood." He'd agree to just about anything at this point, and she was only asking him to stop being an asshole.

She squinted at him. "Honestly? You hear me?"

He reached out, and she didn't flinch away. Grasping her arms, he said, "I hear you. How I've been fucking up—I see it, Jen. I do. You're different, and I see that, too. It was happening even before I went away. I loved it then, seeing you get strong, and I love it now. I don't need you to give in to me. I just need to break the habit of expecting you to. And I will."

"That's...that's a good answer."

"It's the truth."

When she hooked her fingers into the waistband of his jeans, his breath caught. "You can't stay all night. But you can come to bed with me for a while, if you want."

"Jenny. Are you sure?"

"I'm not sure of anything between us but one thing: I love you."

"That's one." He pulled her hand from his jeans and drew her into his arms.

~oOo~

Except for the television, playing at a volume low as a whisper, and the muffled hum and beep of her father's medical machinery, the house was quiet. Jenny led him down the hall, past the closed door of her father's room, the closed door of their daughter's room, into her own, where a small lamp on her dresser offered a soft, incandescent glow. After she closed the door, he heard the *snick* of the knob lock being turned.

Without a word or a pause, she pulled off her hoodie, then her top, tossing them to the floor. She shimmied out of her bottoms and stood there perfectly naked, and he stood there like an idiot, fully clothed and...well, fuck. He was afraid. Afraid to do something to break the spell. Afraid of fucking up yet again, blowing yet another chance she was giving him.

He wanted to fuck her properly, to make love with her. She stood before him naked and ready, and he was afraid to move.

"Mav?"

"You're beautiful."

She truly was. There was no sign on her body that he could see of her pregnancy. He remembered the thick, rich-smelling cream she'd rubbed on her belly and tits, and that he'd rubbed on her as well, every day throughout most of those months. It must have worked, because she was smooth and firm and perfect.

Her dark hair had gotten so long, too. She'd always kept it just past shoulder length, but now it grazed the middle of her back and covered her tits.

Finally, whatever had held him paralyzed gave way, and he reached out to lift a curl from her chest and push it back over her shoulder, so he could see his ink. A heart on fire, his name on a banner across it. He'd seen it last night, too, but he'd been too overcome to speak about it.

He brushed his thumb over the piece, tucked in the angle between her collarbone and her shoulder. "You didn't cover this up or get it removed."

She shook her head.

She'd been his all this time. "Thank you."

"Mav." She grabbed the placket of his kutte and gave it a tug, and he began to undress himself. Jenny watched him, a mysterious hint of a smile dancing on her lips, but she didn't help. She simply waited until he was as bare as she was.

He felt barer, in fact. The balance of power had shifted between them, and Maverick was more than a little disoriented.

Jenny seemed to feel the change, too. Still wearing that odd little smile, she pushed on his chest. He walked backward until his legs hit her bed, and he sat.

Standing over him, she combed her fingers through his hair. There wasn't much growth yet, just enough that he could feel the strands move against her fingers. He set his hands on her hips and closed his eyes, letting himself feel her touch. Giving himself over to her, letting her lead. Not *letting* her. Simply following.

"You're beautiful, too." Her hands smoothed over his shoulders, down his arms, until they were on his hands at her hips. She lifted them and stepped inward, straddling his legs. "You can't come inside me. Last night, we shouldn't have done that. I need to trust that you won't. Unless you have a condom."

He shook his head. "I'll pull out. I promise. But go slow, babe. I'm still out of practice, and I want to make you come this time. I want to be inside you when you do."

She sat on him, drawing her legs up so they were around his waist. Remembering this position, he clasped her hips and lifted her, and she took hold of his cock and positioned it so that he could set her down on it. Her slick heat enveloped him, and his cock surged.

Groaning, he clamped his arms around her and held her in place. "Fuck, don't move. Don't move." Burying his head against her neck, in her hair, he held on and breathed deeply until he could master his body.

He felt her hands at his face; she lifted his head and smiled that smile at him. Leaning close, she kissed him lightly, nipping at his lips, nuzzling his stubbly cheek, pressing her mouth to the damaged ear she didn't yet know was mostly deaf. It was deaf, but it wasn't numb. As she sucked on his lobe, her hips began to flex, picking up a steady and leisurely rhythm.

Maverick took deep, measured breaths, allowing himself to feel her but not to be so consumed by it that he lost control. Since his release, he'd had to learn to control a body that had been entirely subject to outside control for years. Sleeping, eating, moving—all on somebody else's time. At somebody else's whim.

He shoved that thought away and slammed the door on it. No. Not here, not now. Absolutely not.

"Hey," she murmured, coming back to his mouth and running the tip of her tongue over his bottom lip. "You okay?"

Feeling the sudden tension that had shot through his body, he loosened up and cupped her face in his hands so he could deepen their kiss.

When he pulled back, he said, "I'm perfect. I need to suck your tits, though."

Her smile grew broad and bright, and she arched backward, using his shoulders to keep herself steady. He wrapped his arms around her waist and bent forward. As soon as he drew a nipple into his mouth, she moaned and picked up the tempo of her hips.

He sucked, and she flexed, moving with increasing gusto as he worshipped her tits, shifting back and forth between them, favoring neither over the other. Her taste was perfect, like her scent—clean and fresh and just as it had always been. Need pooled and swelled at the base of his cock, waiting, tautening his body, but he held on, devoting his attention to her.

He heard his own grunts, muffled against her skin, mingling with her moans and gasps and whimpers. Her hair swung back and forth, caressing his arms with its cool silk. He groaned and reared back, sliding his hands up to take hold of her head and draw her mouth to his.

He couldn't let her control their movements any longer, or he would blow, and he wasn't sure he'd be able to disentangle himself from her in time to pull out. Before it was too late, he stood up and turned, dropping her to the bed. He meant to keep their connection and lie on her, but she surprised him, pulling back so that he fell out of her. She rolled and came up on her hands and knees, canting her ass up high.

Maybe she was offering her ass, but he wouldn't take it. Instead, he grabbed her hips and sank back where he belonged. She cried out as he hit home, and her hips began to go again, drawing him deep, controlling their pace. But now he had some control as well, and the slow, sensual love they'd been making shifted gears and became something wilder.

He wanted her to come. He needed to feel it, to have that again. Fighting his own need, his body's riotous demand to finish, Maverick gritted his teeth and fucked his woman until she was grunting and moaning and gasping out lusty pleas and prayers. She dropped her chest to the bed and let him have his way, and he slammed into her again and again.

Come, come, come, come! The word was a strained chant in his head. Shit, he wasn't going to be able to hold off, especially since he had to pull out. Just as he thought he was out of time, her hands clenched fistfuls of her bedspread, and she let loose a feral, muffled scream into the mattress. Her body clamped around his, pulsing, and he could not hold back even one more second. But he didn't have to.

"Thank fuck!" he grunted, trying not to be too loud and wake Kelsey, and pulled free. One pump of his fist, and he let loose all over her ass and back, still grunting, this time just an unformed burst of sound rasping up his throat.

Jenny sank limply to the bed, and Maverick fell forward, barely managing to catch himself on his arms. Pulling himself together as quickly as he could, he pushed back to his shaky legs and found his t-shirt in a wad on the floor. He used it to wipe her clean.

Then he stood there, his jizz-soaked shirt dangling from his fist. She didn't want him to stay. Should he just leave? Now? Is that what she wanted? Nothing but a fuck? Still sweaty and panting, Maverick felt his heart sink at the thought.

But then, Jenny lifted her head and reached out to him. "Hey."

He dropped his shirt and went back to the bed, stretching out at her side. She settled at once against him, hooking her leg over his and nestling her head on his chest. He held her, as tightly as he could without hurting her, and kissed her head.

"You can't stay," she sighed. Sleep had already thickened her voice, and Maverick smiled. She always fell asleep after she came.

"I know. I won't. But I just used my t-shirt to clean jizz off your back. Didn't think that one through."

She chuckled and kissed his nipple. "Bottom drawer of the dresser."

"Yeah?"

"Mmm-hmm. Mav?"

"Yeah, babe?"

"I love you."

He kissed her head again, lingering in the scent of her shampoo. "That's two."

~oOo~

For as long as he thought he could, until nearly dawn, he stayed in bed and held Jenny as she slept. He never wanted to leave. But he knew why he couldn't stay, and he had to build her trust in him. So as the sky began to lighten, he eased himself away from the woman he loved. She sighed and drew his pillow into her arms, but she didn't wake.

He took a moment and watched her, her naked body sleek and perfect, her lovely face calm in her rest. Then, full of bittersweetness, a contented disappointment, he pulled on his jeans, socks, and boots. He opened her dresser drawer, and found it full of his old shirts. His Bulls shirts. All of them—t-shirts and hoodies alike. He pulled the top t-shirt out. It was a favorite, the cotton soft and worn, the bull image faded. Pulling it over his chest, he felt Jenny's love in it. A dumb thought. Sappy. Didn't matter. She'd kept his Bulls shirts. She'd kept his flame. She'd never given up on him, not completely.

On his way out of the house, he stopped at Kelsey's room and eased open the door. His little girl slept in the ball she clearly favored for sleeping. Dino was tucked under her chin.

He glanced around her room. The furniture was mismatched, and the dated décor from when the room had been Jenny's was still apparent in the wallpaper and curtains, but Kelsey's flower glowed its pink glow, and the space, even in near dark, burst with color and personality.

He remembered the weeks right before he'd been arrested, when Jenny had been big with their child, and they'd been preparing to bring a little girl into their lives. He'd often imagined exactly this, watching his daughter sleep, tucked into her own bed, loved and warm and safe.

Never in his life had he been happier. His own family. For the first time in his life. He'd meant to do it right.

Recalling that old happiness, Maverick sneaked out of the house his woman and child lived in, determined to have it back and make it true. To do it right.

June 1993

Maverick came into the apartment and hung up his kutte and kicked off his boots. "Jen?"

"In here!" she called, and he followed her voice to their second bedroom. She was sitting on the floor, reading some kind of booklet. Her legs were stretched out wide, and her big belly sat between them.

"Whatcha doing?"

"I think I should have asked you that question a couple of weeks ago." She pointed at a stack of large boxes against the far wall. The top one was open but not unpacked. "You bought a crib. Among other things."

"Oh. Right."

"'Oh, right'? Really? Shouldn't we have picked this out together?"

As her pregnancy advanced, she was getting crabby and combative. Especially during the past couple of weeks, after he'd convinced her to quit her waitress job at The Roost early and give her swelling ankles a rest. But now she was bored, as well as crabby and combative. Their daughter could not get here soon enough. She was due in eight weeks, but it'd be okay with him if she popped out a week or two early.

He sat down before her. "I know. But it was the perfect crib, and the store was having a sale."

"You went to the baby store without me. I wanted to pick out her crib together."

It was his shameful little secret: since Jenny had been pregnant, he'd spent some time wandering around the baby store by himself. Since they'd known she was making a little girl, he'd been there probably once a week. He liked it there. It made him happy to think of things he'd give his child. He liked imagining being her father and making a home for her like he'd never had himself. But he didn't want to confess to being so sappy, so he only shrugged and said, "Sorry."

She closed the booklet—it was the assembly instructions, the cover showing a color photo of the crib he'd bought. "Mav, it's round."

"Yeah, I know. It's different. Cool, right?"

"It has a canopy. And an angel carved into it. With gold wings and a halo."

"You don't like it."

He'd seen it set up in the store, part of a display like a baby's room, all done up with wallpaper and a fake window, and a rocker and bookcase with toys and books. It was different from all the other cribs, and it had just seemed…worthy. He could imagine her sleeping in all that pretty pinkness, opening her little eyes every morning and knowing how special she was, and he could imagine checking in on her every night before he went to bed and seeing her sleeping peacefully, wrapped up like the gift she was.

Even on sale, it had been expensive, but who the fuck cared. He couldn't think of anything better to spend money on than his little girl.

He'd bought out the display—rocker, bookcase, changing table, dresser, linens. And round crib with canopy. The big square box in the corner was probably the rocker. The rest, he'd have to build.

"It's just—I don't know. I feel like it's a bit *much*, maybe?"

He scooted closer, between her spread legs, and picked up her hands. "Our daughter deserves the best. Right? She's going to want for nothing and have a perfect life, and so is her mom. I'm going to make sure my girls have everything. Always. And that will be my perfect life."

Jenny smiled at him. "Okay. A *Lifestyles of the Rich and Famous* crib for our little pixie."

CHAPTER FOURTEEN

Jenny opened the cabinet under the bathroom sink and reached awkwardly over the door from her perch on the toilet. She blindly snagged her box of tampons and knew as soon as she lifted it that it was empty. Dammit. Well, she couldn't blame anyone but herself; she was the only one in the house who used them.

She got down on her knees on the fuzzy bathroom mat and dug back for her emergency stash of maxi-pads. Ugh, she hated feeling that wad between her legs, but it was better than the alternative. She'd have to run by the market first thing.

Once she had her 'feminine hygiene' in order, as she washed her hands and finished her morning routine, Jenny let herself consider her feelings about getting her period. Relief, first of all. She'd been nuts to let Maverick come inside her that night at the bar. She'd been running on adrenaline and hero worship, and she hadn't cared about anything but what the most tender part of her heart wanted—the part that still thought of the life she'd planned with Maverick all those years ago as the life she was 'supposed to have.'

But that was crap, and her brain knew it. No one was 'supposed to have' anything. Life happened. You dealt with what happened or you didn't. For all the plans people made, nobody had any real control over anything, because nobody could control everything.

She was coming to understand that the best chance for making a life with Maverick was if they both stopped thinking they could undo the past and started thinking about how they would do the present. What had been couldn't be reclaimed. They needed to figure out what was, and what would be.

So she was relieved that their heady mistake on the floor of The Wayside had not resulted in a pregnancy. They needed no new complications between them. They already had plenty.

But she was disappointed, too, and it did her no good to deny it. If they'd been living the life they'd been planning, Kelsey would likely already have had a sibling, maybe two, by now. Jenny wanted a big family, and so did Maverick. Her biological clock had been jangling at her for a couple of years now, her nesting impulse growing stronger as Kelsey grew older, and she'd always kicked it away, knowing it was hopeless to even think about more kids when she was alone and always would be. Now, though, Maverick was back, and there was hope.

So she was disappointed that there wasn't a baby coming, and that she hadn't gotten recklessly pregnant and forced the two of them to reckon with their relationship.

Which was sick and stupid. If they needed something like that to deal with their mess, then maybe that mess wasn't worth dealing with.

No—not true. Over the past couple of weeks, since that night at the bar, things between them had been good. He respected her need to go slow. She could see him thinking about the way he spoke to her, and managing his impulse to control everything.

They'd had sex one more time since she'd brought him into her bed, and it had again been beautiful. So much about them was good—had been good before and was good now—that if they could fix the things that were broken, it was worth the effort. There was a good life for them in the future, if they both worked for it.

Maverick wasn't the only one who needed to change. Jenny recognized that she had a hair trigger now and saw him striving to take over even when he was only expressing a different opinion. She'd gone from giving in all the time when they'd been together to making all of the decisions while he'd been away, and Maverick, poor guy, had gotten caught in the middle. Since he'd once controlled her, and he'd still tried, she jumped on him too quickly when he pushed at all.

To his credit, he swallowed his frustration with that. He was trying to be the man she needed. She and Kelsey.

The first problem they needed to sort out was whether each of them was, in fact, the person the other truly needed, or whether they were just stuck in the past.

Today would be a test of that. She was taking Kelsey to the Bulls' clubhouse that afternoon for a family-friendly party. She hadn't seen any of the old ladies since a few weeks after Kelsey was born, when Mo had descended on the house and tried to force her 'help' on her. That confrontation had not gone well, and she couldn't shake the feeling that she was willingly going into enemy territory.

But the club was Maverick's family, and he was in with them much deeper than normal family ties went. There was no Maverick in her life without the Brazen Bulls. That was even more true now than it had been before. If she couldn't get right with them, she couldn't get right with him.

So it was just awesome that she'd started her period, too. Yippee.

~oOo~

When she'd gone to the Sinclair station just before Kelsey's birthday, the Bulls she'd seen had approached her with open hostility, walking toward her like a united front. When she led her daughter up the front walk to the Bulls clubhouse on this day, Eight Ball stood just outside the door, talking with someone she didn't know, someone not wearing a kutte, so a hangaround or just a neighbor; the Bulls had always been friendly with most of their neighbors.

Eight Ball saw her and grinned. Jenny didn't like him—he was ninety-percent asshole and treated women like sex dolls with a pulse, if they were hot enough, like servants, if they weren't, or like nuns, if they were off limits.

He'd glared at her the night he'd come to the bar with Rad to help deal with her attackers. Now, he stepped away from the man he'd been talking to and came toward her. "Hi, Jenny." He turned his smile down to Kelsey, "And hello, pretty lady."

Apparently, she had regained nun status in his eyes. "Hi, Eight. This is Kelsey."

He crouched before them. "I know. We met the other day, didn't we?" He held out his hand, palm up, and Kelsey slapped it.

It still bugged her—a lot—that Maverick had brought Kelsey to the clubhouse without telling her first. She wasn't sure she'd expected him to have asked permission, exactly (okay, yes, that would have been her preference), but she absolutely expected that they would have talked about it first. He knew how she felt about this place. Yes, she'd have to come to terms with the Bulls whether she and Maverick worked out or not, because this was who he was, and she wasn't going to keep his daughter away from him. But it had been deeply shitty of him to bring Kelsey here behind her back.

Finding out that Kelsey had met Eight, and seemed to like him, dug at Jenny more than she'd admit.

He stood up, still grinning. "Mav's out back. He's in the ring with Gunner, so…" he tilted his head toward Kelsey, and Jenny understood. Maverick was fighting. Recreationally. She didn't need his daughter to see him like that.

"We'll go in the clubhouse, then."

Sweeping his arm in a *be my guest* gesture, Eight Ball stepped out of the way. "The ladies are in there. Mo's runnin' the show, like always."

Mo liked Jenny no more than Jenny liked Eight Ball, and that woman could be perfectly nice and still cut an enemy down to a nub. And nobody was more of an enemy than a woman who'd hurt one of her boys.

Jenny stiffened her spine and locked her smile into place. "Okay. C'mon, Kelsey. I think there are some people still for you to meet."

Sad to say, she hoped Kelsey would be a shield. How scary could Maureen Delaney be when Jenny had an adorable four-year-old standing at her side?

~oOo~

Every concern Jenny had about Mo flew straight out of her mind when she came into the party room and looked at the bar.

There weren't many people around. A few sweetbutts tottering about in their ridiculous shoes, obviously doing Mo's bidding. A smattering of hangarounds or neighbors—three teenagers playing on the pornographic pinball machine, a young couple—the guy not wearing colors—standing at the jukebox, a scattered few people watching a Cardinals game on the big television. The weather was good, and there would likely be meat grilling, so most people were probably outside.

Jenny saw all the people in the party room at a glance. When her eyes made it to the bar, she froze. Three women sat in a row, sipping drinks, and she knew them all. None of them was Mo.

Joanna, Dane's old lady. Maddie, Ox's.

And Willa.

Willa. The nurse who'd helped her deliver Kelsey.

Jenny would never, ever forget her. Even in jeans and a t-shirt, even sitting in profile, even sitting at the end of the bar in the Brazen Bulls' party room, the woman was as perfectly familiar as if she'd been her own flesh and blood.

"Willa?"

Willa turned and smiled—not an expression of recognition but of acknowledgement. "Yes? Hi?"

Of course she wouldn't remember Jenny. Willa probably helped deliver dozens of babies a week, and Kelsey had been born four years ago. That was a lot of babies, and a lot of moms. Jenny had had only one. One baby. One nurse. One life changed.

She strode up to the bar so quickly that she could feel Kelsey trying to keep up. She held out her hand. "I know you don't remember me, but I love you."

Willa laughed and shook her hand. Joanna and Maddie laughed, too, but Jenny had no attention for them. "Okay? Wow." Her eyes then drifted down, and her smile warmed and grew with understanding. "Hi, honey." She met

Jenny's adoring gaze again. "Did I maybe meet this little sweetheart early on?"

It occurred to Jenny that Willa had likely made a lasting impression on more women than she alone, and she was a little crestfallen at that. It seemed too important a bond to be shared. "Yes. Yes. I was alone when she came, and I was pretty much losing my mind. You stayed with me, and you got me through. You stayed even after your shift was over, and you were back checking on me the next day. You took her first picture and you…" Jenny was going to cry. "You just…you…" Yep, she was totally crying. "Everything was falling apart around me, and I didn't think I could do it, but you helped me see that I could." She finally released Willa's hand, and she bent down and picked up her daughter. "I'm Jenny. This is Kelsey. Kelsey Marie."

At that, Willa's eyes widened. She remembered. "I do remember. Oh my God. Well, hi!" She held out her arms, and Jenny brought her daughter into them and held on.

Kelsey squirmed uncomfortably. "Mommy, why are you sad?"

Jenny stepped back and gave her a comforting squeeze. "I'm not, pixie. I'm just so happy it's leaking out of my eyes. Miss Willa here helped me have you. She was with me when you came out of my belly. She's a very special lady." To Willa, she said, "I'm sorry I'm blubbering. I just…I'm surprised."

"So am I. How'd you find me here, of all places?"

"I don't think she was looking for you, Will," Maddie answered, casting one artfully shaped eyebrow high and giving them both a droll look. "Jenny is Mav's old lady. This is who we've been talkin' about."

More than wonder regarding what they'd been talking about, Jenny felt shock that Willa apparently belonged here. If she was sitting with Joanna and Maddie like this, talking like this, in the clubhouse, then she, too, was an old lady. These women observed the club hierarchy like it was a religion, and they were devout. "Wait—are *you* an old lady?"

Willa smiled. "Yeah. I'm with Rad. For about two and a half years now."

"*Rad?*"

All three women facing her, even Willa, laughed hard at that. But Jenny was truly stunned. She could not picture her hero, this pretty, sweet blonde, with that gruff, short-tempered jerk. The old lady she'd known—Dahlia—had been more his style. She'd been loud and dramatic, all big tits and dyed red hair. Brassy with a streak of mean. Jenny had been around for a few of their blowouts. The amused way the Bulls watched the show had been one of the things she thought shitty about the whole club. Other people's problems should not be entertainment.

"Yeah, Rad. He's softer than he looks."

Jenny didn't bother to point out that she'd actually known the man, a little, and no, he was not softer. But maybe Willa had softened him. She could see that. So she smiled and gave her head a conceding little wiggle. "I heard he had a kid—so that must be yours?"

"Yep. Zach. He's a year and a half. He's out back with his dad. Mav's back there, too." She slid off her stool. "Come on. I'll take you back."

"Hold on, love," Mo had emerged from somewhere. Probably the kitchen. "Mav's in the ring."

"Right. That's a problem?" Willa turned back to Jenny to ask the question.

"Not for me. Not really, but..." She indicated Kelsey, still in her arms.

"Right," Willa repeated, this time with a true air of understanding.

"I'll go get Leah," Joanna offered. "She can take care of Kelsey."

"Wait!" Jenny's head was spinning. She'd been afraid to think too hard about what to expect of seeing the old ladies again, afraid that they'd all hate her, but even the thoughts she'd allowed herself had not remotely gone like this. Willa was a Bulls old lady. It didn't even matter how Mo or Joanna or Maddie felt, or who this Leah person was, because Willa was in her corner. She had been before, and she would be now.

But Kelsey still didn't know any of these people. "Kelsey. All these nice ladies are family, just like Eight Ball and all your other uncles. This isn't *Miss* Willa, she's *Aunt* Willa. And this is Aunt Joanna, and Aunt Maddie, and...Aunt—"

"Zach calls me Grammo. I like it." Mo's voice rested on a filament between hostile and welcoming, like the edge of a storm front.

Asking her daughter to call Mo Delaney 'Grammo' was a far bridge indeed. Then again, she hadn't thought twice about Kelsey calling her father Granddaddy, and he was a crap human being. At least Mo was loyal to the people she loved, and loved them fiercely.

"What do you think about having a Grammo, pix?"

Kelsey screwed up her face. "Is that like a Grandma?"

"Yep."

"I don't have a Grandma." She turned to Mo. "Are you nice?"

Mo smiled, warm and sweet as fresh-baked cookies. "I believe I am, love. Are you?"

"I believe I am, too," Kelsey echoed. "Do you want to be my Grammo?"

Mo came forward and held out her hand. Jenny wasn't sure, but she thought her eyes sparkled a bit more than normal. "I think I'd like that very much, yes. Would you like it?"

Kelsey put her hand in Mo's. "Yes, please. Maisie has a grandma and a grandpa, and they're nice and make me grilled cheeses and pickles. I have a granddaddy, but he only sits and watches television. Do you make grilled cheeses?"

"I do, in fact. I make other things, too. Do you like brownies? I made brownies today."

"Uh huh. I like brownies and cookies and cake and ice cream and pudding and cookies. I don't like pie 'cuz it falls out."

Mo tossed a question in a glance at Jenny. Understanding, and grateful for the sort-of ask, she nodded, and Mo held out her other hand. "Well, then, let's get you a brownie. And some milk."

Kelsey went to her without hesitation. Jenny watched Mo carry her daughter toward the kitchen, chatting sweetly with her. She'd never seen Mo in grandmother mode; it was a side of her she liked. Maybe being part of the Bulls wouldn't be so hard after all.

Willa put her hand on Jenny's arm. "C'mon. I'll go back with you. Maybe Mav and Gun are done beating each other up by now."

"Was this a fun thing, or a work-out-their-beef thing?" It could also have been a Gun-needs-to-feel-bad thing, but Jenny didn't know if that was still a thing or, if it was, how much Willa knew about it.

"Just for fun." Willa laughed. "Because what's more fun than getting punched in the face?"

Jenny laughed, too. Their men were not like other men.

~oOo~

Leah was Gunner's old lady. *Gunner.* That train wreck of a human had an old lady. Not old at all—young. By the look of her, maybe still a teenager. But she was wearing a pretty engagement ring, and Jenny could see her ink showing under the neckline of her top.

Gunner had an old lady. Rad had Willa, and a blond little boy he was carrying on his shoulders. Dane and Joanna's girls were in college now. More than merely the décor had changed in the clubhouse.

Leah and Rad stood almost side by side near the boxing ring in back. Zach, a toddler in tiny jeans and cowboy boots, cheered and yelled when his father did, like he knew what he was watching. Leah cheered, too. She seemed into it, watching Gunner and Maverick trade blows.

The guys were into it as well, and Jenny couldn't help but smile. She'd never enjoyed watching Maverick fight when he went out to the streets to meet up with shady men in shady places. The rules were slippery in those fights, and the men often beat each other until one simply couldn't get up anymore. That was hard to watch even though Maverick had usually been the one still standing. But she liked watching him fight here, with his brothers, when they weren't trying to really hurt each other. They sparred, but without pads, and they laughed and trash talked all through it and always hugged it out at the end.

That had been one of Delaney's rules, and it probably still held: when brothers fought each other, whether it was play or conflict resolution, they couldn't leave the ring until they'd hugged it out.

She liked watching fights like this because she didn't have to worry, and she could simply focus on her man's amazing body, every muscle tuned to perfection, as he moved about the ring, all grace and fluid motion. The big bull head on his back, still his only ink, twisted and snarled, glimmering in his wet skin.

If Maverick and Gunner had been in the ring since before she and Kelsey had arrived, then they'd been fighting at least fifteen, maybe twenty minutes—and they looked it. Both were soaked in sweat, their bodies red from blows and from exertion.

He hadn't seen her yet, so she waited for the right time, when a distraction wouldn't get him flattened, and called out, "Mav!"

He didn't seem to hear her, but Gunner did and ducked Maverick's next blow. He held out his taped fist, and Maverick turned. His grin at seeing her glowed brightly in his flushed face.

The men hugged, and they came together to the ropes. Maverick ducked through first.

"Hey, babe." He pulled her close, and she didn't resist his sweaty embrace. "You came."

"I told you I would," she murmured so only he could hear. He shifted and tucked his head on her other shoulder. "We'll leave before it gets rowdy, but this is...this is okay. Hey—I started my period this morning." She wanted to get that out right away, and this was a way to do it almost privately but without chance for a big talk.

He pulled back and stared into her eyes. She could see that he was disappointed, but he smiled again. "When we try again, it'll be the right time. Not a mistake."

She nodded and pressed her cheek to his damp chest. That was the best response she could have hoped for.

Willa had gone to Rad and their son when they'd come outside. Now Rad called out, "I hear you and Willa were friends already, Jenny."

Jenny sent him a sincere smile. She felt better about Rad now. Today, she might even be okay with Eight Ball. Maybe. "Yeah, I guess we were. You're a lucky man, Radical."

"Don't I know it."

"What?" Maverick cocked his head at her.

"Willa was working when I had Kelsey. She stayed with me and helped me have her. Seeing her here was...bizarre. And wonderful." There was more she wanted to say about that, but not here, and not now.

"We've never talked about her birth."

No, they hadn't, but Jenny guessed they would do so soon. Again, however—not here. "We will. You should put a shirt on now, though. Kelsey's inside with Mo, and she's been antsy to see you."

"I'm glad you didn't bring her out here. I don't know how to tell her about this." He nodded toward the ring. Big old Ox was climbing in, and a skinny young guy with short blond hair was taking off his kutte and t-shirt. Ox was older, in his mid or late forties, probably, but he was a massive brick wall of male flesh. That kid was going to get wadded up like tissue paper, even in a friendly spar—and Jenny could see that he knew it. He must have been a prospect, or a new patch, because he was being hazed.

"Go easy on him, Slick!" Simon yelled, laughing.

She turned back to Maverick. "Yeah…we'll have to figure that out. 'Daddy likes to punch people' isn't exactly in line with the lessons she's been learning about kindness and peace."

Maverick laughed—he was really happy, and Jenny caught his vibe. It was good to see him like this: the best of him. She felt good. Standing in the back yard of the Brazen Bulls clubhouse, a place where she'd never been comfortable, she felt happy and warm and welcome. That was weird. But good.

He gave her a smelly squeeze and changed the subject. "So, Kelsey's with Mo? That go okay?"

"It did. They worked it out that Kelsey would call her Grammo, like Zach does, and now they're in the kitchen having brownies and milk."

"That's great. See? She's not gonna hold a grudge with you, Jen."

Jenny wasn't yet so sure. She'd always been intimidated by Mo, even before, and Maverick knew it. He also knew that she'd had trepidation about meeting her again, and he thought he knew why. He thought it was because she'd pulled away and denied him Kelsey, the reason all the Bulls had been cold to her.

He didn't know about the last time she and Mo had been in the same room.

October 1993

Jenny didn't know how she could take any more. Kelsey screamed and screamed, right in her ear. She was dry, she'd been fed, she was warm, dressed in a soft sleeper. She wouldn't sleep, she wouldn't nurse, she didn't want the swing, she didn't want to lie down, she didn't want anything but to scream and scream, so hard and loud that she was getting hoarse.

The pediatrician had asked what her temperature was, and, when Jenny had reported that it was normal, he'd told her that sometimes babies just got upset and wanted to cry.

Her baby was upset, and she couldn't fix it. Because she was a terrible mother.

A terrible mother with a moderate migraine, threatening to get worse with every shriek. All she could do was hold her daughter and let her scream, doing laps around this house she hated, bouncing and trying to sing and be calm when what she wanted, what she *needed* to do was cry. Just as loud and long as her baby was. Just give in and wail.

Every time her frantic, exhausted path took her through the dining room, she glared at the papers on the table, the top and bottom thirds standing up from the folds.

Her father's medical insurance would no longer pay for his recuperative care. He'd hit his lifetime limit. There was another policy, she'd managed to discover in the forty-one minutes of sleep Kelsey had had in the past twenty hours, one for long-term care, but the monthly amount of funding was about, at best, a third of the cost of the private facilities her father's caseworker had called.

The last option was a public nursing home. But the Tulsa paper had run a big series of articles about the state of public homes in Oklahoma, and it was not good. Like Victorian England not good. They were understaffed, underfunded, and overcrowded. She bore little love for her father anymore, but she couldn't condemn him to a life of lying for hours in his own waste, with bedsores eating through to his bones. She was a better person than that. She was a better person than *him*.

There was the money that the Bulls brought to her at the bar, but it wasn't enough, and she didn't trust that it was reliable—and it was for her daughter, regardless. Jenny was determined to save every single cent of it so that Kelsey would have it when she was old enough to start her own life. She would never be trapped by circumstances.

The real last option, then, was the worst, and the only: her father was coming home. To live with her. Forever. She was trapped in this horrid house, with a new baby and an invalid father. She was trapped running his stupid, shitty bar, because it was the only job that would allow her to make her own hours and be there for Kelsey and keep this sad little existence running. Forever.

"Please, pixie. Please hush. Please, please, please, please." The books said to stay calm, that babies took cues from their mothers' moods, and getting upset only made an upset baby work up more, but Jenny just *couldn't* anymore. She dropped to the sofa and sobbed while Kelsey screamed on. And on. And on.

This wasn't how it was supposed to be. She was supposed to be with Maverick, living in a pretty house with a big yard, and he was supposed to be taking care of them. He'd promised her a great life for their daughter, and for her, and for him.

The doorbell rang. Jenny stared balefully at it and ignored it. Probably Child Welfare coming to take her baby away because *obviously* she had no idea what the hell she was doing.

It rang again. And again. Then there was pounding. Kelsey kept screaming.

"JENNY! Open up, love!"

Oh *God*. It was Mo. Could this day get any worse?

She hadn't seen Mo since the day of Maverick's sentencing, when he'd gone away for three whole years instead of the few months he'd promised. Mo had called—a lot—but Jenny had deleted every message and hung up on every call she'd had the misfortune to answer.

She wanted no part of the Bulls or anything that had to do with the man who'd left her in this state. Fuck them all. Every one of them.

"Jenny!" More pounding. "I know you're in there, love. Open up, or I'll shoot my way in."

That was no empty threat. Jenny heaved herself and her wailing infant up from the sofa and went to unlock the front door and let the Queen of the Bulls in.

"Well, mercy, what is the commotion in here?" Mo dropped her capacious handbag and reached for Kelsey. Jenny twisted away, but the look Mo gave her was so severe and intent that she found herself turning back and letting her take the baby.

And hating herself for the relief she felt. Even the couple of feet of distance between her ear and Kelsey's mouth was like a cool, soothing breeze. She rubbed at the bone under her right eyebrow, the place where her headache always seemed to dig in.

She was pretty glad, though, that her daughter had not immediately stopped crying when Mo had taken her. If that had happened, Jenny thought she might have just gone outside and lain down in the middle of the street.

"Go lie down, Jenny. Close your eyes for a bit. I'll take care of this little foghorn and give you a break."

Jenny shook her head. There was no chance in hell that she would leave Mo unattended with her daughter. She might wake up and find them both gone.

Mo considered her, disappointment sharp enough to be contempt creasing the space between her arched eyebrows. "Fine, then. At least brush your teeth and put some deodorant on. You stink."

Jenny had to pee anyway, so she turned and shuffled down the hall to the bathroom. She peed and washed her hands, and she was face to face with herself in the mirror. A ghoul looked back at her—matted hair, sagging skin, sunken eyes, and—the best part—stiff, round patches, about the size of softballs, on her shirt, over each boob. She'd been leaking most of the day. All Kelsey's crying and not eating had her boobs filled to bursting.

This was her day off—haha—but it was still nuts that she was walking around at three o'clock in the afternoon in her pajamas and bathrobe. She brushed her teeth, and her hair. She washed her face and put deodorant on. Then she went to her bedroom and pulled on a pair of clean sweatpants and a fresh t-shirt and nursing bra.

Suddenly, the crying stopped. The silence after hours and hours shocked her senses. She wouldn't have been surprised if her ears had popped.

After the initial relief of the sudden wash of peace, Jenny was overwhelmed by jealousy. What had Mo done that she hadn't been able to do? Mo wasn't even a mother! She stormed back up the hall and found Mo standing in the middle of the living room. Kelsey was cradled in her arms, but wrong way up, with her head lying on Mo's hand, her belly on her forearm, and her little legs straddled over her upper arm. Mo twisted back and forth, rocking.

Kelsey had fallen asleep.

"What are you doing?" The accusation Jenny had intended was lost in her whisper. "You're going to hurt her!"

Mo smiled. "This always worked for Clara. She was colicky, too. Drove Joanna nuts until she figured this out. A little pressure on her belly like this made her hurt less."

Jenny couldn't deal with the thought that Kelsey might have been in *pain* all this time. She'd read the book! It had said to watch for her pulling up her legs, but she hadn't done that. It wasn't pain!

Oh God, had her baby been in pain, and she'd done nothing?

Refusing to allow herself to cry in front of Mo, she changed the subject—but she didn't move to reclaim her daughter, who was sound asleep, her breath hitching from the lasting effects of her screams. "Why are you here?"

"You know why, love. Enough is enough. You can't cut us out. You need us, and this pretty lass is one of ours."

"No. She's *mine*."

"And Mav's."

"If Maverick wanted her, then he should be with us now."

"That's absurd, and you know it. He would be if he could be."

Jenny shook her head. He'd made a choice. He'd ignored her and done what he'd wanted, and she was paying the price for what he'd done. Even more, now, than she'd expected. In less than two weeks, when the month was out, she'd have her father on her back. Forever. Because of what Maverick had done.

Mo gazed down at Jenny's little girl for a long time, swinging her gently while she slept. Without looking up, she said, "Seems to me you could use the help, love. You're not doing such a top job on your own, now, are you?"

No, she was not. She was overwhelmed and terrified every minute of every day, whether she was pacing the house with a screaming child, or trying to run a fucking tavern with a baby strapped to her chest, or feeling guilty because she'd left her with the next-door neighbors. She was a shit mom, and she knew it.

But she did not want Maureen Delaney to say it. Worse yet, she was positively horrified at the thought of what Mo might do if she believed Jenny wasn't a good enough mother to raise the child of one of 'her boys.' Mo was one of those scary women who ran straight through and over any obstacle when she thought her cause was righteous.

Pain, fear, exhaustion, and failure boiled in Jenny's heart, and in the battle between fight or flight, or just up and faint, fight won. "And what would you know about it? You can't grow anything in that dried up old cave between your legs, so you have no idea what it takes to be a mother."

Holy shit—had she just said that? Oh no. Where the hell had that come from? That was the kind of thing her *father* might have said.

She'd hit her target, though. Mo's head flew up, and shock and rage surged red blood into her face. They stared at each other. Jenny was afraid to speak again—she couldn't bring herself to apologize, though it was warranted, and she was afraid anything else would make it worse—and Mo seemed too overcome with fury to move.

Jenny knew that Mo was childless not by choice, and not even because she was infertile, but because she couldn't carry a baby to term. She'd had several miscarriages and had been heartbroken every time. Jenny hadn't been around the Bulls when the miscarriages had happened, but it was common knowledge in the club, and Mo herself talked about them occasionally, when she was drunk enough. She was a maudlin drunk.

There was literally nothing meaner or more awful she could have said to this woman. She felt terrible—but also still angry and threatened. An apology was not going to happen. Maybe this bridge needed to be burned so that the Bulls would leave her the fuck alone.

At last, Mo moved. She shook her head like she was coming awake, and she bent to lay Kelsey down in her cradle—on her belly, which the books all said was wrong. She pulled the receiving blanket over her little shoulders, and the baby remained asleep.

Then Mo came straight at Jenny. Jenny held her ground, with effort, and when they were face to face, Mo hauled off and slapped her. Hard.

Mo stood where she was until Jenny had recovered enough from the blow to face her again. Her expression perfectly calm, but her voice trembling, she said, "You want to do this on your own, have at it. I'll not trouble you again."

She picked up her handbag and walked out the front door.

CHAPTER FIFTEEN

Maverick sat at the bar in the clubhouse and watched as the rest of the Bulls, who weren't benched on Russian business, filed in, followed by five members of the Night Horde MC from Missouri.

So much had changed while he'd been away. Not only were the Bulls deep in with the Volkov bratva from New York, beholden to the Russians for the bulk of their income, but they were instrumental allies of that organization, managing the western half of the country and supervising two other, smaller MCs who filled in or finished out runs to Mexico and Canada. Trafficking guns. In quantity.

The Bulls were big time outlaws now. He was having a hard time getting his head around that. In the abstract, it wasn't so much the outlaw work he had trouble with—or, at least, not the fact that it was outlaw. He wasn't nearly as concerned with laws as he was with ethics. The right thing was right because it was right, not because it was legal, and the wrong thing was wrong whether it was legal or not.

But they were playing with bad people now, and that skewed the question of right and wrong, turning black and white into nothing but grey. The Horde had come into Tulsa this afternoon with a box truck full of assault rifles and grenades. There was only one kind of people who bought weapons like that in quantity, and they weren't recreational game hunters. Working with people like that meant doing the things one had to do to survive in that world.

Like kill in cold blood. To settle somebody else's score. As he'd had to do inside. Maybe it was just that clouding up his head—being tasked to kill Lincoln Jennings, a guy he'd known in name only, because a woman he'd never met had wanted him to.

That and the price he'd paid, both in time and in retaliation.

While he mused, the Bulls and the Horde bellied up to the bar. Most of the work was done for the day, and everything had apparently gone to plan, so it was time to party. Maddie had seen to it that there were plenty of women around as party favors, and the Horde seemed eager to partake. They were young men, a couple of them huge—as big as or bigger than Ox.

Maverick tried to remember these guys' names; the Horde had been a friendly club for a long time, but there hadn't been all that much cooperation with them before. There was distance of about two hundred and fifty miles between them, so getting together had rarely been a casual thing. Before, they'd met up at rallies or on stopovers on other business. Delaney had thrown them a few jobs, but nothing like this partnership.

The two big guys...Maverick wanted to say that the dark-haired one was the president's kid. Little Ike, then, though there was nothing little about him, except his age. In his early twenties, mid at the most, Maverick guessed. He was wearing a VP patch already. Damn. And Little Ike's friend, who seemed about Maverick's own age. He couldn't remember his name. He was the only Horde not showing much interest in the sweetbutts, which indicated that he had an old lady and didn't take advantage of the run rule. Maverick respected that.

From his position on the figurative bench, Maverick wasn't really interested in any of it. The Russian shit made him uncomfortable for all sorts of reasons, so he was probably better off on the bench anyway. He sat on his stool and drank his whiskey. He gave the occasional friendly nod, but he didn't bother to make nice.

He was looking forward to getting out of the clubhouse and going to Jenny's.

She was close, he thought, to being ready. They'd spent the past few weeks taking things slowly, learning each other again, understanding what they needed. He was working on talking with her in ways that weren't so intent on getting her to see things his way, and she was working on not thinking every damn word out of his mouth was meant to argue. He'd forgiven her for cutting him out of Kelsey's life, and she'd forgiven him, he thought, for going away.

He would never be sorry he'd beaten her father, but he was sorry about all the ways it had hurt her.

Which was where they were stuck now: what to do with her father. The last obstacle, he thought, between him and his family. He could not live under the same roof as that bastard. Even in Earl's current state, Maverick knew he could not see that face every day and just deal with it.

Earl's insurance wouldn't cover a decent nursing home, and Jenny couldn't afford the balance. The money the club, and now he, had been giving her, she'd been saving for Kelsey's college. Maverick admired that, even as it frustrated him that his girls had been struggling. But he was damn glad she hadn't been using his money for Earl's care.

That was the sticking point: Maverick could afford to cover what the insurance wouldn't pay for a good private home. He'd asked Mo to do a little research, and she'd found a couple of places that looked decent. Not luxurious, but comfortable, with good care.

Even while he was benched, his cut of the Russian business was solid, and he was doing all the other work he could get his hands on. He was in financially good shape.

If Jenny and Kelsey lived with him, and they sold that shithole of a house, and maybe the bar, too, they could make Earl somebody else's problem without any negative impact on their own security.

But Maverick couldn't bring himself to pay for Earl's care. He couldn't get right with the thought of supporting that son of a bitch in any way. Probably the last block between him and the life he wanted, and he couldn't fucking do it.

He hadn't offered, and Jenny hadn't asked, but it was on his mind constantly.

"Mav!" Delaney's shout pulled him out of his reverie. "C'mon, brother, we're in church before we're all too wasted to think."

Maverick spun on his stool and considered his president. The meeting tonight was prep for the runs the next day—gun runs. Not his job.

"Prez?"

Delaney grinned. "You're off the bench, brother. We need you on Galveston. You good with that?"

Was he? Theoretically, he could say no. There'd be consequences, but nobody wanted a guy on work like that who wasn't all in.

Galveston. That meant Mexicans picking up the cargo at the port. The northern run was easier—just up to Nebraska, to relay with another club: the Great Plains Riders. It wasn't clear to him who in Canada wanted Russian steel, but the southern route left no room for pretending they weren't doing business with the worst kind of people.

Seemed to him that, in this business, the Bulls were sandwiched between the worst kind of people.

"Mav." Delaney wasn't asking. "Let's go."

"I'm on release, D. Can't leave the state."

Delaney simply stared, unmoved.

Facing the club president, Maverick felt the ground shudder under his feet. He wouldn't have his patch taken from him if he refused, but he teetered on the edge of a cliff nonetheless. If he said no, he made a choice beyond the work. His reasons for refusing would be about the club, and about his years inside, and about his life—the one he had, and the one he wanted. He was either in or he was out. Even if the club allowed him to lurk on the margins, he couldn't live like that.

Despite Jenny's discomfort with the Bulls—which seemed lately to be easing—Maverick needed the club. These men and their women were the first thing like a family he'd ever had. They weren't enough; he needed Jenny and Kelsey, a family that was only his, to have enough. But he needed the Bulls, too. He could only give his woman and child the life they deserved if he had the club. He could be the man he needed to be only if he had the tether of the club. That was simply true.

So he'd have to get right with the Russians and their customers. He'd have to get right with what Irina Volkov had had him do inside, and the price he'd paid.

And he'd have to hope with all he had that he didn't get caught up beyond state lines. Hope was still a precious commodity to him, hard to come by and painful to lose.

"Maverick."

Maverick finished his drink and stood up. "Yeah. Coming."

~oOo~

Galveston was a five-hundred-fifty mile ride from Tulsa. With the cargo they were protecting, they couldn't go over the speed limit, so it was a long slog. More than eight hours, almost nine with a quick pit stop.

But the weather on this mid-October day was fine—the sun bright and warm, the wind cool enough for the breeze in his face to keep him wakeful and feeling alive. He rode with his brothers around and near the truck, and the roar of big Harley engines filled the air. For the most of the ride, Maverick couldn't have cared less what was in that truck or how far behind him the Oklahoma state line was. He was doing one of the few things he truly loved—riding an open road, the wind filling his lungs, his bike in his hands and between his legs.

The only time he felt tense was just south of Dallas, when a couple of Texas state troopers came onto I-45 and kept pace with them for a good ten miles. You didn't want to fuck with those guys, or give them any reason at all to fuck with you. The two cruisers had obviously decided that bikers sporting colors were up to some kind of trouble; they were just waiting for their chance to pull them over. Maverick and the rest of the crew put on their best friendly-neighbor faces, and Wally, driving the truck, pegged his speed at a couple of miles per hour under limit.

Maverick, riding at the back, considered the situation and worked on keeping his heart quiet and steady. Normally, he'd trust everybody on this run to be cool: Rad and Ox were always solid as steel beams. Gunner, too—he could go badly haywire on his own, but when he had his brothers with him, he was chill. Wally, the prospect, Maverick still didn't know all that well, but he wasn't easily cowed by the patches, and that was a good sign.

But they had a Horde riding with them, too. Little Ike had asked for his club to get a place on these runs. He wanted to know the end point; he wanted to understand the work completely. For some ungodly reason, Delaney had agreed. So they had a kid riding with them, way too young to be wearing that VP patch. Maverick didn't know him at all, and he trusted him even less.

While those troopers rode along, Maverick kept his eyes on the back of the Horde VP and waited for that kid to do something stupid.

But he didn't. He kept his cool like the rest of them. After a while, the cops pulled off onto a ramp. Maverick smirked to himself; those dudes must have been damn disappointed—and little did they know that they'd missed what might have been the collar of their careers.

As they rode under the overpass, Maverick checked his mirror. He couldn't see the cruisers, but they were in his rearview even so, and he relaxed again.

~oOo~

In Galveston, things got tense again, and for real this time. They brought their truck to a commercial dock, near a row of rusting vessels that Ox identified as 'shrimpers.' Maverick wouldn't know a shrimper from a skiff. He'd didn't like large bodies of water and had never been on a boat—not even the little johnboat they had up at the Bulls' cabin. He'd never learned to swim, and the few times he'd been in deep water, he'd felt powerless and panicky. Water was deadly and unpredictable. Even standing on the dock unsettled him. He didn't like the feeling of something that should have been solid shifting under his feet.

That wasn't the true source of his tension or his disquiet, however. The men Rad and Ox were talking to — that had him on high alert, keeping his hand on the weapon at the small of his back. All four men who'd come up to the Bulls were heavily tattooed — including their faces. The one in charge had really extensive face art.

In four years in prison, Maverick had earned what might as well have been a university-degree's worth of knowledge about ink. In the Bulls' world, ink was significant. Club inked declared more than simply affiliation. It meant a commitment, one so deep it was carved directly into the body. That mark of affiliation was also protection, indicating the power of the people at your back. They marked their women for the same reason — that commitment meant loyalty. Trust. An indelible vow to hold each other's secrets, and faith, precious.

In prison, it wasn't much different, but it was even more crucial. Ink often made the difference between life and death.

Maverick had had to fight hard for the right to keep skinhead ink off his body and keep their so-called 'friendship,' and even so, his lack of evident affiliation had branded him, to guards and inmates alike, an outsider. Only a man like him, who could fight for his place and win, could survive prison as an outsider.

As the state penitentiary, McAlester had housed the whole pantheon of bad men and their communities. Maverick knew the inking styles of virtually every outlaw group. The men doing business with Rad and Ox, with the rest of the Bulls and their lone Horde companion arced behind them, were very bad men indeed.

The man doing most of the talking had the name *Abrego 13* tattooed across his forehead, from his hairline to his eyebrows and from one temple to the other, in a style like graffiti. He had hash marks inked below his left eye, in groups of five: seventeen in all. He was marking his kills. On his fucking face.

These guys were Salvadoran, or affiliated with them. A Salvadoran gang. Abrego 13 had started up in in Los Angeles in the Eighties, populated by young men whose families had fled the civil war in their country, and they had spread south toward home, infecting all points between, when the war was over.

This was no drug cartel, no organized business. Abrego 13 was about violence and mayhem. If they were the Volkovs' customer, they were using these guns and grenades for terror, not greed.

Jesus Christ.

Ox's father had been a Mexican immigrant, and he spoke fluent Spanish. He was doing the talking for the Bulls. Maverick spoke no language but English, so he didn't understand, and he didn't think anyone else did, either. But, based on body language, the exchange seemed to be going smoothly — a truck full of guns for two big duffels full of money. They'd drop the money off at a dry cleaners in Galveston that was a front for other kinds of laundering, and the Bulls' part of this nasty business would be over.

Ox and the Abrego in charge nodded. Ox said something to Rad, who turned and motioned to the Bulls and Little Ike that it was time to start unloading the truck.

Yeah, everything was moving smoothly — but for the fact that they were handing war weapons over to a death gang.

Little Ike hefted a crate of AKs and stalked toward the Salvadorans. He met Maverick's look as they passed each other. The kid was pale, and his eyes were wide, but he seemed steady — just, like Maverick, freaked the fuck out.

~oOo~

"Those guys were some kinda fucked up." Little Ike nodded at the server who'd set a fresh beer before him and offered her a lopsided grin. "Thanks, darlin'."

At his side, Rad said, "Don't matter. Not our job to judge the customer. We just move the merchandise."

"And you're good with that? What the fuck are they doin' with the merchandise?"

"Not our job to know that, either. And that meetin' was cordial. Straight business, no wrinkles. You're judgin' books by their covers, Little Ike."

"Isaac."

Rad acknowledged the correction with a tilt of his head. "So they got ink. So do I. Every one of us has our share. How much d'you got, son?"

"Enough," Little I—Isaac growled. "It's not the point. The guy you were talking to—those hash marks. That was a kill count. Seventeen. I don't think he's countin' mosquitoes he's squashed."

Maverick had been thinking all the same things. "The kid's right, Sarge. Abrego 13, they had a presence at McAlester. Very bad dudes. If they're buying Russian—"

"They're not. They're middlemen, just like us. And we all need to shut the fuck up and mind where the fuck we are."

Where they were—a roadside tavern next to a cheap motel off I-45, about halfway between Galveston and Dallas. Now that the truck was empty, the guns delivered and the cash at the laundry, they could ease back and take a load off. They'd ridden clear of the scene and stopped for the night.

The tavern was crowded and loud, and it was unlikely anyone had overheard their conversation, but Maverick understood Rad's caution. He also understood Isaac's worry.

He had to say something, despite Rad's directive to shut up about it. "If they're working for somebody else, that's no better. They'd only work for somebody badder than them."

"Badder or richer," Gunner put in.

"These guys are about power, not money," Mav countered.

Gunner leaned in. "Money *is* power, bro. You think Irina is where she is because she's a badass old grandma? No. She throws bags of money at assholes in her way, and they do what she wants."

"Assholes like us?"

Rad slapped his hand on the table, and everybody's drink sloshed. "You all need to shut the fuck up. We had a job. We did the job. End of goddamn story. You got a problem with that, then you bring it up in church. Not here."

Everybody sat back, and no one said more. They sat in silence, staring at the beers arrayed over the table.

"Bud's not gonna cut it tonight," Mav said and stood up. "I'm getting a bottle of Jack. Takers?"

Everybody nodded. "Make it two," Isaac said.

~oOo~

"Are you home today?"

Jenny laughed. "Well, that's where you called me. So...yeah. Right here."

Maverick returned her laugh. "I mean are you home for the whole day, or are you going to the bar later?"

"No bar today. I was thinking I'd take Kelsey to a movie after school. *Hercules* is playing at the second-run place. She loves that movie. Hey—are you back in town? You want to go with us?"

God yes, he did. "I'm back. Jenny—I want to come over now. I'll bring the Cherokee, and we can pick her up together and go to McDonald's before the movie."

She didn't like him just showing up, so he always called first now. Sometimes she said no, which was why he preferred to just show up. But he was changing his overbearing ways, so he sat with his eyes closed and silently willed her to say yes.

"Sure. That sounds good." She paused, and Maverick listened to Patsy Cline singing in the background. "Mav—you okay? You sound weird."

Not until his family was together would he truly be okay. But that wasn't what she heard in his voice. He'd woken that morning in Texas with a murderous hangover and a conviction that time was up. No more waiting, no more going slowly. Time was up. He needed his family living in the house he was buying for them, and there was only one gate left between him and what he needed.

If the Bulls were in bed with Irina Volkov and the rogue's gallery she brought with her, then he meant to get some fucking good out of it.

He'd decided that it wasn't *his* money that would pay for Earl Wagner's care. It was Irina's. And that bitch owed him. If he thought of it that way, he could do it.

"I'm okay. I'm good. Just want to talk, babe."

Another hesitation, this one heavy with wariness. "Okay..."

"I'll be there in ten. I love you, Jenny."

"That's one. I love you, too."

One more thing to deal with, and there would be nothing left in their way. "That's one."

~oOo~

Jenny was in the front yard, putting fake spider webs and plastic spiders over the overgrown juniper bushes. Maverick smiled; she'd always enjoyed decorating for the holidays—all of them, not merely Halloween and Christmas. At the least, she'd hung a new wreath on their apartment door, but she really liked to do lights and garlands and the whole deal. She hadn't gotten a lot of good holidays growing up. Even the holidays he'd spent at the group home had been better.

She turned when she heard him pull up to the curb, and she came down the front walk to meet him on the sidewalk.

He pulled her into his arms and kissed her, feeling the glad relief he always felt now, with her hesitation and resistance to their relationship over. She melded to him and opened her mouth against his, purring a tiny moan when his tongue found hers.

She wanted him like he wanted her. Her reservations were all about logistics now, and he would handle them all. Today. Now.

When he pulled back, her cheeks were pink, and she was smiling. Strands of dark hair had escaped her braid; they brushed over her face in the autumn breeze.

"Well, hi there." She smoothed her hand over his cheek.

"Hi. Love you."

"That's two." Her smile grew, but concern creased her eyes. "You sure you're okay?"

"Like I said, just need to talk. There a place we can be private?"

She stepped back, and concern quickly overtook the pleasure of their greeting. "Carlena has my dad in the back yard. Kelse is at school. The house is empty. You're scaring me, though."

He pushed his fingers between hers and lifted her hand to his lips. "It's good. I think it's good. Don't be scared."

"Okay." She studied their linked hands. "Come inside."

~oOo~

Jenny led him into the living room, and they sat together on the sofa. "What is it?"

Maverick had a fine line to walk: he wanted to persuade her — he *needed* to persuade her — but if she felt bullied, the whole thing would blow up. He decided to simply be as upfront as he could be. "I have an idea, and I want to try to convince you that it's good, but I don't want to push too hard. I don't know how to do it without pissing you off."

That earned him a smile, which was a pretty good start. "We each get to finish our sentences, and we stay focused and deal with the issues we bring up. We don't shut each other down. That's how. Mav, what's this about?"

"Do you love me?"

"Yes. You know I do."

He grinned. "Good. That's two. Do you want to be together? Really together — you and me and Kelsey living in the house I'm buying?"

Her guards went visibly up, and he saw how easy it would be to blow this chance. "You know there are other things to think about."

It had been nearly painful to let her finish that sentence. "I know. You didn't answer my question, though. We're supposed to be staying focused on the issues we each bring up, remember?"

Now she smiled, and she tipped her head down, abashed and adorable.

"Jenny, do you want it? What I want?"

"Yes." No hesitation at all this time.

"Is there anything besides your dad keeping you from making the move?"

She blinked, surprised, and Maverick saw that she'd been doing her thing where she didn't think hard enough about important problems that needed solutions. Her brain just shut off when she got stressed out. Frustration began to churn in his gut. How she'd managed to keep things going while he'd been inside, he could not say. This was the kind of shit that made him need to take over.

But then she let out a sharp breath and said, "Kelsey. We haven't talked about how we'll parent her together. We haven't talked about rules and routines and discipline. There's the bar and this house and what to do with them. There's us and what our relationship will be like. Have we figured that out yet? I don't think so, and I can't just jump in and hope, not with Kelsey to think about. And my dad is not just one issue—he can't live with us, and I can't afford to place him anywhere good. Even if I could, there are people who are employed to take care of him, people I care about, and I don't want them to lose their jobs. I don't have an answer for any of that."

That was a lot more than Maverick had realized—and it was clear that she had, in fact, been thinking about it.

"Okay. Can I take them point by point?"

A tilt of her head was the only sign that she was willing to hear him, but it was enough.

"Okay. Kelsey. You're a great mom, and you've been doing it on your own for four years. She has rules she knows and a routine that works. I'm not looking to change that. As for discipline, I'm not laying a hand on her, and I hope you don't, either. Time outs and shit like that work. You know I don't yell. Anyway, I'm going to follow your lead, at least for a while. If we disagree about something, we talk—like this. Just the two of us, listening to each other and working it out. Okay?"

Jenny stared so hard at him that Maverick had the feeling she was trying to see straight through him. "Okay," she said at last. "That...that works."

"As for you and me—babe, we're good. We were always good, but now we're better. I know you can feel it. These past weeks, I see you. The woman you are now. And you are fucking amazing."

"I'm not, Mav. Turning me into an ideal isn't going to fix us."

"I didn't say you were ideal. I said you were amazing—and it's true. You amaze me." He picked up her hand. "I see you trying. Do you see me trying?"

"Yes. I really do. It's beautiful."

"So that's what our relationship will be—we'll always try, and we'll amaze each other. That's what it already is."

"Mav…"

"Yeah, babe?"

"You're painting a pretty picture, but it's just a picture. It's not real."

"Why not?"

"Because being a parent is hard and stressful and exhausting. Knowing what to do and doing it are two different things, and knowing what to do only happens like a third of the time anyway. The rest of the time, I've got no idea what I should do, and I'm just flying blind, hoping I don't break her. And us—you say we'll amaze each other, but what about when we don't? What about when we piss each other off?"

Again, Maverick felt that dangerous territory under his feet. It would be so easy to sweep her doubts away as the silly distractions he believed them to be. Instead, he tried to hear the seed of substance in her worry. "I don't think it'll be easy. I think it'll be *easier* when there's two of us taking on the job. I think we can figure out what to do together, and maybe get it right more often. But even when we get it wrong, it'll be together. And of course we're gonna piss each other off sometimes. But it's the amazing part that we'll remember, and that'll keep us from being dicks to each other. Jen, if we just always try, we'll get through the bad shit."

Her quiet laugh heartened him. "Head down, shoulder to the day?"

He offered her a good-natured shrug. "It's a solid philosophy."

"You've thought this through."

"So have you. You see the cloud, and I see the sun behind it."

She smiled. "You always did. Like you think you can will the world to go your way."

Not quite. It was more that he had to believe that there was sun, or the cloud would swallow him up. Even before prison, that had been true. Now, after four years of devouring darkness, he was fucking desperate for the sun.

"It's the only way to get through. Keep going until you have what you want."

She smoothed her hand over his forearm, stopping where their hands were still joined. "That right there. It's the thing I love best about you. It's also the thing that makes me craziest. You don't give up."

"Not when it's important like this, no." He gave their joined hands a brisk shake and got back on point. "That leaves your dad. Everything else seems attached to him. I have a solution."

"Okay. Let's hear it."

"We use my club take to put him in a decent home and pay for the balance after his insurance. We sell this place — and the bar, if you want. His nurses work for a service, right?"

She stared blankly at him, her mouth slack. His question went unanswered, but he knew that he was right. Darnell had already told him as much.

"They won't lose their jobs. They'll be reassigned, and if you want to keep in touch as friends, then just exchange numbers." He'd be secretly happy if she didn't keep in touch with Darnell, but he'd accept it if she did. That twitch of jealousy was his own problem to work out.

"You can't pay for him."

He hadn't expected her to fight that part, not if they were together. "Why not?"

"You made him like he is."

"That's not news, babe."

"You hate him. You'll resent it. And me. If not now, then eventually."

"Jenny, listen to me. You're right. I hate him. I wish I'd killed him that day. Sometimes I think about putting a pillow over his face one night and just being done with it. If he lived with us, yes, I'd probably resent the whole situation eventually. But money? Fuck that." She didn't need to know that he'd struggled with this very point. His struggle was over. "Money isn't going to be the thing keeping us apart. I'm not gonna let that be true. Don't you, either."

He pulled her hand close and clasped it to his chest. "I'm trying not to push too hard, but really listen to what I'm saying. Put your shoulder to that cloud of yours and *see*.

That's the solution. Sell this house, and use that money for his care, too. Sell the bar, too, if you want. You wanted to be a stay-at-home mom, and now you can. I'll pick up the rest of his bills—*we* will, because what's mine is yours. You have a place to live now. You have a real home. With me. You don't have to live his life anymore."

"You're making my head spin." She did, in fact, looked dazed. "You're twisting me all up again."

Maverick saw a field full of land mines in that single sentence, but he had no choice but to walk on. "I need to push here, Jen. If there's a good reason to wait, I'll back off. I'll hear you, and I'll wait. But I don't know what we're waiting for—him to die? Fuck that. I'm *broken* living like this, babe. We're *all* broken. None of us is living the life we should be. Including Kelsey."

His words made her flinch. "We can't go back, Mav. I keep saying—"

"I don't want to go back." He'd cut her off, and she flinched again, but he pressed on, and she didn't stop him. "I want us. You and me. Who we are now. We're a family. All my life, since I can remember, I've wanted what we are. Please. Let's give our daughter the life you and I never had. It's *right here*. I'm holding it out and begging you to take it."

Her hand still trapped in his, Jenny stared at him. Tears filled her eyes and made them shimmer. He didn't know what else to say, how else to beg. There was nothing between them now but her fear, and he didn't know what else he could do to ease it.

This moment, right now, felt like the pivot point. There was no more waiting in him. Not because he was impatient—though, yes, he was that as well—but because he was worn down. From the day of his eighteenth birthday, which had been celebrated at the boys' home with a slice of Sara Lee chocolate cake, after which he'd been sent on his way alone in the world, life had worn him down to a nub. He'd wanted only one thing, since he was old enough to know it was possible: a family of his own. A woman. Children. A home to shelter them, kept warm with their love.

He'd almost had it once, and he'd blown it. Now, it all sat right before him again. Right now. He waited for Jenny to speak and knew that if she didn't give him the answer he needed, the world would have worn him down until there was nothing left.

Nothing at all.

September 1981

"Hey, Rich. Come talk to me."

Rich turned, a sick feeling at the pit of his stomach, and faced Lester, the director of this boys' home. He'd lived here since he was four years old, had never had anyone even consider adopting him, so he knew the score. Today was his eighteenth birthday. He was aging out of the system. And out of the only home he'd ever known.

He hefted the black sack in his hands. "Taking the trash out, Lester."

"Good man. After that, then. I'll be in my office."

His office. Yeah. Well, it wasn't a surprise. He'd hoped for a reprieve, but he hadn't really expected one.

So he went out back and tossed the bag in the dumpster, then went to meet his fate.

~oOo~

Lester Darville wasn't the only director the St. Ignatius Home for Boys had had in Rich's nearly fourteen years as a resident, but he was one of the better ones. He didn't try to be the boys' buddy, and he didn't act like a prison warden. He got a lot closer to 'dad' territory (as far as Rich could tell; he didn't remember what having a father was actually like) than the others.

They'd had a couple of shitty directors over the years, but those hadn't lasted long, fortunately. For the most part, the people who worked at Iggy's were decent. Some were priests or brothers or some other kind of Catholic thing, but others, like Lester, were what they called 'lay staff.'

Despite the name of a saint on the building and the crucifixes on walls in every room, religion wasn't shoved down the boys' throats. They had grace at mealtimes and mandatory Mass on Sundays and holy days, but that wasn't so bad.

The bedrooms weren't overcrowded, just two boys to each, and now there was MTV in the rec room. Some of the boys were assholes, but boys like Rich kept the assholes under control, for the most part. Overall, Iggy's wasn't a bad place to live. He knew it could be worse. From boys who'd come in from other places, group homes and family placements alike, Rich had heard that there was a *lot* worse out there.

He'd known that the end was coming. As a ward of the state, he was only somebody else's responsibility until the day of his eighteenth birthday or when he graduated high school, whichever came later. Because he lived in a home like this, with a waiting list, he was out the door that very day. He'd known that. But it still hurt to sit here in Lester's office and literally be given his walking papers.

Lester had pushed him to think about jobs or college, and had talked to him about how to find an apartment. Rich's response had been to spend all his free time at the boxing gym, in the ring or hanging out with the older fighters. He had a little job there, barely part-time and only minimum wage, but it had been enough to keep him in tape and gloves, and the pros gave him pointers and sparred with him for free.

The things Lester wanted him to think about were too big, too nebulous, too scary. He had no idea how to make it on his own, and he felt small and lost when he tried to think about it. Like life was about to grab him by the neck and fling him into space, with no air or gravity, no control of anything.

But in the ring, he was in control. Life made sense inside the ropes, when everything boiled down to one simple imperative: Be better than the other guy. Strong, smarter, tougher. Just better. Be the one still standing.

He knew what he wanted in life. He wanted to pull into his own driveway and see the lights on in his own house. He wanted to walk in the front door and smell supper in the oven. He wanted a beautiful woman to come to him and wrap herself around him while she asked about his day. He wanted kids playing in the back yard with their dog. He'd only ever seen a life like that on television, but he knew it was the way things were supposed to be.

That life would not come from a job at a burger joint and a basement one-bedroom shared with five other people, which was the best thing he could hope for next, and he couldn't understand how to get from one to the other.

So he went to the ring, where being his best was enough, and when it wasn't, the path to get better was clear: Work harder. Sweat more. Keep going.

As he sat down beside Lester's desk, what Rich wanted was simply to be allowed to stay right where he was, at least until he could understand what his next step should be.

"So, son. You know what happens now."

Rich swallowed so his voice wouldn't shake. "I was thinking…could I stay on if I worked here? Just, like, cleaning up or something like that? You wouldn't have to pay me—just let me stay."

Lester shook his head. "Only counselors live on the premises, Rich. And you know we need the bed." He pushed a manila envelope across his desk. "There's an address in there for a shelter we work with. You've got a bed there for three nights. After that, if you need to stay longer, you'll have to work that out with them yourself. There are a couple of names of people in the parish who'll take in a boarder. There's also five twenty-dollar bills in there, to get you fed while you're looking for a job and a place. And a letter of reference." He bent down and lifted a paper grocery sack, its top folded neatly over. "And our birthday gift to you: brand new set of good clothes for job interviews—khakis, Oxford shirt, shoes, belt, the works. Even a tie. Keep these nice."

"Lester..." his voice shook, and the name broke in two.

"I know, Rich. I came up through the system, too, remember. Aged-out just like this. It's hard. But I got through it, and you will, too. You're strong, and you're smart. If you apply yourself, you'll do just fine. Only one way to move through this world, right?"

Rich nodded, but only to acknowledge Lester's favorite saying, not his faith in it.

"Say it with me, son."

"Head down, shoulder to the day." They said it together, but Lester's voice far overpowered his own.

Lester stood and held out his hand. "Go on up and pack your things, say your goodbyes. I know it doesn't feel like it, but it's better if it's quick. Like pulling off a Band-Aid."

Rich stood tall and shook the director's hand. Lester Darville was the closest thing he had to a father, the closest thing he could remember ever having. "I just want a family," he said as they dropped their hands.

"Iggy's never was that for you, Rich. We do what we can, but we can't be that. You're gonna have to make a family for yourself. And when you do, you hold it close and keep it safe like a precious gift. You hear?"

He heard. "Yes, sir."

CHAPTER SIXTEEN

Jenny's heart slammed back and forth inside her chest. Her head spun and slued. Maverick sat facing her, clasping her hand to his chest, his expression naked with need.

Was it that simple? Just say yes and have what she wanted? Just let him take care of her?

Say the word, babe.

That was what he offered: sell the house, sell the bar, move her father into a nursing home, move herself and her daughter into Maverick's home. Be a full-time mom, have the life they'd been planning to have before.

But she'd been completely dependent on him before. She'd had no job, no apartment with her name on the lease, and in mere weeks, she'd been left with nothing but a brand new baby and an invalid father. She'd been forced back to a life she'd escaped and had found it in ruins.

Maverick had sat here and addressed all her reservations, calmly and without obvious manipulation. He'd made his case, and it was a good one. Airtight. Except for the crack that was her fear.

"What if you go away again?"

He hadn't considered that; pained surprise broke across his face. But he wrapped his free hand around the knot that their joined hands had made, and he squeezed. "I won't. I promise."

"Don't do that. Don't promise something like that. You can't know it'll be true."

"Jen—"

"No." She owed him that interruption. "I know enough about what the Bulls do to know that you can't promise you won't go to prison again."

Now it was despair that shaped his features. "No. You're right. If you need that promise, I can't make it."

His manifest turmoil and fear, written all over that scarred, handsome face, calmed her. Tough as he was, he was afraid as well. She wasn't alone in that.

She put her hand over the bundle of their hands, so they were all clasped together. "I don't need the promise, Mav. I need the answer. What do I do, if everything I have is bound up with you again and you go away?"

He was quiet, his eyes averted, searching for something beyond her. Then he met her waiting gaze again. "The club, babe. They'll be there. They were there before. I think I understand why you pushed them away, but they're there. They'll always be there, and you'll never fall. They're your family as much as mine, if you'll let them be."

She wondered if he really did understand why she'd turned away from the Bulls. She'd felt betrayed by Maverick, she'd felt manipulated and abandoned — she'd *been* all those things — and she'd wanted a full amputation of him from her life. That included his club, which she'd never fully trusted anyway.

To see them as her family, to let them really *be* that, she'd have to find a way to trust them.

Willa. Maybe it was silly, just some lingering hero worship for a woman who'd saved her, but she trusted Willa completely. Willa obviously trusted the Bulls and was a full member of that family — and of the circle of old ladies.

Willa was her touchstone. Even more than Maverick, on this matter, Willa, her mere presence, could guide her in.

"Okay. I'll try."

He blinked. "What?"

"It comes down to trust. I trust you again. And I'll try to see the club like you do and trust them, too. Okay."

"Babe, I'm sorry. I need you to say what you're saying."

She laughed lightly at his confusion. "I want us to raise Kelsey together. I want her to have that life. So you're right. It's time. I love you, Maverick."

"That's three," he murmured. "Holy shit." He broke their hands apart and grabbed her head, slamming his mouth over hers before she could take a breath.

His tongue plunged into her mouth and he pushed forward, lying over her, overwhelming her completely, but in the way she craved. She locked her arms around his neck and gave back all the passion he filled her with, and for a minute she was sure they were going to fuck right there on the sofa.

Then she heard Carlena bringing her father back into the house, into the kitchen.

Maverick heard the same thing and pulled back. "Dammit," he muttered.

Jenny giggled and kissed his nose. "We have to pick Kelsey up soon anyway." When he began to sit back, away from her, she held him close for one more second. "Stay here tonight. All night. We'll talk to her together after the movie, and we can pick this up where we left off after she goes to bed."

They'd only been intimate a few times since he'd been back, and she'd never let him stay the night, not while things were still up in the air between them. But this big talk they'd had, that had been everything landing into place. It was time.

His brow furrowed. "Jen?"

"Do you want to?"

"Fuck yes. Absolutely. I'd rather be in our house, but I will be with you wherever I can."

"I can't spend the night at...our house"—his grin at her pronoun was like sunlight in her face—"until we find a good place for my dad. But you can stay here as much as you want."

He swept his arms around her as he sat back, and buried his face in the crook of her neck, and he held her so tightly that she could feel his heart beating.

"I love you, I love you, I love you," said the man who'd once been so indifferent about those three words that Jenny had taken to keeping count of the times he'd bothered to say them.

"Infinity," she answered now.

~oOo~

Kelsey's teachers were surprised to see Jenny standing on the playground with Maverick at her side. Betsy in particular—she'd been the one to confront him at the fence, back in the summer, and she remembered him. He hadn't been back to Alphabet Acres since that day.

Now, as Kelsey trotted up with her Hello Kitty backpack dangling from one arm, and her jacket sliding down the other, Betsy followed behind her. Jenny could see the woman's narrow-eyed suspicion from ten yards away.

But then Kelsey squealed, "Daddy! You came to my school again!" and Betsy's suspicion turned to shock.

Maverick crouched and caught their daughter in his arms. "Hey, pixie! How was your day?"

"My day was good. I colored a goats that says BOO. That's B-O-O. You said pixie. That's what Mommy says."

Holding Kelsey close, Maverick looked up at Jenny. "Is it okay if I say it, too?"

Knowing he was asking them both, Jenny nodded while Kelsey said, "Uh-huh. I like it. Pixies are like little fairies."

It had once been their name for the baby inside her. Now they would share it for the daughter that baby had become.

"Everything's okay?" Betsy asked, confused.

"Everything is great," Maverick answered.

When Betsy looked to her for confirmation, Jenny smiled. "It is."

~oOo~

"Does she sleep with a different animal every night?" Maverick came into the bedroom and closed the door.

In the middle of her nighttime routine, Jenny rubbed her hands together and smoothed lotion over her leg.

"Sometimes she has a favorite for a few days, but she says she doesn't want any of her animals to feel lonely, so they all get their turn for slumber parties."

As she stood straight and put her foot back on the floor, Maverick stood behind her. "She's a special little girl."

"I think all parents think their kids are special. But yeah. Ours really is." She reached for the lotion again, but Maverick reached past her and picked up the bottle.

His head was at her ear. "I get hard every time you say 'ours.'"

All day, since she'd agreed with his plan and he'd kissed the shit out of her, Jenny had felt different. She no longer watched Maverick constantly, furtively, trying to know what was right, trying to see if she could trust him. She just knew—this was right, she could trust. Picking up Kelsey, taking her for burgers and to see a movie, coming home together, hanging up her 'goats' (which was actually a ghost) on the refrigerator, sharing her bedtime routine—all of it had been normal and good and right. The way things were supposed to be.

They'd talked to Kelsey right before bedtime, telling her that they were going to live together at the house daddy had gotten for them, and that Granddaddy was going to live in a nice place where people could take good care of him. She'd been full of questions, but not of worry. She, too, was getting what she wanted. She had a mommy and a daddy now, and they were all supposed to live together.

Jenny was happy. Until she'd truly felt it, she hadn't considered how long it had been since she last had known happiness.

Four years.

As he smoothed lotion up her arms, Jenny moaned and leaned back against his chiseled chest. "That's all that's making you hard? A little word?"

He moved his head to the other side and kissed her ear. His tongue traced along the edge and back down to swirl a circle on her neck. "Hmmm?"

Okay. What had seemed an odd quirk, some habit she'd thought he'd picked up in prison, of keeping people on his strong side, was clearly more than that. Jenny stood straight again and turned around in his arms. "Mav? Are you deaf in that ear?"

His smile surprised her. When he turned her around and pulled her back into the cradle of his arms and chest, she didn't resist. "Mostly, yeah. Not a big deal, babe. Just whisper your sweet words in my other ear, and it's all good."

"How'd it happen?" She tilted her head toward his strong side. "Why didn't you tell me?"

With his hands freshly coated with lotion, he began to massage her shoulders, letting his fingers slip down, along her spine, under her camisole. Jenny closed her eyes and let his touch flicker all through her body.

"Happened the way you think it did. Got hit too hard too often. I'm about half blind in that eye, too. I fought a lot inside, Jen. A lot of bad shit happened. I didn't tell you because I want to leave that shit inside. In the past. I don't want to relive any of it, and I'd have to, to talk about it. Okay?"

All the time he'd been away, Jenny had clung to her anger. She'd thought about her life, and Kelsey's, and all the things that were wrong, all the ways things weren't as they were supposed to be. She'd felt imprisoned in this life, in this house, full of pain and loss and fear. She'd spared hardly a thought for Maverick's pain, or his loss, or his fear. She'd made him her enemy, and she'd survived on the energy of her anger.

Now, with him again, loving him unreservedly again, forgiving him, she had an ocean of thoughts to spare for him. These four years had been hell for him. That was obvious just to look at him: his body was a map of new scars, each marking a point of pain in his life. His hands were like cragged boulders. His left ear—the one that was deaf—was misshapen. Scars marred his eyes, his nose, his chin. He had scars across his chest and belly and arms, too, scars that couldn't have been made with fists.

He'd been a fighter since he was a kid, and his skin had been marked up well before she'd met him. Yet now he looked like a man who'd been fighting not by choice but for survival.

She'd known. Since he'd been back, she'd known. She simply hadn't wanted to see it.

"I'm so sorry," she whispered now. "God, Mav. I'm so sorry."

He shook his head against her neck. "Doesn't matter. This is all that matters." His hands moved around her waist and up, under her top. Her nipples, already tight and seeking, felt the touch of his hard fingertips like a shock, and she arched her back.

"This is everything I need." His fingers plucked and swirled over her tender, needy flesh.

Jenny raised her arms, hooking her hands behind his head, stretching her body out so that he could have it all. She wanted his touch everywhere. She wanted to be consumed by him.

One of his hands dropped, skimming over her belly and pushing into her panties. When they brushed past her clit and sank into her, she cried out, clutching his head to her as tightly as she could.

"Fuck me." The words would barely come out, so lost was her breath already. "Fuck me so hard."

"Jenny," he groaned. "Jesus." His fingers left her, and he pushed her forward until she let go of him and put her hands on the dresser before her. Her panties ripped and fluttered to the floor at her ankles when he yanked so hard one side tore free.

Behind her, she heard his belt and his jeans opening; he was still fully dressed, except for his boots and kutte. Next, she heard a faint plastic crinkle, and she reached back and grabbed his hand. "No."

With the half-open condom packet between his fingers, he stopped. "Babe?"

She took a deep breath so she could speak. "Don't use that. I want another baby with you. It's time."

"Jen, are you sure?"

She was. This wasn't like the night at the bar, when she'd been half-stoned on adrenaline. Besides, she wouldn't have been disappointed if she'd gotten pregnant then. But tonight, this was a choice. They'd made some decisions. They'd told Kelsey. They were together and moving forward. She was almost thirty years old, and Kelsey was four. It was time.

"Are *you* sure?" she asked, turning his question around.

"Fuck yeah." He dropped the condom. "I want to marry you. Soon."

She pulled her camisole off and tossed it away. "When we get everything sorted out. When we have everything right. Then yeah."

He gently kicked her legs wide. Jenny bent forward again, offering herself. She felt his cock—so hard and hot, its tip already wet—brush between her thighs, and he pushed in, letting out a long, strained groan.

There was nothing better in the world than this. Their bodies joined, moving together. The sounds of his need, his pleasure, his love, mingling with her own. The touch of his skin, the heat of his body, all around her, driving her forward, up and up and up, coiling her nerves and muscles until she was nothing but a snarl of sensation, of pulsing desire.

He bent over her, resting his cheek on her head, heaving greedy gasps into her ear. His hands left her hips, one capturing a breast and the other pushing between her legs to play at her clit as he drove into her, each thrust so deep and fierce that the dresser shook with the force of it, and Jenny could feel her orgasm stampeding toward her, rumbling from the point of their union outward, charging up her spine and through her limbs until she could only grunt and slam her body backward, crashing into him again and again.

"Fuck yeah." Maverick growled at her ear, meeting her hips with ever-increasing vigor. "Come all over me. Drench my cock. That's it, that's it, that's—*fuck*!"

In the middle of her climax, Maverick hit his, and they froze together, rigid and throbbing, until Jenny thought she'd pass out. It let her go at last, and she drew in a wild gulp of air.

Resting on her back, Maverick chuckled. She felt it vibrate through his cock, inside her. "Damn, babe."

Wrung out, twitches of enduring ecstasy still moving through her, Jenny smiled and sighed. "That was amazing." A little yawn rolled up her throat, and she almost managed to hold it back.

Maverick pulled out. "Nope. Don't you fall asleep on me." Before she could decide whether she had the will to stand up straight, he swept her into his arms, cradling her against his chest. "I'm not done with you yet. I got all damn night, and I'm gonna use it. I'm gonna knock you up tonight or die trying."

He swung around and carried her to the bed. Jenny giggled when he dropped her on the mattress.

Then he followed, settling himself between her legs. His arms hooked around her thighs, and his mouth descended to her pussy, still swollen and thrumming. When he sucked her clit between his lips, she was wide awake again.

~oOo~

Even after multiple orgasms and hours of lovemaking, Jenny couldn't sleep. Maverick slumbered peacefully behind her, his body curved protectively around hers, but Jenny's eyes and mind were wide open.

Unlike most of her sleepless nights these past four years, she wasn't worried, or scared, or depressed. This wakefulness was brisk and alive. She was excited. Hopeful. In love. Happy.

Everything would be the way it was supposed to be. She and Maverick had worked it out together, made their way together, and she could believe in that. She could trust it.

How could she sleep when she was so close to everything she wanted?

Dawn had brightened the sky, so there was no point trying anymore. Carefully, she eased from Maverick's embrace, pulling her pillow down so his arm would wrap around it—an old trick from before, to keep him asleep when she needed to get out of bed.

He sighed heavily, almost a purr, and settled again.

Grabbing his t-shirt from the floor, she pulled it over her head. It skimmed her mid-thigh, practically modest, but she got a fresh pair of panties out anyway and stepped into them. A sidelong glance in her mirror showed the braid of the day before to have become a frayed, snarled rope, so she combed her fingers through the mess until it was smooth enough that she could catch it back with a butterfly clip. Presentable, she went out to start the morning.

First, she checked on Kelsey, who'd turned around in her bed. Her head was pressed against the footboard, and she was curled in her little ball, but facedown, with her butt in the air, in a preschool parody of her preferred infant sleeping position. Mr. Teapot, a floppy, spotted dog, strangled in the crook of her arm.

Jenny stood and watched her girl sleep. In that little bed was the only good thing her life had held for more than four years. The reason she was still alive, the reason she'd kept fighting, was that child—as frustrating and terrifying and infuriating as she was delightful and sweet and inspiring, and absolutely perfect.

If she'd allowed Maverick to have that strength, if she'd stayed with him, supported him, let him look forward to days like this, when he'd be with them, would his time in prison have been something he could talk about? Would he have fewer scars?

He wasn't a man who let the past chew on him. He never had been, but he'd never had to avoid it, either. The past had simply been what it was, and he always focused on moving through the present toward the future.

She would never ask him to talk about things he needed to lock away, but she knew him, and his need to lock the last four years away spoke loud and long about how bad prison must have been. He had scars she couldn't see.

She bore some responsibility for that. It wasn't her fault that he'd been arrested, that he'd done time, but it was her fault that he'd done it alone, that he hadn't had Kelsey to keep him strong.

With a sigh, she closed her daughter's door. As she stood before her father's, she heard his machines, making the sounds of his wakefulness. Normally, unless there was trouble, she left him alone and let Carlena handle him when she came on shift at nine, but on this morning, feeling happy and melancholy at the same time, she pushed his door open.

He was awake, trying to fuss with his CPAP machine. His motor skills weren't good enough to take it off; all he could do was slap himself in the head, and get increasingly agitated about it.

"Dad, calm down." She went in and pushed the button on his bed to raise the head. He couldn't breathe without help when he lay flat, and he couldn't sleep when he sat up. Once he was safely elevated, she turned off the CPAP and took the mask off his face. "There. Better?"

"Jen." Sometimes he could nod, but she hadn't heard him say 'yes' or any version of it since he'd been hurt. 'No,' he had down, and a couple of other words. Her name had come to stand for everything else.

"Good morning. Carlena won't be here for a while yet. You want me to turn on your TV?" He had a small set that they'd set up on a wall shelf for him. His room was almost indistinguishable from a hospital room.

"No."

"Okay." She patted his hand and turned, meaning to go. An impulse stopped her, and she turned back. "I have something to tell you, Dad."

He had the mental capacity of a six-year-old, they said. Not much older than Kelsey. The same age Jenny had been when her mother had died. Would he understand? Would it be better not to tell him, to simply move him and explain when it was all done?

She didn't know. But the need to tell him had come on her with force. Was it malice? Did she mean it to hurt him? Searching her heart, she didn't think so. With Maverick back and their future on track, she didn't feel her old pettiness for her father. He'd been mean and erratic, but even if that was still in him, he was harmless now. He'd be harmless forever now. And he'd always been sad. Always broken.

It wasn't malice, but she didn't know if it was right. The words simply needed to be said.

"Daddy." She hadn't called him Daddy in twenty years. "Some big changes are happening. Maverick and I are together again, and we're going to make a family with Kelsey."

He grunted, and his hand slammed at the side rail.

"I know you're afraid of him."

"No!"

She was upsetting him, but now that she'd started, she couldn't just leave that news out there on its own. "Okay. Well, I know you don't like him. I understand. So we're going to find you a good place to live. A place that'll take care of you better and give you a bigger life than this little house."

"Jen! Jen!"

She smoothed her hand over his stubbly, fleshy cheek. "It's okay. Everything's going to be good. The way it's supposed to be."

He grunted again, and his face went red.

"Jen."

At Maverick's voice, Jenny spun around, feeling strangely guilty and protective. He stood in the doorway, wearing only his jeans, his hair up at all ends. She'd done that, raking her fingers through it again and again.

Her father grunted again, angrily. She patted his hand again. "It's going to be okay, Dad. I promise. I'll check in on you later, after I get Kelse moving." She turned the television on and put it on the ABC channel, so *Good Morning America* would play when seven o'clock rolled around. He liked that show. For now, he could watch the farm report.

When she went to the door, Maverick was staring at her father. Silently. Icily. She grabbed his arm, pulled him out of the room, and closed the door

The sooner these two men never had to see each other again, the better.

"Pisses me off to hear you call him 'Daddy.' That's what Kelse calls me."

She cupped his cheeks in her hands. His stubble had turned into a beard. "I haven't called him that since I was little. It just came out. And he *is* my father."

His lip curled in disdain. "Biologically, yeah. But that man was never a father to you."

Maverick was wrong, actually. It would have been easier if her father had never been a father to her, if he'd never been her Daddy, if he'd never shown her love or affection, or remorse. But he had. She'd spent her whole life trying to be good enough to deserve only that part of him and not the other.

December 1976

Mrs. Turner stared out the window over her kitchen sink. "Looks like your daddy's home, sugar. How about you pick out some cookies, and you can take 'em back over with you."

The Turner's funny kitchen table—shiny red and white and sparkles, with drawers in it—was strewn with Christmas cookies, cooling on racks and arrayed on trays. It was Christmas break at school, so Jenny spent whole days next door, not just the afternoons until her daddy came and took her to the bar and made her stay in the back.

Ever since her mommy had done the bad thing and gotten herself killed, Jenny had to go to the bar with her daddy when she couldn't stay next door. She wasn't sure why she couldn't always just stay next door, but she couldn't. When she'd asked Mr. Turner, he'd told her to ask Mrs. Turner. When she'd asked Mrs. Turner, she'd said her daddy had his reasons. When she'd asked her daddy, he'd told her to shut up.

So when he came and took her to the bar, she went. Sometimes, when the sun was out and there weren't many people there, he'd let her stay up front and spin around on the bar stools or play with the bowling machine. But when it got dark outside, and crowded inside, she had to go in the back and stay there.

She hated being in the back. It smelled funny, and there were long shadows in all the corners. And sometimes there were rats, but she wasn't supposed to say that. There was an old recliner back there by Daddy's desk, and she was supposed to do her homework, eat her sandwich from the deli down the street, and go to sleep, but it was hard to sleep when maybe a rat would come out. If she was sleeping, it could get on her face, and they had sharp little feet like tiny, bony hands with claws.

She liked it better when she could stay next door. Mrs. Turner made good food for supper and had little pink glass bowls for ice cream or pudding for dessert, and Mr. Turner let her read the funny pages of his paper. They had a girl named Rhona, but Rhona was a Big Girl, in high school, and she didn't pay much attention to Jenny—or her parents. She spent a lot of time upstairs, in her room. When the phone rang, it was usually for Rhona.

On this day, Mrs. Turner and Jenny had made pretty green cookies that looked like wreaths and pushed Red Hots in while they were still soft and hot, to look like berries. And Santas with red sugar sprinkles and Christmas trees with green sugar sprinkles. And chocolate balls covered in something like white fur. Coco-nut. She didn't like those. The coco-nut tasted funny and stuck on her tongue.

Mrs. Turner brought over a big plastic tub that used to be for margarine. "Come on, sugar. Pick your cookies. You want to be ready when your daddy comes over. He don't like to wait."

She plucked up the two wreaths she thought were prettiest. The Red Hots were exactly even, and the red hadn't smeared on the green. She chose some Santas and Christmas trees, too, but not the coco-nut ones. She selected each cookie carefully and set it in the bowl. While Mrs. Turner put the lid on, Jenny went to the front hall and got her coat off the hook.

Her daddy knocked on the back door as she came into the kitchen, and she went and opened it. When she saw him, she got scared. His hair was messy, and his eyes were droopy. It was hard to be good enough when he looked like that.

"Let's go, Jenny." His breath smelled like booze. When she was little, she used to think of it as grownup soda, but now she was older and she knew it was booze, like at the bar.

Mrs. Turner came up behind her and set her hand on Jenny's shoulder. "Jen was a very good girl today, Earl. She helped me bake cookies, and she cleaned up."

He nodded, but he didn't look up at Mrs. Turner or Jenny. He just stood on the little back stoop, one step down, and waited, rocking a little. It was cold, but he wasn't wearing a coat.

"Let's go."

Mrs. Turner's hand didn't move from Jenny's shoulder. It squeezed more tightly instead. "We're happy to keep her the night, if you'd like."

"It's Christmas Eve. I want her home."

"Of course you do." Mrs. Turner crouched at Jenny's side and gave her a quick hug. "Merry Christmas, sugar. You have a good day tomorrow. Come on over later, and see what Santa might've left at our house."

Jenny didn't believe in Santa anymore. Not since the first Christmas after her mommy got herself killed. But Mrs. Turner was nice, and Jenny didn't want her to be sad like she'd been, so she didn't tell her that Santa was a damn lie.

Her daddy held out his hand. "Don't meddle, Elma. I got it handled."

Mrs. Turner stood up. "Alright, then. Merry Christmas, Earl."

Jenny's daddy made a weird noise and yanked her out of the house and down the porch steps.

When they got into their own kitchen, her daddy snatched the big margarine tub from her hands. "What's this?"

"Cookies. We made cookies today, and I picked out the best ones for you."

He tore off the plastic lid and tossed it away. It flew across the room like a Frisbee. Rooting through the tub, he plucked out one cookie after another, tossing them away, one by one. They dropped to the floor and cracked into pieces and crumbles. One of the green wreaths landed, and two of its Red Hots fell off and rolled away.

When the tub was empty, he tossed that away, too. Jenny stood, still wearing her coat—creamy fur with a big hood and pretty sewing up the front, the prettiest coat in the world, which her daddy had given her for her birthday—and stared at the cookies all over the floor.

Her daddy went to the cabinet and pulled down a bottle of booze. As he walked out of the kitchen, he grumbled, "Clean that fuckin' mess up."

~oOo~

"JENNIFER!"

Jenny jumped at the slurred shout.

"JENNIFER MAE WAGNER! GET YOUR ASS IN HERE!"

It was going to be bad, but it was worse not to come when she was called. She set her Nancy Drew book aside and left her room.

He was standing in the kitchen. Barely standing. More like slumping. He was barefoot, and he'd taken off his shirt and wore only his sleeveless t-shirt, slouching halfway out of his pants. The buckle of his belt gleamed in the light from the lamp hanging over the table. His eyes were red, and his cheeks were wet, but he didn't look sad. Maybe he'd been sad before, but now he was mad.

"What the fuck is that?"

He pointed at a little red dot on the kitchen floor. A Red Hot. She must have missed it when she'd swept up the cookies. It was squashed flat; he must have stepped on it.

She didn't answer.

"I asked you a fuckin' question."

"It's a Red Hot. From the cookies. I'm sorry, Daddy. I thought I cleaned everything up. I tried to do a good job."

"But you didn't, did you? You left food on the floor like a fuckin' slob. Get over here and pick it up. Hands and knees. Get down close and make fuckin' *sure*."

She went and got on her knees. The candy had squished into bits when he'd stepped on it, but she stay on her knees until she had all the pieces cupped in her hand, even the ones the size of a speck of dust. When she had them all, she got up and took them to the plastic trash bin by the door.

She'd done the best job she could, but it wasn't enough. She wasn't good enough. She knew that because she heard the faint jingle and the terrible whoosh of his belt being unfastened and pulled from his pants.

"Daddy, I'm sorry. I really did try to do it good. I tried to do what you said."

"Get over here and touch your toes, Jennifer. It's time to take your punishment."

Jenny went and touched her toes. It didn't matter that it was Christmas Eve. Santa was a damn lie.

~oOo~

Later that night, Jenny woke with a start and a squeal.

"Shhh, shhh, shhh. It's just me, Twinkle." Her daddy lifted her from the bed, bringing her quilt with her. He cradled her in his arms and tucked the quilt around her. Her bottom was still sore from her punishment, but her daddy was holding her tightly, snugly, and humming, so she didn't mind the discomfort. "Let's go outside—it's Christmas and it's snowing!"

He carried her into the living room and grabbed the old crocheted afghan from the sofa, and then he carried her through the house, to the back, and onto the screened-in porch. He sat on the rusty metal glider, holding her to his chest, and looked out at the falling snow.

Jenny was cold, but her daddy wanted to hold her, and she wanted to make him happy. She wanted to be good enough that he'd always be like this. So she tried not to shiver, and she snuggled down deep under the quilt that had been on her bed. She tucked her head under his chin. He still smelled like booze, and cigarettes, and his aftershave.

He squeezed her tight. "We don't need nothin' else, do we, Twinkle? You and me and nothin' else."

Jenny snuggled closer. If they could be like this all the time, she didn't think they would need anything else.

CHAPTER SEVENTEEN

November had come in gloomy, cold, and rainy, with several days in a row of heavy clouds and intermittent storms, occasionally threatening to freeze. But on the day Maverick finally got his family right, the sun broke through and warmed the air, like Nature herself celebrated with them.

They'd started early, the very next morning after they got Earl moved into the nursing home. When they'd begun planning, Maverick had thought there wouldn't be much to move—he had furniture for most of the rooms already, and he'd figured that Jenny wouldn't want her father's crap—but he'd been wrong. She'd wanted most of the kitchen, and everything from the dining room, which had been her mother's, and her grandmother's before that, and all of Kelsey's things, of course, and…a lot. He hadn't considered that, as unhappy as she'd been in that house, it had still been her home. She was in those walls as much as Earl was. And Kelsey had known no other home.

So it took the entire Bulls family, the new club van, and five pickup trucks four hours to move his woman and child where they belonged.

Four hours, and four years.

Once Jenny had finally said yes, Maverick had put his considerable will, and the combined power of the old ladies, to the matter of getting it done as quickly as possible. Mo and Joanna had done more research on nursing homes, and he'd taken Jenny on a few tours. When she'd found one she liked well enough, it had had a waiting list. So he'd asked Willa if she had any contacts at the hospital who could help. She did.

Jenny had been uncomfortable with the idea that they were 'cutting the line,' but she'd been almost as impatient as he, once she'd made up her mind, so it hadn't been hard to persuade her that they'd both been on a cosmic waiting list for four fucking years.

They didn't have the house on the market yet—Jenny wanted to fix it up first—and she hadn't decided yet whether she'd sell the bar. But those were tiny details, comparatively. On a sunny November day, with his house full of his family, Maverick knew it would all work out.

He'd allowed himself to have hope, and now he had all he could have hoped for.

"You need a swing on this tree."

Gunner looked up into the branches of the sycamore they stood under; Maverick followed his line of sight. "Yeah?"

"Yeah. That branch is *perfect*. Every kid needs a tree swing."

"I was thinking about one of those sets they have at the lumber yard."

"Those are okay, too. But you gotta have a tree swing. Used to be one on this tree. Look—you can see the scar where the rope was. Fuck, I could run back to the station and get what we need to make one today."

"He's right, Mav," Simon agreed, bringing over fresh beers. "Kid can't grow up right without a tire swing."

Maverick had never swung on a tree swing in his life, and no one in his thirty-five years had ever extolled the virtues of them before. There'd been a rickety metal swing set behind Iggy's, and he remembered that the big game had been to see if you could swing hard enough to get the front legs to leave the ground completely without sending the set over. They'd also had a metal cage of a jungle gym, and a set of metal bars, in three ascending heights. All of it over hard-packed dirt. His childhood had been a collection of scrapes and bruises even before he'd discovered the ring.

But he'd been pretty good at rocking the swings—and at what they'd called the 'dead man's drop' off the highest bar.

He shrugged and took a swig of his beer—Rolling Rock; Rad and Willa must have brought it. "Okay. But hold up. Let me talk to Jenny first." He'd promised to follow her lead until he had his feet under him as a father. He needed her buy-in before he let their daughter have a tire swing.

Gunner laughed. "Damn, son. You are *whipped*." Simon chuckled, too.

"Fuck you, bro. Don't play like you wouldn't ask Leah the same fucking thing."

He flipped his friends off and scanned the yard. Rad, Griffin, Apollo, and Becker were lounging on the new picnic table, drinking. Delaney and Dane were checking out the new grill. Kelsey was playing house with Zach in her cottage. Jenny stood on the patio with Willa and Leah. The other old ladies and Bulls must have been inside.

Jenny and Willa laughed at something Leah said. That was something he hadn't heard before—Jenny having a good laugh with the old ladies. Before, she'd been intimidated and shy around Mo, Joanna, and Maddie, all of whom were over forty and had been old ladies for decades. Maverick thought they'd been kind to Jenny, but she'd felt patronized. And maybe she had been. They were tough, assertive woman, all three of them, and Jenny, before, had not been.

But Willa was close to Jenny's age, and Leah was younger—and she, too, had had a toxic relationship with her father, according to Gunner. So maybe Jenny had simply needed someone more like her to connect with. He hadn't seen it then, but he'd had a club full of men like him. He hadn't seen why she couldn't value the club, the family that they were, the way he had.

This club, as it was now, offered Jenny family. Not before, but now. There was a lot he hadn't seen before. And a lot he hadn't heard. Now, with half his hearing gone, and near half his eyesight, he could listen and see clearly.

He saw his own place in the club again, too. His doubts and reservations, the grudge he'd harbored at the bottom of his heart for all the men who'd been living their lives while he'd been away, all of it eased, standing in his own back yard, on a crisp autumn afternoon, watching his woman and child blend into his club and become one.

~oOo~

"Can I do that?" Kelsey watched Gunner shimmy down the rope.

Crouched beside her, Maverick pulled her close. "No, pixie. The rope isn't for climbing. It's to hold the swing."

"But Uncle Gun was climbing."

"Just to hang the swing, so it's safe for you," Gunner said. He gripped the rope and pulled, making the tire spin gently. "Now it's good and strong and ready."

Kelsey stayed where she was, leaning back on Maverick's chest. "It's not a swing, though. We got swings at school and they're not like that. That's for cars."

Jenny came over and held out her hand. "Let's try it, pix."

With her mother's encouragement, Kelsey went forward, and Jenny picked her up and helped her get her legs through the tire and set her bottom comfortably. Gunner backed off, and Jenny gave the tire a little twist, just enough to rotate a couple of times.

Kelsey giggled. "It makes my tummy tickle! Can I go more?" Jenny twisted her a couple more times and let go, and Kelsey squealed with delight. "More! More!"

Still crouching nearby, Maverick felt his chest tighten, and he understood what people meant when they said their heart swelled. His felt like it was going to push straight through his ribcage.

Zach came toddle-bounding over, his arms up, headed for the swing, and Rad ran after him, sweeping him up in a wide arc and landing him over his shoulder. Zach screamed and kicked, yelling, "WANNA FWING! WANNA!"

Rad winced at the shriek in his ear. "No you don't, buster. You're not big enough, and your mama will have my balls for earrings."

Maverick laughed. If he was whipped, he wasn't the only one. They all were, from Delaney on down.

When you had the right woman, there was no other way to be.

~oOo~

"Babe, stop." He grabbed the stack of paper-wrapped plates out of Jenny's hands. "It's late. This'll all be here in the morning."

Their family had left, at long last. Maverick had bathed Kelsey and put her to bed. He'd sent Jenny to take a shower and had thought he'd find her in bed, waiting for him, but instead, he'd closed Kelsey's door and heard rattling and thumping and rustling in the kitchen. She was still unpacking.

"It's not late. It's eight-thirty."

He set the wrapped plates on the counter and grabbed the knot she'd made in her flannel shirt, at her waist. "Yeah, well, I have other plans for the rest of the night." He pulled her close and bent to taste the skin beneath her ear. "We've never fucked in this house. I want to do you in every room."

Her sultry chuckle rumbled over his tongue as he traced a line down her throat. "Not Kelsey's room, I hope."

"No. Not that one. Or her bathroom. But all the others. Thought we'd start with the kitchen." He grabbed her hips and lifted her onto the counter.

"You sure she's really asleep?" Jenny was already breathless and undoing the knot of her shirt.

Maverick pulled open his jeans and released his cock. "Sound asleep." He opened her jeans, and she helped him wriggle them off of her. Her panties hadn't come down with them, but he was too impatient for that. He yanked them aside and shoved into her, groaning in harmony with her gasp. Pulling the cup of her bra down, he latched himself onto her tit and began to thrust.

"Oh, Mav," she panted, winding her limbs around him. "I love you so much."

She'd always said that it didn't count when he was inside her, but he'd never agreed. "That's four," he rasped against her chest.

~oOo~

As the Bulls dismounted, Delaney sidled up to Maverick. "You steady, brother?"

"Yeah, yeah." He looked around the shadowy lot. This half-empty industrial park had been the site of more than a few of Montgomery's underground fights, and he knew it well.

The president nodded. "Let's see how bad this shit is. Everybody, stay back from Rad, Dane, and me. Stay alert and frosty. Getting the kid out in one piece is our priority. If we can do that and get out of here without anybody getting off a shot, we'll regroup in the chapel and work out what's next." He turned to Maverick again. "I know you're still holding onto that grudge with Dyson. I need you to keep holding it. We don't know the field right now. Understood?"

"I said I'm good, D."

Good wasn't the right word. But he was in control. His hatred for the Dyson crew was way down on his list of priorities now. He'd had Jenny and Kelsey with him for only a few days. His main priority was to keep that life intact. He'd never forgive or forget what Dyson had done to him, but his grudge was a cold stone in his heart. Something to feel, but no longer something to do. Killing Ellison Carver had been the last of the doing.

A steel door in one of the abandoned warehouses opened with a protesting creak, and dim light wedged out onto the cracked pavement. An unarmed man stepped out, little more than a silhouette against the pale light.

"Okay," Delaney gruffed. "Let's see what's what. We're crossing enemy lines, boys. Alert and frosty. Don't get dead. Let's get Wally and get out of this shit alive."

"Should some of us stay back, watch out here?" Gunner asked

"No," Rad answered. "We don't know what's in there, or what's waitin' out here. We stick together. Don't want a locked door splittin' us up."

"Could be an ambush, though. They could end the whole fuckin' club," Eight Ball observed.

Delaney nodded and wiped a hand over his beard. "Yeah, could be. Expect it. But where? In there, or out here? They got the leverage right now. That's why we get Wally and get out. We'll handle the beef later, on our terms. They set this table, and I don't want to choke down any more of what they're serving than we gotta."

"We're in the fuckin' city limits," Dane groused. "This is not how we work."

"Tonight, it is. Let's go."

Every member of the Brazen Bulls walked toward that open door. Delany, Dane, and Rad walked abreast in front. Ox, Eight, Becker, Apollo, and Simon made a second row. Maverick, Gunner, Griffin, and Slick brought up the rear.

The door itself was a pinch point, a vulnerability for the men walking blindly in. Maverick looked around, trying to see trouble in the lurking shadows.

He felt the weight of the gun at his back, and the second piece on his ankle. The brass knuckles in his pocket.

He felt the greater weight of his family. He'd made arrangements; Jenny wouldn't be without support, no matter what happened to him. But he'd only had this life for a few days. The thought that it might end already leaned hard on his shoulders and made his knees want to shake.

They went single file through that steel door and followed a wending path down dank corridors, into a wide space that must have once been stock storage. Massive steel racks had been clustered against one wall. The rest of the space was empty. Hooded lights stretched down from the ceiling and made a pattern of spotlights on the damp concrete floor, leaving the rest of the space in eerie darkness.

Under one of those spotlights was a metal chair. Bound to it, beaten and unconscious, was their prospect. Wally.

"Jesus fuck," Rad growled and pulled his gun. All the Bulls did likewise.

A rustling clatter of assault rifles being aimed answered the act, and about thirty black men — double the size of Melvin Dyson's crew, and more than double the Bulls — emerged from shadows around the room.

"Where's Melvin?" Delaney called.

Four seconds passed in silence before a man stepped out of the darkness and stood under one of the lights. He appeared to be unarmed.

At Maverick's side, Gunner muttered, "Oh, fuck me."

At the same time, Rad again grunted, "Jesus fuck." Ox did the thing he did, where he seemed suddenly to get even bigger. His back flared out and his shoulders spread. He was already enormous, so everybody called it 'Hulking out.'

These guys knew who that man was.

"D," Rad said, but Delaney held up a subtle hand to stop him.

"I know." To the man in the light, the Bulls president called, "Booker Howard. We haven't been introduced."

The man smiled. "But my reputation precedes me, looks like. And yours does, too, old man. Brian Delaney. King of the Bulls."

"Just president. I take it Melvin's not here."

Booker Howard laughed. He wore tidy slacks and a good-fitting Polo knit shirt. He was dressed like a man who had dinner plans after golf. A conservative businessman. Except for the ostentatious, gold-and-diamond Rolex glinting in the hard light.

"That's why I called this meeting. To serve you notice. The twenty-first century is coming up fast. The time has come for old men and old ways to make room. Melvin...let's say he retired. There is no more Dyson crew. The Street Hounds own Northside now. *I* own Northside. My ways aren't old ways."

He hadn't moved from his place under that light. He hadn't even gestured. With his hands at his sides, he'd rattled off that speech like a prepared oration.

"Good for you," Delaney snarled. "Why'd you take our boy?"

"Because he was easy, and I wanted your attention. You need to know how things are gonna be now. The Hounds want Tulsa. All of it. And I aim to make that happen."

Delaney laughed. "Boy, you got no idea how deep you just sank. Declaring war on us is a stupid fuckin' move."

Howard finally moved, reacting to Delaney's use of the word 'boy.' Maverick didn't think he'd meant it as anything other than 'young man,' as he'd used it to refer to Wally moments before, but Booker Howard took it to mean something more offensive, and his smile disappeared.

"I got your whole club locked in this room, and I could wipe you out with a snap of my fingers." He held up his hand as if to snap. That watch glittered. "I'm not declaring war, old man. I'm serving you and your redneck brothers your eviction notice. And one more thing." He stepped out of the circle of light, moved through shadow, and stopped in the next circle, about six feet from Delaney and Rad. He extended his arm, his finger pointed at the end of it. "I want him."

Gunner. He was pointing at Gunner.

"What the fuck?" Maverick muttered and moved in front of Gunner. "Fuck you."

Howard cocked his head. "I don't know you. Which one are you?"

"Maverick," he snarled. He felt Gunner's hand on him, trying to pull him off, but he shook it away. "You want him, you gotta get through me."

Finding his smile again, Howard answered, "I *do* know you. You're the one killed Jennings inside. I heard Clem Carver made you his bitch for that."

Maverick flinched against the whip of those words uttered with his brothers all around him, but he kept his eyes locked on Booker Howard. "I'm no man's bitch. You can ask Carver about that."

Delaney moved then, stepping between them and breaking Maverick's sightline. "You don't get Gunner. Not gonna happen."

"Then I keep the one I got." Howard snapped his fingers, and one of his men stepped forward and aimed his rifle at Wally's head.

"No!" Gunner shouted and tried to push forward, past Maverick. Releasing his two-handed hold on his gun, Maverick grabbed his friend and held on.

"Easy, Gun. Let D play it out," he muttered at his ear.

Delaney's voice was calm. "If you think you're gonna cause me pain over makin' a choice between 'em, you don't know shit about us. That boy there is not a patch, so my choice is easy. You don't get Gunner. But you kill that boy, and you will learn all about the Bulls. We will teach you every lesson we have. We will take our time and make sure you learn."

"Big words from a man leading a club I can wipe out right now."

"With a snap. So you say. But you won't. You're gonna give us our boy, and we're gonna walk out of here pretty as you please. While you watch."

Another curious head tilt from Howard. "You think so?"

"I know it. You're smart, Booker. I see that. You gotta be to take over a fifty-year-old organization and end the son of the man who started it. Melvin's roots went deep in Tulsa. So you must have worked some smart strategy to land where you are. You've done your research, I wager. You know who backs us, so you know what kind of power we have on our side. My bet is the Hounds are more than themselves, too. You have people to answer to. And they have bigger concerns than Tulsa. So you won't start a war right here."

"How's it a war if I wipe you out?"

Delaney didn't answer. Maverick couldn't see his face, but he had the strong impression that the president was smiling.

The scene seemed to freeze. Delaney and Howard stared at each other. Except for them, and the still-unconscious Wally, every man in the space was armed and aimed somewhere. But no one moved or spoke.

At last, Howard moved. He flicked his hand back toward his men. "Cut him loose." To Delaney, he said, "Take your *boy*. Get your asses out of here. But you remember tonight. We're coming for you, old man. You and your *club*."

~oOo~

"We gotta lock down," Rad said. "Bring our women and children in."

A rumble moved around the table as members agreed. Maverick was sure on board—though he worried how Jenny would take the news that already he'd brought danger to her and Kelsey. It hadn't even been a week since they'd moved in with him.

But Delaney shook his head. "We can't lock down. Not now. Not yet."

"What are you talkin' about, D?" Sitting beside Maverick, Gunner surged forward. His leg was going like a rabbit on meth; Maverick hadn't seen that kind of nervous energy in his friend since he'd been back. "That bastard is talking about a fucking *war*. He means to wipe us out. He took out *Dyson*. We can't leave our families unprotected."

"He was gonna kill Wally right in front of us," Apollo added. "Just snatched him off the street. To send a *message*. We're not gonna let that stand, right?"

Just about everybody had something to say then, and Delaney used the gavel to shut them up. "Enough. Talking all at once isn't gonna get us anywhere. We go in turns. Me first. Think about what a lockdown says. He makes his big threat, and we run home and pull up the drawbridge? That is the wrong fuckin' answer to his message, and you all know it. We need a show of strength."

Slick, who normally stayed quiet at the table, like just about every new patch Maverick had ever known, slapped his hands on the wood before him. "Wally's out there getting patched up. It's the second time in a few months that some Northside assholes tuned him up. Please tell me we're gonna do something about it."

"We are, son," Dane answered. The VP spoke quietly, and Maverick sensed him trying to settle the table.

But Slick wasn't finished. He turned on Delaney. "You were gonna let them cap him. Just walk away? Because he doesn't have a patch? Who the fuck are we, then?"

That quieted the room in a way neither Delaney nor Dane had managed. The president set down the gavel he'd still held, and he leaned in, crossing his arms on the table. "We are Brazen Bulls. We are brothers. Only us, around this table. I will choose any one of my brothers over any other man, and I won't blink before I do. Wally hasn't earned his patch yet. He is not my brother until he does. So I would have walked away. To save one of our own, we all would have."

His eyes narrowed. "And if you wouldn't, Slick, then that shiny new Bull on your back isn't your fit."

Slick sat back, his righteous anger deflating while they watched. "We came in together. He's as loyal to the club as I am. I don't know why I'm sitting here and he's not."

"Because your sponsor put your name up, kid," Rad replied. "Wally's didn't. Simple as that."

Everybody turned to Ox, Wally's sponsor. The big man shrugged. "He's loyal, yeah. Good kid. Hard worker. Tough. No initiative, though. He needs to step up more. He's not ready."

"He's bled for this club. He's bleeding for this club right now," Slick insisted.

Ox shook his head. "A patch isn't a consolation prize, brother. When he's ready, I'll put his name up."

"Not everybody at the table has to be a leader. Loyal and hardworking might be enough. Especially now. We're gonna need the bodies if we're about to start a war." Dane stubbed out his cigarette and looked down the table at Ox. "Just something to think about."

Ox nodded once, acknowledging Dane's observation but not agreeing.

"We won't start it," Delaney corrected. "Howard already has. But we'll damn well finish it. There anything more to be said on the question of a lockdown?"

Yes, there was much more to be said. Maverick pulled a fresh beer from the tub in the center of the table. It was going to be a long meeting.

~oOo~

Three hours later, Maverick pulled onto his driveway and parked next to the Cherokee. He sat there for a minute, astride his bike, and studied the front of the house. The windows glowed warmly as the lights inside beamed through the sheer curtains into the night. That was one of the best sights—his house, lit up in the night though he hadn't been home, because his family was. He imagined Jenny in there, putting Kelsey to bed, sitting in bed with her and reading her a story while she hugged the night's choice for slumber party guest.

Just like the dream he'd held close most of his life. His family. At home.

He was frazzled and half-drunk and scared. The word 'war' had been thrown around like a goddamn ball all night. They'd spent half an hour arguing about whether to lock the clubhouse down, ultimately voting not to. Delaney's insistence that it was too soon and too weak had eventually persuaded most of the table.

Maverick had voted for the lockdown, wanting to do whatever they could to keep their people safe. But at the same time, he'd been afraid that it would go through. They hadn't had a lockdown while he'd been with Jenny before, and she'd been uncomfortable enough with the club. Now, she was finding her place in it, but what would she do if he told her that his world had become so unsafe she and Kelsey had to be locked away? Could he lose them again?

No. She'd made her choice. She knew enough about the Bulls, and about him, to know what being with him meant. They were together, and he wouldn't lose them again. End of story.

Something landed on his leg, and he jumped as several little points of light pain sank into his calf. He looked down and saw two gleaming eyes looking up at him. While he tried to decide what kind of critter was claiming him, it mewed. A kitten.

"Hey, shorty. You alone out here?" He picked it up and brought it to his chest. Just a tiny thing, more fur than animal. It made its little squeaking mewl again and began to purr, its chest rumbling against Maverick's gloved hand, and its front paws paddling back and forth. "You got a mom out here? Kitty, kitty? Here, kitty?"

He called a few times and made kissing sounds, trying to draw a mother cat into the open. The kitten did its part, too, crying. He dismounted and rooted around the yard, but found nothing. Just this tiny puff in his hands, purring and mewing and shivering.

He'd wanted to get Kelsey a puppy or a kitten. He'd been thinking Christmas, but maybe Fate had a better idea. "You need a home, shorty? I just happen to have one right here. Brand spankin' new."

The turmoil of the night forgotten for now, Maverick carried the kitten up to the porch—in the light, he could see that it was grey stripes with white feet—and into the house.

Jenny sat in the living room, watching television. She muted it with the remote and stood as he worked his way out of his gloves, kutte, and jacket while holding the kitten. It mewed, opening its mouth wide for that tiny sound, and Jenny stopped in her path toward him.

"What d'you got there?"

Maverick grinned, hoping it was charming. "Found it outside. Climbed right up my leg. I don't think there's a mom around. I looked all over. It's too cold to leave him out there."

He held his breath for her reaction and released it in a puff when she smiled. "Definitely too cold. Probably too cold for fleas, too, and that's a good thing." She took the kitten from him and turned it over. "Girl." Scratching at its little grey belly, she seemed to be examining it. "She's skinny. But looks like no fleas." Her beautiful eyes came up, and she smiled. "Kelsey's still awake. She's been telling herself her books. She won't sleep for a long time if you bring that to her now."

"Should I not?"

"Go ahead. I'll keep her home tomorrow if she doesn't get enough sleep. Seems like this is a day to make our family bigger."

That seemed an odd thing to say. As the kitten escaped her grip and climbed up her shoulder, Maverick picked it up again. "What's that mean?"

Jenny's smile was wide and happy, and as her mouth began to form the words, he knew what she would say. "I'm pregnant."

"Holy shit!" he shouted, startling the kitten, who promptly sank all her claws into his chest. He could not have cared less. He grabbed Jenny and crushed her close, slamming his mouth over hers. The kiss was wild, frenzied, and brief. When he broke away, he said, "Marry me, Jenny. Marry me now."

She laughed. "Right now? Not sure we can put it all together at ten o'clock at night if you want it to be legal."

"As soon as we can, then." When she nodded, he kissed her again. "Thank you, babe."

"You don't have to thank me. Just love me."

"That's easy," he said and kissed her again. The kitten crawled onto the back of his neck.

~oOo~

Late that night, as Jenny slept at his side, and Miss Shorty—so christened by their ecstatic little girl after hearing him call her 'shorty'—slept on his pillow, purring loudly, Maverick lay and stared up at the ceiling. His brain was too busy for rest.

He wasn't upset. The bliss of his evening at home with his family, of Kelsey staying up long past her bedtime to play with her new baby and finally simply falling over on the sofa, unconscious, and of Jenny, pregnant and, as far as he was concerned, already glowing—that bliss had eased his worry away. So he wasn't upset.

But he was aware. Alert. Needing to process everything about the day, and about so much more. He had everything to lose. But he wouldn't lose it. He would keep them safe and healthy and happy, and he would do it smart this time. Delaney had been fucking brilliant in that warehouse, and Maverick trusted him again one-hundred percent. If he said Irina Volkov would have their backs, then Maverick would believe it.

He still believed that Volkov owed him. Big. But what he felt for her was no longer a grudge. Just a debt he would expect to be repaid. A substantial debt. He had killed for her and paid dearly for it, and he had not been compensated. It was a favor in the Bulls' bank. Delaney believed her to be honorable. If she was, then Maverick could trust her to feel that obligation. That would keep the Bulls and their family protected.

Maybe, then, what had happened inside, had been…not worth it, never that, but at least something good might balance out its bad.

He hadn't really considered that people outside would know everything that had happened. As far as he was aware, until tonight, his brothers had had no idea, and he had absolutely intended to keep it that way. If they'd understood what Howard had meant, none of them had said so, or even looked at Maverick askance. But none of his brothers was an idiot. They'd heard, and they knew. Maybe it would come up in some way, someday. If so, he'd deal with it then.

Howard had gotten it wrong. Never had he been Carver's bitch or anyone else's. He'd been ambushed, and he'd been badly hurt, but that was different.

And he had made Carver pay.

July 1996

The hit had gone down smoothly. A shiv had been delivered to him, he'd found Jennings in the showers and slammed it repeatedly into the man's neck while Jenning's eyes were covered in shampoo suds, and he'd dropped it in the mop bucket, which was full of bleach, as instructed. He'd done the hit naked himself, so he'd rinsed off, dried off, and gone back to his dreary routine.

One, two, three, done.

A week later, the guards had turned everybody's cell over, looking for evidence. They'd found the shiv in his bunk. He'd been fucking framed for a murder he'd actually committed.

He hadn't reacted, and he hadn't fought, but the guards had been brutal anyway, getting him into the hole.

Now he sat here, with probably a few busted ribs and a concussion, at least. Four walls hemmed him in on all sides, and he was alone except for his thoughts—and those thoughts were black as pitch. Once upon a time, he'd been slated to do a few months in county jail. Instead he'd gotten three years in the pen, and the guards here had seen immediately to it that he wouldn't get parole. Now, with mere weeks left of his full sentence, he sat in solitary, waiting to be tried for murder.

He was going to die inside.

~oOo~

He'd lost track of how many days he'd been down here, but the lights were out, so it was probably night when the door slammed open and light from the corridor blinded him for a second. He could only make out shapes, but he could hear, and smell, that men had entered his small cell. Men, in the plural, slamming into his cell in the dark.

Maverick jumped to his feet, just as the cell door clanged shut and near-total darkness took over again.

But he was used to the dark, and his eyesight, faulty thought it was, improved once the blinding light from beyond his cell had been doused.

Five men. There were five men in here with him, in his tiny cell. He could make out their shapes, could see them arc around him, wedging him into the corner.

He didn't need to spend a single thought to know who it was: Dyson. He'd figured already that it must have been them who'd planted the shiv. A murder sentence wasn't enough retaliation for Jennings' death, apparently.

They'd cornered him, but he'd fought in the ring for years, on the streets for longer than that, and in here, fighting the most brutal battles of his life, since the second week of his sentence. He knew how to use his environment. He could use the walls, and the dark, and the simple mass of them all, against them.

"This is for Linc," said one near the door. He knew that voice. Clem Carver. Head of the Dysons at McAlester.

Carver stood near the door, but the others came at him all at once.

He grabbed the first body he could and jumped, putting his bare feet on the wall and climbing up, jumping over, holding on, trying to wrench the head he'd gotten hold of. His still-broken ribs screamed in his chest, but he was fighting for his life, and he let the scream out through his mouth. He never yelled, not in fighting, not in life, but he yelled now. He roared.

The body in his arms dropped as he took a heavy punch to his face and the darkness lit up with stars. Ducking low, he slammed blindly forward, taking another body in the fleshy middle, and he reached out, ignoring the blows and kicks raining all over him, and wrapped his arms around two legs. He heaved and arched back, feeling his ribs separate, the fragile healing they'd started breaking free. The body in his hands came up, and he heard a satisfying crack as some part of it—the head, he hoped—hit the metal edge of his bolted-on bunk. Two down. Two to go. And then Carver to deal with.

He could taste blood coming up with his breath, and his head clanged and whirled, but he wasn't going down. He fucking was not.

"Enough. I'm bored. Time to make some memories."

Maverick heard the words but had barely made sense of them before fiery pain sliced across his gut and folded him forward, and he felt a wash of hot liquid spread over his belly and down his leg. And then another blaze of pain in his side. He'd been shanked. Twice.

Fuck it. He was *not* going down. He roared again and turned in the direction the shiv had come from, but one of the men he'd put down got up again, right under him, and sent him headlong to the floor. His chest crashed into his bunk, and he couldn't breathe.

"Get him down. Let's go."

He tried to fight without air, but there were too many hands, too many fists, too many arms. He was yanked up as he finally managed to drag white-hot agony into his lungs, and they slammed him onto his bunk.

Face down.

Knowing what was next, Maverick was already trying to shout again when he felt hands at his prison-issue pants, tearing and yanking. *NO!* His desperate lungs held onto the little bit of air he'd given them, and his shouts, his screams, were silent.

NO! NO!

They held his arms, pulled his legs apart, pressed down on his back. And then there was a heavy body on him, skin to skin.

Carver's voice was soft at his ear, almost sensual, and that—his quiet ease, his *enjoyment*—made everything all the more horrible. "This is what you get when you fuck with Dyson, son. We fuck you right back. You're gonna remember that for next time."

~oOo~

Maverick woke with a breathing tube down his throat and knew immediately that he wasn't in the penitentiary. The room was too big and bright, too cheery. He was shackled to a bed, but there was a window at his side, without wire or bars, showing bright sun and blue sky.

He was in the local hospital. They'd fucked him up bad, then. Bad enough that the infirmary couldn't help him. He'd almost died.

That would have been a better result. An end to this miserable existence.

But he was alive, and they'd send him back the second he was strong enough not to die of his injuries. He'd go back in, and every single day, probably for the rest of his life, he would face the men who'd done this to him.

Four of the men who'd attacked him were nothing but dark forms, faceless, anonymous. He'd have to take down all of Dyson to be sure to get them, and that was impossible. Even if he strengthened his relationship with Groddo and his band of idiots, they wouldn't take on a war like that. Evans and the other guards would tear them all to pieces.

But he'd known Clement Carver. That voice in the dark, in his ear. Carver was the one who'd really hurt him. He was their leader, but he was not invincible.

Carver had told him he would remember. And he did. He remembered every fucking second.

He would never forget.

He would make him pay for all of it.

CHAPTER EIGHTEEN

They were married in the clubhouse, a week before Thanksgiving.

Not long ago, Jenny would have sworn up and down and all over that she'd never even step foot in the Bulls' clubhouse again, much less hold her wedding ceremony in the party room, next to the bar and the pool table and in full sight of the obscene pinball machine.

After the night that she'd told him she was pregnant and they'd decided to hurry the wedding up, they'd spent about a day talking about the wheres and hows. Maverick had suggested they just go to the courthouse, but he'd visibly flinched when he'd said the word, and Jenny didn't want their marriage associated with his other experiences in that place—she had her own bad memories of the last time she'd been in the courthouse.

So then where? It was November, and the blush of warmth they'd had when they'd moved had faded. The weather was grey and cold, so they couldn't exactly go to a park or something like that. A church was out of the question. When he'd suggested a banquet hall, some generic, tacky box of a place, Jenny had seen the obvious: there was only one place they could get married.

He'd been surprised when she'd suggested the clubhouse, and he'd resisted for reasons not unlike hers for resisting the courthouse. He didn't want her to be uncomfortable. He wanted their memories of this event to be only good.

But she wasn't uncomfortable with the Bulls anymore. She didn't love them all, but she'd found friends—Willa and Leah, and Gunner, too. Even Rad. Mo was…Mo, and Jenny had some rough history with her, but she was being nice.

Everybody was being nice and not overly condescending or suspicious.

What was more, she herself was less suspicious and tentative. Maybe it was just that she'd been on her own and lonely for such a long time, but she felt less vulnerable to judgment and, consequently, she felt less judged.

Whatever it was, she'd noticed it on the day she and Kelsey had moved in with Maverick, when the entire Bulls family had helped. Watching Maverick with his brothers, with the other old ladies, watching them all love Kelsey and show that love freely, she'd seen it: they were her family, too.

So they got married in the clubhouse, with Gunner and Willa standing with them, and Kelsey standing between them, holding their hands. And Mr. and Mrs. Turner standing right up front.

Jenny wore a crème lace dress that she found at the mall, and a pair of simple pumps. Kelsey wore a mint-green dress with shiny black Mary Janes. They'd had their hair done together that morning, matching updos, and tendrils fell in little airy ringlets down the back of Kelsey's neck. Maverick wore jeans and his kutte, over a black button shirt.

The Reverend Matilda Fielder, of the Glory to the Savior Fellowship Church, the storefront church at the other end of the block, presided, and after the five-minute exchange of vows and plain gold bands, after Maverick kissed the shit out of her while their daughter looked on and the club cheered, the Bulls opened the doors to the neighborhood, and they all partied.

It wasn't the kind of wedding that magazines featured on their covers, but it was just the right wedding for them.

~oOo~

"Hey, Mo." Jenny stepped beside her at the Delaneys' huge dining room table and picked up a stack of china plates. "I'll help."

Mo gave her a sidelong look. "Thanks, love."

The warm rumble of family chaos filled the silence as the women set the table. With all its leaves in and a folding banquet table at the end, the table extended through the large dining room, well into the living room. The whole thing was covered with crisp, smooth white linen, and would hold the entire Bulls family and then some. Mo Delaney did not think small when she entertained.

Jenny had made a decision, but now that she meant to act on it, her brain had seized up. But this was a good time. It was Thanksgiving, and they were, for now, alone together, almost in private. Finally, after she had circled the table, placing a plate before each chair, while Mo laid out silverware, she screwed up her courage and said, "Can I talk to you for a minute?"

"Sure." She answered without looking up, arranging a knife on a folded linen napkin.

"No." She put her hand on Mo's arm to stop her work. "I mean really talk."

Mo stopped and stood up straight. She met Jenny's regard head on and waited.

Before her brain could fail her again, Jenny jumped in. "I want to tell you I'm sorry. Truly sorry."

"For?" Mo asked, but Jenny knew she knew.

"I said something terrible to you once. I think it's the meanest thing I've ever said to anyone. God, I hope it is. I hope I've never been *worse* than that. It was terrible, and I'm sorry. I know you and I are never going to be great friends, but I just...I just want you to know that I hated myself for saying it then, and I've always been sorry."

Jenny had no idea how old Mo was. In her fifties, maybe? Something like that? She was a severely beautiful woman—a striking kind of beauty, all in contrasts. Fair skin. Dark, nearly raven-black hair. Black, arching brows. Pale, piercing blue eyes. Cheekbones for days. There was nothing at all approachable in that beauty. To Jenny, she looked almost exactly like the Evil Queen in *Snow White*.

The expression that Jenny's words had provoked was a picture of the Queen's imperial contempt, and she instantly regretted opening her mouth.

Mo set her handful of silverware on the table with a tinkling clatter. "Do you know why Thanksgiving is my favorite holiday, Jenny?"

Jenny shook her head, afraid to make more dangerous words.

"It's the only holiday of the year that's truly about family. However you make up your family, Thanksgiving celebrates it. You don't have to have a picture-postcard life to bring the people you love into your home and feed them and be grateful to have them. There's no one relationship that's more important than the others. Christmas—that's about the children. Halloween, too. Valentine's Day is for lovers. Mother's Day. Father's Day. They're all about one kind of love or another. Thanksgiving is for all kinds of love, and however you love, whoever you love, whatever kind of family you made, you can have them with you and love them and feel their love back."

She swiped at her cheek. Jenny wouldn't have known she was crying otherwise. Just that one brisk swipe, and she continued. "I don't have the picture-postcard family. The Bulls are my brothers and sons. Their women are my sisters and daughters. Their children are my grandbabies. We don't fit on any card you can buy at the Promenade, but we're family just the same. I had to make mine up all on my own, and I love them just as hard and deep as anybody ever loved anyone. The Lord didn't see fit to let me have babies of my own. He let me hope, but He didn't let me keep them. That was a source of bad pain for a very long time. So aye, what you said that day was awful. But I know why you said it. You wanted me to stay away, and you knew I wouldn't unless you hurt me enough. You were right about that. You were wrong to do it, but you were scared, and it's hard to do the right thing when you're scared."

Mo paused, and Jenny got the feeling she was giving her a chance to respond, but there wasn't anything she could say.

"You say we won't ever be great friends, and perhaps that's true. But that won't be because I harbor bad feelings, or because I don't want to love you like a daughter. You answer me one question, and, for my part, you and I are squared up fine."

"Okay." The word barely came out.

Stepping closer, so there was only the width of a high-back chair between them, Mo crossed her arms. "Are you all in? Whatever happens, are you in with Maverick, and with all of us? Not on the edges, but right here in the heart. Are you family?"

Jenny looked down at the gold band on her finger. Nothing flashy, just simple, gleaming gold, a match to Maverick's. The only ring he wore. The only ring she wore.

She lifted her head and met those arctic blue eyes. "I didn't have the picture-postcard family, either. Mav gave me the best family I've ever had. He gave me Kelsey." She spread her hands to indicate the huge table dressed for a feast. "He gave me and Kelsey this. I'm all in, Mo."

Mo was quiet, studying her. Then, her red lips curving into the slightest smile, she tilted her head. "Well, then. We'd best get this table set so we can give our family a proper Thanksgiving feast." She picked up the bundle of silverware again.

Just that head tilt. No hug, no heartwarming moment of tearful reconciliation. Just acceptance.

It was exactly right.

~oOo~

Twenty-four people sat at that long table—eleven on each side, and Mo and Delaney at the ends. All of the Bulls, all of their old ladies, Gunner's father and sister, Wally, the prospect, and Kelsey. Zach was down for a nap. Kelsey sat between her parents, her eyes wide and her head swiveling all around, trying to keep up with all the talk and laughter.

When all were seated, Delaney put his fingers in his mouth and whistled, and everyone quieted down. Keeping with Mo's longstanding tradition, starting with Delaney, they went around the table and told something they were thankful for. For most, it was mundane stuff—they were happy for their families, for a new bike, for some good news they'd gotten. When it was Maverick's turn, he cleared his throat.

"I got a lot of things I'm thankful for, and I'm thankful even to be able to say that. I'm thankful to be free. I'm thankful to be at this table." He grinned and looked around at his brothers. "I'm thankful for all you assholes." Chuckles rose up around the table, as well as a few middle fingers.

He reached around Kelsey's back and brushed his fingertips over Jenny's cheek. He looked at her as he said the rest. "But most of all, I'm thankful for my wife and child. This beautiful woman, and the perfect little girl she made me." He winked then, and Jenny had that flash of a second to know what he was about to do. "And I'm thankful that she's making me another one as we speak."

They hadn't even told Kelsey yet. Jenny stared at him, stunned. All around them, their family shared the same stunned silence.

"Wait," Gunner finally said. "Jen—he knocked you up again?"

"Damn, bro," Maverick laughed. "Leave it to you to kill the magic."

As the table caught on and erupted with good cheer, Jenny turned to Mo. After the talk they'd had less than an hour earlier, it seemed like the wrong time to announce her pregnancy. But Mo returned her look and gave her that same accepting tilt of the head, this one with a fuller smile.

"Well done, love," she said under the din.

Willa and Leah and the other women converged on her at once, and she accepted all their hugs.

Kelsey tugged on her sleeve, and Jenny turned. "What is it, pix?"

"I don't know why everybody's hugging you and hitting Daddy's hand."

"They're happy. When Daddy said I was making him another one, he meant that there's a baby growing in my belly."

"Now?" She frowned at Jenny's flat stomach. "In there?"

Jenny picked up her daughter's hand and set it on her belly. "Right inside there. It's just tiny right now, but it'll keep growing and growing, and in the summer, maybe close to your birthday, you'll have a baby brother or sister."

"Really?" She patted Jenny's belly. "Is it a boy baby or a girl baby?"

"We don't know yet. We'll find out in a few months. And then you can help us decorate the baby's room and get everything ready."

The table was settling down again, and Kelsey turned away from Jenny and pulled on Maverick's arm. "Daddy! I want to say a thankful, too! Can I?"

Maverick picked her up and set her on his lap. "Sure, pix. Go ahead."

She looked all around the table, like a queen surveying her realm. Then she took a big, serious breath. "I'm thankful that I have a mommy and a daddy and we all live together in a house with a princess house and Mommy is making a baby and I used to want a boy baby but now I want a girl baby 'cuz Maisie got a boy baby and he pees in the air." She swooped her little arm up high, drawing a fountain spout in the air, to demonstrate.

When the table erupted yet again, this time with laughter, Jenny saw Kelsey startle and frown. She reached over, meaning to ease her daughter's mind, but Maverick tucked his face close and spoke to Kelsey until she grinned.

A storm of happy tears loomed on Jenny's horizon, and she knew she'd make a mess of herself when the table settled again and it was her turn to be thankful. But that was okay. She knew just what she'd say.

~oOo~

On their way home that evening, they stopped at the nursing home to see her father on Thanksgiving.

Maverick waited in the Cherokee. He would never budge on his feelings about her father, and Jenny would never expect it of him. He didn't understand why she'd want to visit, and he wasn't happy that she wanted to bring Kelsey with her, but they'd talked it out, he'd listened, and he hadn't pushed her to change her mind.

But he didn't want her going alone, so he was there, waiting in the car. Jenny knew that that was pressure as much as protection. More than protection. There was nothing her father could do anymore to hurt her. But Maverick waiting outside meant that they wouldn't linger inside.

A little manipulative, yes. But first they'd had a full, fair talk; he'd listened, and he'd conceded. That was such an improvement over before that Jenny was content to let him have this small measure of influence on the situation.

The home they'd found was a good one—in a decent suburb just west of the city proper, with up-to-date facilities and resources, and pleasant, thoughtful décor. On her own, she'd never have been able to afford it. It didn't even smell. Every place they'd visited had had the same odor in the air—disinfectant, bland food, and decay, with a persistent hint of human waste. In the cheaper places, that smell had been nearly overpowering. In this place, it was there, but only noticeable if you tried to smell it.

He shared a room with another man, an elderly gentleman with dementia, and Jenny knew that he hated that. But a private room was beyond their means without unduly burdening their own life. She'd brought as many of his things as she'd been allowed, and she'd hung his favorite pictures on the walls around his bed. She'd made it as nice as she could for him, and it was nicer than the house they'd moved out of, except that it wasn't his.

As they walked through the halls, Jenny smiled at the staff they passed, and Kelsey pointed out all the decorations—lots of construction-paper turkeys and headdresses and pilgrim hats. The home had arrangements with a few nearby preschools for children to visit and spend time with the residents, and they did art projects together.

His room was empty, so they went down to the cafeteria, which doubled as a recreation room when meals weren't being served. They found him in his chair, in front of the television.

"Granddaddy!" Kelsey let go of Jenny's hand and skipped to her grandfather. She stood at his side, where he could see her, and patted his hand. "Hi, Granddaddy. Did you have a good Thanksgiving? I did. We went to a big house and had a big turkey and there was chocolate pie and I don't like pie but this was good and had white stuff on it that tasted like marshmallows and Mommy is making a baby!"

Jenny's father flapped his hand, and Kelsey caught it and held it. "I hope you got turkey and pie like I did."

"Jen."

"Right here, Dad." She came up on her father's other side and bent to kiss his cheek. It was smooth, and he was dressed in khakis and a plaid shirt. Somebody had dressed him for Thanksgiving. "Happy Thanksgiving. Did you have a good day?"

"Now. Now. Jen."

With so few words in his vocabulary, it wasn't easy to know what he meant. Jenny had gotten as adept as she thought it was possible to be in 'Dadese,' but he could have been saying that it was a good day now, because she and Kelsey were there, or he could have been asking her to take him away right now. She elected to hear the first one.

She smiled and pulled up a chair to sit beside him. "I've got some news to share. Kelsey told you that we're having a baby. Next summer. And Mav and I got married last week."

"Yeah, Granddaddy! I got a pretty dress and had my hair like Mommy's and then Daddy kissed her and everybody clapped."

Her father's eyes moved back and forth from daughter to granddaughter, and his mouth moved, but he didn't speak. Knowing that news wouldn't bring him happiness, she changed the subject.

"I heard from Darnell. He got promoted. He's in administration now at the service. And Carlena's got a new assignment. They're both doing good. I've decided not to sell the bar. I'm going to keep The Wayside. Is that okay with you?" She knew it was. The only thing in life he truly loved was that bar.

"Jen."

"I'm not going to run it day-to-day anymore, though. I made Dave the full-time manager, and I'm hiring more staff. I'm going to stay home with Kelsey and this new one, but The Wayside is a neighborhood institution, and when it comes down to it, I can't sell it to somebody who'd change it up too much. Russ and the others, they'd practically be homeless if they couldn't camp their butts at the bar."

His hand flailed out and grabbed at hers. She let him catch it. "Jen. Jen."

She remembered the day she'd brought him back to the house, after his insurance had cut off his hospital care. On that day, when Kelsey was only two months old and still colicky, Jenny had known utter despair and felt nothing for her father but furious, hateful resentment. There had been no pity for his circumstances, no hint of the tormented love she'd grown up feeling for him, no glimmer of hope. She'd only hated and despaired, and she'd been sure she'd never feel anything else.

The television had caught Kelsey's attention, and she'd taken a couple of steps toward it. Jenny turned her hand so that she held her father's, rather than the other way around, and she brought it to her mouth and kissed it. "I'm happy, Dad. Things are the way they're supposed to be now. I know you don't want to be here, but taking care of you was crushing me, and Kelsey, too. In just the few weeks you've been here, everything inside me is lighter. How I feel about you, about the kind of father you were, that's lighter, too. I can forgive you now, Daddy. I do forgive you."

How much could he understand? Jenny didn't know. But he grew calm, and he stared back at her, and his hand seemed to squeeze around hers. "Jen," was all he said. The word he'd said more than any other in the past four years.

Her name.

"I love you," she was able to say, and to mean, for the first time in years.

October 1993

Jenny stood in the dining room and watched as Darnell, her father's new nurse, and the ambulance drivers or technicians or whatever they were pushed her father's gurney up the ramp she'd had installed on the side of the porch. He was still in a gurney, unable to support himself upright, but his insurance wouldn't pay for any more time in the hospital.

They got onto the porch and swung around.

"Hold on, hold on," Darnell, in the lead, said.

A male nurse. A big black male nurse. Jenny wondered what her father thought about that. He wasn't racist, exactly, he served whoever came into his bar, he was cordial to the Turners next door, and he was civil to the people he met, but he thought black people weren't as smart or industrious as white people.

Actually, yeah, he was racist. He had been, anyway. Jenny wasn't clear on how much of who he'd been still remained inside that silent, jerky body. How would he feel about Darnell feeding him and bathing him and changing his diapers?

His other nurse was a heavyset, muscular Native American woman. Would he like that more? Or less? Did it matter, if he couldn't say? Would he learn anything, being dependent on people he didn't respect? Was he capable of it? Had he ever been?

Strapped to her chest in the Snugli, Kelsey popped Jenny's boob free and started to fuss. Jenny began bouncing at once—since she'd discovered that Kelsey would be quiet if she was in the Snugli while Jenny bounced and swayed, she felt like she was never still—and shifted her to the other boob. She didn't bother to close the 'done' side of her bra.

"Gurney won't fit," Darnell called to the ambulance guys. "I'm gonna need to take the doors off." He leaned into the house and sent Jenny a questioning look. "That okay by you, ma'am?"

No one had ever called her 'ma'am' before Darnell. It didn't sound right. "Yeah. Whatever you need."

Darnell had been to the house a few times in the past few days, giving her tips about how to get ready for her father. They'd made sure the wheelchair her father got would fit through the doors and hallways of the house, but they hadn't measured for a gurney.

Was nothing about this ordeal going to just be easy? Just happen without a hitch? Nothing at all? Wasn't it bad enough that it was happening at all?

"You got tools? A screwdriver?"

"Yeah. The garage. I'll get 'em." She turned, and Kelsey lost the boob and began to cry. Jenny dug into the Snugli, perfectly aware that her left boob was showing at its side, still dripping milk, and not giving a ripe fuck, and tried to get her squalling child to latch back on.

All at once, with no warning, Jenny was crying, too. "Please, pixie," she begged an infant who couldn't understand.

"You know what? Never mind. I'll carry him in." Darnell stepped back out. After a minute or two, he came in, her father cradled in his arms like he weighed nothing, and carried him back to his bedroom.

Kelsey latched. Jenny was still crying, almost getting it under control, when she noticed one of the ambulance guys standing just inside the front door. "What?"

"Sorry. I need you to sign." He held out a clipboard. She went and scrawled her signature on the line he indicated, and then he and his colleague pushed the gurney away. They left two bright yellow plastic bags on the porch.

Inside one of the bags, Jenny could see the blood-spattered checkered pattern of the shirt her father had been wearing they day he'd last beat her, the day that Maverick had done this to them all. She stood on the threshold, feeling the rhythmic draw of Kelsey's suckle, her other boob out for the world to see, and stared down at that piece of shirt.

"Ma'am?" Darnell stood right behind her.

"Jenny." She turned around and faced him. "Please call me Jenny." That seemed supremely important just now. She needed a friend, and Darnell was the closest candidate. A friend wouldn't call her 'ma'am.'

He reached out and pulled her shirt over, covering her boob. "Jenny. It's gonna be okay."

She shook her head, disappointed in his empty words. It was not going to be okay.

But he pulled her inside, picked up the yellow bags, and closed the door. "It is. I've been doing this job a while now, and I know that families find their way. It's like learning a new dance. When you don't know the steps, you trip over yourself, making mistakes all the time. But once you figure it out, you move smooth, and everybody thinks you're magic."

The image of this big man dancing, like Astaire and Rogers, made her smile. "You dance?"

"I do. Met my wife that way. Got a wild hair and took a class. Latin dancing, if you can imagine. She was teaching it." He grinned. "I looked a fool, swingin' my big ol' legs and arms every which way, trippin' over these boats in my shoes, but she didn't give up on me." His grin softened. "Don't you give up on you. It'll be okay. You'll figure out the steps."

Jenny offered him a nod. She wasn't convinced, but she appreciated the encouragement and, for the first time in months, she didn't feel completely alone.

Maybe Darnell was a friend.

CHAPTER NINETEEN

"Hold up. You see that?"

At Gunner's question, Maverick and Apollo stopped and looked. Becker, who'd come up from behind after paying their tab for supper, ran into Maverick's back.

"Shit, sorry, man. Why'd we stop?"

Maverick didn't know yet. But Gunner had sidestepped into the alley, and instinct drew Maverick and the others into cover as well. They didn't need to know why to be cautious. They trusted their brother that there was cause.

Looking over Gunner's shoulder, Maverick focused on the storefront across the intersection—a mom-and-pop pho place that the Bulls frequented. One of those excellent little places that locals kept a secret. They'd actually bickered this evening about whether to eat there or at the burger joint they'd landed at. Beef and beer had won out.

A white Lincoln Navigator was parked at the curb, its high sheen reflecting the rainbow of Christmas lights that swagged across the streets in this part of town.

"That's Derrick Ammons' ride," Gunner said.

Becker put his hands on Maverick's shoulders and rose up on his toes, rubbernecking. "You sure?"

"Yeah. Look at the wheels. I'd know that bling anywhere. He treats that truck like a woman. Probably fucks the tailpipe." The wheels were super-high-end chrome spinners. Even on the parked car, they threw light back like jewels. Gunner looked over his shoulder and met Maverick's eyes. "They're on our turf."

Since Booker Howard had pounded his message into Wally's head, the Bulls had been preparing for war. More than simply gearing up, they'd put Apollo on intel, and he'd dug deep. Derrick Ammons had been a mid-level operative in the Dyson crew, but he'd been promoted since Melvin Dyson's 'retirement' and was now the distribution chief for Street Hounds.

Still leaning on Maverick's shoulders, Becker said, "They're still owed for Wally."

If they moved on somebody that high up as retaliation for their prospect, it could set the fuse alight on the keg of gunpowder that sat between the Bulls and the Hounds. Maverick shook his head. "We gotta get to a phone, call D in on this."

"I got this." Apollo dug into his kutte and pulled out...a phone. Once of the cell phones Maverick had seen ads for on television. Nokeys, or something like that. He figured them as toys for rich businessmen. The guys who'd already had car phones.

Keeping an eye on the restaurant, Maverick heard Apollo's call connect. "D, it's Apollo. I'm with Mav, Gun, and Beck, over by Pho Ha's. We got a situation.... We're standing here looking at Ammons' SUV."

After a beat or two, he set the phone from his ear. "Anybody see a guard on that thing?"

"Not out here," Gunner said. "They might have somebody keeping their eyes peeled inside." He turned his whole body to face Apollo. "He wants us to hit the *truck*?"

Delaney had obviously heard that, because they could all hear him through the earpiece of Apollo's toy. "GUN! SETTLE!"

Becker chuckled. Maverick couldn't keep the smirk from his lips. Apollo beamed a grin bright enough to illuminate the alley. Gunner flipped them all off.

Apollo put the phone back to his ear. "What should we do, prez?" He listened, nodding, "What's everybody carrying?" he asked, then held the phone out among them again, so Delaney could hear.

Maverick pulled his kutte open to show his shoulder holster. "My Glock, same's always."

"My Sig," answered Gunner.

"I got my Sig on me," said Becker. "But I got Boom Boom in my saddlebag."

'Boom Boom' was Becker's fifty-caliber Desert Eagle. A ridiculous handgun.

Apollo put the phone back to his head. "And I got my Beretta." He listened again. "Okay, D. I'll call when it's done."

Shoving his phone back into his kutte pocket, Apollo pulled his sidearm. "Everybody mount up and lock and load. And get Boom, Beck. We're killing the truck."

They mounted their bikes and rode up, spanning the street. Going through the intersection, they braked, aimed, and all at once, fired, unloading four mags into the Navigator.

Thunder exploded from Becker's Eagle, and the SUV rocked and bounced with every bullet. Glass sprayed, tires exploded, water hissed from the engine. The alarm wailed until a bullet struck it and shut it up.

They fired fast and emptied their mags just as the door to Pho Ha flew open and four black men surged out, their guns already drawn.

In the sudden break after the Bulls ran out of bullets, Maverick heard Bing Crosby's voice, coming through the open restaurant door. Ol' Bing was dreaming of a white Christmas. The mounds of shattered auto glass on the street and sidewalk, glinting back the festive Technicolor of strung Christmas lights, seemed to be giving Bing what he wanted.

After a beat of shock, the Hounds aimed their own weapons, which, Maverick assumed, were not empty. "GO, GO, GO!" Apollo yelled, and the Bulls turned and flew down the street to a much less festive chorus of gunfire.

~oOo~

"We whole?" Maverick asked, once they stopped, tucked in an alley, out of range of danger. "Anybody hurt?"

No one was. Not a single bullet had hit them, not even their bikes.

"WOO-HOO!" Gunner crowed, laughing. "That was FUCKING AWESOME!" He whooped again and slapped Maverick on the back. "Damn!"

Maverick laughed. He'd forgotten how good the surge of adrenaline in a life or death fight could feel. He'd spent four long years in a nonstop life or death fight, but this something entirely different. When you had power in the situation and hope for the outcome, life or death was a choice. He chose life.

He was going to lean on Delaney to get Kevlar vests for the club.

~oOo~

Maverick smiled as Eight Ball picked Kelsey up so she could reach the top of the tree. When she couldn't make the angel stand up straight, Eight put his hand over hers and helped. Cheers and applause greeted her success, and she looked around shyly, grinning and blushing, and then strangled Eight Ball in one of her death-grip hugs around his neck.

Glancing toward the bar, where Jenny sat with Willa, Leah, and Patrice, Griffin's girlfriend, Maverick watched his lady watch their daughter and Eight Ball. Jenny didn't care much for that particular brother. As far as he knew, Jenny and Eight hadn't had any specific interaction that had gone bad. He supposed there might be something he didn't know about, but he doubted it. Eight would never move on a brother's woman, damn sure not the mother of a brother's child, and he wouldn't go out of his way to do wrong to a woman, either, not even one who'd abandoned a brother.

He thought it was probably that: Eight Ball didn't go out of his way for women, period. Other than Mo—he had a mama's-boy devotion to her—Eight barely noticed women at all. They had his attention when he was looking to get off, and they were invisible otherwise. Rumor had it that he had some freaky tastes in the getting-off department, too. A lot of women seemed to be able to scent that on him. Some of them liked it, and others did not. Jenny did not.

Fine by Maverick. But he watched her pay attention to how Eight Ball was with their daughter, and when she smiled, he felt relief. If she could find some trust for that brother, then she was well and truly settled in.

"Should I be worried about that?" Gunner sat down at the other end of the leather sofa.

Maverick finished off his glass of Jack. Tyra, a sweetbutt, was there in a flash, taking his empty away from him and sashaying to the bar to refill it.

"About what?"

Gunner nodded to the pool table. Gunner's older sister, Deb, was playing pool with Simon. Maverick watched as Deb set up her shot, bending sidelong over the table. Simon's eyes seemed to be focused not on her shot but well to the side, about the location of her ass.

"That's a thing? Si and Deb?"

"I don't know, man. I don't think so. She hasn't said anything about it. He sure as fuck hasn't said anything to me. But he's lookin' at her like she's laid out on a plate with parsley." Gunner slammed his beer bottle to his lips and swallowed down a long pour.

Maverick took his refill from Tyra with a chuckle. "Easy, bro. She's a hot chick in tight jeans, bent over a pool table. Si's a red-blooded Bull. 'Course he's gonna look."

"My sister is not a hot chick."

Yeah, she was. Deb was about Maverick's age, and he'd be lying if he said he hadn't had a thought or two about her. He'd hooked up with Jenny not long after he'd met Gunner and his family; otherwise, he might have made a move on Deb.

"To answer your question, no, you shouldn't be worried. It's probably nothing. If it's something, they're both well over the age of consent, and Deb deserves some good times, don't you think?"

"Not with a Bull, though. Not with all the shit goin' on right now," Gunner groused.

He had a point, and Maverick turned to his own family again—his pregnant wife, laughing with her friends. His little girl, helping Zach hang paper snowflakes on the twinkling clubhouse tree. On this Christmas Eve, the clubhouse didn't seem like a clubhouse at all. It was a home, filled with family. There were even Christmas carols playing.

But outside, a storm brewed. Not the kind that might bring a white Christmas, but the kind that might bring a red winter.

"It's quiet for now," he said to his friend.

Booker Howard hadn't retaliated for Ammons' SUV. Though the Bulls remained vigilant, Howard seemed to have decided that the truck wasn't worth escalating trouble too quickly. He'd spent the past few weeks building up his organization, transitioning Northside from the defunct Dyson crew, cleaning that house, establishing relationships. Melvin Dyson had been an important man on the north side of Tulsa. Howard likely had to tread lightly to build up the support he needed. He couldn't just lay waste and claim the rubble.

The Bulls watched carefully as it happened. Delaney and Dane were doing what they could to strengthen the club's relationships, ensuring that their friends stayed friendly, and seeking Volkov support.

And they were arming themselves heavily, preparing for battle. They had vests now, too, and wore them whenever they were out in colors.

Out in the open, Tulsa seemed like its usual self, but anyone who moved in the underworld was on alert for war. DEFCON 1.

"Won't be quiet for long, though," Gunner said. "You heard D—they're probably waiting to hit us on the next Russian run. When we're scattered."

Every eight weeks or so, Russian guns came in, and the Bulls split up to handle the north and south legs. Generally, in a peaceful Tulsa, they left one man or two at home, just in case, and the rest of the club went on one leg or the other. Normally, that was good sense, with enough coverage everywhere. But in a civil war, it made them weak at home and on the road both.

Maverick would not live his life in fear. Not now, not when he had everything he wanted. He shifted his seat so he could face Gunner straight on. "Then we won't be scattered, Gun. We'll work it out. We'll figure out a new schedule and keep everybody whole. We're strong, and we've got stronger friends. Trust D. Howard is a hemorrhoid on the asshole of the world. He won't win. We will."

After a contemplative silence, Gunner sighed. "Okay, yeah. We need more men, though. I'm thinkin' of putting a name in."

A beam of pleasure lightened Maverick's mood again at once. Sponsoring a prospect was serious business. A prospect's success or failure landed on his sponsor's back. Maverick had, a few times, worried that sponsoring Gunner, the human tornado, would end his own time in a Bulls patch. Now Gunner had settled down enough to think about mentoring, shaping, another Bull. That was real growth. He slapped his friend's back. "Yeah? You got somebody in mind? Hangaround?"

"Nah. He's been to a few parties, and Dane knows him, but he doesn't hang around. Somebody I know from the races. Osage Indian kid. Caleb Mathews. He's cool."

"Yeah—bring him up in church next. That's great. You're still racing, huh?"

Gunner shrugged. His attention had moved to the bar, and their women. His woman in particular, Maverick had no doubt. Pretty little Leah. "Yeah...sometimes. Not like I used to." He huffed a quiet laugh. "Now I'd mostly rather just be home."

Maverick's eyes landed on Jenny, and she looked over right then. Their eyes locked, and she smiled.

"Yeah. I know what you mean, Gun. I know what you mean."

~oOo~

Maverick came into the bedroom and stretched, pushing his fists into his lower back and arching over them. "Damn. The people who make assembly directions on toys need to take some English classes. I don't know why they bother putting those worthless sheets of paper in the box at all."

Propped up in bed with a book, Jenny smiled. "Did you get it all together?"

"Yeah." He stripped down and slid in beside her, and she set her book aside. "It looks pretty great out there. I can't wait for Kelsey see it all for the first time." He brushed his fingers over her forehead. "How's your head?" She'd gotten one of her 'auras,' signaling a migraine on the way, while they were at the clubhouse.

She caught his hand and brought his fingers to her lips. "Good. I got home to bed quick enough. It only lasted like an hour. Thanks for handling all that. I almost came out to help you with the toys after, but there was swearing, and I thought you were probably better off on your own."

"Yeah. The parts on some of those things weren't machined too well. Muscle and cussing was required to make 'em fit. I'm glad you're okay." He laid his head on her belly and slid his hand over her hip. "How okay are you?"

Her muscles shook with her laugh, and he felt her fingers dance over his neck, down his spine. "Very okay. Very very."

"That is very good news." He hooked an arm around her and dragged her down flat on the bed. "Very very." He bent his head and tasted her sweet mouth, soft and willing under his. As he shifted a leg over hers and brought his hand up to cup a breast and tease a nipple, she pulled back—not far.

Her lips brushed his as she said, "Mav...you can tie me up if you want. We haven't done that since..."

Since before he'd gone away. Since before she'd gotten big with Kelsey. He'd loved tying her up, binding her to the bed with scarves or silky ropes, wrapping her wrists up together or splaying them wide, making her subject to him, under his control, at his whim...

He stunned himself by going soft, and not gradually. His cock deflated. Jenny felt it, too, and shared his surprise—he saw it in her frown and the flare of her eyes. He pulled away.

"Mav?" She held his arm, not letting him go far.

Allowing her to hold him, he turned and sat up. "Sorry."

"What's wrong?" She sat up, too, drawing the sheet over her chest—in that move, he saw that he'd made her self-conscious.

So was he. But he had no idea why. He *loved* tying her up, seeing her sleek limbs pulled taut, her slender wrists and ankles wrapped with pretty silk, watching her hands twist and her toes curl as he found more and deeper places of pleasure in her body and kept at them until she begged and begged...

He shuddered. Jesus Christ, what the fuck?

"Mav—please tell me what's wrong. Please."

With a flash of image, he knew. He flinched against the memory and jumped out of bed.

"Mav!"

He had to tell her. He swore he'd never put it into words or sound, but now he knew, standing naked next to the bed she was in, their bed, in their room, in their house, on Christmas fucking Eve, that he was going to have to tell Jenny.

"I can't do that anymore. Tie you up. It's not...I can't do that to you. Take control like that, where you can't stop me."

Her worry changed. She'd been afraid she'd done something wrong. Now she was worried for him. "Mav, it's okay. You never forced me. I liked it. I trust you."

That made a stabbing pain in his heart, and he flinched again. He *had* forced her. A little. He'd ignored her resistance, sure she'd like it—and she had. But first she'd been afraid, and he'd forged on, heedless in his arrogance.

She'd liked everything he'd done. But what if she hadn't? Would he have apologized?

No. He wouldn't have. He would have tried harder, thinking she simply needed to relax and be more open to it. He hadn't been worthy of her trust.

He'd been a fucking bully. A gentle bully, but a bully nonetheless.

"I can't hold you down. I can't."

When she stood and blocked his path, Maverick realized that he'd been pacing. She cupped a hand over his cheek. "Maverick. What's wrong?"

And here it was. He could make something up, deflect, lie, set it aside, leave it buried. Or he could tell her and hope—trust—that she would understand.

He turned his head and kissed her palm. "Something happened to me inside."

~oOo~

"You gotta say something, Jen."

He'd said it all, said more than he'd meant to, and now she just sat at his side. Tears streamed down her face, but she wasn't crying openly, no warp of her features. Only those wet rills, dripping onto her bare chest. They sat on the side of the bed, both naked. Maverick felt far more exposed than merely his skin.

"Babe, please," he pleaded when still she wouldn't speak.

Without a word, she slid off the bed, to her knees. She pivoted until she faced him and maneuvered herself between his legs. He wasn't ready for what it looked like she intended—he was soft and freaked the fuck out, and horrible memories slammed unimpeded back and forth in his head, let loose for the first time since they'd been made.

Carver had sure as hell been right about that: he would never forget any second.

"Jen—" He stopped when, rather than take hold of his cock, she bent forward, folding all the way down, and kissed the top of his foot. Her lips lingered on the highest point of his bridge. He could feel her tears wet his skin.

"Jen..." he said again, on a breath. He didn't know what she intended, but her touch was gentle and calming.

She moved to the other foot and did the same thing. Next she moved to that foot's ankle bone, and to the other. His shins. His calves. His knees—pressing a single, soft, unhurried kiss to each point, working her way up his thighs. As his brain finally began to push the memories back to their lockbox, he held her head, twisting his fingers into the fluid strands of her long hair.

His cock had begun to stir when she made it to the top of his thighs, but she moved away from it, scooting closer, pressing her lips from one side of his belly to the other, then up, over the center, finally to kiss each nipple. From her knees, she couldn't reach any higher than that. Maverick lifted her face and bent his to hers until their foreheads touched.

She still hadn't spoken, and tears still streamed, but he didn't need her to say anything now. "I love you," he whispered. "How many is that today?"

"Infinity," she answered, and kissed him.

~oOo~

A few hours before dawn on the first Christmas morning he'd spend with his wife and child, Maverick sat alone on the sofa, a glass of whiskey in his hand, and stared at the glowing colored lights of their Christmas tree. Under the tree and for several feet around it sat the shiny packages that Jenny had so carefully wrapped, and the assorted toys that he had so intently built. They'd gone more than a little overboard with Kelsey's presents—*he* had gone more than a little overboard.

Jenny was worried that she'd be overwhelmed, that there was far more here than Kelsey could focus on, but Maverick didn't care. His girls hadn't had much these past four years, and he was going to make up for it now. He couldn't wait for her to wake up and see.

She didn't believe in Santa. Jenny had never told her about the jolly old elf; she had a bad history of that fantasy herself, and she didn't want her little girl to feel the hurt of finding out Santa was a lie.

It hurt his heart. Santa wasn't a lie; he was a gift—wonder and mystery and joy on Christmas morning. He'd never believed in Santa, either, but he'd been brought up in an orphanage, with no family or traditions. He wanted his little girl to have perfect Christmas memories, the kind that kids with families got to have.

So they'd have to start now and make up some that were just their own.

That was why he was awake at four in the morning. Not because he was tormented by those memories that had vandalized his brain earlier in the night. Jenny had kicked that shit right to the curb, and she'd done it with hardly a word. She'd simply lavished love and desire on him, adored his body with her own, until he had control over his memories and was hard again. Then she'd brought him off with her mouth, and again when she'd straddled his lap and taken him in.

He'd never thought before of Jenny taking care of him, only of him taking care of her and Kelsey. Everything about his love and his drive to make his family whole had been focused on taking care of them, on being Jenny's husband, Kelsey's father. Making the family he needed. But tonight, he'd realized how much of his desperate need was for himself. He needed somewhere he could be weak. He needed to be taken care of, too.

So no, he wasn't awake with tormented thoughts. He was awake with anticipation. With happiness. He was fucking *alive*. He sat on his sofa and appreciated the view of his new, beautiful life. The quiet, glowing tree, its colored lights reflected in shimmers on the shiny paper Jenny had used to wrap gifts. The stone fireplace beside it, festooned with pine boughs and shiny red balls, three stockings hanging from the mantel.

Maverick had felt that tight twist in his chest when Jenny had pulled from a box a bundle of white tissue paper and shown him what was inside: the same stockings she'd brought home on their first Christmas together, matching, with their names embroidered on the cuffs. Now there was one for Kelsey—bigger, with a sparkly Christmas tree sewn on it. It bulged with candy and small gifts.

Jenny's had a little something weighing down the toe of hers, as well.

Wrapped up in his Christmas reverie, Maverick didn't hear Jenny come up behind him. He jumped when her hands slid over his chest and she kissed his cheek. "Hey. Are you okay?"

He smiled up at her. "Yeah. I'm good. Come sit." He set aside his glass as she came around the sofa. She sat beside him and tucked herself under his arm. She'd pulled his t-shirt on; he loved it when she walked around in his shirts. "You remember our first Christmas? The real first?"

"You mean when I was pregnant?"

He nodded. They'd been dating the Christmas before that, but they hadn't spent it together.

"Of course." She laid her head on his shoulder. "I'd known I was pregnant for like two weeks, and you bought that ridiculous present for a baby girl."

"It wasn't ridiculous."

"It was when we didn't know what the baby would be. But you were sure she was a girl."

"And I was right."

She answered with a playful slap of his bare belly. Then her mood quieted. "I remember it all. I was still so scared about the baby, and you were so confident, like always."

He winced. "I'm sorry about that. I should have listened."

"It's okay. You listen now. And I think…if I'm honest with myself…I think I needed it sometimes back then. When I get trapped in my head, I need help getting back out. That's not nearly as true as it was, but back then, I didn't know how to think for myself."

"You sure do now."

She laughed. "Yeah. Now I'm a mouthy bitch." When he only chuckled, she poked his side. "You're supposed to say, 'No, dear, you're not a mouthy bitch.'"

His silent grin earned him another poke, and then a nipple twist. Laughing, he grabbed her and flung her down on the sofa, lying on top of her, but he didn't pin her. "You're not a mouthy bitch, dear."

Her arms looped around his neck, and they stopped talking or laughing or wrestling, or marking time.

When they came up for air, Jenny brushed her fingers through his beard. "You saved Christmas for me that day. You showed me what it could be, to have our baby together. Like you could *see* it. I wish we could have had that."

He looked down into her eyes, which glimmered with festive lights, and possibly some new tears. "We do have it, babe. Now. This is what I saw. This is exactly what I saw."

December 1992

"Hold up, hold up." Maverick crouched before the fireplace and pushed the button, and fake flames rose up into the fake logs with a gentle cough. He stood up and surveyed their work. "There. Now it's perfect."

Jenny crossed her arms. "It's not bad, I guess."

"What do you mean?" He uncrossed her arms and pulled her close. "It's perfect. The tree, the stockings, the fire. Like a Christmas card. And next year, it'll be even better, because there'll be another stocking next to yours." He rubbed her belly. It was still flat, she'd only been pregnant for a few weeks, but he'd become fascinated with her belly and could hardly wait for her to get big.

They hadn't planned for this baby, and he hadn't been thinking about being a dad yet, but now that she was coming — she was a she, he could feel it — Maverick was all but marking the days off on the calendar.

Jenny, on the other hand, had spent the past couple of weeks, since she'd taken the test, in a daze. It scared him, and he hated that feeling above all others. He kept trying to find ways to get her excited. Sure, she was scared, a lot of changes were going to happen to her body, and the biology of the whole thing freaked him out a little bit, so he could hardly imagine what it felt like to actually grow a human being inside your own body, but if he could get her focused on all the good stuff, she wouldn't be so scared. Jenny was like this about all the big things — she needed to be distracted from her worries and focused on the goal.

Meanwhile, Maverick was having the best fucking Christmas of his life: in love with a beautiful woman, baby on the way, Christmas tree, fireplace, stockings hung with care. He was making a family of his own, just like Lester had said, all those years ago, when he'd aged out of the system and gone out into an unforgiving world alone.

"Jenny." He pulled her to the sofa and sat her down. "What's wrong, babe?"

Staring at their cheap fake fireplace and its bright orange flame, she sighed. "I don't know...I guess...I'm scared. What if I suck as a mom? What if I turn out to be like my dad? What if...I don't know. Just what if. I don't feel like I'm ready for this, Mav." She was going to cry. Dammit.

Maverick didn't think he'd fully relax until she was too far along to do anything about the pregnancy. He didn't really think she'd do anything like that, certainly not without telling him first, but still...maybe once all the options were truly gone, she'd stop finding dumb reasons not to be glad about this. "Who cares if we're ready?" She laughed soggily and tried to pull away, but he held her hands in his firm grasp. "No, I mean it. Who cares? Who's ever ready for this? To hear Joanna talk about it, their girls were planned, and she still had no clue what she was in for."

"That's not helping."

"It's Fate, babe. It's right because it happened. All my life I've wanted exactly this: a family just like this. At Iggy's, we had those little cheap felt stockings, you know the ones they sell at the drugstore? They're like five inches long?" She indicated that she knew what he was talking about. "We had those, and we'd write our names in Elmer's and dump gold glitter on them, and then we'd use thumbtacks and stick them on this paper fireplace that the staff taped to the wall. We had a tree in the dining room, but the presents under it were empty, like the stockings. Just for show. We got presents, the church would come by and drop off shit the parishioners donated, and we each got something from the staff, but it wasn't any kind of Christmas you saw on television. Even the Cratchits had more Christmas than we did."

"Cratchits?"

"Yeah—from *A Christmas Carol*."

"Oh, right. Duh." She smiled a little, and Maverick had some hope.

"We didn't have much Christmas because we weren't a family. We were just a bunch of boys who didn't have anybody. No donation dump of cheap toys and six-packs of socks makes up for that."

Before she could start feeling sorry for him, Maverick changed direction. "When I went to bed on Christmas night, this is what I thought about. When I was grown up, I was going to have a family, and I was going to have a real tree with real presents under it and a real fireplace, and real stockings full of gifts. This is the first time I ever had it. Even at Mo and D's, I've been just borrowing theirs. This is ours. Yours and mine. And next year, when the baby comes..."

He kissed her hands and got up.

"Mav?"

"Hold on a sec." Crossing the room to the front door, he went to his kutte, hanging on the rickety coat rack, and rummaged in an interior pocket. "I was gonna wrap this, but the box is pretty enough. I got the baby something."

She smiled. "The baby that's the size of a pumpkin seed? That baby?"

"The one and only." He resumed his seat and handed her the sparkly silver box.

With a curious twist of her brow, she lifted the lid, and then she gasped. "Mav, what?"

He took it from her and lifted out the dainty sterling chain. A small, heart-shaped pendant dangled from it. "You see what it says?"

She lifted the pendant on her fingertips. "Mav, what if it's a boy?"

"She's a girl. Trust me."

"But what if it's not? I don't know if the *baby* knows what it is yet. Are you going to be disappointed?"

"To have a son? Fuck no." He grinned. "I won't give him this, of course. Might confuse him. I'll give him something else and love him just as much. But she's a girl, Jen. I know it. A little girl, and I'm gonna treasure her and carry her around on a puffy pillow so she never gets hurt, and I'm gonna love you and take care of you both so good. Next year, we'll have another stocking on the fireplace, and there will be a *fuck ton* of presents under the tree, and she will be perfect and sweet and not spoiled at all even though she'll have everything she could ever want. All my life, I've been working for this one thing. I'm not gonna screw it up. I promise. I *swear* to you—we are going to have a perfect life and a perfect family, and there is nothing you will ever need to worry about. I will take care of you forever."

He took the pendant from her and set it back in its box, with the heart front-side up. Sterling silver, engraved in elegant script, with tiny diamond chips dotting the 'i's.

Daddy's Little Girl

CHAPTER TWENTY

Lying on the sofa under Maverick, illuminated only by the multihued glow of the Christmas tree, Jenny looked up into that handsome, scarred, beloved face, into those searching blue eyes, and saw a bottomless reservoir of love for her and their children, and of hope for their future. His hope was better than his reckless confidence of before. That confidence had been heedless of her or anything but what he'd wanted, and he'd dragged her along in his wake. She'd gone willingly, for the most part, but not on her own power. His hope, on the other hand—his hope saw her, heard her, needed her. She was a partner in that hope.

She thought of what he'd told her, of the things he'd gone through in prison, of the horror and powerlessness he'd experienced, and her heart broke that he'd been alone, abandoned, for all those years. She had left him alone. She had abandoned him.

He had left her, too, but to a different kind of torment. An easier kind.

So much of what they'd had before had been good and right—what they had now was a testament to what had been good before—but it had been built on an uneven, unstable foundation. What they'd both needed then they still needed now, but they hadn't known how to get there—he'd known only how to lead, and she'd known only how to follow. They'd been like two half-selves, unable to make a whole. In their loneliness since, in their turmoil, they'd learned the rest of themselves and come back together on stable ground.

They'd finally made their whole together.

She shifted under him, settling her legs on either side of his hips, and he groaned as her movement pressed his cock against her mound. She wore only his Bulls t-shirt, and he wore only a pair of sweatpants. She slid her hand down his side and pushed at his waistband, reaching between them to find and free his ready cock.

"Fuck me, Mav. I need you inside me."

He obliged without a word, letting her take hold of him, letting her feed him into herself, and his mouth locked on hers as he thrust deep. Swallowing her moan, lapping it up with his tongue, he rocked his hips, and Jenny pushed her hands into the back his sweatpants and grabbed, digging her fingers into the flexing, muscular meat of his ass.

As Jenny felt her nerves begin to twist together into the pattern of their ecstasy, felt the hot flood of need loosen her joints, she broke free of his mouth, desperate for breath, and bit down on his shoulder.

Maverick grunted and slammed into her. In a sudden move, he tossed a back cushion from the couch, making more room on the seat, and grabbed her head, dragging a fistful of her hair, yanking her mouth from his shoulder and claiming it for his own again.

In her hands, his muscles flexed and released, harder and faster each time until the sofa began to move under them, short, stuttering shifts with each slam of their hips together.

Jenny was coming, sweet *God*, she was coming, and she needed to breathe, but she didn't want to lose any part of their union, not even their tongues, and she was going to pass out, and she didn't care. She could hear that he was close, too—his breathing was as desperate and insufficient as hers, great noisy drags of air through his nose, but he wasn't going anywhere, either.

When the climax landed, she couldn't control anything, and she screamed into his mouth. He grunted wildly at the same time, almost a scream of his own, and her eyes flew open—and she found herself starting right into his. He'd already been watching her.

They came down together, gradually slowing to a stop, pulling back from their mad kiss at the same time, swallowing heaps of air together. Then, when satiation brought sanity back, they lay together, still connected, and stared into each other's Christmas-lit eyes.

She lifted her head and kissed his nose. "This is what I saw, too," she murmured.

He smiled and brushed his lips over hers. When he pulled out, she hung on, unwilling to let him go far, but she needn't have worried. He simply adjusted his sweatpants, tossed the other back cushion to the floor, pulled the knitted throw that had had been a gift from Mrs. Turner over them, and settled in behind her, with his arms around her.

Jenny fell asleep cocooned in his strong embrace, feeling the cozy glow of their Christmas tree on her face.

~oOo~

"Mommy. Mommy, it's Christmas!"

Jenny's eyes fluttered open. Kelsey had her face right up in hers, barely an inch between them.

"Morning, pix," she yawned and blinked herself to wakefulness. Maverick's arms still held her snugly, but she could feel him waking, too.

"It's not morning, it's CHRISTMAS!" Kelsey corrected, jumping up and down in her flannel holiday nightgown. Miss Shorty, trapped in her arms, seemed surprisingly comfortable with all the ruckus. "Daddy, it's CHRISTMAS, AND THERE ARE SO MANY PRESENTS! Are they for *me*?"

Maverick kissed Jenny's shoulder and sat up, bringing her with him. "A lot of them are, I think. But there's some for Mommy, too, and some to take to Grammo and Grampop's house later, too."

"And some for Daddy, too. Can you find your name on the tags, Kelse?" Jenny asked. She needed to distract her for a few minutes, because she had a mission to complete before the gift-opening got started.

"Uh-huh. K-E-L-S-E-Y. That spells Kelsey."

"Good girl. Okay—you find the Kelsey presents, and Daddy and I will be right back."

Maverick cocked an eyebrow at her, but she simply grabbed his hand and pulled him back to their bedroom.

Once there, he tried to catch her, thinking she meant more fooling around. She pushed him away. "Easy, tiger. That's for later. Just hold on a second." She went into the closet and pulled the old lockbox down from the shelf. Her father had used it long ago, when he'd brought the till home with him every night after he'd closed the bar. Its lock had been broken for years, but Jenny used it to keep special mementos of Kelsey's life—things like their hospital bracelets from her birth. A lock of hair from her first haircut, tied in a thin scrap of satin ribbon.

A little sparkly silver gift box.

Standing in the closet, she took that box out, put the lockbox back in its place, and went back into the bedroom, where Maverick waited, clearly perplexed.

"What's goin' on, babe?" he asked, wearing an uncertain smile.

"I love you," she said, holding the box behind her back.

His smile widened. "That's one."

"We don't have to keep count anymore. I know how you feel, and you tell me in so many ways, including with words."

He came up and tried to take both her hands, but she only gave him her free one. "I like keeping count. It's our thing. And I want you always to know for sure, every night when you close your eyes, that you heard those words on that day. On every day for the rest of your life. I love you."

God, she loved him so much. "Okay, then. That's one." She brought her hand forward and held out the little silver box.

He knew what it was at once. His eyes widened and came back to hers. "Jen. You kept it?"

"Of course I did. I never gave it to her because...well. I didn't. Besides, it's yours to give to her, nobody else's. It's the first gift you ever got her."

"Jesus Christ," he muttered, and Jenny saw with a start that he was near tears. In all the time they were together before, she'd never seen him cry. He was not a man who gave quarter to tears—unless the reason for them was his love for their daughter.

He hadn't taken the box from her yet, so she lifted his hand and set it on his palm, curling his fingers around it.

"There are bows in that bag in the corner, if you want to dress it up. But I think the box is pretty enough just as it is."

He lifted the lid and stared down at the tiny silver heart. "Jesus Christ, babe."

"You were always her daddy. I always knew that." She stepped close, bringing her body against his, and closed him up in her arms. He laid his head on her shoulder, and they stood quietly, together.

"Mommy! Daddy!" Kelsey was just on the other side of their closed door. "COME ON!"

Maverick laughed and pulled back. He hadn't cried, but his eyes glittered, and he took a deep, sniffling breath. "Let's go. We've got a first Christmas to get started."

He kissed her, closed up the box, and went to open the door. "Merry Christmas, Kelsey. I love you."

"I love you, too. That's one, Daddy. Merry Christmas!"

"Let's go see what's under the tree."

Jenny stayed back and watched him sweep their daughter up and set her on his hip. Kelsey put her little arms around his neck, and Jenny was slammed by a memory, striking her so hard she put her hand over her heart—seeing, only a fantasy in her mind's eye, exactly that, Maverick with a pretty little girl on his hip, her arms locked around him just so. She'd been standing in the women's section of Wal-Mart, six years ago, when her mind had conjured that image.

As he carried Kelsey toward the living room, Jenny saw him talking, and he handed his little girl the silver box.

She'd leave that memory to just the two of them, and she'd hold her own close to her heart.

A first Christmas, he'd said. It wasn't, really. It wasn't their first Christmas together as a couple, and it wasn't Kelsey's first Christmas. That day had been sour and dark, full of longing for the life she'd lost and despair for the life she'd had.

On that day, she'd been at her weakest. But she'd survived. And Maverick had survived. Their love had survived. And now they all had the life and family they wanted.

Maybe this was a first Christmas after all.

December 1993

Jenny's father grunted as he fell awkwardly back into his wheelchair. "Sorry, Dad." She lowered his bed a little more, until the mechanism wouldn't go any farther, and tried again. Tucking her head and shoulder under his arm—it made her think of Maverick's thing, *head down, shoulder to the day*—she wrapped her arms around him and heaved.

This time, he landed on the bed, at least well enough that she could wrestle him around and get him on it right eventually. He'd been home for two months, but she still hadn't mastered getting him between his bed and his wheelchair.

He wasn't paralyzed, but he might as well have been. He was like an infant, with little ability to control his body. He'd been a strong but not a large man, and he'd lost a lot of weight since he'd been hurt, but he was still bigger than Jenny and just about more than she could handle.

But she couldn't afford full-time nursing, so she had to handle him one shift a day, and on weekends, and on holidays. Holidays like Christmas. Like today. Christmas Day. Kelsey's first Christmas. Ho, ho, fucking ho.

During the week, she could leave him in bed for her overnight shift, but she couldn't do that on the weekends. She'd tried once, and when Darnell had come back on shift, he'd been able to tell and had been firm with her about the danger of bed sores. So she struggled to do it right and get better at it.

Once he was mostly on the bed, she pulled and pushed, as gently as she could, getting him to the middle and his legs and arms and head oriented properly. While she worked, he lay there, inert, his eyes following her back and forth around the bed.

"Okay. Okay. Let's get you changed." That was a sentence she found herself uttering several times a day, to her infant daughter and her invalid father both. As she lifted his hospital gown—she hadn't figured out how to dress him when she was in charge, so she left him in the gowns he slept in—and took a long, steadying breath before she began to open his diaper. Just like Kelsey's, only much, much bigger, and with more Velcro tabs.

The combination of soft foods he could eat and the meds he was on made his stools soft, sometimes nearly liquid. Would she ever get used to changing her father's diaper, to cleaning his flaccid dick in its spare grey thatch, to heaving up his legs to wipe his ass, a grotesque parody of her care for her daughter?

No. She absolutely would not.

Just then, Kelsey woke and began to scream from her crib, that awful, head-splitting, heartbreaking wail she'd developed over the past few days, worse than even her colic shrieks. She had a bad cold, with a sinus infection and both ears infected as well, and she was in more pain than Tylenol infant drops could manage.

Jenny tried to hurry her father's change, but it was impossible to hurry when she was maneuvering a man who still weighed substantially more than she did. While she went as quickly as she could, Kelsey's screams became more and more desperate. She couldn't breathe from her nose, and each long, terrified, agonized whoop stuttered out into horrifying silence.

Finally, Jenny slapped the last new tab closed and slammed the bedrails up. Leaving the noxious used diaper open on the table beside the bed, Jenny ran down the hall, into the bathroom to wash her hands as fast as she could, then to Kelsey's room, yanking her shirt and bra open as she went.

Steam from the humidifier had made the dark room muggy. "I'm here, pixie. I'm here."

Kelsey's nose was crusted with yellow gunk, and the tears streaming from her eyes weren't clear. Jenny didn't bother to check her diaper. She picked her daughter up and swiped her face with the end of her shirt, pinching her nose lightly as she did it, trying to clear it out. Then she offered a breast. Kelsey settled as she latched, and Jenny sat down in the rocker.

Congested as she was, Kelsey couldn't hold the latch, but Jenny kept wiping her nose and offering her breast, back and forth, until she was fed and soothed. Jenny rocked as her little girl fell back to a restless, but hopefully healing, sleep.

"Jen! Jen! Jen!" Her father called, like a recorded message. The only word he could say.

Jenny tried to ignore him. She rocked and held her daughter, and she stared at the elaborate, absurd round canopy crib. She didn't cry; she was too tired and beaten down to cry.

This was not the life she and Kelsey were supposed to have.

~oOo~

That night, while both her charges were asleep, Jenny threw away the few Christmas decorations she'd bothered to put up. She hadn't really liked Christmas since she was a little girl, but it had been Kelsey's first, and she'd had a momentary urge to make something of it. Dumb—Kelsey was four months old. What did she know?

She considered the tub of cookies and fudge that Mrs. Turner had brought over from next door, with a pretty little card showing a baby girl in Santa's arms. *Merry First Christmas, Sweetheart!* the glittery text read. That right there, cookies from Mrs. Turner, was the only gift that had come into this house. She hadn't even gotten herself together enough to buy her own daughter a gift. So much for making something of her first Christmas.

Jenny tore open the lid, stomped on the foot lever to the garbage can, and dumped the contents. She tossed the tub in the sink and snatched the card and its red envelope, meaning to send it in right after the cookies. But she stopped, seeing Mrs. Turner's perfect, Palmer-method handwriting, and opened the card.

She'd opened it when Mrs. Turner had come over, but she'd only made a show of reading it and being grateful. Now she read it. A message for her as much as for her daughter.

Sweet Kelsey, we've loved your mama since she was little as you, and you're a lucky girl, because she's full of love and strength, and she'll give all that to you. Always remember, beautiful flowers grow in the darkest dirt. Your mama is a beautiful rose, with a thick, strong stem, and you will be, too. Happy first Christmas! Love, Mr. & Mrs. T.

Ps. Next door is home, too. For you both.

Discovering that, in fact, she was not too tired and beaten down to cry, Jenny collapsed into a chair at the table and wept.

~oOo~

That card from the Turners was the only memento of Kelsey's first Christmas there was. The day had been awful, but it had held this bright spot, this sole reminder that there was more in their lives than misery. There was love, too. Jenny slid the card into its envelope and took it back to her room.

She took down the old lockbox from her closet shelf and sat on her bed. She'd begun to keep mementos of Kelsey's life in it. She hadn't collected many, yet; little so far had felt worthy of remembrance. The strip of ultrasound photos. Their hospital bracelets, and the pink bassinet card, from her birth. The Polaroid that Willa, the nurse, had taken for her, which was the only photo she had of the day Kelsey was born.

The silver box. Maverick had bought it for the baby right after she'd found out she was pregnant, and he'd shown her at Christmas. Just the year before. Jenny opened the box now and took out the silver pendant and chain. *Daddy's Little Girl.*

So like Maverick. She'd been barely pregnant, but he'd been totally positive that the baby was a girl. So positive, he'd bought this necklace for the daughter he hadn't had yet.

She tried hard not to think of Maverick with any emotion except anger. Only anger got her through these days. But now, feeling broken and vulnerable, with Mrs. Turner's sweet message of encouragement trying to bolster a mood that had been damn close to suicidal, she let herself wonder what Maverick's first Christmas in prison was like. Was he alone, too?

Well, yeah. He was in prison. Even surrounded by people, even if the Bulls visited every single day, he was alone. He wasn't where he belonged.

He belonged with her and Kelsey.

He would have been a good father. He'd loved Kelsey from the moment the test stick had turned. He'd been lavish in his devotion while they were planning for her arrival, and he would have been lavish in his devotion now.

He'd torn it all down, but if he hadn't, Kelsey would have been surrounded and swaddled in love.

Jenny hated him so much because she loved him so much. There was no good life without him in it.

She supposed he knew about Kelsey; the Bulls knew, so he must. But Jenny had never written to tell him anything. Was that fair? No, it was not.

She put the pendant back in its box and returned it to the lockbox. Why was she keeping it? A memento of what could have been, but not what was, brought only pain. But she couldn't throw it away. If she did, then even the shade of could-have-been, even the fantasy of might-still-be, would be lost, and Jenny would be lost with it.

The Polaroid rested beside the silver box. Turning her brain off before it could think, she took the photo out and brought it to her desk. She pulled a plain white envelope from her bill-paying drawer and dug the Oklahoma State Penitentiary card out of her address book. She addressed the envelope to Richard Helm, listing his inmate number—written on the back of the OSP card—and the address. She put a Santa stamp on the envelope

She considered writing a letter, but she had nothing to say—or too much to say to know where to start. Before she slid the Polaroid into the envelope alone, she wrote across the white space at the bottom: *Kelsey, 8/21/93*.

Not allowing her brain to start up and change her mind, she pulled her coat on over her pajamas and hurried the envelope out to the mailbox on the sidewalk in the front of the Turner's house.

As the mailbox door clanged shut, snow began to fall. Jenny looked up into a deep, dark blue sky swirling with white, like a snow globe. A tiny, feathery nothing of a hope trembled on the floor of her heart.

EPILOGUE

"Sir! Wait! You can't just—"

Ignoring the nurse, Maverick hurried down the hall where the examining rooms were. He opened the first one—empty.

"Sir! Stop!"

He crossed the hall and opened the second. A woman who was not his wife had her belly exposed. A man in a dress shirt, sitting at her side, said, "Hey!"

"Sorry, man." He closed the door and went to the next.

"I'm calling security!" yelled the bitch in the flowered scrubs.

But Jenny was in the third room, her belly likewise exposed. Fuck, he loved that round little bump. "I'm here! I'm here!" He slammed his ass onto the stool beside her, grabbed her hand and pressed it to his mouth, then grinned up at the technician. "What'd I miss?"

The technician blinked.

"She hasn't started yet," Jenny said. "But you cut it close, Mav."

"Sorry, babe. Rough morning."

"Hounds stuff?"

He glanced back at the technician, who watched them with great interest, the ultrasound thing in her hand. "Yeah. It's okay. We'll talk later. Right now, let's see our baby."

~oOo~

"It's big."

Jenny laughed and snatched the grainy photo out of his hand. "It's so little she had to draw a circle around it so we could see it."

"What? You're crazy. That circle is because it's so impressive. Look at that thing. It's a fire hose. He's gonna walk funny."

Rolling her eyes at him, she tucked the photo into the folder they'd given her and slid it into her purse. "How do you do it?"

"Do what?" He opened the door of the Cherokee and offered his hand to help her in behind the wheel.

"You wanted a girl, and we had a girl. You wanted a boy, and we're having a boy. You always get your way."

Still holding her hand, he pulled, keeping her from getting into the car. "Just lucky, I guess. Or maybe I just want the right things. Like you. You and Kelsey and our little boy. All my right things."

She smiled and framed her hands around his face. "You're our right thing, too."

He bent his head to hers and kissed her. "I love you."

"I love you, too. That's four."

He helped her into her seat and closed the door, then motioned for Jenny to put the window down. She did. "Okay. Caleb's staying on you all day, until I get home.

Don't drag the guy all over creation. Get Kelsey, get home, and stay put. Got it?"

"Got it. Mav—how long is it going to be like this?"

He'd have given up a limb to have had the answer to that question. In the three months since Christmas, war drums had been sounding all over Tulsa. For the most part, the action so far was more posturing than anything. Bulls and Hounds and their respective allies all feeling each other out. Some property damage, lots of nuisance, some crimp to everybody's bottom lines, but no serious harm to people yet. The Bulls had had two Russian runs so far this year, and they'd gotten them done. But the massive extra security was slowing them down and costing them dear. They had protection on their families, too, on kids and old ladies, and they were stretched thin. If Irina Volkov hadn't offered some of her men to bolster security on the runs all the way to their end point, they wouldn't have been able to manage it all.

They'd patched Wally in and brought in two new prospects in addition to Caleb Mathews, trying to fill out the roster enough to keep everybody protected and healthy and get their work done. Maverick was nervous about so much inexperience in the crossfire, but they had no choice.

He was open with Jenny about as much as he could be. Once they'd locked down for the first time, he hadn't felt like he could evade her questions, but she was rolling with the situation like a pro.

"I don't know, Jen. We're trying to work through it, figure out a solution. We will. But if you trust me and let me lead on this, I will keep you safe. I promise. I won't let anything happen to us."

"I trust you."

Those words were almost as powerful as the others he loved to hear.

~oOo~

Home late that night, well after his girls had gone to sleep, Maverick parked his bike on the driveway. The house was dark, but Jenny had left the porch light on, and he knew there'd be a plate in the fridge, his portion of the dinner she'd made, ready for him to heat and eat.

She still owned The Wayside, but she'd filled out a whole staff to run it, and she went in once or twice a week, just to check in. Jenny was a full-time mom, just like she'd always wanted to be, and she'd taken to it with gusto.

They had a perfect home and family. Everything he'd ever dreamed of.

Once the Hounds had been put down, they would have a perfect life. In the meantime, Maverick would make sure that Kelsey continued to think that everything was already perfect.

He'd been out before dawn that morning and had only managed that hour or so away from the club to be with Jenny for the ultrasound, so he hadn't even laid eyes on Kelsey all day long. After he hung up his kutte and kicked off his boots, after he sent the prospect on watch home, before he went to the kitchen for the food and beer he desperately needed, he went to his daughter's room and eased open the door. Miss Shorty galloped from the room as soon as the door was open. She hated to be closed in anywhere, and Kelsey badly wanted the kitten to sleep with her every night. They had an ongoing 'negotiation' on the matter.

Her blanket was wadded at the foot of her bed. Maverick tiptoed in and drew it up, tucking it over her balled-up little body. She sighed in her sleep.

They'd gotten the club lawyer, Percy Clayton, to help change Kelsey's birth certificate. Now she was Kelsey Marie Helm, and he was listed as her father. Things were, as Jenny often said, the way they were supposed to be.

Maverick knew of no other way to live than to aim for what he wanted and push until he got it. He didn't let the bullshit of any one day break him down. For Jenny, he'd learned how to cooperate, how to bring a partner in, someone to strive with and for, but his will remained unchanged. He got what he wanted because he fought for it. No matter what.

He didn't know how to give up, how to settle, and still live. He'd given up once, and he'd just about died, even while his heart had kept beating. For his blood to really pump, he had to strive.

Right now, there was trouble in each day. He got up early, rode away from his family, and faced risk. But he wasn't afraid. That trouble—meaningless bullshit. What he came home to every night—this was real. He'd fought hard for it. And he had it.

He would keep it. He always got his way.

He brushed his daughter's hair from her face and kissed her cheek. "Good night, pixie. Daddy loves you."

"That's one," she sighed, peaceful in her cozy nest.

Susan Fanetti is a Midwestern native transplanted to Northern California, where she lives with her husband, youngest son, and assorted cats.

She is a proud member of the Freak Circle Press.

Susan's blog: www.susanfanetti.com

Susan's Facebook author page:
https://www.facebook.com/authorsusanfanetti
'Susan's FANetties' fan group:
https://www.facebook.com/groups/871235502925756/

Freak Circle Press Facebook page:
https://www.facebook.com/freakcirclepress
'The FCP Clubhouse' fan group:
https://www.facebook.com/groups/810728735692965 /

Twitter: @sfanetti

Brazen Bulls Pinterest board:
https://www.pinterest.com/laughingwarrior/the-brazen-bulls-mc/

Printed in Great Britain
by Amazon